To Ange

CW00734805

THE HURT

(A TRILOGY: BOOK 1)

EVA BIELBY

Love & Best Wishes.
Eva
x

ACKNOWLEDGMENTS

I would like to take this opportunity to thank my son
and daughter for their never ending support over
the last few years. I love you both to the moon and back.
Also, I would like to thank many of my friends
and author friends from around the world,
who have given me constant support, encouragement,
and advice, whether acted on, or not!
Thanks again for making this journey
an absolute pleasure.

Eva xx

CHAPTER 1

From being an only child I was lucky enough to have the most amazing parents in the world. Unable to have any more children after I was born, they lavished me with all their love and attention and I wanted for nothing. Yes, I was totally spoilt, but they were also sensible people and down to earth enough to not let me become a brat, or a snob. Dad inherited a substantial sum of money from my grandparents when they died during my early childhood years. After he left University, and down to his hard work, he soon owned his own advertising agency. During my teenage years, an apartment in central Paris and a villa in Marbella (for the golf, he told his friends) were also added to the family assets. Our home, which they purchased when I was four years old, was a fairly modest four bedroom detached, and was situated in one of the most pleasant areas in Richmond. Mum was lucky in that once she married Dad, she never needed to go out to work.

They paid for me to have the very best private education but only as a day pupil. I don't think I could have coped with life as a boarder. I had it all though – the ballet lessons, the ponies, the violin lessons, and as I approached my teens and throughout the teenage years, I always had the latest fashion in clothes, holidays abroad, almost everything a girl could ever want – except friends. I never had any genuine friends, and particularly, not a best one. I was occasionally allowed to tag along with a small group of girls who tolerated me, but that was it. I was bullied constantly from first starting school and right through the senior school years too. I never found out the reasons behind it all. They just tended to hit me whenever an ideal opportunity presented itself, but nobody ever actually told me why. Their nickname for me was Morticia, which I assume was because of my long dark hair. I had a few theories both then and ever since, but I suppose only the bullies themselves could give the real reason, although it is most unlikely that I will ever see them again to ask why.

One theory was that they were all snobs. Despite my very privileged upbringing I was always down to earth and never looked down on anybody as they did. I treated everybody exactly the same, wealthy or poor. An additional theory I had was that their parents didn't appear to have as much money as my parents were fortunate enough to have behind them. It always seemed as if the other parents were scrimping to give their kids a private education, but there was little left over for the holidays, ponies, and clothes, except perhaps for those with mounting credit card debts. My final theory was that a whole gang of them caught me aged eleven, and Alex Baker-Thompson (best looking lad in the school) behind the bike sheds. As a gang of the bullies approached from the playing field, Alex had his hand groping up the leg of my knickers, and it surely couldn't escape their notice that his flies were open.

It further didn't help matters that I was more sexually aware than they were. Without wanting to sound cocky, a lot of the lads seemed to fancy me (and some were more skilled than Alex in their first sexual attempts). I was pretty much attracted to most of the good-looking guys, but mainly the older ones. Word also got around the school, thanks to James Barton, that he fucked me in the P.E. equipment storeroom one particular Friday lunchtime (which was true). James took my virginity when I was fourteen years old. More gossip which hadn't helped my cause where the bullies were concerned. I tended to have a lot less bother with the bitches if I ignored the lads completely so I tried hard to do that most of the time and blend into the background, at least when other girls were around.

Whatever the reasons for the bullying, I was well and truly alone at school. I never told Mum and Dad about any of it. I didn't want to be labelled a cry baby and most of all I didn't want to give the bullies the satisfaction of letting them know they got to me. I just took the slapping and not once was I even tempted to run away. I'm made of tougher stuff than that. Quite a few of the teachers were aware I was having a tough time with the bullies and they would make sure their presence was noticed when on duty on the school playing field. I always tried not to let it bother me, but sometimes I'd silently cry myself to sleep and vow to keep in the background and unnoticed the next day at school. Surprisingly enough, my lessons never suffered and I determined to get my revenge on the bullies by making sure my exam results were second to none. I left school with 3 'A' levels, all 'A' grades in Maths, English and Geography, which met the entry requirements for the London School of Economics.

University was a whole new chapter in my life. Although I felt quite shy and wary for the first month or two, I managed to make some genuine friends and one in particular, Roberta, known to her friends as Bobbie, became my first ever close friend. We worked hard, played hard, smoked some weed (nothing worse than that though) and life was good. Again, I never went short of money and didn't need any student loans. Dad paid for everything.

Bobbie was always tired. She worked in a bar three or four nights a week to help pay her way through Uni. I was amazed at how she always managed to get to her lectures on time. Her Mum would come down every couple of months to visit, staying in a hotel just around the corner from Bobbie's student flat which she shared with two others. She (Bobbie) hadn't seen her Dad in eight years. It was a shame really, he would have been proud of her. She was pretty, well-mannered, very amiable and extremely intelligent. Her degree was a formality. I loved her to bits. She was the first female who genuinely liked me and it was a big thrill for me. At last I was liked instead of being tolerated. We had so much in common; our love of music, men, visiting the City's art galleries, fashion, and generally having a good time.

During my second year at Uni I met Gavin. I wasn't out with Bobbie that particular night as she was at work in the bar as usual. I was with three of our mutual friends who were taking the same degree course in Accountancy and Economics. We decided one night to try a new wine bar that recently opened which wasn't too far from the main university building and the student flats. The four of us downed a bottle of vodka before leaving my flat and were just getting our night into full swing when four or five guys walked in, ordered their drinks and headed straight over to our table. They proceeded to pull up extra chairs and made themselves at home. Anna, Beth and Jennifer, my friends, mouths gaping in surprise at suddenly being surrounded by so much testosterone, were soon lapping up the attention. One of them made a beeline for the vacant seat beside me and gave me his undivided attention. He was amusing, flirty and not to mention, scorching hot! We soon became so engrossed in our conversation we were oblivious to the fact that his friends and mine were still sat at the same table. Other than disclosing his name, Gavin, he said little else about himself and seemed more interested in finding out all there was to know about me.

We chatted endlessly for almost two hours, except for the half-dozen times he went to the bar to replenish our drinks. He was fair haired, had the deepest blue eyes and had a look of the fabulous rock legend, Jon Bon Jovi. By one in the morning I was smitten. How lucky was I tonight? Polite, well-mannered, interesting and more importantly, he was interested in *me*, not my looks or my body, just *me.* In the time that passed, I barely noticed that the other girls had partnered up with Gavin's mates and discreetly disappeared, I'd been so rapt with my new drinking mate. Eventually we called it a night and he walked me the short distance to my flat sometime before dawn. We made a date for the following Saturday, he pecked me quickly on the lips and was gone. I was impressed, a man who wasn't out to get laid immediately he met a girl!

We met mid-morning just outside the Natural History Museum the following weekend. We both had visited the Museum previously, but the date was more about us spending some time together rather than further educating ourselves in historical knowledge. It was a very pleasant few hours and spent in such awesome surroundings. Later in the afternoon, we went on to Covent Garden and found a quiet little restaurant where the prices were reasonable compared with many of the others in the vicinity. We decided, during our meal, that we would return to 'our' wine bar, the one where we first met. He walked me home around one in the morning. We indulged in a little passionate kissing for five or ten minutes, before we said our goodbyes and he went on his way. What a perfect day. What a perfect gentleman. Ten minutes later I was snuggled in my bed intending to read, but my thoughts were consumed by Gavin.

Two to three weeks later, and after more than a few boozy late nights with our friends, we decided it was time for just the two of us to have a quiet night in. I lived alone so my flat was the perfect choice, whereas he would have to bribe his roomies to go out and even then it was not guaranteed. We had no booze, no weed; a KFC bargain bucket, a bottle of diet coke and a DVD. We loaded the DVD but it ended up playing to itself as we chatted about our degree courses. (I learned during our first date that Gavin was in his final year at King's College and studying chemistry.) The conversation flowed easily between us; our parents and families, future plans, films, our friends…until our music tastes cropped up.

Taking his cue at the mention of music, Gavin switched off the TV and explored my CD collection, finally opting for an Aerosmith album. We listened, snuggled up and we kissed. It was the most natural thing in the world when we slowly undressed each other and indulged in the most meaningful and deliciously exciting foreplay I ever experienced. Each move on his part was tantalising, barely touching my skin, and his fingers were so gentle in their probing, his tongue teased my nipples until they stood, roused and hard. I shuddered in anticipation and my stomach ached for him. He drank in every minor detail of my body and whilst doing so he took my hand in his and guided it onto his impressive piece of manhood. It excited me to explore its length as I gently rubbed every inch; so slowly at first and he gasped in pleasure, savouring every moment until the time felt right. As we continued on our journey of discovery, I tensed as he rubbed my clit and tentatively probed into my vagina, pushing further and further in. The moment arrived sooner rather than later as we moved together onto the floor, not wanting to lose our connection and with his hands cupping my face. His cock needed no guidance and it was my turn to gasp as he eagerly shoved it inside me. It felt like heaven. His thrusts were gentle, slow and loving. He awakened all my senses, and that feeling of being aglow was amazing. I held myself back, not wanting to let go too soon. I wanted our first moment to last forever. He was so considerate in his moves, watching my face expectantly all the time, discovering what pleasured me the most and revelled in his discoveries. When he sensed that I could hold back no longer, his thrusting became faster, for minutes only, and we climaxed together, explosively...our juices fusing for the first time. Shaking in each other's arms with the intensity of the moment, I cried. I had just experienced what it was like to really be made love to. We made love twice more during the course of our first night together.

Time moved forward at a pace I struggled to keep up with. Life was like a dream. Gavin and I were out socialising quite a lot with our friends and when she wasn't working, Bobbie and her new boyfriend, Phil, were also included in that circle. I was quite surprised that I could ever get any work done, I was always tired or hung-over. I was also too rapt with Gavin and our love-making and the time we spent together. I had friends, a best friend and the best boyfriend I ever had. I truly loved Gavin. He made love to me, and I loved being made love to. This was not the emotionless fucking or shagging I experienced in the past. My heart melted each time I saw him and I couldn't wait to make love at every opportunity. Before too long I gave Gavin a key to my flat, and gradually he stayed over more often until he was living with me permanently.

During my third year of University, my bubble of happiness was popped one day when I received a very upsetting call from Mum. Dad had been rushed into hospital with a suspected heart attack. After leaving my lecture, I left a message for Gavin back at the flat and hurriedly threw a few clothes into an overnight bag. Shooting off in my car to see Dad in intensive care at their local hospital, my journey was filled with dread. I was afraid for him, and for myself and Mum. How would I ever cope without my wonderful Dad if something happened? I loved him so much and he was far too young to die. I worried for Mum and wondered how she would cope without him if he died. Crying throughout the journey, my tears made it difficult for me to drive. I couldn't concentrate but I couldn't get there fast enough. My break-fast also threatened to re-present itself. I felt I wanted to vomit and was terrified of getting to the hospital too late.

By the time I enquired about Dad in A & E, the diagnosis had already been made. It was confirmed that Dad had indeed suffered a minor heart attack but I was assured he was going to be okay. It hurt me to see Mum so distraught and wrapping my arms around her we comforted each other as we waited in the family room to be told when we could go in to see him. He looked reasonable but exhausted, which was not surprising considering what he had been through. He was still hooked to the ECG machine when we were allowed in. He joked that he was over the moon to see Mum and I again as he thought his time was well and truly up. I berated him for that, telling him that it was no joking matter.

Bobbie called me later in the evening to see if Dad was doing okay and to ask if Mum and I were coping. I assured her that Mum and I were both doing alright and Dad was making good progress. She went on to tell me that she parted from Phil, her latest in a long line of suitors, along with some other trivial bits of news from Uni. She didn't sound as if she needed any consoling about her break-up with Phil, so I said I would see her maybe in a week's time and we ended our call for the time being. Later, as I was heading to bed, Gavin rang me to say he was missing me and I succumbed to a few tears when I finally put the phone down. I ached to be with him but my parents had to be my priority.

Three days later, Dad was discharged from hospital care and was told he must take things a lot easier than he had been doing of late. It was nice to have him back home and Mum and I fussed around him endlessly. I ended up staying with them for another five days. My calls to Gavin continued each night. I was missing him more with each day that passed, my heart ached to be with him. Leaving Mum at home to look after Dad one day, I went out to get some food shopping for them. I stocked up with fresh supplies and enough freezer things to last for at least a month. Once I was happier to see Dad with much more colour back in his face and feeling so much better, I set off back to my flat, Gavin and Uni.

Finding a vacant spot, I parked up and made my way into the building. I scanned my fob and struggled through the security door and along the corridor with the carrier bags of supplies I bought earlier. As I turned the key in the lock and pushed the door open wider with my foot, I could hear the Aerosmith CD playing. The memory was brought to mind in an instant; Gavin and I when we made love for the first time, and that was what I was looking forward to in the next five minutes. I was already in the mood and couldn't wait. I crept towards the lounge to surprise him. It was unlikely that he would be expecting me so soon or that he heard the key in the lock with the volume of the music. The door to the lounge was slightly ajar and I held the shopping bags out in front of me to push it open wider. I was frozen to the spot at the sight that greeted me. Bobbie was on her knees bent over the armchair and my Gavin was shagging her from behind. Judging by his groans of ecstasy and her very vocal gasps, I guessed they just finished. I felt physically sick, numb and unable to move; rooted to the spot. Consumed in their moment, they weren't even aware of my presence. My so-called best friend and the man I loved… fucking in my flat! I felt as if my heart stopped beating. To make them aware of my presence, I intentionally let the bags drop from my hands, each landing with a thud onto the hardwood floor. They instantly spun around, guilty eyed and mouths gaping in surprise. Gavin pulled out of her muttering,

"Oh fuck! Oh fuck!" and made a rapid exit to the bedroom - *our* bedroom. Hell, it was *my* bedroom. Bobbie stood up and grabbed at the nearest cushion in an attempt to cover her nakedness, as if it made a difference to me.

"Get your fucking clothes on and get out of my flat. Get out of my life for fuck's sake, you bitch!" I screamed, my anger rising rapidly,

"I loved you. I trusted you, and you've abused it all. You come to my flat and screw my boyfriend and all while I have been helping my Mum care for my sick father! I never want to see you again! FUCKING GET OUT!"

I was at boiling point and her lack of emotion was swiftly pushing me well beyond that. I didn't trust myself to act and feared I would go too far, so I remained near the lounge door, trembling with rage. Within two minutes, she was dressed. She strutted past me and was gone, without a soli-tary word to say, not even a sorry. Gavin shiftily slid back into the room when he heard the door slam shut. Whether he thought it was me or her who had gone, I don't know. He'd put on his dressing gown and from the look on his face, he thought we were going to sit and have some cosy little chat, in which he would try to talk me round.

"Babe…I…" he started.

I couldn't bear to look at him and I was about to lose control, I was shaking so much. In that moment, I hated him.

"Save your breath, you bastard! Just get your clothes on,

get all your things and fuck off! Don't you ever fucking come near me again!"

The pained expression on his face served to anger me even more. "But where will I go? They've got somebody in my old room. I have nowhere to go!" he tried pleading.

No thought for the shock and pain he just caused me. He was thinking only of himself and it cut through to my core like a laser.

"That's *your* fucking problem, Gavin! Did you think I would still want *you* in here, in *my* flat, when you've just been fucking found up to your nuts in *her*?" I screamed.

He fled.

Do all men look so stung and hurt when you kick them out for sticking their cock up another female? Like it's you that's the bad, cruel bitch? Are they for real?

It was fifteen minutes before he emerged from the bedroom with his black bin bags. His eyes looked tear-stained, but I could not bear to look at his face for more than the fleeting glance. Was he genuinely sorry for hurting me or just sorry that he'd been caught? I don't know and I don't care. He came towards me, arms outstretched, until he saw me recoil. He staggered backwards.

"Babe…I…love you, since we met. Always!"

The bloody nerve of him!

I reached the end of my patience.

"GET THE FUCK OUT MY FLAT – NOW!" I screamed at the top of my voice.

All I could find in the fridge was some dregs (maybe one glass, at a push) of Pinot. In my desperation to numb the pain I threw it down my neck then rummaged through the side-board to see what spirits I could lay my hands on. Half a whiskey tumbler of Jack Daniels…his! What the fuck? URGGH…I knew there was a reason I never tried it before. I downed it anyway and almost instantly brought it straight back up again... tasting worse on its way out than it did going in, if that's at all possible. I must have cried solidly for almost two hours. With insufficient booze to drink myself stupid I turned the music off and sat in silence, thinking things through. I thought of the plans we made together for our future, how much I would miss him, how much I would miss our lovemaking and my heart broke. Struck with a sudden desire to get out of the flat, I sprang into action. My flat which I had always loved, the flat I had shared with *him*, I now hated. I needed to get out, I couldn't breathe. The hurt was all consuming. My toiletries were still in my overnight bag. I grabbed the few bits of washing that were in the bag, threw them into the washer and replaced them with some clean undies, denims and a T-shirt.

Within ninety minutes I settled into a room in a run-down hotel at Piccadilly Circus, the only one available that night. I made two resolutions during my waking hours. I told myself I would never get too close to a female again. Secondly, I didn't want to fall in love again...*ever*! Just for good measure I added a third one...never to cry again over any man.

On returning to the flat the next morning, I called Uni giving 'personal reasons' for my decision to quit. Secondly, I called the estate agent, giving them four weeks' notice to terminate my tenancy agreement from that day. My final call was to Mum and Dad to inform them that their daughter was returning, full time. By late morning all my clothes and personal things were packed, loaded into my car and the flat was fully cleaned throughout.

CHAPTER 2

*T*hey were looking out of the lounge window and on seeing my car pull alongside their Range Rover, came out to greet me. After a quick hug, Mum and I took the cases and some other heavy items to the front door. Dad grabbed a handful of lightweight carrier bags which contained bits of clothing that I was unable to fit into my already stuffed suitcases. He was still having to take things cautiously. Once he deposited the bag in the front hall he came up and folded his arms tightly around me. I didn't cry. I rested my chin on his shoulder and took comfort from him, the one man in my life who I have always been able to rely on. He didn't say a word; he didn't pry, he didn't judge, he never would! He never even asked me what had gone wrong. They wouldn't push me; I would talk when I was ready and they respected that.

Mum prepared my favourite meal in an effort to cheer me up. We sat around the dining table enjoying a glass of wine and discussing Dad's progress. We covered the same ground as the previous day before I left them to return to Uni. The events of the past twenty four hours seemed like it happened a life-time ago. When we left the dining table to relax in the lounge, Mum brought through a second bottle of Chardonnay and the topic of conversation turned to current affairs, the weather, Uncle David's stocks and shares, in fact any subject that skirted around my 'issues'. I understood, they were sparing my feelings. I guess they may have already suspected my reason for returning home, but knew I would reveal all in due course. I drank far more Chardonnay that night than the pair of them, relaxing at first but turning maudlin as the night turned into the early hours. Dad needed his rest though, so not wanting them to feel obliged to sit with me all night, I made my way upstairs about one in the morning. I heard their bedroom door close shortly after. I wept (silently, I hope) and much as I fought against it, I could not help but relive the horrendous scenes of... was it just thirty six hours ago? My mind flitted back to when I was at school and I compared this new type of hurt to that which I experienced from being bullied. This new hurt was totally off the scale. Sometime around dawn, when the stress, exhaustion and heartache finally wearied me, I succumbed to sleep, restless though it was.

It was late morning when I heard the sound of one of my parents trying to open my bedroom door without making a sound. Thoughtful as ever, not wishing to disturb me in case I was sleeping, but nevertheless, he or she just had to check to see if I was okay. I waited until the door softly clicked shut then shouted, guessing it would be Dad,

"I'm awake, Dad. Tell Mum to get the coffee on, I'll be down in ten!"

He paused for two or three seconds before answering, "Okay, darling, when you're ready."

Until I dragged my weary self into the én suite, I didn't realise exactly how exhausted I was. I splashed my face with cold water and caught sight of my reflection in the mirror. I looked pale. Dark rings encircled my eyes, (in part, due to the mascara I hadn't troubled to remove before climbing into bed) and all I could think of to ask that reflection was, 'Why me?' The reflection had no answers…nothing to say!

I padded downstairs in dressing gown and slippers. I hadn't even brushed my hair but just gathered it all up and clipped it in place for the time being. As I approached the dining room I could see Mum and Dad were sat in the conservatory. A fresh pot of coffee and a plate of enough toast to stave off hunger for the rest of the day sat on the coffee table.

"Hi, sweetheart," Mum greeted me as I sat down to join them, concern showing in her eyes despite the smile. "Don't try telling me that you slept, because I shall know that you're lying."

I smiled weakly at her. "I won't!" Although I knew my parents wouldn't push me, I recognised that I was under close scrutiny.

"We thought that since it's such a lovely morning, it would be nice to have coffee in here for a change."

It was beautiful outside, the sun was shining, a gorgeous day, if you aren't hurting; if your boyfriend hadn't just fucked your best friend, yes, it might be a nice morning.

"Well it's certainly brighter than my mood." I mumbled.

I realised I had to get it out there and then, make Mum and Dad understand how I was feeling. I couldn't just sit around depressing the hell out of them for days without them knowing and understanding the reasons why.

"We are not expecting you to talk, darling" said Dad "if it takes months until you are ready, we will respect that."

"Dad, I have to get it out in the open now, a problem shared and all that. If not, it's going to eat me up inside, so when we've eaten, I'll put you in the picture."

The mountain of toast was wasted (apparently, they

already had breakfast earlier). The last thing I wanted to do was eat. I felt physically sickened but empty at the same time so I nibbled slowly on a couple of slices, just to keep Mum happy, or else she'd lecture me on how I must look after myself better. After a few minutes, I struggled to force down any more of the toast so I discarded it and started talking.

They never needed me to tell them how happy I was when I first met and fell in love with Gavin, they saw the evidence of that for themselves over the last year. I told them about all the special times we shared, how much we laughed together. (The only details I omitted were about our raunchy sex life.) I talked for ages; places we visited together, the meals and restaurants we visited, films we watched together, how special he was to me. I also mentioned our joint plans for our future together and how we talked about perhaps going to live in New York. Devastated yet again at the thought that New York would not be happening, at least not with Gavin, the tears started to roll.

I stopped talking and poured myself another cup of coffee. Yet again I took another piece of toast that I didn't want and by doing so, I bought myself a little more time. It was going to hurt to have to speak about that scene. It hurt for me to relive it in my mind and it was going to further cause me pain to tell them.

"Darling, I think we both know what's coming. You're not ready! Leave it for now." pleaded Dad.

"It's going to hurt, whether I do it now, or in ten years' time. It has to be now."

Omitting the vulgarity of the scene that greeted me when I arrived back at the flat, I revealed all. I never heard either of my parents swear or use obscenities, so I described how I found Bobbie, bent over the lounge chair, and how Gavin was doing it to her, like a couple of dogs. My tears continued to flow. Mum kept handing me the tissue box, my voice felt raw and croaky and I couldn't stop shivering. Taking a few more minutes to collect myself, I fought to keep calm long enough to finish my story. Describing Bobbie and Gavin's reactions on realising that I saw it all, I felt the bitterness inside pouring out.

"That bitch, Mum! My so-called best friend moved in on the man I love while I was here, with Dad seriously ill. How could they do this to me? I would like to bet it wasn't the first time it happened."

"Sweetheart, whether it was once, twice or twenty times is irrelevant, it's cheating." She threw a quick glance at Dad and hesitated for a few seconds before confessing "To be honest, darling, we haven't really been too keen on Bobbie since you first introduced us. There was *something* about her."

I was a bit shocked to hear her say that, they had always been perfectly pleasant to Bobbie when they saw her.

"Why didn't you tell me what you thought? I would have listened to you both. I always trusted your judgement."

"Darling, we know how happy and excited you were to have a best friend for the first time. How could we spoil that for you by expressing our doubts? Also, we might have been totally wrong about her. It would have spoilt a good friendship for you." Dad explained.

"It might have spared me this heartache though." As soon as I said the words I instantly regretted them. It sounded as if I was now laying the blame on my parents, though they hadn't flinched.

"Did you ask them how many times it happened?"

"I wanted to know…but I didn't want to know, so no, I didn't. I've already been punished, Mum. Why add to it? I really wish you told me about your doubts. It would have saved this heartache but I understand why you kept the thoughts to yourselves. It's not your fault. They are the ones that have hurt me, not you two."

For the rest of the day, putting Gavin and Bobbie out of our minds, we talked about me possibly going to live abroad and leaving London behind, but more so about my decision to quit University. Mum and Dad made some suggestions, offered advice, and I listened to it all. I stressed to them that I was incapable at that point of making any life changing decisions. I didn't know what I wanted. The clocks turned back, to before Dad's heart attack? No. That wouldn't change anything. I would still have rushed to be with Dad. When would I be over this waking nightmare? I didn't know anything anymore. I know they were upset about me quitting University but Dad assured me he wasn't too concerned about it. He said he was confident that when I was ready, I would have a lot to offer future employers, whichever path I chose to follow.

For the next two weeks I hung around home most days, except one occasion when Mum and I went out for a much needed girly day. At home, I would read for much of the time and became engrossed in some of Mum's thrillers, an author I hadn't heard of before. He was an excellent writer. I became addicted to the stories and fell in love with all the characters. My reading was only ever disturbed though, by thoughts which crept up on me...of Gavin. One question that kept plaguing me was if Bobbie had been out with us that first night, would Gavin have been attracted to her instead of me? Try as I did to put that question to the back of mind, the lack of an answer haunted me.

Dad pottered around his garden (for the moment, pottering was all he was capable of). Sometimes, he would creep in through the back door, tiptoe in his stockinged feet into the conservatory and lean over the back of my chair, hug me and plant a kiss on the top of my head. He's always been like that. I sometimes surprised him by doing the same to him. Under normal circumstances we would laugh at these surprise hugs, so full of affection. This time though, the laughter wasn't appropriate, chiefly due to my dark moods.

If I wanted to be alone, I went up to my room. This was usually when I needed to think or wanted to feel sorry for myself. I would put on a DVD or a CD for a bit of background noise. Sometimes I didn't realise what disc I was loading (the first one I grabbed) and got drawn into some of the films, usually my old favourite chick flicks, reaching out for the tissues before the end, which brought my own misery and worries back to haunt me again.

Every night after our evening meal we sat at the dining table for hours, talking about anything but my troubles and enjoying a couple of bottles of wine between us. I was lucky to have such wonderful, caring parents who were as supportive to me as they always have been. They loved me and would do anything for me, buy me anything I wanted…if there *was* anything I wanted. I didn't want material things though. I just wanted to be there with them. They never did anything to hurt me and never would. They were the only ones who could get me through this.

Half way down our second bottle of wine on one such night, Dad went into the kitchen and returned with an armful of holiday brochures.

"Your Mum and I need a break, darling, and so do you. We've all been through a tough time recently, so no arguments. You choose. I'll go anywhere you fancy but preferably somewhere we've not been before. Just bear in mind when you're going through the brochures, I want no sightseeing tours or traipsing around cities, museums or temples. I'm going for a rest, so I want sunshine, sun-loungers around a pool and doing absolutely nothing."

Whilst I was appreciative of their generosity, the last thing I desired was a holiday. I wanted to stay at home and mope but I knew they would only fret if they went without me. The last thing Dad needed was to spend a holiday worrying, so for two days I concentrated on browsing the internet, looking at the countries that we were yet to visit. After some discussion with Mum we came to a mutual decision, Cuba; a place we wanted to go in the past but still hadn't managed it. After Dad visited his doctor and was given the all clear to fly, he booked the holiday through an online travel shop. The next six days were spent frantically shopping for lotions, potions and new bikinis for Mum and I. Dad paid a visit to his office for the first time since before his heart attack. He wanted to check up on things and to see how his new recruit Anthony was settling in. Planning to return to work after our travels, he said his goodbyes and picked up the latest set of management accounts to peruse by the pool.

Although Cuba was still very much a poor country, we found everything about the place charming and quaint, if somewhat run down in places. Our holiday resort at Cayo Coco was reasonably new and had everything that we required. The food was good (we had heard negative reports on the meals served in nearby hotels), our rooms were immaculately clean, and the staff were efficient and attentive. We heeded advice not to leave towels, sandals, and swimsuits on the loungers overnight, otherwise they would disappear. After a day or so Dad looked fit and well again, considering what he went through recently. He was fully relaxed, and was either sleeping or reading the days away, with a little gentle swimming once a day and some short walks thrown in.

After three or four days of chilling out with Mum and Dad I decided to give them some space. Also, I needed some 'alone' time. My darling parents when we were together talked incessantly. Most of the time it was to keep me occupied, I know that much! If they were getting my attention I didn't have time to brood. I needed some 'me' time though, I wanted to brood, to get things straight in my mind. I wanted to make sense of everything that happened and start thinking of a way forward. Basically I wanted to put all the shit behind me. I went to see one of the tour reps and booked myself a day's sight-seeing in Havana, a salsa night on the beach and a dolphin experience. Swimming with dolphins, I was told, could be quite therapeutic – and I needed therapy. Dad looked at me, a question in his eyes when I told him about the three excursions I booked. I instinctively knew what he was thinking. He was wondering if I could cope on the tours when it was highly likely that I would mostly be accompanied couples. They understand me so well. Clearly they knew I was seeking time for myself as Mum did not offer to accompany me, though I got the impression she would love to come along too (well, perhaps not the salsa).

It was only a short flight to Havana and the sight-seeing tour once there, was an education. I never realised that Ché Guevara was such a national treasure as history was never my thing, even though museums hold a big fascination for me. I was enthralled by their old American cars and couldn't visit Havana without having the obligatory ride in one. Later in the afternoon when my car trip was over, I found a tourist market and purchased one of the many oil paintings of those cars. Just as Mum and Dad predicted, the seats on the plane and the tour bus were predominantly occupied by couples, so the tour guide paired me (for the tour and the lunch included) with Keith, a single Canadian guy. He never told me his age, but I suspected him to be mid-thirties. He seemed like a nice enough guy but reminded me of a puppy dog. He hung onto my every word with his tongue practically lolling out. I would have been blind not to notice the fact that he was attracted me. I enjoyed our conversations to a point; he was intelligent, amusing at times, and we shared some similar tastes in music and film, but I was trying to recover from the Gavin incident and Keith was not my type.

We were back at the pick-up point for the coach in plenty of time and I was looking forward to relaxing for what remained of the evening. The busy day's walking left me physically drained. When we arrived at our hotel later in the day, Keith gave me a peck on the cheek and made his way to his room. At least I didn't have to put up with him anymore, it had been a few hours too many. During our conversations at the latter part the day, I deliberately avoided telling him of my plans for the remainder of the holiday.

I was in for a shock when the tour bus arrived at the venue for the beach salsa three nights later. Whilst gathering around for instructions from the tour guide before our short walk to the beach, I noticed Keith, the last person to get off the bus. I was one of the last to board the bus back at the hotel and failed to notice that he had been seated at the very back. He came over to me and, putting his arm around my shoulder said,

"Looks like we could be partnering each other again, honey."

Oh, fucking crap!

My stomach sank and I felt so irritated. So much for my plans to find someone interesting to spend the evening with!

There was no choice in the matter as the rest were couples, so we partnered for the salsa and as we were learning we laughed at each other when we got the steps totally wrong. After the salsa finished, Keith entered the men's limbo competition and dared me to enter the one for the ladies. His limbo was so good and managed a close second to the worthy winner of the competition. I was eliminated about half way through my contest when I leaned too far back and fell flat on my back into the sand. To me, it was an excellent night, good company and plenty of laughs, but to Keith it was many steps nearer to getting into my knickers, or so he thought!

Back at the hotel after we left the bus, his arm went around my shoulders yet again and he pushed me towards the wall behind the reception building as we were passing. Before I had chance to protest he planted his lips on mine, kissing me hard and urgently. I struggled to get my head from between the wall and his lips but finally I edged free and pushed him away, seething.

"Stop it, Keith! You've spoilt what has up to now been an enjoyable evening!"

"Honey, don't worry, what happens in Cuba, stays in Cuba." he muttered, as he came towards me again.

"Look, I think you're basically a nice guy, but I don't like you in that way. I don't want a relationship, sexual or otherwise with anybody right now. I haven't come on holiday for that!"

"Then why bother coming on holiday at all? You're the best chick there is around this resort, surely you realise that every man here wants to fuck you?"

Yeah, sure mate. And like all those men, like Gavin did, you'd probably be another one that ended up fucking my best friend.

I didn't utter the words, but it was the first thought that crossed my mind.

"No, Keith, they don't. You're the only one who's tried, nobody else."

At that, I turned my back on him and walked away, wondering if I would ever rid myself of all the bitter thoughts. I just wanted the whole episode behind me. I joined Mum and Dad the next morning and after breakfast we gathered our books and towels and claimed our loungers for the day. I was still furious about Keith spoiling my night out and I was having visions of him turning up on my dolphin day. I made a real effort to read but I was unable to get beyond the first few pages of my book.

"Are you alright, darling?" asked Dad. "I wouldn't ask but

every time you've gone for a dip, I can't help noticing that your book has been open at the same page each time."

"I'm fine, thanks. Just going over things in my mind, you know."

As it turned out, I needn't have worried too much about my unwanted Canadian friend. Keith *was* on the dolphin tour as well but had found another lady (or ladies) to work his charm on. I was already on speaking terms with them, having seen them in the swimming pool on a number of occasions. They were enjoying a girls' holiday, having left their husbands hard at work in the U.K. I don't know whether they made Keith aware that they were married but if so, it was not deterring him from giving it the full charm offensive. Good luck to him. I wasn't going to let him affect my mind enough to spoil another day.

The dolphins were marvellous, I swam with them, stroked them and attempted all the tricks. The day was as therapeutic as promised. I was in awe of the wonderful creatures; their intelligence, their intuition and mostly of their interaction with humans. I cried, it was such a moving experience. Somehow, I managed to steer clear of Keith and his lady friends all day until it was time to return to the coach. His arm was around the taller of the two women and I noticed him give a playful slap on her bottom as she boarded the bus ahead of him. I saw both women in the pool the next morning. We stopped swimming to have our daily chitchat. I mentioned that I saw her at the dolphins with the Canadian guy and asked how she got along with him.

"Don't ask." she replied, "Story is...he was after a shag. I told him I was married and that I wouldn't cheat on my husband but he didn't seem to care. He said 'honey, what happens in Cuba, stays in Cuba'."

I laughed, and seeing the quizzical way in which they looked at me I felt obliged to tell them of my own experience. They were disgusted, but relieved that I handled the situation well enough. He apparently turned rather nasty when she, Dawn, had refused to give him a kiss but luckily two couples were walking past at the time. The two guys stepped in to help her and Keith ran off. Thankfully, none of us saw him again.

I was relieved when we were walking up the driveway, back home again. Unable as always to sleep on the plane, I couldn't wait to get a shower and go to bed. Despite being tired though, I was starting to feel better in myself. The holiday had been a godsend to me and Dad was looking fantastic again having been forced into relaxation with no gardening, no worrying about the business, and no worrying about me, because I had been where he was able to keep his eye on me.

CHAPTER 3

*O*nce we returned home from Cuba, two weeks passed us by before we had time to gather our thoughts. Dad started going into the office two or three mornings a week and he was looking tanned and healthy after our break. He tried to convince Mum and I that he felt better than he had done in a long while, but I wasn't so sure. It didn't stop her though from worrying constantly for every minute that he was away from home. I managed to persuade her not to be calling the office or his mobile every five minutes to check up on him, even though I was sorely tempted to do so myself. With a little encouragement she busied herself with some of her voluntary work in the local 'Mind' shop. She also returned to the Ladies Circle and pottered about in the garden, though what Dad would think to her re-positioning of the pots of bedding plants and statues I hadn't a clue. It kept her busy, kept her off my case and it gave Dad a peaceful time while he was at the office, so I didn't think he would have any objections.

Though I was feeling better after the recent events in my life, I couldn't understand what was wrong with me since returning from Cuba. When Mum and Dad were out of the house (and therefore unable to bear witness), my daily routine started to involve cleaning the house from top to bottom. If their activities kept them away from home for long enough I would start at the top and work my way down all over again. I couldn't understand what the hell I was doing. Their house is always immaculate, due to the conscientiousness and thoroughness three times a week of Anita, their cleaner. I have never done this before and can't understand why I've suddenly started being obsessive about cleanliness, particularly as I am a naturally untidy person. Now, I pick things up after myself, put dirty laundry into the washing basket, scrub the bathroom and polish the bath and sink until they sparkle. I plump up the cushions, wash windows, change bed linen every day and use antibacterial cleanser on every square inch of the kitchen. The bookshelves in Dad's den have become an additional obsession. I sit for hours organising the books along the shelves. From the tallest books on the left, I arrange them in size order right along each shelf. I place ornaments in perfect symmetry as well as the magazines on the coffee table. I can't stop myself. My other thing is to wash my hands and arms, right up to my elbows. I scrub with a nailbrush, twenty or thirty times a day.

The three of us went out for a drive early one Sunday afternoon. We stopped for a carvery lunch at a charming country inn and later went for a pleasant walk around a local beauty spot. After we walked for half an hour or so, we sat down on a bench so Dad could take a breather and Mum edged closer to me.

"Sweetheart, we've been getting worried about you and your behaviour since our holiday. You've not been yourself lately and we think you need some help."

She certainly caught me off guard and my immediate

reaction was to go on the defensive. I even shocked myself when I snapped back at her,

"To what behaviour are you referring exactly? The fact that I am trying to pick myself up after my boyfriend cheated on me?"

I watched the impact register on her face. I have never spoken to her like that before and much as I don't like myself for doing it, it didn't stop me. I carried on venting.

"That's not *behaviour*! It's something I will get over in time. It doesn't happen overnight! You've no idea what it's like!" Her face softened and she reached out.

"Look Helen, see these." She lifted my hands in hers and shook them gently. "I've seen them. Sweetheart, you've scrubbed them until they are almost bleeding. That's the behaviour I mean...and the rest!" she nodded knowingly.

I looked away, avoided her gaze and she took that to be my acknowledgement of her stated facts. She pulled me towards her and folded her arms around me, not saying another word. I sighed heavily over her shoulder, my silent admission to the truth. So they know what was going on. I must have been crazy to think that they wouldn't. Dad noticed his books and the meticulous placing of each and every one of them. Mum couldn't fail to see each night they went to bed, that the sheets and duvets were fresh, the persistent smell of bleach in the bathroom; never present before, even after Anita's days cleaning. Then there was Anita herself, reporting back to them about my manic routines during their absence; telling them how tidy my room was these days, no CD's or DVD's to pick up anymore, no clothes to put to the wash or hang up, no bed to make. She crept around the house watching me rearrange the books in Dad's study. Anita was also the first to witness the obsessive scrubbing of my hands and arms.

First came the visit to our family doctor. Dad accompanied me after I persuaded him and he prompted me at times whilst I told the story of the last few months and the affect those events were having on me and my life. Despite my resolve, I cried. I tried holding it back I really did, but the doctor asked me such direct questions, I felt like I was backed into a corner. There was two ways out of that corner...cry, or answer the questions. I did both. After listening for nearly twenty minutes (each appointment was ten minutes only and hadn't I grumbled many times before about people taking too long?) Dr Jack opened his mouth to speak but Dad instantly cut him off.

"I know what you're about to suggest, Richard, but forget it. She is not starting on anti-depressants. No way. I know people who have struggled to get off the bloody things..."

"But it doesn't have to be..." he tried to cut in.

"No! She needs some proper help, not medication. I want her to see a clinical psychologist or a counsellor. You can do that for her, can't you?"

Dad laid down the law and Dr Jack stared back at him, twiddling his pen around in his fingers, deep in thought.

"Okay, I will write a couple of letters. You should hear something over the next few weeks."

He asked how Dad was coping since he returned to work and, apparently satisfied, he saw us back to reception where he shouted the name of his next patient.

Mum tried her hardest to organise the next couple of weeks for me. She cut down her charity shop hours to almost nothing, and the Ladies Circle was forgotten about, yet again. She arranged some outings for the two of us; a spa day, trips out for lunch, shopping sprees and a couple of musicals in the West End. Dad did his little bit too by taking me to his golf club, telling me it would be good for me and it would give me something to focus on. He enrolled me as a member and afterwards, stood grinning for half an hour watching my feeble attempts to hit the ball get worse with every passing moment. I know they are only trying to help, but it kept me busy, entertained, and away from the house, bleach, vacuum cleaner *and* the soap, water and nailbrush.

Mum and I had a really lovely day at the spa. In the morning we ate cream cakes by the swimming pool as we read our magazines…in the nude, like most of the other ladies present. A variety of beauty treatments and holistic therapies were on offer. I chose a non-surgical face-lift, a set of acrylic nails with a French manicure and an hour of reflexology. Mum decided on an Indian Head Massage and Hot Stone Therapy then finished the day with a facial. It was a wonderful feeling to be utterly pampered and we giggled like a couple of school girls as we walked back down the street to the tube station. Dad surprised us both and prepared one of his special stir fries for when we got home; my favourite chicken and pineapple with some saffron rice and mixed salad leaves. We took our meals out in the garden and sat around until after dark. Mum and Dad drank a bottle of red. I consumed a considerable amount of water (being good and healthy for once) as recommended by the reflexologist. (Apparently, it helps rid the body of toxins following a foot massage.) With some beautiful classical music playing behind us in the conservatory, the birds twittered their good-night calls to each other at dusk, we whiled away the evening; Dad completed his Daily Telegraph crossword and Mum and I enthused over our spa day, promising to do it again soon. We reminisced about my childhood days and I felt more relaxed than I had in a long time, and without one mouthful of alcohol passing my lips.

It was nearly four weeks after my original visit to Dr Jack at the surgery before I received my appointment through the post to visit clinical psychologist, Mr Gillespie. The appointment was for a Friday, just over two weeks away. Mum and

Dad were chuffed the appointment came through fairly quickly as sometimes people waited months for these type of appointments. I think they were happy; thinking that their little girl was going to get some help with her problem and that they would soon have her back to normal again. To be honest, I don't really feel that I have a problem, not a psychological one anyway. What was so wrong about me wanting everything to be clean and tidy for once in my life? The way I see it, I'm helping around the house, something I have never done before, but not before time. Mind you, there's still the obsessive hand washing and I have to admit to myself, *that* really is a predicament. I feel more than a little apprehensive about the forthcoming appointment though and truly wonder if there is anything that can be done to help me. There is another appointment I need to make too...and pretty soon.

CHAPTER 4

$\mathcal{T}$he other appointment came first; one that Mum and Dad don't know about and don't need to know about. I'm roughly eleven weeks pregnant and for the last six weeks I've been throwing up every morning. I've been on the pill since I was sixteen and I couldn't understand what the matter was when I missed my first period. I *never* missed a pill, I always made sure of that. They're always on the top of my bedside cabinet and I never fail to take one each night before going to sleep, even when I've been drunk. Thinking back, the only possible explanation I have come up with is that I took antibiotics for ten days for a particularly bad chest infection and they've counteracted the effects of the pill. Still, there's no time to be wasted wondering how and why, the matter needed my urgent attention. I'm too young, not too fond of children anyway and I need a career. A part of me wondered what it would be like to gaze down into a cot and see a little boy or girl with Gavin's eyes and nose. But I don't let myself dwell on the thought for too long. For the most part I can only see the negative side…it would probably turn out to be a cheating, conniving bastard like its father. I won't be responsible for bringing another of those into the world, there are more than enough already.

I told Mum and Dad I'm going into the city for the day; a bit of shopping, some mooching around an art gallery and maybe even a museum. Mum offered to come with me but I rapidly quashed that idea. I told her I need some time to think and plan for my future. I'm scared. I was almost tempted to tell her what I was about to do; to have her come along, hold my hand and let me cry on her shoulder after it's over. I got a shiver within the depths of my body. I hated having to lie to my parents but I'm only doing it to protect them from the hurt and disappointment they would inevitably feel.

"I'll be fine, Mum. Stop worrying. I'm having a day alone, that's all. I need to think."

Whether it was still the morning sickness or just pure nerves I don't know, but the nauseous feeling never left me during my journey on the tube. My appointment was for ten o'clock in a private hospital not far from Harley Street. I had a ten minute wait after I checked in with the receptionist. I suppose like every other young woman who've done this before me, I seriously considered walking out of there. I know what I was about to do was morally wrong but to have a child is not right for me. It was my fear that made me want to run. Fortunately, somebody came to take me into a little side office before I had a chance to run. There was some form filling to do and a quick consultation. By teatime I was out of there. It was over and done with. I felt so strange when I woke up…to know that the last little bit of Gavin which had been growing inside me had gone. I felt a sense of relief. I got rid of his foetus and hoped by having rid myself of it, would also help get him out of my mind, permanently…like a type of exorcism. I caught a cab home just in case I started to feel queasy after my surgery, but the nausea I did feel was more to do with guilt. At least I had no worry of passing out on the tube.

"So, darling, did you get any thinking done whilst you were out?" Dad asked as we settled down after our evening meal.

The guilt gnawed at my insides again and I hoped they wouldn't see the red flush that I felt glowing up my face.

"Yes. I'm going to have my appointments with the clinical psychologist. After that I'm going to get a job, if I can," I told them, "in accountancy. That's always what my intention was. I'm just taking a different route now."

"I may be able to help with that, sweetheart" said Dad, "leave it with me for a few days."

My heart melted at his protectiveness of me and his offer of assistance, but it also made me feel small. I didn't want his help. I just robbed them of a grandchild. I didn't deserve any help. I suppressed a short-lived urge to scream out my shame. I needed to do something for myself for once. My parents have already done so much for me. They gave me a very privileged start in life. Now is the time for me to go it alone, without any strings being pulled on my account. Determined that I would sort out my own career but wanting to show my appreciation for his support, I muttered,

"Thanks, Dad."

The appointment with Mr Gillespie soon came around. The first initial visit involved me telling him all about my life from my earliest memories and right through my school years, which was mostly to do with the bullying. It was hard work; there was no prompting from him whatsoever. He hardly said a word, just nodded occasionally to acknowledge that he understood what was being said; his elbows on the desk, the fingers of each hand interlocked together. The half hour appointment dragged while I was in there and once finished for the session, he told me to see the receptionist on the way out so I could book my next appointment. He suggested two weeks as an ideal gap.

Those next weeks passed by quick, and uneventfully. I continued with my daily cleaning routines to the house and unconsciously trying to remove the top layer of skin from my hands and arms through the constant scrubbing. Mum and Dad persisted in watching over me whenever they were able. I really wished they would stop fretting. I'm not about to do any serious harm to myself; I don't have my finger poised over some self-destruct button. My routine is getting me through each day in the way I know best. I don't harbour any guilty feelings about getting rid of Gavin's baby. I know it had been the right thing to do...at least where I was concerned it was. I think I would have resented it, looking at his or her little face and seeing Gavin in every expression and mannerism. Not once did I ever consider that it may have looked like *me*, having *my* facial expressions, *my* temperament, maybe all *my* genes. I won't let those thoughts enter my head, though. I can't. Any guilt I feel is only for the loss that my parents are unaware of...their loss, not mine.

At our next appointment Mr Gillespie started the proceedings by asking about my life at University. He asked how I coped with the coursework, what my plans were for the future at that time, both before I quit and afterwards. I told him about the university social life, the constant partying, meeting Gavin and the events leading up to his betrayal with my best friend. Yet again, as I talked, he sat, fingers as usual entwined, sometimes watching me, sometimes gazing out of the window...but he listened intently. I hadn't failed to notice that on both occasions there was very little note-taking involved in the appointments. Perhaps he wrote up his notes afterwards so as not to suddenly lose his patient's train of thought by hurriedly picking up his pen to start furiously writing lest he forget some minor detail. It might leave me, his patient, wondering what he's writing about me, and did it involve the words total nutcase, loser, raving lunatic or recommend mental institution for the rest of his or her natural? Our time ended promptly when my thirty minutes were up. On leaving his room I called by the receptionist's desk to make my next appointment.

I already decided I wasn't going to waste the next fortnight waiting for session three with 'the shrink', as I now referred to him when speaking with Mum and Dad. Making a valiant effort not to clean and scrub as much, I sat in front of the computer and composed my introduction/enquiring if you have any vacancies' type letter which I planned to send out to all chartered accountant practices throughout the London region. I thought the letter through with utmost care, the wording had to be spot on. I wanted to create an instant good impression and really sell myself. My aim was to make them want to know more about me and subsequently, invite me for an interview. It took me four hours in total. I edited, re-edited, made some additions, deleted a couple of words here and there and finally I was happy with it. One thing that worried me was the fact that I quit university...would they even consider me? I stated in my letter without going into detail, that my reason for me leaving university was personal. Would they just disregard me anyway and label me as a quitter to save themselves disappointment later in the day? Or would they give me a chance to explain those personal reasons during an interview? I couldn't see myself explaining to them 'well, I quit Uni because I caught my boyfriend fucking my best friend.'

I was in a rush to get all the letters sent out as I wanted something sorted before Dad could start speaking to some of his contacts and, as he put it 'pull some strings'. I was desperate to make my parents proud of me. My second reason for rushing to get a job was the shrink appointments...I want them over with. My way of thinking was if I get a job (something to occupy my mind), the O.C.D. will just automatically disappear. The day after I finished the letter I printed off fifty copies and used Google to search for accountancy practices in the Greater London area. I hoped fifty would be sufficient, but if I wasn't successful with any of those there was plenty more practices I could try.

I had a pretty good feeling about the exercise and was quietly confident that I could land myself a position of sorts. I still had the quitting Uni thing niggling at the back of my mind but I was sure that there was someone, somewhere, who would be willing to offer me an opportunity by giving me the benefit of the doubt. I seriously needed some interviews. If I could achieve that much, at least it would help restore some faith in myself.

A few days after I mailed all the letters I paced around the lounge and hallway each morning waiting for the postman. The frustration when I shuffled through any mail to find the letters all addressed to Mum or Dad was unbearable, but I am not the most patient person at the best of times.

Why do people take so long to reply to letters? I've never been able to understand that. To me, it's simple. You get a letter, you answer it. Just a straightforward 'yay' or 'nay' would do...why take days, weeks even?

Two days before my next 'shrink' appointment was due, I opened my mail to find not one, but two letters from accountancy practices willing to offer me interviews and both suggested a date and time. One was three weeks away, a Thursday at four pm, and one on Wednesday, just a week away at ten thirty. I was thrilled. I already received about ten rejection letters in the previous two or three days, some stating 'unfortunately, we do not have any vacancies at this current time' and the remainder saying 'sorry to inform you that your application has been unsuccessful.' Now, I needn't give a thought to those. I was overjoyed and gave a beaming grin as I thrust the interview letters into Dad's hand later that day.

"See? I can do it, Dad." He grinned back at me and gave me a huge bear hug, delighted to see me looking more positive.

"I always knew you were capable, darling. Never doubted you for a second. I hope the interviews go smoothly. You will be an asset to any company, I'm sure."

I hoped so too. I needed this.

I went along to the next appointment with Mr Gillespie two days after receiving my interview letters. This time he wanted to know all about my obsessions. When exactly had it started, how often did I indulge in my obsessions? Was it every day? What did I feel I was achieving? How many times a day was I scrubbing my hands or showering? Did I think that this had all been triggered by Gavin having sex with Bobbie?

Stupid bloody question!

Did I feel mentally contaminated because I couldn't rid myself of the vision of the two of them indulging in such a way?

What sort of question was that to ask? Wouldn't anybody feel the same way, having witnessed those two shagging like a couple of dogs?

Why was I arranging Dad's books in perfect symmetry? Was I trying to get my life back in order?

It was a total waste of my bloody time.

I've come here to see this guy and he sits there telling me what is patently obvious.

He ended the day's session by confirming that I have Obsessive-Compulsive Disorder and that as things only recently started occurring, he was quite sure that with some additional help, cognitive behaviour therapy quite soon, it was possible that I could get past this stage in my life before it really took a hold. He would make the referral and the therapist would write to me offering an appointment. On the journey home I was feeling rather disgruntled and pissed off with everything. I badly needed *not* to have to go through with the ridiculous therapy.

I parked my car in the drive, ambled up the path and in through the door. Mum was in the kitchen preparing the vegetables for the evening meal. She turned to face me.

"How was today's session, darling?" and without pausing for another breath or waiting for an answer,

"There's some more mail for you...well, one letter...on the coffee table. The post arrived just after you left."

I left Mum alone in the kitchen, muttering as she continued to attack the swede with a touch too much enthusiasm. As I ripped open the envelope and read the contents, I started to smile and couldn't stop myself from punching the air. I had another interview, ten o'clock on Monday morning the following week.

By eleven am at the start of the next week I was offered a position. No waiting whilst hundreds of other hopefuls had interviews too, no hanging about waiting for the rejection, or in my case, acceptance letter. My interviewer told me immediately that there was a position and possibly a future for me within the practice. I liked the gentleman, Mr Hopkins, from the first impressions I got and it was all I could do to keep myself from flinging my arms around him and kissing him. He gave me all the necessary information with regard to salary, holiday entitlement, sickness, and training and promised to get the employment contract drawn up immediately. Finishing up, he asked when it would be convenient for me to start. I left the office on cloud nine and with an overwhelming desire to dance down the street as I walked back to the underground station, knowing I would be starting my new career in a week's time.

Mum and Dad were delighted for me and after some persuasion regarding me wanting to discontinue the therapy, eventually agreed that it would probably be more beneficial than seeing any therapist. They reminded me the next morning to call the other accountancy firms and inform them I had been offered and had accepted a position elsewhere. I made the calls to those companies and wrote to Mr Gillespie telling him that I did not wish to carry on with our appointments or to pursue a meeting with the C.B.T.

CHAPTER 5

*L*ife was quite dull and uneventful for the next two years. I spent most of my spare time studying for my A.A.T. (Association of Accounting Technicians). I loved working for the Hopkins Partnership and my first impression of Mr Hopkins had been right. He was an excellent accountant and had the utmost patience when dealing with trainees. He always explained things clearly and concisely and was willing to help with my studies if I ever found myself struggling to understand the assignments. Fortunately, I never needed to ask for that help. Another thing I was fast learning in my work environment is that there was nothing Mr Hopkins loved better than joining in with a bit of fun and gossip in the staff kitchen at lunchtimes. All the staff were extremely fond of him (as were his clients) and at practical jokes he was second to none.

My studies for A.A.T. would take two years and if I managed to pass my exams I intended to do further studying and become a Chartered Accountant. Mr Hopkins gave me every encouragement and constantly reminded me that his offer of help was always there if I needed it.

I didn't bother much with a social life; I hardly ever went out other than the occasional hour or two in the pub with colleagues after work on a Friday. I had a decent holiday with my parents during that time plus the odd visit to their apartment in Paris. Occasionally, I went out on some dates and I'd had a couple of steady boyfriends but nothing lasting more than two or three months. They didn't work out and I quickly lost interest. I tried to find the kindest way to end the both relationships. One thing that did please me was that my obsessive behaviour rarely surfaced. I was a little over the top about having a tidy desk and bedroom and I still wash my hands more than anybody I know, but the frantic cleaning of the house and scrubbing my arms with the nail brush had stopped completely.

Some days at work ended up quite tiring where audits were concerned. I often had to travel, along with one or two of my colleagues, to various limited companies to carry out an annual audit after their financial year end. Some firms made us really welcome and went out of their way to clear spare desks for us and yet there were places that almost had us sitting in what could best be described as a store room where the radiator didn't work, if there was one, and our only work surface was a decorator's pasting table. Often at some of these businesses we could go all day without even being offered a cup of tea or coffee.

On one of the audits during my second year of studying I was stunned to bump into Alex Baker-Thompson in the corridor on my way back from the loo (the boy from my senior school days who was caught by the bullies fingering me behind the bike-sheds). We chatted in the corridor for a while. He was employed as a draughtsman at the company we were currently auditing. He asked how my uni days had been. Not feeling the need to mention the Gavin situation I told him I was really ill so was forced to quit. We saw each other most days for the next fortnight until the audit was complete. On my last day there he asked me out, as friends. I didn't think it could do any harm (and he was still quite attractive). Maybe he would be able to tell me what had happened to some of the other people from school - where they were now, who was married, or any other gossip about them, so I said yes. I didn't particularly care about where the bullies were but I looked forward to having a proper catch up with him. We exchanged mobile numbers and he promised to get in touch over the following week or so.

We met outside King's Cross early one Saturday evening later that same month and walked arm in arm around London for a couple of hours. We exchanged our family news, shared holiday experiences and things in general. I felt a little sorry for him when he told me about a girl he had been seeing for five months. Her father had taken some sudden dislike to Alex and told her in no uncertain terms to call it off. It was quite clear that Alex really liked the girl and was still puzzled over what he had done to make her father turn against him.

After a few minutes of searching we came across a cosy little restaurant and over our meal we got around to talking about some of the kids from school. Alex hadn't been in touch with his school friends for quite some time and had very little gossip to report. However, he had read in one of the national newspapers that one of my bullies (Ann Stead) had died in a tragic car crash, about eighteen months previously. Though I intensely disliked the girl throughout our school years I couldn't help but feel some sadness for Ann and her parents.

We enjoyed a couple more nights out before Alex asked if I consider us becoming an 'item'. It came right at me when I least expected it and I just gaped at him in shock not knowing what to say, but my head started spinning wildly. I was over Gavin, but I still hadn't been able to forget the hurt he caused me. After a brief battle trying to find the right words I told Alex that I wasn't looking for a relationship and explained that my studies consumed almost all of my spare time. Adding to that and hoping he wouldn't feel too bad, I said I would like it if we could still continue to meet up as friends. He barely hid disappointment but grudgingly agreed.

We met up regularly for three or four months and then one night after we both had way too much to drink, he tried to stick his hand down my undies when we were heading to the cinema to see a late film. Feeling disgust that I couldn't hide I lashed out at him with a force I didn't realise I possessed and his back connected hard against a wall. He was shocked and responded aggressively,

"Come on, Helen. You didn't push me away behind the bike sheds. You loved getting poked and *plenty* of lads poked you."

I was appalled. Had I really been that trashy? He made me sound like a slut and I didn't see it in the same way he did. We had been kids for fuck's sake, experimenting, doing what is natural – becoming sexually aware. I felt mortally wounded by what he just implied.

"Alex, I always thought of you as a nice guy, good-looking, funny, and I valued your friendship but I'm sorry, you've destroyed it. I was a young girl back then, just finding out about sex and experimenting, maybe a little too much, I concede. You thought I would be cheap...a dead certainty you would get laid! You've blown it, Alex!" I walked away, hailed a cab, and tortured myself the rest of the night until past sunrise.

CHAPTER 6

y lack of a social life returned. With no close friends and no boyfriend I became a hermit again but if I was to be honest with myself, I wasn't too bothered. The only social life I had, if you could call it such, was spent with Mum and Dad. I sometimes met up on a Saturday afternoon with my colleagues from work. We mooched around the shops and went to a pub for a few drinks. They went home to prepare for dates with their boyfriends, I went home to Mum and Dad and my studying. Not wanting my co-workers to think I was totally dull, I invented a boyfriend, Justin. I had some exciting dates with him, got fed up with him and a few weeks later I was seeing John (my next creation). I wasn't proud of myself for the white lies, but it was far easier than having to explain why I wasn't interested in men and why I preferred to study. What would they think if I told them the truth? I would probably have earned the label 'oddball', getting strange looks from them all and would never get invited to the Saturday shopping sessions or anywhere else ever again.

Dad tried getting me back to his golf club (where I was a

fully paid up member) but that wasn't for me either. He started dropping hints in a bid to tempt me, that there was a few eligible bachelors with a really good handicap.

"You'd like Mike, sweetheart. He's quite a dish. Well the ladies seem to like him, anyway."

I laughed at what he was saying,

"You're not very subtle, Dad. Stop trying to get me off your hands. Studying comes first. I'm too young, for heaven's sake."

There was cause for celebration later in the year when I achieved my A.A.T. qualification. My parents were thrilled and as I started making preparations for further studies towards getting my chartered recognition, Dad told me I needed a break from studying for a while. He booked a cruise for the three of us, my first ever, for during the Christmas and New Year period. The weather in England was wintry and horrible, lazing about in the Caribbean sun relaxing on a lounger reading thrillers instead of accountancy, economics and contract law, or doing nothing else but daydream sounded excellent. The day we boarded I met people who were my age group and we swam together, dined together and danced until the early hours. The weather was perfect and I thoroughly enjoyed everything about the cruise. When the end of the holiday came we all swapped addresses, phone numbers and email addresses, swearing to keep in touch and true to form, nobody did.

Mr Hopkins was of the same opinion as Mum and Dad and thought I needed a break from studying. Whilst all three of them thought I was having a few months' rest, I was going to bed early but my bedtime reading was the text books that I already purchased. I never left the study books on my bedside cabinet for Mum and Dad to find and kept them hidden in a drawer beneath all my undies. I couldn't help but overhear a whispered conversation between them one day.

They both were of the opinion that my studying had become another obsession and was perhaps another outlet for the O.C.D.

I made more of an effort to get out. I joined a badminton class where some of my work colleagues were also members. I went to the cinema once a month with the same crowd. I was amazed to find how much I enjoyed the badminton after the first four or five sessions. Those first sessions were exhausting, which was to be expected really as I hadn't done much in the way of physical exercise for so long. Once I learned more and was hitting great shots, winning some points and understanding the scoring system better, my competitive streak came to the fore and I was eager for Tuesday night to arrive each week. The Saturday shopping and drinking outings I enjoyed more than ever, because I was now able to join in with the conversations about badminton or the latest films. I was fitting in at last and the people I always referred to as colleagues were now friends. The six of us that were unattached started to plan for a holiday together. We knew the time had to be taken between Christmas and New Year while the office was closed, otherwise there was no way we would all be allowed to take annual leave at the same time. Finally, it was all booked and my excitement on Christmas Day put smiles on Mum and Dad's faces throughout.

We had a glorious week in Spain. It was the first time I ever spent a holiday with friends and it was also the cheapest holiday I ever had; three star accommodation on a room only basis. The cleanliness left a bit to be desired and the beds were barely comfortable but I *didn't* feel the inclination to get the bleach out for once, I was too busy enjoying myself. We flirted, we were drunk almost twenty-four seven, we sunbathed when we managed to drag ourselves out of bed in daylight hours, and we danced the nights away in the seedy little bars and discos. My new found friends would often cast me some looks of amazement, they were seeing me let my hair down for the first time. I shocked them even more so when I made the first move to chat up the odd guy who caught my eye. Not with the intention of getting laid or emotionally involved - I just wanted someone attractive to dance with, laugh with and share a kiss at the end of the night. I was also trying to get my confidence back. We all had a fantastic time and I was quite sorry when the week came to an end. On arriving back at Gatwick on the second of January we vowed to do it all again at the end of the year, but somewhere different.

I continued my studies on a regular basis but didn't let it interfere with my social life anymore. I found it was quite beneficial to resume my studying after the odd nights and days off as I was more refreshed and able to focus better. Mum and Dad went on holidays without me which was a good sign. They obviously didn't feel the need to watch my every move any longer. I went to Paris with them for the occasional long weekend but that was it.

Not long after our holiday in Spain, Cindy, the receptionist from work announced her marriage. She first met Adam a couple of months before our holiday. Once she was back from Spain they became an item. He proposed on Valentine's Day and the wedding was planned for August. I felt honoured, not to mention so happy, when she asked me to be a bridesmaid along with Gemma, our office manager. We eagerly accepted and with only six months until the nuptials it was back and forth to the seamstress every two or three weeks, shopping for the right sandals and hair accessories and a trial run at the hairdressers. It was a busy time for us and Cindy's excitement was infectious. I felt quite envious at times. The wedding came and went. Cindy looked radiant, pretty and happy. I was pleased for her. Gemma and

I didn't look too bad either. There was a weird moment when Cindy threw her bouquet into the eager crowd of waiting singles. I stood and watched, an innocent bystander, totally bemused at all the young ladies and their eagerness for the exquisite, airborne blooms and berries to fall into their grasp. When the flowers hit me on the forehead, landed in my arms and knocked off my headband in the process, there were howls of laughter along with some jealous mutterings from the wannabe brides.

As we all stood and watched the classic Rolls Royce, adorned with the old boots and tin cans as is tradition, pull away from the Majestic Hotel, Gemma whispered in my ear,

"That's one less for the holiday to Tenerife. We're down to five now. So don't you go off and fall in love will you?"

I widened my eyes in horror.

"I'm off men, Gemma, so that's not bloody likely to happen."

Christmas came around again along with the chaos that the British weather was causing since early November. After a quiet but pleasant Christmas day with my parents, Boxing Day morning arrived. The pre-booked mini-cab picked me up at eleven am, after Gemma, then after collecting Nina, Gillian and Janet, our other friends, it was Gatwick here we come. We had yet another good holiday together doing exactly the same things that we did in Spain the previous year, along with two or three bits of 'excitement' that we could have done without. Gillian left her handbag in a bar one night and on returning there to look for it, found that it was gone and nobody had handed it in. Her credit cards were in there. She managed to call the card companies to get the cards cancelled and thankfully, before her account had been used. Fortunately, she hadn't taken too much cash out with her that night but obviously she was upset. Then Nina, despite protecting her very pale skin with a high factor protection *and* avoiding spending too long in the sun, still managed to get quite badly burned. We all attended the hospital emergency clinic with her and sat around for four hours before she was even attended to.

Next was an incident which involved me. I was doing my forty lengths one morning while the pool was fairly quiet when some stupid kid, not looking where he was going, dive-bombed into the pool and straight onto my back. I seemed to be under the water for ages, panicking and gasping for breath, but I finally managed to surface. I was laid on the poolside in shock and in absolute agony with my back while a small crowd gathered round. The parents of the kid, sat on the opposite side of the pool, were glowering in my direction with looks that implied 'how dare I be in the pool when their little boy was having some fun', or 'stupid woman, it's her own fault'. 'Serves her right for getting in the way!' My back ached badly for a couple of days but mercifully, I suffered no lasting damage.

We managed to have plenty of fun despite those events and like all holidays it came to an end all too soon and we were back at Gatwick again. As we stepped off the plane into the horrendous winter weather, I wondered how many of us would be holidaying together the following December.

CHAPTER 7

I took a week's annual leave just before I was about to sit my final exams. I knew I would have the house to myself during the day and it would be peaceful for my final round of studying. Dad was busy at work and Mum was out most days doing more voluntary work than she could really cope with. I studied hard and for long hours, mainly concentrating on the elements where I knew my weaknesses lay. I read, re-read, made a list of the key points and then focused on letting them sink in. By Wednesday night I felt like my head was in overload and I was in need of some time out. I told my parents I would be taking some time off on the Thursday. My father asked if I would like to visit his office for a few hours to check out some new design software package that had recently been installed on all their computers. He was particularly excited about it and as I hadn't been to his office in the last four or five years he thought it would make a pleasant change for me. Just to keep him happy I agreed to a visit, promising him I would be at his office for eleven am.

As I pulled into the car park and parked my Mazda, I was

aware that I was being watched, and not just from one window. Dad obviously made all his staff aware of my visit and they were all waiting to catch a glimpse of the boss's daughter, most of them for the first time. I was disappointed to find that only two of his original staff remained; Dorothy, his aging secretary and Graham, the financial controller who was also heading towards his sixties. To bring me up to speed Dad gave me a guided tour of the office. So much had changed since my last visit which had been not long after I went off to uni. He introduced me en-route, to all the staff that I didn't know. Once we sat down in his office fifteen minutes later, Dorothy provided us with coffee and biscuits and Dad gave me a demo of the new software as promised. It was way over my head but I tried to show an interest. He was expecting Anthony, a staff member, back from a business meeting around twelve thirty and as they planned to go out for a spot of lunch, Dad invited me to go along too, or rather, he insisted.

Anthony had been a new recruit just before Dad had his heart attack and five years on he was the marketing director and Dad's right hand man. It was gone twelve fifteen when he knocked on the office door and realising that it wasn't closed properly, he stuck his head around the gap.

"Is it okay for me to come in, Ken?" he spotted me sipping at my coffee and winked.

"I can come back if…"

Ginger hair and green eyes. Definitely not my type.

"Come in, Tony, yes."

I did a quick appraisal as he came towards me to shake hands; smartly dressed, nothing spectacular but certainly not unattractive. I detected too, a hint of cockiness about him.

"Let me introduce you both. This is my daughter, Helen… Helen, this is, Tony Pawson."

He shook my hand firmly, a little too confidently in my opinion, and smiled.

"Pleased to meet you, Helen. I've heard so much...your father never stops..." he nodded as Dad cut in,

"Of course I don't stop. I'm a doting Dad." he chuckled as Anthony still gripped my hand.

"Glad to meet you too, Anthony," I uttered, easing my hand away, "though I can honestly say that Dad hasn't spoken of you much. Probably because Mum doesn't like him talking about work at home. She blames work for the heart attack." and I shot Dad a faux stern look.

"Helen's joining us for lunch. Shall we get going?"

My stomach juddered. I had a feeling I was going to regret coming to Dad's office and joining them for their mid-day banter.

Thirty minutes later, ensconced their favourite gastro pub with lunch ordered and a gin and tonic in hand, we sat down at a table situated in a large bay window. Whether he wanted to hear it or not, Dad gave Anthony a detailed biography of my life since birth. I sat and cringed, hoping Dad would stop...and soon. There were several embarrassing moments for me but Anthony appeared to be enthralled and smiled across at me from time to time when Dad paused in his story-telling for a few seconds.

Anthony requested our first order of drinks to be put on the final bill so I wondered what on earth Dad was doing getting up to go to the bar for drinks when the waitress would soon be bringing the food. He could have ordered direct from her when she served our food. Not my idea of being subtle. Even Anthony was amused as he commented,

"I think he's giving us time together, Helen. Don't be surprised if when the barman has put the drinks on the bar, Ken will pay a visit to the toilet...to give us more time alone."

It struck me how well he seemed to know my father.

Either that or they'd gone through this before. Maybe Dad had tried fixing Anthony up before, in a similar way. I was a tad suspicious.

"Okay, I say let's play him at his own game. You stare around in the opposite direction to me, I'll start searching through my handbag or sending a text or something. No talking, let's make it look awkward."

Sure enough and exactly as he predicted, we watched as Dad made his way from the bar and over towards the corridor where the toilets were situated. We had a brief conversation about how my studies were progressing and he asked if I had any long term plans for my future, enquiring as to whether I intended to stay at the Hopkins Partnership or search for pastures new. That was where the conversation came to an abrupt end as Anthony, with a better view of the toilet door, mouthed

"He's on his way."

I snatched up my handbag and shuffled through it, making a determined effort to look stony faced. I chanced a quick glance at Anthony, who was doing a sterling job of looking disinterested.

I couldn't resist commenting once Dad was back at our table,

"Dad, didn't you go to the bar to get drinks? You've come back without them."

"What? Oh...I'll go...."he stammered "I thought you two would be busy getting to know one another?"

Anthony and I glowered at each other before he uttered,

"Ken, we...um...well...I'm not sure that Helen's sufficiently enamoured with me. I seem to be boring her."

It was hilarious watching Dad's face as he stood open-mouthed, looking in disbelief, first at Anthony, then back and forth between us both. I shot a quick look at Anthony which confirmed he was struggling to stifle the laugh that was trying hard to fight its way out. Only seconds separated the guffaws that escaped from us both a minute later and Dad's expression remained one of disbelief, still open-mouthed trying to understand what the big joke was.

"What's...what is this? What's so hilarious?" he pleaded, trying to understand. The waitresses were approaching with our order.

"Sit down, Dad, we'll explain while we eat."

"We know what you're trying to do, Ken. Acting like you work for a dating agency. Pah! We might *not* like each other. Did you consider that?" asked Anthony.

Dad emphatically denied the accusation and tried to convince us both and perhaps himself, that his invitation for me to come to his office was strictly to offer a change of scenery and routine; a break from studying and home.

"So why the dinner invite?" I demanded. "Surely after Anthony's business meeting this morning you have things to discuss. You didn't need to ask me to come along." His lips were moving and I could tell that he was racking his brain for some excuse and he finally managed,

"How often do I get the chance to take my daughter for lunch? Tony and I can talk later after you've gone home."

The food was excellent and I could understand why they used the place whenever they entertained clients. I had to admit to myself that it made a pleasant change. I secretly enjoyed Anthony's attention and made a mental note to call into Dad's office a little more often in future.

As we drove back I told Dad that I would just go straight home and not bother to go back up to the office. I sensed a note of disappointment in his voice so I explained that I needed to make a few phone calls. Once we were back at the office car park, they both walked me over to my car. After a few more pleasantries Anthony shook my hand, said it had been a pleasure, and as Dad started to walk away he lowered his voice and asked me out to dinner that coming Saturday night. I hadn't envisaged being asked out by him, or so soon. I was delighted but had to warn him,

"Do me a favour, don't tell Dad. Don't give him the satisfaction, please. I couldn't bear to see the smug look on his face for the whole of next week and beyond." He laughed.

"Okay, you have my word, Helen."

Somehow, we managed to arrange a time and place to meet fairly quickly, so as not to give Dad any satisfaction from a lengthy goodbye on our part.

CHAPTER 8

$\mathcal{I}$ couldn't believe how fast the time was passing, probably due to all the studying I'd done. I'd been dating Anthony for almost six months and still without my parents' knowledge. Before I knew it I was a certified chartered accountant at last and the news came as a bigger relief to my parents than to myself. They were proud and loved boasting to family and friends. I got the impression that they saw my achievement as a sign of 'normality'; like you have to be *normal* to pass exams?

My dates with Anthony had been *just* that, dates only; trips to the cinema, meals out, a drive out into the country and 'Phantom of the Opera' at Her Majesty's. I refused to get further involved and had stressed that I didn't need any involvement whilst in my final days of studying. The exams were first and foremost in my mind. No emotional issues, no sexual relationship or anything else that bore the potential to create complications.

With exams well and truly out of the way and my qualifications now firmly under my belt, Anthony pushed me a little more each week to make our relationship public. More than anything, I think he was desperate to take it to the next level, and for my father to know, which I understood to mean he wanted our relationship to become physical.

"So what are we going to do then," he asked, "about telling your parents? Do I casually mention at the office that we have been seeing each other? Or should we do it together, go back to your parents' house one night and just tell them?" I wasn't expecting him to push the issue this soon. I'd not once considered telling my parents until now. I suppose I would have to meet his parents as well at some stage.

"Let me give it some thought for a while."

"Whatever you decide to do I am happy to go along with it. I think it's time they knew though."

He was right of course and I felt a little embarrassed at having been so secretive where both sets of parents were concerned. The conversation turned to other things as we dined that evening but by the time we left the restaurant my mind was made up.

"I'm telling my parents tonight when I get home. It will be better coming from me."

"Okay! What do you think your Dad will say?" he was eager to know.

"Not a great deal I think! He was trying to get us together anyway so what could he possibly say?"

Two hours later I got my answer. My parents were happy, especially Dad. He hadn't even been that shocked to learn how long we had been seeing each other. He thought it was more than a coincidence that Anthony's mood around the office changed dramatically since the day I joined them both for lunch. He was also further suspicious when people in the office kept asking Anthony why he was on a high and he'd been deliberately evasive and avoided any further questions.

"Things are good! That's it really." He'd fobbed them off and shrugged his shoulders dismissively.

"He's a good guy, darling. I'm really pleased. Excellent prospects and he's going to be running the business for me when I decide I'm ready for part retirement. I trust him with the business and I trust him to look after you."

It worried me listening to him, and my tummy started churning. What he said about Anthony, it sounded like he was giving me the 'Anthony's an eligible bachelor' talk, telling me what good prospects he had. But we only spent such short periods of time together and I didn't know if we were sufficiently compatible at that stage.

"It's early days, Dad. We've only been dating up to now. I like him a lot and he's keen on me too but let's just wait and see."

Mum wanted to meet Anthony and she couldn't wait. She got a shopping list started and invited him to a dinner party for just the four of us the following weekend. She was keen to make a good impression when he met her. I felt that Anthony might have preferred something a little less formal, like popping in to say hello for half an hour when he took me home one night but he seemed quite pleased that Mum was going to such trouble for him.

The evening arrived and the dinner party went well. Anthony was his usual charming self. Mum went a little over the top trying to make him feel welcome and fussed over him endlessly. Dad talked business whenever he could manage to get a word in as Mum bombarded Anthony with her never ending questions about his family.

He took me to meet his parents a couple of weeks later. We were in their house for just over an hour and other than nodding their heads at me and a grudging grunt of a greeting, I was ignored for the most part. I didn't take it too personally and told myself they were probably shy when it came to meeting people.

Meeting the parents was the proper start for our relationship. It was out in the open at last. Days later we slept together for the first time. We got engaged within six months and planned the wedding for eleven months later.

We both had fairly small families so the majority of the guests were my friends from work and Anthony's and Dad's mutual friends from their office. I invited a few other 'non-work' friends from badminton, and Anthony invited some guys from the golf club. Cindy and Gemma from the office were my bridesmaids, but as Cindy was now six months pregnant, the seamstress made a much looser version of the figure hugging navy silk dress that Gemma wore. They both looked stunning as they watched me step into my bridal gown in our suite at the hotel. As non-believers, we had picked a top class licensed hotel as the venue for the civil ceremony, wedding breakfast and evening reception/disco.

I was proud to have Dad, head held high and looking the business in his morning suit, walk me down the aisle. At the same time I was overwhelmed with love for Anthony as we made our vows. A love I hadn't expected to feel again for any man after Gavin. I was the epitome of the happy blushing bride. My cheeks flushed with embarrassment at being the centre of attention, as Anthony, and then Dad, made their very witty and lovely remarks about the bride. Dad also used that well-worn expression about 'gaining a son'. I smirked and couldn't help but think when he said it that he already regarded Anthony as a surrogate son before we had even been introduced. It was the perfect wedding day. Another big moment after the wedding speeches came when Ted walked up to me, envelope in his hand and welcomed me to the Hopkins Partnership as his junior partner, his personal wedding present to me! I was ecstatic, getting married and achieving my greatest ambition on the same day!

One small matter that kept eating away inside me was the distance that Anthony's parents seemed to be keeping. Not once throughout the whole day did they come over and offer their congratulations to the pair of us, nor was there any polite chitchat or fun to be had with them as we posed for the group photos. It seemed like Eileen, his Mum, didn't care much for me and also that his dad, John wouldn't be *allowed* to like me.

On the Sunday morning we left for a honeymoon in Vegas, our mutual choice. Dad drove us over to Gatwick and as he left us at the drop off point with our luggage, he gave me a big bear hug.

"You looked beautiful yesterday, Helen. I am proud to be your father, but you've always make me proud…and now you're a partner at the practice, too!" His eyes filled with tears as he turned away and climbed back into his car.

I soon discovered why Anthony had been eager to honeymoon in Vegas, the casinos. He never gambled before in his life other than the occasional horse race like the Grand National and the Epsom Derby. Many of his friends who holidayed in Vegas had expressed their enthusiasm for the casinos, how it had been addictive for them; the click of the chips, the constant supply of alcohol to those playing the machines, blackjack, other card games, and roulette wheels, it was 'magical' they told him.

We fell into a daily honeymoon routine. Anthony was exceptionally loving and attentive throughout the week. We made love every morning, explored the sights and attended some shows in the afternoons. We dined early each evening before visiting the casinos allowing Anthony to indulge in his new found passion. I occasionally played a few of the machines but I was cautious, setting myself an affordable limit and once I reached it I gave up and was content to sit watching Anthony's game play.

He also started off cautiously, but having had some decent wins in the first few days he started getting reckless, gambling with higher stakes and not quitting while he was ahead. I panicked at times as I watched him use his winnings as his next stake.

While I had no desire to spoil his fun, I worried that he was gambling with our joint savings; savings which we intended to keep for furnishing our new home in Windsor. We had only been able to afford it because of the sizeable deposit given to us by both sets of parents. As it turned out I needn't have worried…by the time the honeymoon was over, the balance of our savings account had increased by $14,500. It was nice to suddenly have a boost to our finances, though I didn't take much comfort from it. He was already talking about visiting a casino in London, and having seen the look on his face as he played, I was concerned that he was addicted.

CHAPTER 9

*O*ther than my concerns about Anthony's new found love of gambling, the first eight months of our marriage were almost perfect. Anthony continued to be loving and attentive and our new house had been beautifully furnished throughout that time. We had some great times and we laughed a lot. We went out two or three times a week together. I continued with my badminton and Anthony went to golf, sometimes with my Dad and other times with his friends. Cooking became a new hobby for me and I soon discovered how much I enjoyed experimenting with different flavours.

Anthony was enthusiastic about the meals I prepared so I bought more cookery books. Dad got an herb garden started for me as he knew Anthony was hopeless at anything that involved DIY or gardening. We got into the swing of holding small dinner parties every two or three months and inviting friends over. I enjoyed being hostess and considering that I had done very little cooking before getting married (university life had been mainly takeaways or nothing more adventurous than beans on toast and pot noodles) I was proud of some of the culinary delights that I managed to serve up.

The moment I dreaded arrived soon enough. It was mid-week and we had just finished our evening meal, Anthony complimenting me on one of my Indian concoctions. He was a little too enthusiastic about something that I thought to be mediocre. I sensed I was being softened up. First came the suggestion.

"Darling, should we have another dinner party on Saturday night?" he asked. I was surprised by this as we only had one recently. Much as I enjoyed the evenings, it usually involved me spending the whole day in the kitchen. I found them quite wearing so I didn't relish the thought of another so soon.

"Oh, Anthony, do we have to? I've just recovered from the last one." His smile faded slightly, so I caved in a little.

"Who were you thinking of inviting?"

I knew it was coming.

"My parents!"

I felt my face drop…and he was on it in an instant.

"What's the matter, Helen? Darling, they haven't even seen our house yet. And you haven't seen them since the wedding. It's nearly eight months!"

I felt cross with him and I could feel the tension start in my neck. It was like an accusation aimed at me. I wanted to ask him what I'd done wrong to them. It wasn't my fault they hadn't been to visit, I had invited them. Didn't he understand that? He was waiting for me to say something…so I told him.

"Well…it's just that I have asked them to visit us on quite a few occasions now, when your Mum has rung you here… and you've not been in. I honestly don't think they'll come for dinner, Anthony. To be honest with you, I don't think they care for me much." His eyes widened in surprise…he looked stung. I instantly regretted my words.

"Don't be ridiculous, darling, of course they like you. You're imagining things. What on earth makes you think that? I'll call them tomorrow and ask."

I felt a sinking feeling in the pit of my stomach as I gave him a nod to say 'okay then.'

Crap!

Not only did his parents not like me, I didn't like them. I would be mortified if they accepted his invitation.

The following day, I had been home from work half an hour and our evening meal was well under way when I heard Anthony's car pull into the drive. I could see him from the kitchen window as he opened the rear passenger door to get his laptop. He turned around and waved, a big wide grin on his face and I hoped the reason for that was that he had a good day at work.

"Sweetheart, you'd better get your menu sorted out, they're coming, Mum and Dad! I told you they would." he blurted as he came into the kitchen.

"Oh! Okay, that's not a problem." I managed, trying to put what I really wanted to say to the back of my mind...and wishing I was half way around the world. I finished off preparing the vegetables but my enthusiasm for that evening's meal had deserted me. All I could think about was how much I dreaded seeing his parents again.

When we finally sat down to eat, Anthony had sensed my mood change.

"Darling, you've gone very quiet, what's bothering you? Don't you want to make an effort for my parents?"

Me! Again!

I was fighting to stay calm and wondering why he couldn't see what was staring him in the face and had been since he first introduced us.

"No, no, it's not that." I lied, "I just don't have a clue what sort of things your parents eat. You know…their likes and dislikes?"

"Right, well then, you should have said. Let's see…no fish, no pasta, nothing too spicy. You'll be fine. I'll trust your judgement on the food. I'll buy the wine tomorrow."

No getting out of this one then!

My worst nightmare was about to happen. I felt as if I was backed into a corner, trapped! I searched my mind for a way out and couldn't see one. Anthony was looking at me expectantly…for what? I didn't know!

"You had better cast your eyes over the menu when I get it planned then. I'd hate to serve up something that they don't like. Maybe there's something they dislike that you have forgotten to mention?" He appeared deep in thought, eyes looking to the ceiling for an answer, finally

"No, I don't think so."

I picked up a handful of recipe books and took them into the lounge so I could browse as I drank my glass of wine. It wasn't out of eagerness to plan the menu, but more an excuse to avoid speaking to Anthony, who seemed to be deliriously happy that his Mum and Dad were coming for dinner. I really didn't trust myself to speak lest I reveal my true feelings about them. Before we went up to bed I presented my proposed menu to him for his approval; Glamorgan sausages with red onion chutney and a small side salad for starters. For the main course I selected lamb shanks, vegetables and potato gratin, dessert would be white chocolate cheesecake with fresh raspberries on the side. As an added touch, I planned to serve a blackberry and elderflower sorbet between each course to freshen the palate.

"They've all been tried and tested at some of our other dinner parties." I told Anthony "Do you think the menu's alright then? I don't want to try anything new in case I make a mess of things."

"This menu will be fine, trust me. They'll love it." He replied confidently.

I'm not so bloody sure about that!

The dreaded evening arrived. Anthony went out to welcome them as their car pulled into the drive. I peered out of the kitchen window hoping I wouldn't be seen by them. Always brought up to believe that it is good manners when you get invited out to dinner, to take a gift along; a bottle of wine, flowers or even some chocolates, I wasn't sure what to expect from them. I noticed they were both empty-handed. I walked over to the door to greet them as they entered the kitchen and held out my hand,

"Eileen, John, how lovely to see you again."

"Hello." She grunted, poker-faced as usual as she glanced at my proffered hand and pushed straight past. John put his hand out, fleetingly shook mine and swiftly pulled it back out of my grasp. Hell fire, did he think he was going to bloody catch something from me if he held on too long? I looked over at Anthony to see if he noticed their reactions towards me...he had. He shrugged his shoulders at me and asked them both if they wanted a glass of wine. Eileen said she'd have a glass but quickly followed with,

"Your father won't want one, he's driving."

Like he had a choice in the matter!

"Would you like a tour of the house, Eileen?" I offered politely.

"I'll show myself around, or Anthony can give me a tour. You get back to heating the ready meal." She walked off leaving me totally flabbergasted. I heard her footsteps on the stairs seconds later. Again I looked at Anthony for support and mouthed the words at him *'get back to heating the ready meal up?'* He mouthed back,

'Shhh!' and shook his head. I gave him one of my looks and stomped back to the kitchen. So he was going to let his mother get away with everything. Maybe *he* would, but I was definitely not going to!

They took their seats in the dining room half an hour later and I served up the starter before sitting down myself. Eileen stared at her plate a few seconds too long, looked over at Anthony and asked,

"What on earth is *this*?" I just couldn't resist,

"Why don't you ask me, Eileen? Anthony doesn't really remember, and it was me who did the cooking." She didn't even acknowledge me or cast a look in my direction.

"They are called Glamorgan sausages (pointing at them), and that is red onion chutney" I said (pointing again), and indicating next the few lettuce leaves and cherry tomatoes, "and that's a bit of salad on the side."

I could feel Anthony's eyes burning into the side of my face and I didn't give a damn!

"Is it cheese?" She asked.

"Yes. Caerphilly."

She pushed the plate away from her, remarking, "Cheese gives me a headache."

"Forgive me, Eileen." I said in my sickliest of voices, "I never realised." I caught a disapproving look in her direction from her husband. The main course also met with disapproval,

"I do think lamb is so terribly fatty. We hardly ever eat it."

I chose to ignore the comment, carried on eating, and listened to her continued, scathing remarks to Anthony about the décor in our bedroom, our choice of leather suite in the lounge and how we rushed in to marriage far too soon. She pushed her food around the plate as she talked and I noticed the determination on her face. The bloody woman had no desire to eat anything that I cooked and furthermore, she was hell bent on insulting me at every given opportunity.

I could see that John was starting to feel very uncomfortable with her behaviour, and perhaps feeling a little sorry for me. He ate everything on his plate and complimented me on the menu, despite the glower he got from his wife. He was interested in, and asked me intelligent questions about my work and badminton, which he apparently had been pretty good at in his younger days. The guy was actually good company and pleasant to talk to. I was pretty adept at being able to hold a conversation with one person and pick up on things being discussed in a second conversation and sure enough, Eileen carried on spewing out her cynicism.

As I served up dessert and placed Eileen's in front of her I couldn't stop my sarcasm surfacing,

"Eileen, if the dessert is not to your liking I can get you some ice-cream from the freezer...something that *I've* not prepared." It was a waste of time, the woman was so thick-skinned. I was by now, avoiding all eye contact with Anthony and John couldn't fail to see the warning looks from Eileen while I had been in the kitchen as he became very quiet again. I ate my cheesecake and decided I had enough tension for one night. Pushing my chair back and standing up, I announced,

"Do excuse me folks, I have a headache and I'm going to bed. It has been nice to see you again, John."

"Too much *wine* darling?" Anthony asked me sarcastically.

"No! It must be the cheese in the Glamorgan sausages. Good night!" and feigning calmness and serenity I walked out and left them.

I heard their car pull out of the drive fifteen minutes later, which was rapidly followed by Anthony's footsteps thundering up the stairs. He shoved the bedroom door wide open, hitting the chest of drawers behind it and pointed at me accusingly,

"YOU" he shouted loudly "have embarrassed me tonight, Helen. How dare you treat my mother in that manner?" I'd already calmed down and was ready for the onslaught I knew was coming.

"So it's just fine then…the way she has been trying to belittle me all evening? You did not find anything wrong with the things that she said to insult your wife, Anthony? That is acceptable is it…for her to speak to me the way that she did? Does my father talk down to you? Does he insult you at every given opportunity? He *never* would do that though, he has better manners, and at least he *likes* you. But if he didn't, I would still defend you, Anthony. That is what a husband and wife should do after all, support each other. *She* hates me! I think your dad likes me but he has to do *her* bidding. I feel sorry for him." I struck a chord. The truth hurt! He was beyond furious. Unable to defend his mother further he screamed,

"FUCK YOU, HELEN!" and with that, he slammed the bedroom door and was gone. For the first time since we married, I woke up alone the next morning. Anthony slept in one of the guest bedrooms for the night.

CHAPTER 10

*I*t took a while for us to get over the disastrous dinner party with Anthony's parents and I resolved that until Eileen started to treat me with more respect there would be no more dinner invitations to our house. I genuinely tried to make more of an effort with them. I visited them in their home with Anthony a few times after that night but there was no imminent thaw about to occur in the foreseeable future. Rather than insult me anymore she reverted back, as she did before we got married, to punish me by ignoring me. She made no eye contact whatsoever or any attempt to include me in conversation. I gradually started building a wide selection of excuses to avoid the monthly visits. There was no way I was going to continue to put myself through it again and again.

Our life carried on in pretty much the same vein as it had before. We did our usual things together, laughed a lot and had fun but something changed since that night...our love-making. I don't suppose it could be called love-making anymore. We were having *sex* instead. Fucking! Sex with a vulgarity, a particular crudeness to it...and strangely enough,

I loved it. We indulged in acts that were for our individual sexual gratification only, rather than one mutual act done in a loving, as one, and sensual manner. It was as if we were taking out our mutual anger on each other...wild! But no less enjoyable!

We never discussed having children. Anthony gave the impression that he wasn't too bothered about having a child and to me it wasn't essential to have an end product of a marriage. If it happened it happened, but if it didn't I was certainly not going to lose any sleep over it. Mum and Dad would quite enjoy playing the doting grandparents to, maybe a little boy, since they had not been blessed with a son. They never asked me if we planned to have a family and I didn't have the heart to tell them that it might never happen if they ever did drop any hints. I wasn't the maternal type. Other people's babies scared me...and the thought of the over-whelming responsibility for the upbringing of a child abso-lutely terrified me.

Within the first year of our marriage and as a result of the honeymoon in Vegas, Anthony visited casinos on three or four occasions with some friends of his and his luck held up well. His risk-taking soon ventured down a different route however, and he started dabbling in the stock market. I was thankful that I have my own bank account, despite his persistent pushing for a joint account, and that was the way it was going to stay. I didn't trust his luck to hold out, or, unlike my father, his judgement.

Over a four or five month period I also became suspi-cious about his drinking habits. He was arriving home from work at his usual time but when he walked in the house he occasionally seemed unsteady on his legs. I could often smell whisky on his breath even though he had to drive five miles home from the office. Whether he was leaving work early for a late afternoon session or secretly drinking in the office, I didn't have a clue and I was unwilling to challenge him of have any confrontation. I had enough of those already given the short length of time we'd been married. It didn't stop at the unknown amount of alcohol he consumed before coming home either. He downed a bottle of wine each night with our evening meal and as a result, would fall asleep on the settee. On such occasions I would eventually go to bed alone. He rarely joined me on those nights, remaining semi-comatose in the same position until morning came around again. I worried about him…and the direction in which our marriage seemed to be veering.

The frequency of our rude, crude sex sessions was dwindling due to the drinking. Our conversations were brief, to the point and occurred at meal times only. Weekends didn't show much improvement and they seemed to drag. It was an advantage that he didn't work on Saturdays and Sundays, so at least it enabled me to try to talk and find out what was troubling him. He was evasive about what his problems were when I asked if it was to do with me. He insisted that our marriage wasn't causing him concern but couldn't come up with a valid reason for the way he behaved towards me. He denied drinking too much and told me to chill out and stop whinging. Apparently, there wasn't any problems at work that were upsetting him, yet I intended to speak with Dad and ask if the business was doing alright. He was adamant that I had done nothing to upset him. I just couldn't get to the bottom of things. All I knew was that our problems started immediately after the disastrous dinner party with his parents and things were escalating. It was a major concern but I tried my best to hide how I was feeling. I didn't feel loved anymore. I felt more like a possession than a wife and lover, and to me at least, it felt like our marriage was over. I cried myself to sleep most nights.

CHAPTER 11

*T*ed Hopkins arranged a meeting for me with a prospective new client, a limited company whose offices were roughly forty miles away. The structural steel firm struggled to stay afloat during the early nineties recession that had seen so many casualties within the industry. The managing director made redundancies, ran the place on a shoestring and kept the overheads to a minimum. He priced jobs at break-even just to get the work and successfully kept the place ticking over. Each month of every year since, was a struggle. He re-mortgaged his home and injected more cash to keep the business afloat, staying focused on his determination not to close the doors. His gamble finally paid off. Over the last two years he gradually needed to recruit more staff and now had a forward order book worth more than six and a half million pounds.

I arrived at the office of Martin Farrer Structural Fabrications Limited with fifteen minutes to spare before our twelve o'clock meeting. His receptionist, Julia, provided me with a coffee and introduced me to the accounts office staff before taking me along to Martin's office and introducing us.

During our business lunch which lasted approximately two hours, we made arrangements for the company's first audit before I set out for the forty mile return journey. As the journey took me in the opposite direction to work Ted told me not to bother returning to the office and to go straight home.

I was surprised to see Anthony's car in the drive when I pulled in. It was extremely rare for him to arrive home before me and it was only just past three o'clock. My first thought was to wonder if he came home ill. I entered the house quietly in case he was asleep. Depositing my handbag on the kitchen worktop, I crept through to the lounge.

I felt my body sag and was mortified by the overwhelming sense of déjà vu at the scene in our lounge. My eyes and head struggled to believe what was happening in front me. Anthony was reclining on the settee, trousers and undies around his ankles. A young man was knelt on the floor fondling Anthony's balls and bent over giving him an enthusiastic blow job. They were engrossed and didn't realise I was there. One pair of denims and boxer shorts had been unceremoniously thrown into the armchair. Anthony looked to be shit-faced drunk. I don't know where I summoned the self-control from. Though proud of remaining calm, I could feel vomit rising into my throat and my hands trembled but I held it together. Without any screaming and shouting or being predictable, I casually walked over to the settee, offered my hand to the lad and said,

"Pleased to meet you! I see you've met the prick and are getting along just fine already." He jerked on hearing my voice and dropped my husband's scrotum as if he'd just been bitten. His mouth gaped and Anthony's cock went from seven inches to shrivelled-up slug in seconds as it fell from the lad's mouth.

"Helen…I…I…it's not…" stammered my twat of a husband.

"How it looks, Anthony? Is that what you were going to say?"

The kid was hauling his clothes back on in desperation and made a bid to get past me for a quick exit via the kitchen. He was barely in his early twenties, if that. My heart went out to him. Anthony must have brought him here. Strangely, I didn't feel any malice towards him.

"Did he pay you, love?" I asked him. "How much did he promise you?"

Staying in his way to block his escape, I reached the kitchen before him and snatched my purse from the work-top. He could hardly get a word out,

"It's…it's ….okay. Sorry."

I thrust five twenties at him. "I hope this covers a cab back to wherever...take it." He looked me in the eyes and after a few seconds hesitation, took the money. As he closed the back door behind him Anthony made his entrance, with a drunken stagger.

"How…how much did you give him?" I battled to stop the Gavin and Bobbie scene which started to replay in my mind, wondering if there was ever to be an escape from it, and that's all Anthony could utter? I swung round to face him.

"A hundred…you owe me a hundred pounds, you fucking arsehole!" I almost laughed at him. His eyes all but popped from their sockets.

"Twenty is what I agreed with him. What the fuck do you think you're doing giving him a hundred fucking quid and expecting it back from me?"

"He deserves it for having to put up with all this...this shit…what a shambles! Call it embarrassment money. He's not much more than a kid! What are you playing at, Anthony? You were married for fuck's sake!"

My earlier calm was dissipating. My hands started to shake again as the bombshell kicked in! The impact hit Anthony like a sledgehammer as well...what I said to him had hit home.

"Helen...*were*...? What...your Dad...? I..."

"Don't worry about your precious position, Anthony!" I screamed, my anger building with each passing second, "I'm not even going to waste my time telling Dad. He thinks the sun shines out of your every orifice...Mr Perfect!" then, "I...this is what I...we'll do...we carry on as normal. But from now on we lead separate lives, Anthony. My parents are not to know about this. Just don't you ever come anywhere near me!"

"Babe...Helen...I love you...!"

I felt the hurt yet again...I'm always hurting. I wanted to cry. The tears threatened and I spat my next words out with such venom,

"Love me? You haven't loved me for ages, Anthony. I've never felt loved since your parents came for dinner. It's a marriage of convenience for you. It lets your parents think you're.... that you're normal! You're anything *but* fucking normal! You couldn't even defend your wife against your mother! You fuck around with rent boys and expect me to believe you *love* me? You don't love me! You haven't made love to me in months, you've fucked me! *Love?*" He stood there, mouth wide open, looking...not sorry, but worried and I could almost read his thoughts. What he was showing was not concern for me, he was worried for himself and his position in my father's business.

"Helen...your Dad...I..." he stammered.

"I won't be telling him! And let's get one thing straight... I'm doing this for my father's benefit, Anthony, not yours!"

There was nothing I would have loved more than to be able to let my father know what an utter bastard Anthony turned out to be, but over the past couple of months Dad was very quiet again. He never complained or said he was feeling ill but there was something troubling him. I know he worried about his health and fitness. I know Mum asked him several times to cut back on the hours he was putting in at work, which he'd done just to pacify her. I trusted that we would be seeing an improvement over the following weeks due to his part time hours and I didn't want anything to spoil that.

CHAPTER 12

*T*he problems that Anthony and I were having in our marriage, if it could be deemed as such any more, prompted me to start getting out and about more with the girls from the office. I hadn't been to badminton for the last six months or so and it felt good to be playing again and get some physical activity back into my life. I joined Nina, Janet and Gillian on the Saturdays out again, but we tried to do something different this time. Once a month it was shopping, but on the others our outings could involve anything from a drive into the country for a walk, a pub lunch, a cinema trip or a visit to an art gallery.

It made life interesting and was a vast improvement to hanging around at home, watching Anthony recover from yet another hangover and having to listen to a thousand reasons why he should never have married me. Shit, I couldn't believe what I was listening to on a daily basis. I wasn't the one paying bloody rent boys or gambling and drinking my life away! I gave in trying to converse with him. I didn't even wish to know why he'd changed and was treating me in this way. I didn't want to know any more.

Things were beyond that. Though as far as anyone else knew, all was still perfect between us. There was nothing to be gained from disclosing the harsh reality to my friends and colleagues, and mostly my parents.

One particular Saturday, after our monthly shopping trip, we stayed in the city much longer than normal and hailed a taxi to take us to Covent Garden where we sauntered around for half an hour trying to agree on a restaurant. It was a fun filled afternoon. We didn't actually make any purchases other than a few bits and pieces like make-up and hair clips. None of us were in any particular hurry to get home. Nina's husband was away on business and Gillian and Janet's boyfriends (who were friends) were both in Prague for a stag weekend. I assured them that Anthony wouldn't mind me staying out and went outside to call him, or so they thought. After we settled the bill for our meal we roamed around the area looking for a suitable pub where we could rest our aching feet, park our backsides and concentrate on getting smashed, for the first time in ages. By the time we reached a pub called the Lamb and Flag we no longer cared,

"This will do, won't it? Nina urged "I need to pee, so it will have to do."

Inside, it was anything but quiet. The place was rapidly filling up and the atmosphere was almost party-like but we managed to find a table in a corner. Janet and I went to the bar to order the first round of drinks and were immediately surrounded by a group of young men who clearly had been on the drink for a few hours.

"Why don't you young ladies come and join us at our table over there?" one of them asked. Janet didn't waste any time trying to knock them back.

"Look guys, it's no use trying to hit on us. We're all in relationships, and in fact," she gestured towards me, "she's happily married, and so is Nina." She pointed to where Nina was sat with her back to the window. If she only knew the truth about my marriage and the sham that it is!

"Okay then, that put us in our place. Look, come and join us anyway. We're only out to get pissed and have a laugh. Go on, you know you both want to. Go and ask your friends. We promise we'll try to keep our hands off you." Janet still looked dubious and raised her eyebrows. Knowing what awaited me back home, I was hell bent on having some fun.

"What harm can it do, Janet? I'll go and ask Nina and Gillian."

Five minutes later we were sat around the lads' table, all introductions made, and Ed, the loud one amongst them, had gone to the bar for the next round.

"Come on, ladies. Drink up! Your second round is here!" he shouted as he approached the table with the tray of drinks for us females perched precariously on one hand like a waiter. After slopping them down on the table in front of each of us and doling out the wrong drinks to the wrong girls, he set off back to the bar to collect the drinks for the six of them. We girls shuffled the glasses around until we each had our requested tipple in front of us.

"Somebody go and help him," Nina suggested. "I don't fancy his chances with six pints." Two of his mates whose names I already forgot, staggered over to be of assistance to him.

They were an assorted bunch; two mechanics, one builder, an IT manager and a plumber, the sixth one being unemployed, the conversation at times was nonsensical, but they were flirty, fun and harmless. Even Janet despite her earlier reservations, managed to relax and enjoy their company. By half past eleven we were all pissed and singing along with the songs playing on the jukebox. I let my hair down and was enjoying myself for the first time in…a long time. I can't even remember what time it got to when Gillian said she had far too much to drink and was ready to leave, so we all made our excuses. The guys came to the door and gave us hugs and agreed how much they enjoyed our company. When Ed asked us if we had plans to return there in the near future we broke into fits of giggles and joked on in a silly and flirtatious way, but were teasingly evasive.

Much later, after I removed my sandals in the kitchen and climbed the stairs to bed, I realised exactly how drunk I was. I was making what I thought to be a conscious effort to keep quiet so I wouldn't disturb Anthony as I passed his room. It wouldn't do to wake him up. I couldn't cope with a full on confrontation, the state I was in. I stopped, wobbling a little outside his door, and listened…all was quiet. After I splashed some cold water on my face and brushed my teeth I flopped onto the bed, unable to stand a moment longer in case I should fall. As my head hit the pillow I drifted off to sleep without even removing my clothes.

Totally unaware of how long I'd been sleeping, I was horrified to be awakened by somebody roughly pulling my tights and panties off in one swift move. How could somebody be in my room? I always bolt my bedroom door…don't I? It all came back to me in a rush, how pissed I'd been, how pissed I was still feeling…when Anthony rammed his cock up me with the force of a madman and started nipping and squeezing my breasts so hard it was excruciating. I lashed out, pummelling hard into his chest with my fists before wildly aiming a slap at his head. He was causing me tremendous pain, both in my private parts and my belly. I realised I was hurting because I wasn't submissive…my inner muscles were tense and I fought every powerful stab at me. He dodged my blows, but not once did he stop ramming into me. I squirmed beneath him, trying to wriggle free…away from the brutality of his selfish need. I was appalled at what he was doing to me…making me feel trashy, like scum. I tried to scream out as he continued, to alert anybody who might happen to hear. Furious, he let go of one of my breasts and slapped his hand firmly across my mouth.

"Shut the fuck up, you stupid bitch…you're my wife!" he snarled.

I continued thrashing at his arms, chest, or any part of him that I could reach as I tried to scream back at him.

"This…not…a marriage…this…is rape…you bastard!"

I managed to mumble to no avail, his hand blocking my words. I'd lost though. I didn't have any fight left in me, due to my booze weakened body and I was hurting…everywhere. He continued to fuck me in his raging and violent manner and all I could physically do was lie there and take it and pray for it to end soon. I cried, silently. It felt like it would never come to an end. One hand stayed firmly over my mouth. The fingernails of his other hand raked at and dug into my breasts. He threw his head back, fucked me hard and rough, and even harder as his intent to damage me drove him into some obscene fantasy. It brought about his climax. I couldn't bear to look at him and with one hand I pulled a pillow over my face and sobbed into it.

I felt him pull out his disgusting, dripping cock and…he laughed,

"You always were a good fuck, Helen. I see that hasn't changed." From within my depths, the rage I felt suddenly exploded from me in a final fit of energy and I threw the pillow from me.

"YOU…BASTARD!" I screamed. I kicked out at his back as he moved to stand up, a move I instantly regretted. He turned and slammed his fist into my right eye. Once he left my room I staggered over to the bedroom door, bolting it this time…as I should have done those few hours earlier.

CHAPTER 13

*N*ot surprisingly, I didn't sleep for the remainder of the night. On waking, I got out of bed, showered, scrubbed at my body and sobbed uncontrollably. I laid on the bed breaking my heart and there was no one to listen or care. The people who *would* care couldn't ever know about this. The plans we made two years ago were ruined, as they had been for a while. Even though the last few months were a living hell, I was devastated and shocked at what Anthony had become. My whole body pained me. I felt dirty in the most horrible way that a woman could; forever tainted, cheap, and yet I had no reason to feel cheap! I hadn't heard another sound from him during the night. I didn't know where he was, whether he had gone downstairs or back to his bed. I knew I wasn't leaving my room until I was absolutely certain that he left the house.

Once showered, I tiptoed around the bedroom and packed a bag. I also vomited on and off for an hour or so while I waited. Fortunately, I didn't have too long to wait. I heard his car pull out of the drive just after nine. I was desperate for coffee; something to eat and drink, thinking it might settle my stomach, but I wanted to be out. Just in case he wasn't gone for long, and happened to return before I seized the chance to be gone, I grabbed my bag, ran down the stairs and within five minutes of him driving away, I was in my own car and pulling out of the drive, tyres screeching as I sped down the street. I headed in the direction of home. Mum and Dad were away for their anniversary...cruising. They were somewhere in the middle of the Indian Ocean for three weeks. I wouldn't have wanted to arrive at their house in my physical and emotional state if they had been at home. I would have plenty of time to sort myself out; they'd only been gone three days.

When I arrived at their house and let myself in, I made coffee and toast and took it upstairs to my old bedroom. I sat on the dressing table stool whilst I drank my coffee and stared at myself in the mirror. The swelling around my eye and upper part of my cheek looked angry. The blackness was coming out. I looked a mess. Not only did I look at my physical injury, I inspected myself carefully, trying to delve deep under my skin. I was looking for a sign; any sign that gave me a reason as to why, why my husband would rape me, hit me, and leave me in this state. What did I do to warrant this kind of behaviour from him? Had I deserved all that I got? I couldn't think of anything, but perhaps other people could see something in me that I wasn't able to.

After finishing with my breakfast, I lay down on the bed and started thinking about what to do. I couldn't report it to the police. I couldn't put myself through that. Hell, I couldn't put my parents through it! What this could do to my father with his heart problems was not a thought I wanted to dwell on. The only thing I knew for certain was that I could not go in to work on Monday morning looking like this. First thing on my 'to do' list was for the week, I needed to phone Ted.

I drifted off to sleep at some point and when I woke it

was four in the afternoon. For a few seconds I wondered what I was doing there. Smacked in the face by reality when the memory returned, a fresh flow of tears rolled. I got the sudden urge to shower again and I all but ripped the clothes from by body. Under the almost scalding water I scrubbed at myself in a frenzy for a long time...until my skin was raw.

For all the time I spent in my bedroom, the only item I managed to get on my agenda was to phone Ted Hopkins the next morning. I was relieved that my parents had a well-stocked freezer. I had no wish to go out for shopping. I didn't want to see the stares and questioning glances from people if they caught a glimpse of my eye. I fixed something to eat and made a point of writing down the items I used from their freezer. I would replace everything like for like before they returned home. I didn't want them to know I'd been staying over. Dad hadn't been too well before they went away and I wasn't going to add to their worries.

I suspected work was behind it all, but he always kept things work issues from Mum and I. Anthony would prob-ably be the person to ask if everything was alright at the office, but at the minute I couldn't even contemplate asking him. I would have to go back to our marital home sooner or later but I didn't relish the thought. Previously, he never hurt me when he's been sober and I've seen him drunk on plenty of occasions and never been hurt by him. Why was last night different? Was he cross because I stayed out late and not let him know? I quickly talked myself out of that thought though. Lately, he didn't give a shit where I was. He didn't communicate with *me* if he decided he was staying out late and there were many times when he stayed out all night. I never questioned him anymore and didn't feel the need to. We're not a couple. It didn't interest me where he was. He usually gave an explanation when I next saw him...like I cared! Since the day I found him with his rent boy in our house, I didn't want to know. I would sometimes think that he was probably in a gay bar searching for another twenty pound blow job.

I tried to shut out my thoughts for the rest of the evening by pouring a glass of wine and putting a film on TV, but while I looked at the screen the film rolled on unwatched. All I could see was a rape scene repeatedly playing out in front of me, with me as the victim, time and again. I sat in silence, replenished my glass periodically and carried on drinking in an attempt to blot out the events of...was it really just hours ago, this same day? Bleary eyed from drink and my tears, I pulled my legs up onto the settee...and slept.

When I called the office it was Gillian who answered. It seemed she wanted to indulge in idle chit chat about Saturday night so I snuffled and sniffled into the mouth piece.

"Listen, Gillian, can you please offer my apologies to Ted? I'm feeling rough. I think I'm getting the flu, I ache all over and I'm really not up to it."

"Gosh yes, you do sound a little snotty, Helen, I hope you feel loads better soon. Oh Hell, we were all out together on Saturday night. I hope you've kept it to yourself, honey, but I'll warn the girls. You get back to bed and stay warm. Dose yourself up." Her obvious concern for my welfare left me feeling guilty for lying, but how could I let them know the true reason for my absence?

"If anybody should need me urgently, Gillian, get them to ring my mobile please. I'm staying at Mum and Dad's, Anthony's away for a few days on business."

"You've done the right thing Helen, getting the oldies to look after you...you'll soon be better. Keep us informed. Now, go to bed!" I mentioned a few weeks back that my parents were going on an anniversary holiday, but she'd assumed...I didn't correct her.

The only reason I'd sounded snotty was that I was yet again crying. I hated lying to Gillian and the other girls. Well no, I wasn't really lying to them, merely being economical with the truth. They thought I was happily married and for the time being, there was no reason for them to know anything else. I can only imagine their horror if they could see the state of me. I stayed off work for the full week and when Saturday morning came around, I thought I would pop back home to get some more of my make-up and some clothes that would be more suitable for my return to work on Monday. Anthony would hopefully be at the golf course so I wouldn't have him to contend with. I wasn't too concerned about his car being in the drive when I pulled up. He was picked up by one of his friends every other week and it was clearly not Anthony's weekend to drive this time. Letting myself in through the back door I could hear music, maybe from the television. I hoped he wasn't going to be in and my whole body stiffened, genuinely scared of coming face to face with him...my rapist.

It was like a scene I remembered from a movie I watched years ago. Three motionless figures, two laid in uncomfortable looking positions on the lounge floor, one of them a man wearing nothing but a tee-shirt. Another was sprawled full length on the settee, his mouth wide open emitting gurgling noises in the back of his throat. As my eyes adjusted to the semi-darkness I could see that one of the people on the floor was female, bare-breasted, her skirt up around her waist and her genitals on display. I wasn't so much shocked... as livid. I stepped over them and flung the lounge curtains wide open, ignoring their reactions. Daylight streamed in and my eyes were drawn straight to the coffee table. There were specks of white powder on the glass top which vaguely indicated where the cocaine had been in lines. A pack of drinking straws was opened, half a dozen of which were scattered and bent up on the floor. Three or four bottles of various spirits were half empty. Beer and lager cans were strewn everywhere. A loud snore from him drew my eyes back to the guy on the settee. It was Anthony's friend, Paul, a fellow golfer.

The moans and groans of his house guests didn't deter me from stomping up the stairs to see how many had partied last night. First port of call was my bedroom and I prayed that nobody had been screwing in, or been sick in it. A cursory glance revealed it was left untouched since he raped me in there the previous week. I quickly closed the door on it, needing to focus on what I was going to do next and to evade those memories that sought to engulf me once more. Opening the door of the spare room next, again to semi-darkness, I could just make out two male and one female form spread-eagled across the double bed. All were in various stages of undress and seemingly dead to the world, either through drink, drugs or a combination of the two. There was an open condom packet laid on the bedside cabinet, the unused condom fallen to the floor and left there. Perhaps they'd been incapable of unrolling it onto an erect penis, or maybe there hadn't been an erect penis….which wouldn't surprise me judging by the amount of alcohol that had obviously been consumed by them, and that was without taking into account the drug usage.

I didn't bother them with a greeting. I doubted even one of them would wake from their heavily intoxicated sleep. I slammed the door without a care as to whether I disturbed them or not. Crossing the landing towards Anthony's room, I realised that there was nothing that man could do now that would surprise me. When I flung open his door I wasn't even taken aback that he was in bed with two females, both naked and Anthony in the middle, also naked, mouth wide open and snoring loudly. The two girls stirred in their sleep and one of them, a girl with short blonde hair and I guess about twentyish, suddenly sat bolt upright.

"Who the fuck are you?" she asked in a defensive tone, eyes glaring at me.

"Me? Oh, don't worry about *me*. I'm only *his wife*. Not that it's any concern of yours. We live separate lives." I watched her face waiting for a reaction but there wasn't one. "I would say your biggest worry at the moment is…do you actually know where that prick has been?" I paused a few seconds, giving her time to digest my question,

"Yes! That dick!" I gestured towards my sleeping husband, "The one who was obviously stuck into the two of you last night?"

She raised her eyebrows and woke up a little faster than anyone normally would. I recognized the flash of panic in her eyes.

"Shall I tell you where it's been?" I didn't wait for her reply before carrying on "Not so many weeks ago that dick was shagging a young man up the arse. Who knows what you might have… just a little food for thought!"

She leaned across Anthony and poked her friend, (who had drifted back off to sleep), in the ribs.

"Emma! Emma, come on! Let's get out of here, now! This guy apparently doesn't care…Emma, come on! This is his wife. We need to go, wake up!"

Emma was fully alert in no time, panic showing in her eyes too. They both sat on the edge of the bed looking for their clothes in the half light. Anthony was still oblivious to it all. I left them to it and returned to my bedroom. I threw a few clothes into my suit carrier, grabbed some toiletries from the en-suite, and headed back down the stairs. The bodies in the lounge were still comatose so I passed through to the kitchen, slamming doors behind me in anger. I grabbed a few favourite titbits out of the kitchen cupboards and the fridge and quickly stuffed them in a carrier bag. Before I was finished, Emma and her friend (or shagging partner for want of a better description) came tearing through the kitchen…obviously in a rush to get away. They cast me a quick glance before lowering their eyes. They were going to leave without saying anything so I just couldn't resist.

"You two should think very carefully about who you sleep with in the future. No condoms spells unwanted preg…" Emma's friend cut me off mid-sentence,

"We're both on the pill and…" I stopped her right there and jumped in quick.

"Oh, I'm pleased to hear it, I'm sure. What about sexually transmitted diseases; AIDS…HIV? Have you considered those little gems, too?"

They exchanged stupefied looks and I eased up on them, knowing I had a similar matter to attend to. I lowered my voice this time.

"I'd get yourselves checked over if I were you. As I said… you don't know where that dick's been."

They shot me one final glare and were gone. I finished my grocery gathering and locked the door behind me. I drove past the girls hurrying away further down the street. I didn't feel it appropriate to offer them a lift anywhere. They got themselves into their own mess. Hopefully they would learn something from it.

There was only a slight yellow tinge to my eye by the time I woke up on Monday morning. After I applied my make-up nobody would ever know that I had a black eye. The staff showed their relief as I walked through reception, down the corridor and into my own office.

"Are you over the flu, Helen? Are you sure you're going to be okay?" "You should have taken a few days longer." and "You still look a bit peaky pale."

"I'm fine girls...still a little tired, but I've been bored. There are only so many chick flicks you can watch. It's been nice to stay there though, with Anthony being away." I crossed my fingers behind my back as I continued to play along.

It felt good to be back at work and some sense of normality. I lied about being bored because over the last week the O.C.D. was back again. I cleaned my parents' house right the way through each day for the previous four days. Any more hurt in the future and I know it will keep coming back. I'd been raped, scrubbed myself red raw, and when there was next to no skin left to scrub I turned to the house. It was a good thing I was back at work. I had friends in the office, my social life and I had clients to see. I made a promise to myself...no more cleaning! I made excuses one lunch time for not joining everybody in the staff canteen and went out. I visited a private sexual health clinic not far away, for an assortment of tests to be carried out. The wait for the results was going to be tense.

CHAPTER 14

I moved back into our house three days before my parents were due back. Once I made sure that Anthony was out at work, I called for a joiner to come and fit a proper security lock to my bedroom door. I wanted to feel safe should he decide to try and help himself to my body again. I also wanted to be in the house before he came home rather than have to walk in when he was already there.

I was making myself something to eat when I heard his car pull into the drive at seven o'clock. I hadn't announced my return to him and wondered what he would think when he saw my car in the drive. I didn't dwell on the thought too long and already felt extremely nervous. I plated up my meal and hurried through into the lounge with my tray and sat down. I grabbed the remote, switched on the television, made myself comfortable and started to eat. I didn't want him to see that I was intimidated by him.

Probably because he wasn't looking forward to facing me, he stayed in the kitchen. I could hear him as he pottered about making something to eat for himself. The microwave pinged after about fifteen minutes and I wondered if he would eat in the lounge but he must have thought it better to stay put. A bottle chinked against a glass so he was evidently getting himself a drink. He came sauntering through, avoided eye contact with me and plonked down into one of the armchairs. I was trying hard to stop myself from shaking. It wasn't easy, although looking down at my hands they didn't show a flicker of what I was feeling deep within me, my stomach was lurching.

His face and body were turned towards the television as he walked into the room and sat down. After total silence between us for a few minutes or so he finally turned towards me.

"Helen, can we talk please?" his voice sounded strained.

Oh shit, did we really have to? I had no wish to begin a confrontation!

My stomach continued to churn and I could feel every beat of my racing heart. I hated him, how could I possibly talk to him? But somehow, after clearing my throat, trying to rid myself of what promised to come out as a nervous croak, the sarcasm came confidently spilling out.

"*What* exactly would you like to talk about, Anthony? The *weather*? That's usually a good starting point. Or how about today's news headlines? How's about the price of petrol?"

I stared directly at him, noticed his pleading eyes, the puppy dog expression.

"Come on, Helen, hear me out…please."

I didn't answer and continued to give him my ice cold stare. He took this as his cue to carry on talking.

"Helen, I am so sorry, I truly am."

Somehow I found that hard to believe and I couldn't understand why he even had the gall to make an apology that he wouldn't genuinely feel the need to do.

"What are you sorry for then, Anthony? Sorry for raping me? Sorry that I caught you all after your little orgy two weeks back? Sorry for marrying me? Sorry for being a complete bastard? Go on, enlighten me!"

Proud of my venomous little outburst, I still stared at him intently, watching his body language and his facial expressions as he tried his hardest to convince me how sorry he was. I wanted something to pick at while my brain was in an endless struggle to understand why.

"I…what I did to you, three weeks ago. There…I've said it. I don't know what came over me. It must have been the…the weed I smoked that night. It can't have agreed with me."

Weed? He expected me to believe that?

He was avoiding my gaze, inspecting his fingernails. I was astounded but determined I wasn't going to start kicking off.

"You must think I'm stupid, Anthony. You've smoked weed before, I know you have. It's never made you like that. You *raped* me. You abused my body and you punched me in the eye. I had to stay off work for a bloody week so nobody would know. Are you telling me you remember all of it? You remember you raped me? Do you remember punching me in the eye, huh? If that's what cocaine does to you, those girls got away quite lightly didn't they? It's making you violent, Anthony. When will the next time be? Who will be your next victim?"

His eyes met mine and I could see he was close to tears. I racked my brain to find some sort of emotion for him. I didn't feel sorry for him. Despite everything I didn't even hate him. I felt nothing whatsoever…just …indifference. It saddened me to realise that.

"I honestly can't remember hitting you, Helen. Truly I don't recall that. I am so sorry. You never deserved that."

"So I *deserved* to be raped then? Is *that* what you're saying?" I snarled.

"No! Helen, no! Don't twist things! That's not what I meant and you know it! You didn't deserve any of it. You've done nothing wrong. It's me that's at fault here. Everything is *my* fault."

Yes. It was his fault. He raped me, there was nobody else to blame but him, but I started to get upset, I must be guilty too. I had done something wrong, surely? He stopped loving me...months ago. I need to know why.

"That can't be true. I must have done something to make you hate me, Anthony...there must be. I've tried to be a good wife to you...where did it all go wrong?"

He got up and started to pace the lounge, his eyes staring down at the carpet. He appeared to be deep in thought and I didn't think he was going to answer my questions.

"It's not you. It's work, Helen. I assure you that *you* have done *nothing* wrong at all. Just a few worries at work and I haven't been coping with them. I know I've been drinking too much, the...drugs as well. I shouldn't have done any of it. I've let you down."

My first thought on hearing this was that he must have made some serious fuck ups at work in Dad's absence. I could feel my anger building again and snapped my next words at him.

"You sure have, and you've also let my father down. I hope there are no problems at the office for him to come back to. You know he hasn't been well lately."

"I *am* aware of that, Helen." he snapped back "The problems at work are things that I can sort out without worrying your Dad. Are you planning on telling him about us...erm, things?"

I was close to boiling point at his selfishness. The things he put me through, rape, his drunken orgy and drugs, and all he was concerned about was his position within my father's company. I managed to keep my voice a bit calmer as I answered him.

"Of course I'm not going to tell him. Tell him that I've

married a total bastard? A bastard who hasn't treated his daughter right? That would be an understatement wouldn't it, Anthony? Dad's been close enough to another heart attack as it is, without me adding *you* to his problems, don't you think?"

He turned away from me, unable to meet my eyes any longer.

"Yes, I suppose you're right, Helen!"

"I know I'm right!"

My heart was pounding. I was struggling to breathe. I needed to calm myself. I had to lay down some ground rules if I was to continue to stay, or worse still, allow him to remain in the house.

"I've moved back in here today. Mum and Dad are home in the next couple of days and I don't want to be at theirs for obvious reasons. Let's get things straight. I don't want you bringing friends or people over here. This is my house as well. I don't care what you do anymore, Anthony – but don't do it here. I don't want your bloody drugs in this house."

He nodded and gave a sigh, probably relieved that I still wanted my parents to have no knowledge of all that had transpired.

"And now, I need your promise that you won't ever… touch me…rape me…"

"Helen, never! I wouldn't, I promise."

A flash of understanding, he knew that I meant business. I decided not to mention to him the extra measures I'd taken for my personal security.

"Message understood."

I felt a sense of relief that it was out in the open. It was not going to be easy living under the same roof. We'd already been doing so for months, but things had changed. My thoughts turned to my parents and how long Anthony and I could keep up the façade.

He sat quiet with his thoughts for a while before asking if I minded him watching some documentary or other. I said I didn't have a problem with that and as I got up to go to the kitchen he told me there was a bottle of Vinho Verde in the fridge and I was quite welcome to pour myself a glass if I wished.

"Thank you. I assume you are telling me this because *you* would like one?"

Without a doubt that was the only reason he mentioned the wine to me.

"When have I ever refused?"

"Precisely!" I responded, in what came out with an acidic tone to my voice.

He wasn't capable of refusing alcohol. It wasn't many months ago I would have been delighted to pour him a drink but we were no longer together as a couple and he had pushed my buttons too far.

We watched a nature documentary in pure silence while we drank a couple of glasses of wine. When the programme credits rolled, I realised how exhausted I felt after our earlier exchange. I stretched as I got up from the settee.

"I'm tired now. Goodnight!"

"Okay. Goodnight, Helen."

I cringed, irked by the way my Christian name still rolled off his tongue.

CHAPTER 15

J went to visit my parents on the Saturday morning and stayed the full day. They arrived back on the Friday afternoon, three days after I left their house.

"What's Tony doing today, darling?" Dad asked. "I thought he would have come along with you. I'm dying to ask him what's been happening in the office in my absence. Has he mentioned anything at all?"

"No. I never talk shop with him, Dad, you should know that. I think he's either gone into the city for the day or he's golfing. I'm not totally sure. He did tell me, but as usual I wasn't paying much attention."

I heard all about their cruise and the tours they had been on each time the ship docked. We spent the late morning going through their holiday photos. As we were still seated at the dining table after lunch, I enquired as to whether Dad was feeling any better for his long rest from work. He was perhaps a little too quick to assure me that he was well rested. I followed this up by asking if he was worried about anything at work. He was suddenly alert.

"What makes you ask that, Helen?"

"You were keen for Anthony to be here so you could ask what's gone on while you've been away. All you had to do was answer 'yes something's worrying me' or 'no, of course not!'"

"There's nothing for you to trouble your little head with. I trust Tony to sort out any issues that may crop up."

That's exactly what worried me. I wasn't impressed with Dad's effort to look cool about everything. He skirted around the subject rather niftily, but instead of voicing my opinion we just moved on to the next topic of conversation. Mum as usual didn't have much to say, but I noticed she kept giving Dad a look of concern when she thought he wouldn't notice.

By six o'clock I made my excuses and went off to meet the girls from the office for a few drinks. We had no late night planned - just a few drinks and hopefully a lot of unwinding. When I arrived home just after eleven, Anthony was already up in his bedroom. A peaceful night for him, which meant a perfect peaceful night for me too.

CHAPTER 16

*D*ad returned to work and was managing to toe the line with his new part time hours. Things were ticking over in much the same fashion. Anthony and I were avoiding each other as much as possible when we were both home. I socialised with my friends and he with his. I knew the day was fast approaching when Mum would be inviting us around for Sunday dinner and having already discussed this matter with Anthony, we agreed to both go for appearances sake. It should be quite easy really. If we turned up just before lunch was due to be served, there would only be the meal to get through. Mum and I usually ended up in the conservatory and Dad and Anthony would be in the lounge watching Sunday afternoon sport or else they would stay at the dining table and talk business.

Three weeks flew past since their holiday and we still hadn't been asked over for Sunday lunch. It suited me down to the ground. Anthony was also not relishing the inevitable.

In our home it was unavoidable that we met up in the lounge some times and shared the odd bottle of wine but that is as cosy as it got. We discussed only what we needed to discuss and nothing more. I remained as pleasant as could be expected under the circumstances. Anthony seemed to find it quite hard to make any eye contact with me whatsoever. He was hopefully feeling ashamed and guilty…as he should be!

To my knowledge, no friends of his visited the house when I was out and that's the way I wanted it to stay. I wasn't sure how long we could continue to co-habit without any more incidents or without my parents finding out. I hadn't asked if he told his family about our relationship. I didn't really want to know. I'd no doubt that if he had done, or when he eventually did, all the blame would rest firmly on my shoulders as far as they were concerned, or more appropriately, as far as Eileen was concerned. Should there ever be any grief directed at me from his mother I would have no qualms about telling her that her son raped me. I could quite easily reveal to her that he preferred the company of young men, enjoyed snorting cocaine and occasionally indulged in threesomes with young ladies. There were plenty of stories for her to think about regarding her son, although it would no doubt be me that led him astray and caused him to go off the rails, in her opinion.

I took the plunge one night and decided to ask Anthony how my father was coping at work and if he thought he still had health worries. He thought long and hard, continuously staring at the television for a few minutes before answering.

"I don't know. He spends most of the time in his office and doesn't have much to say unless it's about business. He looks well enough and is always pleasant to everybody in the office, the true gentleman as always." He then added, "If you're worried about him, why don't you ask your Mum?"

I didn't really know what to make of his answer and was curious whether he would keep any worrying facts from me, not wanting me to fret more than was necessary.

"Well it was Mum who told me to ask you. She keeps

asking him at home if he's feeling alright, and he assures her that he's fine."

He leaned forward in his chair and gave me a re-assuring smile (I wish he wouldn't!).

"If he's telling her he's fine I expect it's because he *feels* fine. I'm sure she's fretting about nothing...as you women always do."

He turned his face back towards the television and I mulled over his last words and shook my head, astounded by them. Being married to him, I had plenty to fret about. It was *not*...nothing.

Mid-morning during the next day at work, I closed my office door and placed the call that I should have made nearly two weeks earlier but had put off time and again. After a short wait 'on hold' I was delighted to hear from the clinic that the results of all the tests taken came back negative. I cried with relief.

That same afternoon I had a meeting to attend in our office with some new clients. The two gentlemen purchased a country pub a year ago and now had a development plan in mind for building some chalets around the pub's car park that could be rented on a short or long term basis. They required our assistance to produce some projected figures to show their bank. Ted and I would be joining them at their pub for lunch after the meeting to discuss matters further. With my home being mid-way between the office and the pub, Ted told me to follow him in my own car. It would save me driving all the way back to the office.

Leaving the men behind after our successful meeting and lunch, it was three fifteen when I left the pub. Turning into our street half an hour later, I could see there was a car parked directly in front of our house, and as I drove another thirty feet past the large hedge that blocked the view of most of our drive, I noticed Anthony's car was there. He was stood on the front doorstep exchanging envelopes with a guy. They were engaged in some animated conversation. My suspicions were instantly aroused. Anthony was never one for leaving work early unless it involved alcohol. My last experience of him arriving home early was not a particularly pleasant one. It didn't look as if there was a rent boy involved this time, but the exchanging of envelopes is never a good sign. I groaned out loud.

Whether he saw my car approaching and deliberately got rid of the guy I don't know, but the man reached his driver's side door, got in and pulled the door shut just as I pulled into the drive. As I climbed out of my car, I watched the vehicle pull away, trying my utmost to get a good look at the driver's face. Anthony already closed the front door before I arrived. No doubt he would try to deny seeing my car approaching home from down the road, and whatever it was that the driver of the car passed to him, would by now be stashed safely out of my way.

Rather than have Anthony insult my intelligence by telling me a pack of lies, I decided to play it cool and not ask too many questions. Using the back door as always, I walked into the kitchen just as he was filling the kettle.

"Tea or coffee, Helen? I haven't been in long, I'm having a tea!"

I was a little taken aback by his cheeriness but answered him politely.

"Tea will be fine, thanks."

I couldn't appear too interested or he would be suspicious but my curiosity was getting the better of me. I was eager to watch his reactions so I chanced it.

"Who was the guy at the front door? I haven't seen him before." Then I added, "The one driving away as I pulled up?"

He was busy pouring the hot water into the cups with his back to me. I couldn't see what expression he had on his face.

"Oh, him, Joe? He did some design work for us a few weeks ago, while Ken was on holiday. I promised to pay him in cash. He only recently started up in business and has struggled along with his household bills in his first month. It's to tide him over until his cheques start to come in. I arranged it when your Dad was away, as I know he doesn't like making cash payments."

He must have rehearsed that one quickly, or he plucked it from thin air on the spur of the moment. I didn't believe a word of it. He would only have had a maximum of three to four minutes from seeing my car until the minute I walked in the back door. I wanted to scream at him, to ask him exactly how naïve he thought I was and also, what about the envelope that was handed to him!

I did some tidying up in the kitchen as I was drinking my tea, puzzled all the while about what I saw. He sat at the counter reading his newspaper. There was a long silence between us as I carried on with some little jobs. Suddenly, he looked up from his paper and remarked,

"You're home early today."

I didn't need to answer as there hadn't been a question. He made a statement, but I felt that if I did answer it would at least keep things chatty and casual for the time being.

"Well, we had a meeting with some new clients and went for lunch to the pub they own. They have plans to develop and build some chalets around the car park. It looks like it could be a money spinner for them. I left Ted there with them still discussing things. It made more sense to come straight here rather than drive all the way back to the office."

I never took my eyes off him. It could have been my imagination but I thought I caught a flicker of something. Realisation that, whatever he was up to, he came too close to being caught? When I removed his empty cup from in front of him he stood up and calmly announced,

"Just so you know, I'm out tonight. I'm going to a casino with some friends. You'll have the house to yourself for the night."

He grabbed the jacket of his suit from the back of the kitchen chair.

"I'm going for a shower."

It was music to my ears to hear that he was going out. I loved having my own space but tonight I had a mission, I was going to have a private little treasure hunt. Not wanting him to see me look so delighted, I scowled and delivered my perfect nagging tone.

"I'm warning you, Anthony. Don't you dare bring anybody back here or come into my room, for that matter."

I'd hit it perfectly. Immediately on the defensive, he bristled and snapped back.

"I'll probably stay out all night. Don't worry. I told you I was sorry. That won't happen again."

"I know you did. I'm just reinforcing the message."

After he went upstairs I heard the door close and the lock engage on his bathroom door. I crept up after him and hearing the shower running, darted into his bedroom and quickly checked his jacket and trouser pockets for the envelope the mystery guy handed him...nothing. I checked his drawers and under his mattress...again, no joy. I was disappointed, but knew that if he wanted to hide something from me he wasn't going to make it easy to find.

Going back down the stairs as silently as I went up, I made a swift search under the cushions of the settee and chairs, in the drawers of the bureau and every possible hiding place I could see. No envelope! I remember he was in the kitchen putting the kettle on as I walked through the door. Having a re-think to myself, I wonder if he realised the kitchen was his quickest option when he saw my car approaching. I expected he would be downstairs in the next minute or two so I didn't have time for a large scale search. I would stay in the kitchen until he went out. That way he wouldn't have any opportunity to retrieve what he'd hidden…if he *had* hidden it in the kitchen. My best option was to do some cooking and look busy.

Ten minutes later, he left. He walked into the kitchen, shrugged his shoulders and before closing the door behind him, said

"You should be relaxing, not cooking! You've been at work."

While I was stood at the kitchen sink staring out of the back window, it hit me…the greenhouse. It was situated to the right of the double doors that led onto our patio; the one place on our property where Anthony thought I would never set foot. I sat at the kitchen table deep in thought for twenty minutes or so, giving him chance to get some distance away. I paced it all out in my mind and in practice, from Anthony closing the front door, a dash to the greenhouse and getting back into the kitchen again. He would have about a minute to spare. I was a little hesitant to carry out the actual search, scared of what I might find, but I knew it had to be done. I had to know.

I got my answer within twenty minutes. After a thorough search of every corner, the envelope in question came to light inside the bottom one of a stack of large, unused plant pots. The envelope was unmarked, sealed, and from its weight and substance, contained something like a powder. I returned it to its hiding place and left everything as I found it. My worst fears were confirmed. Drugs…it had to be!

I returned to my cooking, finished up and went to bed rather early for once, but I wanted to lay in the darkness and think.

CHAPTER 17

$\mathcal{I}$ kept a close watch on the greenhouse at every opportunity over the next few days. During Anthony's absences I checked on the envelope. I made a point of indulging in casual chit chat when he was home, to see if he would let slip what his plans were and where he was going each time he left the house. I realised that once I discovered the envelope missing, I would need to recall where he said he was going to at least give me some idea of where the final destination was for the disgusting stuff! I couldn't decide whether he was stupid enough to sell direct to the end users or whether he was just an insignificant courier in a large operation.

Late Friday night of the same week he received the envelope, I resolved to be awake early on the Saturday morning and keep myself busy in the kitchen. Anthony would be going out to play golf and it was his turn to pick up his partner. If there was any convenient time for him to remove the envelope, I thought that it would likely be the weekend. I gave no thought as to what I should do if I managed to see him retrieve the envelope. I hadn't given consideration yet as to whether I would involve the police, my parents, or whether I would actually confront him. I could not yet see beyond my sole aim...to prove something to myself. I only want some confirmation that he is the scumbag I think he is, even though deep down, I already know the answer to that!

I came to with a start...the slam of a car door and an engine turning over being my rude awakening. It slowly dawned on me it was Saturday morning. I sat up quickly, my eyes searching out the alarm clock. It was nine thirty. I shot out of bed and grabbed my dressing gown. It must have been Anthony's car that I heard. Without bothering to put anything on my feet, I put my gown on and ran down the stairs and through to the kitchen. I paused for a few seconds just outside the patio door. I vocally chided myself at the breakneck speed at which I just descended the stairs. What I found or didn't find in the greenhouse within the next two minutes, the situation would not change within the next few hours, so why the rush?

My forage into the plant pots revealed that the envelope was still there. I was surprised. I genuinely thought he would have removed it that morning, his first real opportunity.

He stayed out all Saturday night and didn't return until the Sunday evening. I somehow doubted the envelope would be moved until the following weekend now as he wouldn't want to leave something like that in his car when he was at work, but I intended to check the greenhouse as often as I could.

An opportunity to leave work an hour early presented itself the following Tuesday. I hand delivered some audited accounts to a client on my way home but as her office closed at five o'clock I needed to be there sooner in case she wanted a few words. By twenty minutes to five I was out of her office and fifteen minutes later I was home, thirty five minutes earlier than usual. After I dumped my bags on the worktop, I opened the patio door and stepped outside. The sliding door to the greenhouse was not quite in position. I was stunned at first but then started to doubt myself. I desperately tried to remember whether I was in a rush the last time I checked. Perhaps it was me who'd been careless? I always tried to make a conscious effort to leave it fully closed, but had I done so after the last time I checked it?

The envelope had gone. Somewhere between the hours of my departure for work and four fifty-five it was removed and taken who knows where? I made a mental note to speak to my father as soon as I could. I needed to know where Anthony had been and without Dad suspecting a thing.

CHAPTER 18

*N*ot long after the envelope went missing from the greenhouse, I found out that Anthony *had* been out of the office for around four hours that same Tuesday. I hadn't needed, after all, to wheedle any information from my father. He called me on the Thursday evening to tell me he went for his check up at the hospital that morning and that the consultant was thrilled with his progress. I could hear Mum's voice in the background, prompting him at times as we chatted on. I was on the verge of saying goodnight when he suddenly remembered something.

"By the way, Helen, I was relieved when Tony told me that Eileen's feeling much better now. He was really worried when he dashed off to see her on Tuesday morning. He was still a little upset when he got back to work mid-afternoon. All that time with her analgesia not working too well."

Our call ended shortly after that…I finally had my proof. I knew Anthony would have mentioned his wonderful mother being ill if there was a grain of truth in it. He talked about her quite often, probably to yank my chain. He knew there was no love lost between us. But thoughts of *them* drifted from my mind as my head was suddenly filled with visions of addicts waiting for a fix, young girls being given drugs and then forced into prostitution. The question came back to me again…what role was he playing in all of it? I was shaking with anger and I felt sickened by my past relationship with him…and that I bore his surname!

CHAPTER 19

$\mathcal{M}$entally, I was finding it increasingly difficult to cope with everything that happened in the space of the last few months. Living under the same roof as Anthony was taking its toll. I was suspicious of every move he made and I know he sensed it. Whereas at the beginning of our estrangement, we tolerated each other and shared a forced politeness, we'd reached a stage where we bickered constantly, about everything! Bills, jobs around the house, even the television held potential for a massive row. Any visits to my parents' house were made by me alone and I still led Mum and Dad to believe all was well and made excuses for Anthony's absence through jokey comments about his busy social life.

Work was causing yet another problem for me, due to my forgetfulness and a total lack of concentration. It was the girls, my friends who were the first to start making comments,

'Hello? Are you with us, Helen?' 'What planet are you on today, honey?' and 'Is anyone at home in there?' I also became aware that most of the staff watched me from time to time out of the corner of their eyes. I seldom saw smiles in my dealings with any of them...those were replaced with subtle concerned scrutiny. The comments *and* the looks got me worrying even more. I knew that if I didn't get myself in check soon, there would be more awkward questions coming my way. Awkward questions with even more awkward and deceptive answers to them. I needed to be more alert, more self-aware.

When the new working week started I was full of determination. I dug into my depths and walked into the office with a refreshed, more cheery persona, it could almost have given the impression that I just recovered from a nasty virus...or pre-menstrual tension. I kept up the happy person act for most of the week, whilst also being conscious of *every* move I made.

As the week went by the results of my self-observations were greatly disturbing me. I struggled to eat my lunch and it was as if I couldn't swallow. I lined pens up in neat rows, stacked files neatly at the very corner with the files perfectly square with the edges of the desk. My blotting pad also had to be lined up square and my doodling on the blotter also had to be symmetrical. The extreme washing and scrubbing my hands and arms reared its ugly head once more. I was out of control. My obsessive behaviour was now visiting me during working hours.

I was totally out of my depth and tried in vain to come up with a solution. Another outlet was needed instead of letting it interfere with my working life. Ashamed to say it but I recognised that I'm a threat to my own professionalism. Being obsessive at home was out as Anthony would notice. He already called me a 'fucking weirdo' so there would be more rows. I wouldn't put it past him to tell my father. Dad would want to know what was causing it. I couldn't bear the thought that if Mum and Dad were to find out they would push me towards seeing Mr Gillespie again and he would press for the cognitive behavioural therapy this time. I felt as if millions of grains of sand were raining down, their very weight threatening to totally engulf me. I couldn't see a means of escape.

I knew I had to take immediate action. I made an appointment with a different GP at our surgery for Friday night after work, not wanting to face Dr Jack again, after Dad's insistence to him last time that he didn't want me on any tablets.

This time, I walked out of Dr Bell's office clutching a prescription for Fluoxetine, an anti-depressant frequently used in the treatment of O.C.D.

CHAPTER 20

For over three weeks I took the prescription drugs every day as recommended. My patience was non-existent as I waited each day for some sign of improvement. I expected to see at least *some* indication that they were going to calm me, get my O.C.D. in order and make me feel normal again. After the time spent taking them and with no apparent advancement, I began to despair feeling that normal for me, would never return. Throwing the three month supply of anti-depressants into the bin was looking like the most sensible option.

It wasn't however, the gradual improvement I anticipated. It happened overnight. I woke up one morning feeling like the old me again, totally calm and without the overwhelming compulsion to disinfect the whole house or poison Anthony. The obsessive desire to scrub everything with bleach, my hands and arms included, had gone. I felt more positive that I could get back on track at work. One Saturday morning, I chose a book off the shelf in my bedroom and read it in one sitting. I hadn't read in months. I even found everyday things to smile about; a programme on the television, the politeness and genuine smile from a check-out operator at the super-market. It was a nice feeling, to be back in control.

It was a pleasure to go to work and come away each night, achieving the finalising and signing off of accounts which had awaited my attention for several days. I was rapidly getting through one of the obsessively neat piles of folders stacked on my desk and noticed the acknowledge-ment in the face of, not just Ted, but each of my friends and colleagues, that I was back.

Janet brought some letters for me to sign before Friday lunchtime and as she waited for me to go through them, she asked hesitantly,

"Helen, we're all going out tonight, we haven't done it for ages. Not the city centre though…we thought maybe Ascot Village. Are you up for it? It'll do you good. You haven't been too well lately, have you?"

I looked up at her and smiled, touched by her concern. It sounded just the thing to get me back into socialising with the girls whose company I adored. I didn't hesitate before giving her my answer.

"Janet, I would love to! Thank you for asking. It will be the ideal opportunity to celebrate the fact that I feel better."

She was happy. She gave me a gentle nudge on the arm before uttering,

"You'll love it, girl!" She scooped up the signed letters and left.

A night out! I almost forgot what it was like to enjoy myself. It was an exciting thought that I would soon find that enjoyment once more. The butterflies of nervous elation swooped up and down in my stomach as I started thinking about what to wear. We gathered in the staff canteen at lunchtime and made our final arrangements.

Not too many hours later we were in Jigz in Ascot; chosen because it offered everything we wanted...food, a nightclub and a choice of bars. There were six of us, Janet, Nina, Gillian, Gemma, myself and a recent addition to the trainees, Leanne. We dined early and had a couple of drinks in one of the bars. It was packed with people and the atmosphere was electric. Although there was no music playing in the bar we were in, the incessant buzz of different conversations all around us was deafening. We could barely hear each other speak to indulge in our own chitchat. Leanne, being the youngest and by far the liveliest of us all, was eager to dance and she kept pointing to the door, miming the famous moves of Travolta in Saturday Night Fever. We giggled like schoolgirls at her craziness but obediently followed as she led the way.

If we thought it noisy in the bar, it was nothing to the volume that was pumping out of the colossal speakers in the club. Conversation was impossible. There were groups of people standing all around the packed dance floor, each person at a different level of intoxication. With talking being completely out of the equation, the only thing to do was to dance, whether the music was to our liking or not. Nina and I couldn't keep pace with the others and every four or five dances we got off the dance floor for ten or fifteen minutes to catch our breath.

It was during one of our dancing sessions I became aware of a guy who stood at the edge of the dance floor staring hard in my direction. He appeared to be with three or four other men, obviously friends of his. I was straining my eyes to get a look at him, but it was hard work with the strobe lighting pulsing away to the music. I lost sight of him for a few minutes and then almost jumped out of my skin to find he was suddenly leaning in close to me. I jerked my head away from him quickly but seconds later a flash of light passed across his face...Alex Baker-Thompson.

He grabbed my hand and led me off the dance floor. Cupping both his hands to my ear he bellowed something almost inaudible. The only words I managed to make out were "...somewhere....quiet...talk..." I nodded in agreement. I managed to grab the attention of Nina and Leanne, pointed at Alex and the door and covered my ears and hoped they would get the gist of what I was trying to say. Once again, he took hold of my hand to guide me through the throng. As soon as we were clear of what was the noisiest experience of my life, he asked,

"Fresh air? Or one of the quiet bars?" I considered for a second watching him comb his fingers across his hair, and his wedding ring glinted under the corridor lighting.

"Fresh air, please! The heat in there is nauseating." He smiled, his shoulders sagging a little, releasing some of the tension,

"I'm so glad you said that. I must be getting old. I can't cope with the noise these days...and to think that I used to love it all."

His arm around my shoulder, he guided me once more through the crowds waiting around outside for cabs.

We sauntered along for five minutes, me grasping onto his left arm for support, my high heels threatening to unbalance me should I place a foot on some unseen bump in the pavement. It was fresh and peaceful outside in the half light. Cars drove past us but any sound from them was insignificant. I wondered what we were doing...what happened to the talk? I tried to think of something to say and he beat me to it.

"You're married then, Helen? I've noticed the ring."

I didn't see any reason to lie.

"Yes. I'm married...estranged. I wear the ring because of

…well, appearances. There are people who don't need to know right now. Long story! You wear a wedding ring too. Where's your wife, Alex?"

I turned to look at his face as we continued our leisurely stroll but he didn't face me. He was deep in thought, eyes staring ahead.

"She's…um…with her mother. She cheated on me. I kicked her out."

I was astonished. It didn't only happen to me then? I couldn't think of anything to say to him.

I wasn't sure how far we wandered in silence but we took a left turn into a road with less traffic. In quite a clumsy move, he suddenly swung around to face me.

"Helen, I'm really sorry! I am! We parted on bad terms last time and I didn't want that."

He was waiting for me to say something and I couldn't find the appropriate words. Such a long time had passed and I just had an apology I never expected. I tried to remember how long ago. He'd dragged me out here to say sorry!

"Wha…" I started to comment but he cut me off quickly.

"Helen, I made you feel cheap. I tried it on with you, poked into your pants…I…"

His words were somehow like a trigger.

Poke into my panties!

My head was about to explode, a pleasant tingling coursed through me. I wanted to be fucked again and I recognised I was about to lose control in that need.

I snatched out for his hand and shoved it straight up my skirt and into my pants.

"Do you mean poke like…like this, Alex?"

I rubbed his fingers over my pussy. I moaned out loud and releasing my grip on his hand, his fingers found their way inside me. His lips were hard on mine in seconds, his tongue forced its way in, but I wanted it urgently and needed his warmth in my mouth. I parted my lips for him. My hand fumbled desperately with the zip of his denims. As my breathing grew heavy and my need increased, I abandoned that attempt and reached down the top of them into his underwear. I felt his stiffness grow as I fondled him right there in the street.

As our wildness became more urgent, we edged our way along the road, not noticing our steps. I groaned in frustration as he pulled his fingers out of me, my inner muscles throbbing in wait as, struggling with the zip that held his pulsing cock in place, he finally succeeding in freeing it. I pulled away from his probing tongue and as I bent over with the intention of going down on him, he grabbed my arm and hurried me another twenty yards down the road and through a gap in the hedge which led into a small park.

His lips found mine again, one eye watching behind me as he steered us backwards, his fingers still inside me. I felt the back of my knees make contact with something and his hand had gone again. He eased me into a sitting position and I detached myself from his lips and took his cock into my mouth. Lengthwise, he wasn't big but his girth was thick. I sucked and marvelled at his thrusts into my mouth and let my mind race ahead, imagining how it would feel to have that thickness inside me, hammering at me and filling me with his cum. I still had my panties on and they were wet.

It all came pouring out of me...months of sexual frustration. My eagerness to be fucked was turning me into a wanton, wild woman! I couldn't wait a second longer, insatiate. I needed this; I wanted to be fucked! I pulled my mouth away from his cock.

"What are you bloody waiting for?" then half screaming at him, "Fuck me, Alex!"

I sensed he was feeling a similar wildness. I stood and pushed my panties down my thighs. In his urgency to give what I asked, he bent down and pulled my panties off one leg. He lifted me off the ground in both arms and as I clasped around his neck with my legs around his waist, he lowered me towards his cock. I held on tight and he released my waist. One hand supporting my bottom, his other hand guided his cock inside me! He staggered ten or twelve feet, managing to keep inside me all the while, towards a tree trunk and once there, pushed my back firmly into it. Breathless, he stammered,

"Helen...ca...can't...believe...you!"

He was on his toes with every upward thrust into me. His girth was grazing me, each nerve alight, pubic bone rubbing fiercely against my clit. Within two minutes I'd cum, my juices free flowing over his length, my mouth wide open with the shock of an experience long forgotten. I felt greedy, I wanted more.

"Alex!" I urged "Don't move, leave it all the way in. Don't move!"

The frustration was evident on his face, he wanted to carry on fucking, but I stopped him. I was breathless, way too hyped, but it would only take me a minute. As he stood still, all my weight bearing down on his cock, I could feel every nerve of it as he throbbed within, alighting every tendril inside my folds and beyond. I screamed out with the intensity as I came again. My eyes closed and I held my breath, savouring every glorious, awakening moment.

When he pulled out and backed away, I couldn't wait to get him inside me once more. Dropping to my knees, I hitched my skirt up to my waist and the anticipation sent me into a new frenzy. What was taking him so damned long, I wondered?

"Alex, what the...*hell* are you doing? Hurry up...shove it... back in, *now!*"

"It's...on it's...way! Babe, you...you're... *fucking* impatient!"

I felt his fingers slide down beneath the cheeks of my backside and at that same moment the head of his cock touched my labia in its new search for warmth. I tipped my head back, my eyes crossed and every bloody nerve throughout my body felt engulfed in flames. That mere hint of more action to come...the end of his cock against my fleshy outer parts, sent me into paroxysms with a new release of cum. It was beyond pure heaven!

I felt him twist my hair around his hand and pull on it as he fucked me like a madman.

"You're...turning...me...into a...raving...fucking luna... lunatic...Helen."

He blurted, a word with each rough thrust into me, a perfect rhythm. Riding me, on and on, my hair the reigns in his grip as I enjoyed second, every stroke of being re-acquainted with sexual wantonness!

I felt a new wetness develop, his pre-cum, as with his free hand, he delved into my bra and squeezed tightly on my left nipple. I groaned at the new pain, and moaned at my ecstasy down below. I heard his throatiness close to my ear as his thrusts continued, a new fiery urgency in each,

"Same...again...Helen? Shall I...stick it...deep...in you... and...hold...as my...as my...cock...spurts...my cum?"

"Yes! Please...now...do it...to...me!"

I was almost screaming again as one final, his hardest thrust hit deep into me, pulsing strongly against the walls of my pussy as he let go, his warm juices spurting deliciously as I excreted my own cum again...

"You're...fucking...amazing...Helen!" he whispered as his breathing started to slow.

As we traced our steps back to Jigz, he placed his arm around my shoulders. I was deep in thought about how I was going to pass this one off with my friends, who must all be wondering where the hell I disappeared to. We approached the door and Alex suddenly stopped and faced me, his lips seeking mine. I froze and stepped backwards.

"Helen, can't we...?"

I cut him off sharply, sensing what was coming.

"No, Alex! We can't. It's been a one-off. Exciting, but a one-off."

My head held high, I turned and walked into the club, straight to the ladies room.

I spotted the girls quickly enough. They were taking a breather at the edge of the dance floor during a brief pause from the music system.

"Where the hell did you go? Who was that guy?" blurted Leanne, not in quite the discreet manner that the other girls would have used should they have had their chance to enquire first. She winked in an all-too-knowing expression as her questions came out. It was nice to communicate without shouting for the first time that night.

"Oh, him? We went to school together, that's all! We've just had a catch up outside...so we could hear one another."

They all looked toward the door.

"Jeeez! What did you do to him, Helen? He's looking pretty pissed off!"

I turned to look. Alex's eyes searched the room for his friends.

"Oh! He made a move on me, so I left him out there."

And as I said it, I saw the reality of what really happened. He just had the fuck of his life and any further chances were snatched away from him in an instant.

I relived some of those wild moments with Alex as I waited for sleep to come. I was a slut. On the same day I got my test results back; found out I hadn't contracted HIV or any other sexually transmitted plague, I have a one-night-stand for the first time in my life. I didn't care much for Alex. I simply gave in to my wildest needs. The self-respect I once had for my body was gone.

Heavenly, wild and dirty sex…without the complications of even liking the guy who fucked me.

"Thank you, Anthony!" I said the words out loud. "This is all your fucking fault!"

CHAPTER 21

ork was great fun on the Monday that followed our visit to Jigz. It was Ted's 60th birthday. We organised everything the previous Friday. Helium balloons were delivered to the office. One of the girls saw some classy desk gadget and we all chipped in to cover the cost. Hilary, his wife, came along to the office mid-morning with freshly cooked bacon baps from a café further down the street and there were cream cakes to follow. She also brought a couple of bottles of champagne along and at dinner time in the staff kitchen, we toasted his health and behaved rather unprofessionally in our champagne induced silliness. Fortunately, no client appointments were booked.

I was still on a high from my recent visit into the depths of sluttish behaviour and the intense pleasures I experienced…my sexual re-awakening! Surprisingly, my good mood prompted me to make sufficient food for Anthony to partake of. Again, something I hadn't done for quite some time. Knife in my hand, chopping onions and mushrooms, I was singing along with the radio to the Madonna song, "Like a Prayer." I knew I would have to be careful when I told him that he could eat with me. I didn't want him reading anything into it. I shuddered at the thought, paused in mid-lyrics, and felt my happiness wane a little. As he walked into the kitchen some time later I was plating up my meal and gave him a cheery smile.

"There's plenty left if you want some...spag bol."

Seeing his eyebrows raise in surprise, I quickly added.

"I did far too much just for me, it's a shame to waste it."

I saw his mouth watering as he looked at my plate long-ingly. I nodded towards the wall unit,

"Get yourself a plate."

"Thanks, I will. It looks good enough to eat."

And as he laughed at his own little joke, it struck me as sad how we used to be happy together, laughing so much and enjoying life. This was far removed from those times. Looking at me curiously as he piled up spaghetti on his plate and followed it with a generous serving of the bolognese, he said,

"You're in a good mood tonight."

"Yeah, it's been a nice day at work. It was Ted's 60th today. We had champagne and precious little work got done."

After I cleared the dishes away, Anthony switched on the television and started watching a history documentary. Our pleasantries for the day were done. I loaded the dishwasher, wiped the worktops down and went back through the lounge. Picking up the new book I started reading the previous night, I settled on the settee to indulge myself. The volume of the programme he was watching was extremely loud at times; WW2 bombs raining down on London and I found it somewhat distracting. I grabbed my MP3 player from down the side of the cushion, pushed the buds into my ears, pressed play and my reading was melodically accompa-nied by Beethoven instead of blackouts and bombs.

The music was soothing as I read. The suspense of the

story was building and I was enthralled but fighting against the weight of my eyelids. I jumped in such a panic as Anthony gently shook my shoulder.

"Helen, there's somebody knocking at the door. Are you expecting anybody?"

My eyes darted up to the clock on the mantle...it was nine forty seven. Pulling my ear buds out, I rubbed my eyes, and wished I'd gone to bed to read instead of dropping off downstairs. With a groan, I managed to say,

"No...not!"

I heard the loud banging, was it for the second or third time? A thought quickly entered my head and I was alert in an instant, and wondered if it was one of his contacts. He stood and looked at me...too long. I wondered if the same thought occurred to him. Trying hard to shake off the remains of my tiredness, I snapped him out of his thoughts.

"Anthony! Go and bloody see who it is! Now! It sounds urgent."

Seemingly reluctant, he left his programme to answer the continuous pounding.

I struggled to hear what was being said, the low mumblings indistinguishable. Anthony closed the lounge door after him when he went into the front hall to answer the knock. I could hear a deep, male voice, then a different one, not quite so deep. The front door closed and Anthony came back in through the lounge door, walking purposely towards me, his face unreadable. Behind him were two police officers. I stood up, the tension crept through my body and I didn't know which way to turn.

"Helen...I..." stammered Anthony.

Oh shit, they've come for him!

I was holding my breath, waiting for him to tell me. My thoughts drifted, I wondered what my father would do or say when he finally found out what Anthony, his dependable surrogate son had been up to. I cringed at my own cynicism.

"We'll take over from here, Sir." the deeper-voiced of the two said to Anthony, then he turned to face me.

"Are you Mrs Helen Pawson?"

What the hell question was that? I was petrified. What would he want me for? I started shaking, coldness striking through me, my knees suddenly feeling weak. I nodded, unsure.

"You may want to sit down, Mrs Pawson. We have some news for you…its bad news!"

My parents had been involved in a fatal accident. My father, who was driving, had suffered a major cardiac arrest at the wheel. He died instantly. The car veered into the path of an oncoming lorry. I listened to his words and thought he must be lying to me. Surely I was dreaming and he was at the wrong address. My mother was apparently, critical and on life support. I couldn't take it all in. All the while he was speaking it was surreal. It wasn't really happening to me. It was happening elsewhere. The voices were speaking to someone else and not me…in slow motion. I felt numb and barely aware of what was going on around me. Somebody put a coat around my shoulders…Anthony. And, was it really him, saying,

"I'll take you, Helen…to the hospital."

We were too late. By the time we arrived at the hospital, my mother's life support machine had already been switched off. Anthony was taken away to make a formal identification of them both. It galled me that I had to leave everything to him, but I needed him. I didn't have anyone else to rely on. He called my relations on both Mum's and Dad's sides of the family to break the news, he organised the joint funeral, organised the flowers. For once, I was glad he was there. I was good for nothing. They had been my life and now they were taken from me. My heart was savaged, torn apart. And I felt such devastation. I wanted to die too....to finally be free from the hurt...

CHAPTER 22

$\mathcal{I}$ spent the first week after my parents' death in either total disbelief or utter devastation, alternating between the two. After Anthony drove us back home following the funeral and wake (which was held in a posh hotel in Richmond, not far from their home), I crawled into a corner and howled the place down. A box of tissues constantly by my side, I took to pouring brandy down my neck all day, every day. It didn't go down very well with my medication. It did fuck all to numb the pain for me. I reached a stage where the waterworks ceased completely. There were no more tears to cry.

Anthony didn't go into the office for ten days. For all the past explosive moments we went through, I think he was genuinely worried about me. He made sure I tried to eat something substantial at least twice a day and stood over me to make sure that I did.

The days all merged into one and subconsciously I drifted into the rocking stage. I would sit cross-legged, arms around my knees, and rock for hours at a time. Anthony called our local surgery and a GP came out two nights in a row to give me a sedative so at least I could try for a little sleep. He also left a new prescription for Anthony to collect from the pharmacy, an increased dosage of my anti-depressants.

Three weeks after the funeral I went into the office, but not with the intention of doing any work. I hadn't been in touch with anyone since my parents died, though Anthony called the office to explain, at my request. I realised I wasn't being fair to Ted, I'd behaved badly but I just couldn't face seeing anyone or even speaking to them. I relied on Anthony far too much to protect me from people. I knew that it needed to stop sometime and this was the time for it to end. I needed to see Ted Hopkins. I knocked on his door, popped my head around,

"Can I come in please, Ted?"

"Helen, please do." He gestured towards the chair opposite him, "I didn't expect to see you back yet. Surely you need a little more time. Take all you need, it's not a problem."

I was racked with guilt. I'd been inconsiderate and didn't want him to be nice to me. I couldn't even look him in the eye, the tears threatened again.

"Ted, the reason I've come in is…" I hesitated, "I can't return, I just can't! It wouldn't be fair to you or to any of the staff. I've not been pulling my weight lately. You know that, so does everyone else. My parents…I'm devastated. Besides that, I have serious problems in my marriage and I've other issues too, which you can't fail to have noticed. I know some of the girls have witnessed my behaviour. I can't concentrate, I can't work. I'm no good to anyone, so it's only fair that I should leave. It will give you the chance to employ somebody or take another partner on. Someone who can give one hundred percent. I'm not even capable of giving ten percent at the moment and I can't see that improving in the near future. It is going to take me a long time to get over this… Mum and Dad…my marriage. I don't know how long…"

"Helen, could you not even think this through for…who knows, however long it takes? Three or possibly four months even? We could get by. You're jumping the gun, it's still early days."

Ted was such a lovely man, compassionate and he had empathy. I hated doing this to him. The trouble was it could be detrimental to the business if I was to stay and couldn't give it my all. I couldn't do that to him.

"But it's not just the grieving, Ted, it's all the other issues. My marriage is wrecked. I can't keep my O.C.D. in check. I *am* leaving, Ted, I *have* to."

His eyes showed his disappointment although he smiled kindly at me.

"Well, you're still a partner here. You can continue to receive your percentage of the profits. I can't say fairer than this. I'll get an agency worker in to help with the workload. Take what you need, one year or maybe more, but come back, please."

I couldn't give him my promise so I didn't say anything. He came with me to my office and watched as I cleared my personal bits and pieces from the desk. There wasn't much, a few of my favourite pens and a picture of Anthony, which I intended to sling in the nearest bin once I left the office. My laptop was already at home so there wasn't much else. I tried to give Ted an update on the files that I'd been working on to bring him up to speed, although with everything that happened to me, my recollections were vague. I stepped towards him and put the pile of files in his arms. Ted being the way he is, immediately put them back down onto my desk and held his arms out to give me a hug.

"I am so sorry, Helen. Please stay in touch. I really hadn't expected this bombshell today, but I want you to know, I do understand your reasons, I really do. If there's anything I can ever do to help…"

"Thank you, Ted. Can I just ask one more thing of you, please?"

"Certainly, what can I do?"

"Would you please mind telling the staff after I've gone? I love them all dearly but I can't face them, the way I'm feeling. Tell them I will be in touch when I'm ready."

"Consider it done, my dear."

"Thank you again, Ted."

I walked out of the door relieved to have one less thing preying on my mind. Remembering the picture of Anthony in my handbag, I tossed it in a waste bin at the end of the street, though I took little pleasure from doing so. I didn't know where I was going, or what I was going to do. Just over the road from the waste bin, I spotted the tube station and crossed over. I got on the first train that pulled into the platform. I had no idea which direction it was going or where I was going to get off.

I don't know for how long I'd been travelling when I woke up from my daydreams, but the train had just stopped at Oxford Circus tube station. I must have been unintentionally staring at the man who sat opposite me because he glared back at me as if I was a weird creature from the deep. He made me feel uncomfortable, so I snatched up my handbag and left the train. Once out of the station and back into the open again, I walked...and walked. Half of the time I didn't know where I was but I just kept going, changing direction without realising and totally unaware of the length of time I'd been walking.

It suddenly dawned on me that people were looking at me and I couldn't understand why. I started to taste the tears that rolled onto my lips. I realised that I couldn't make out the faces of the people who stared; they were blurred. Feeling embarrassed, I turned to what I thought was a shop window on the pretext of window shopping. Only it wasn't a dress shop or any other shop for that matter. I was looking straight at the job vacancies of a recruitment office. *Chambermaids wanted, apply within.* I quickly dabbed at my eyes and went in.

An hour later, I emerged from a top London hotel with a bag containing two chambermaid uniforms and instructions on who to report to the following Monday morning. When I arrived home (it seemed stupid but that's how I still referred to the marital house I shared with Anthony), I ignored the mess in the house. I ignored the mail sat on the doormat near the front door and went up to my room. Opening the bag, I took out the uniforms, stared at them in horror and wondered what the hell possessed me. I was a qualified accountant for heaven's sake. What on earth had driven me to apply for a job as a cleaner in a hotel? I started an argument with myself there and then.

'Yes girl, but you are an accountant who can't even do her job anymore. Too much going on in your life, you can't concentrate, you can't do anything right any more. So you've found yourself a job that you can actually do, haven't you? You can clean. You can make a good job of this. You've got O.C.D. for heaven's sake. Just turn up there on Monday morning. Do it. Get out of the house, away from him. Nobody need know what you are doing.'

'But Mum and Dad would go crazy if they knew about this.'

'But they will know! They'll be watching over you, Helen. That's what they always did. Watch over you.'

The argument within, carried on for over two hours, covering the same ground, asking the same questions, answering with the same answers. My mind was made up. I would turn up for the job on Monday morning. Anthony needn't know. I wasn't going to make him any the wiser and there was nobody else to tell him.

CHAPTER 23

*I*t was my first day and I turned up at the hotel with ten minutes to spare. I checked in with head housekeeper Mrs Fenwick first and filled in my personal details on the form she handed me. She handed over my name badge and showed me to the locker room where I needed to change into one of the little black dresses and crisp white maid's aprons that had been provided. One of the girls, Sandra, took me to the floor that I would be working on and introduced me to Jodie, the girl I was to spend the day with, so she could show me what to do.

Jodie turned out to be a nice kid, more mature than I would have expected for an eighteen year old and unusually conscientious for someone of her years. As we chatted our way through the morning, I happened to mention to her that I detected more than a hint of iciness in Mrs Fenwick's manner. She laughed and agreed with me and let slip that all the staff referred to the head housekeeper as 'Frigid Flo.' I enjoyed Jodie's constant chattering and at least if she was doing all the talking, I didn't have to say much. I preferred to keep it that way, it would keep things simple. I made up my mind that I wouldn't reveal any details about my recent devastating news or my disastrous private life.

I was relying on my O.C.D. to help get me through each working day and it struck me as ironic that my mental health issue actually had a use. I cleaned, scrubbed and took a genuine pride in my work, or so Jodie thought, but she was unaware of the inner demons I was attempting to rid myself of. There were more than a few occasions when I caught her glancing at me suspiciously, and it didn't shake me in the slightest when she posed the question,

"Have you done this type of work before, Helen, because you're making a great job of these rooms? It surprises me because you don't actually look the type. You look kind of… educated, if you don't mind me saying so."

Chuckling, I returned her smile as I quickly scoured my head for further things I could say. I sensed that if I didn't volunteer something about my private life she would keep pushing.

"Thank you, Jodie. You're right! I did have a good education."

Her eyes were agog. She plonked herself down on the bed we just made, laid on her side, propped up on one elbow. Getting comfortable for a heart to heart, she wanted more and looked at me expectantly. I reluctantly obliged.

"I *was* married but he…he cheated. Sadly, I've still got the bills to pay so I do anything I can to earn money. It's very hard living alone but it's what I have to do to keep my home and pay the bills. I work from home as well, doing business on the internet, which I can do on a night and weekends. I work as many hours in a day as I possibly can."

She seemed to quite happily accept what I told her and we got on with the rest of the day's work on our floor. I wasn't happy with myself but I couldn't tell her that I used to work in accountancy or that I suffer with O.C.D. I liked the girl a lot and her chitchat kept me amused for the most part. At other times, I tried to switch off from her constant babbling. I also tried attempting to visualise my parents, but it was hard. I hoped they wouldn't think bad of me or be disappointed, seeing what I'm doing now and think that I'm weak for giving into my grief and throwing away my career.

Mrs Fenwick came out of her office to see me the next morning. Apparently she heard excellent reports about my work from Jodie *and* the shift supervisor and from that morning onwards, I would be working alone. She handed me the details of the rooms I needed to work on that day. The solitude of working without supervision was perfect. I cleaned and scrubbed, only focusing on what was in front of my eyes. I didn't have to think, or concentrate. I disinfected, I cleaned out my mind; cleared it of hurtful thoughts, nightmares of Gavin, Anthony, rape and my grief over the death of my parents. But the hurt returned with a vengeance each time I left the hotel. It didn't feel like I would ever be over it. For the first in my life, I wished I had a brother or sister, a sibling, someone who would share a mutual understanding of the grief, sibling support and something in common, a shoulder to cry on.

I wondered if I could have better coped with my grief if I didn't have so many other issues; if I had a loving husband at home to talk to and care for me. It further grieved me that I didn't even have *that*!

Anthony was absolutely clueless where I was going or what I was doing each day; I left home in my car every morning, parked up in a car park near the tube station and caught the train into the city centre. It wasn't likely that he would ever find out. He never phoned me at work *before* we became estranged and I doubt he would do that now.

CHAPTER 24

I carried on going to work each day, Monday to Friday. When interviewed, I specifically requested not to be given weekend shifts, mainly because I didn't want Anthony to realise what I was doing. Our indifference towards each other was as much a routine for us now as our working hours. We shared a bottle of wine on an evening occasionally, but conversation between us remained almost non-existent.

After I'd been working at the hotel for no more than a few weeks, Mrs Fenwick told me I was to be promoted to the top floor where all the penthouse suites were situated.

"They are much bigger than those you have been used to. The standard of cleaning must be exceptional, Helen. There's more to do but you don't have so many of them." She continued to tell me, "I'm bringing down one of the other girls. She's been missing a few things lately and we've received complaints. I can't afford to let that happen where special guests are concerned. Don't let me down on this, please. You've worked hard and are now my best chambermaid, so I'm giving you this opportunity, putting my trust in you."

It was ironic. My O.C.D. served me well. Was I expected to be pleased? I tried to find some emotion from within but I came up with...indifference. My good manners however came to the fore.

"Thank you, Mrs Fenwick, I'll make certain not to let you down."

I was told by the other staff that she very rarely made an appearance on the top floor to check the suites and I would need to check my own work. I knew my pride would be hurt if she ever received any complaints. Every shift from then on I made my way up in the lift to the top floor; Garden, Kensington, Thames and Tower suites.

She wasn't wrong about the extra work. The bathrooms were large, the bedrooms bigger, plus there was a decent sized lounge with a dining area to each unit. I tried not to think of the job as cleaning for an employer. I rather fancied that each of these little apartments was my home and I was keeping them immaculate for my own satisfaction. There were times I met some of the V.I.P. occupants and whilst there was the odd one or two who talked down to me, the majority were fairly respectful and chatted to me as I worked. The male clientele were especially attentive, or at least they were when they didn't have wives or lovers with them. I could always feel their eyes burn into me as they drank in every detail of my body

About ten days after I started working on the upper floor, I knocked on the door of one of the suites and waited for a response. It was a male guest who opened the door to me.

"Come in, young lady. Put the latch on the door behind you. I don't want to be disturbed by anybody else. I'm busy working so start in the bathroom and bedroom, please. I shall make myself scarce when you want to do the living area."

"Yes Sir, I will."

I latched the door as he instructed and quietly made my way into the bedroom. The door was ajar, and while I was working I could see that he had his laptop plugged in over on the desk, although he was actually sat on the settee with a pile of buff folders next to him. He was reading the contents of one of the folders. I busied myself with the dusting and polishing and changing the linen on the bed, deciding that I would do the vacuuming when he eventually disappeared as he said he would. I was out of the bedroom after about thirty minutes and set to work in the bathroom next. I disinfected the toilet, washed the tiles around the toilet area and moved the used towels onto the floor so that I could clean the bath.

I was bent over the bath reaching to the furthest edge and without any warning at all, I felt my skirt suddenly being raised up my back followed by my tights being tugged down to my knees. As he pushed my panties to one side, a couple of his fingers slid inside me. I froze.

"Sir, what do you think you are doing?" I asked him, careful not give out a trace of rudeness in my words.

He breathed heavily, his mouth close to my right ear.

"I've been watching you working from the bedroom. You didn't hear me, did you? You've got a very hot body and I would love you to show me how hot it can get."

He continued to probe around inside me and I stayed put. I hadn't had sex of any description for two or three months and I almost forgot how good it felt; the excitement coursed through my whole body.

"I…I'm supposed to be…working. I don't do things like that, Sir. T…Take your fingers out, please. I can do my job and you can do yours." As I listened to my own words spill out, I realised from his expression that he wasn't convinced.

Hell, I struggled to convince myself. "That's…what we're… both here for. If my boss knocked on the door…I wouldn't have a job anymore."

The shock kicked in and I realised this was a big problem. It was sexual harassment in the workplace…by one of the special guests. My problem was that I wanted it to continue. I actually *wanted* him to keep poking me…fingers…his cock. I was on fire and the flames had to die out naturally. I didn't want them extinguished. Beautiful feeling…beautiful flames. I turned my face to look into his eyes. Did he realise he was playing with fire? That if I lodged a complaint…but he was *not* playing games. His eyes showed how much he wanted me *and* his determination to get what he wanted.

"Come on…! You know you want to. You would have moved away by now if you didn't."

That much was true. I finally moved to my left and his fingers slid out of me with the move. I tried to persuade myself that I didn't feel horny.

"Wouldn't you rather be fucked than finish the cleaning? I won't tell anyone. I want to fuck you. Come on, how much would it cost me? Name your price."

I was astounded, didn't know what to think. The guy, a special guest, was suggesting I prostitute myself. I turned my back on him, wriggled my tights back up my thighs and straightened the skirt.

"Okay, so if you won't name a price, I'll suggest one. Come on, honey, play the game. I want to fuck you real bad."

I want to be fucked real bad too!

He wasn't particularly attractive, at a guess around fifty-ish, but there was something…or was it just my need to have a shag after weeks without? His first offer was *one thousand pounds*! I shook my head without saying a word. It wasn't about the money. If only he'd rip my clothes off instead of talking money, he would be able to fuck me for nothing…my body was awakened and I was gagging for it. I remained firm.

"I'm just going to get on with my work. Please forget it, Sir. I'm not a prostitute."

He kept raising his price. I continued shaking my head and repeating,

"No! I'm not doing this."

Undeterred, he kept upping the offer. I stopped shaking my head so often, pausing in thought for a few seconds between his bids. When he reached the figure where my interest took a sudden lurch, I turned and looked at him.

"Do you actually have that much money on you? I'm nobody's fool. It's got to be cash or it doesn't happen…your choice."

He broke into a sweat and his hands were shaking, his eyes were undressing me and he started to stutter.

"I'll…I'll…go to my bank later and…br…bring the cash back for you."

"No. You'd better get the cash now…or I'll just do my job and get out of here."

He donned his suit jacket and five minutes later he was out of the door with his briefcase. I asked myself what the hell I thought I was doing and I couldn't come up with an answer. My work came to a standstill; I was unable to concentrate because my mind was now focused on one thing only, getting laid. Somehow I didn't expect him to return. Once he was out on the street with me out of his sight, he would come to his senses and realise he couldn't cheat on his wife or partner.

Half an hour later, my heart leapt as I heard his card bleep in the lock. He replaced the security chain once he closed the door. Beckoning me over to the dining table, he opened his briefcase and showed me the cash. I stood gaping…but not at the cash. What *had* caught my attention, giving me my second big shock of the day – the guy was a barrister. The curly white wig was laid at the side of some A4 Oyez legal forms. Backing away, I intended to return to my duties, suddenly wary of him.

"You could make yourself a fortune with your body and your looks. A nice side-line for you; get you away from all this."

He gestured towards the housekeeping trolley.

I looked directly into his eyes, thinking that he was quite attractive after all and throwing caution to the wind, I asked,

"What do you want?"

He smiled, his brown eyes glowing with desire and he came up close and whispered in my ear.

"I want to play with you, taste you and fuck you. I want you to make it really nice and welcoming for me. Treat me like all men want to be treated. Do it right and you get all the cash that's in the briefcase! You've seen it, now let's see if you want to earn it. Nobody will ever get to know, trust me."

I don't know whether it was because the guy was vaguely handsome, or whether it was the thought of the amount of cash, but I was hot and clammy, my panties still damp from his earlier exploration. It would be yet another escape from my current existence and depression. He started peeling off his clothes down to his tight trunks as he walked towards the bed. His almost nakedness showed him to be slightly over-weight with a hint of a paunch, but not unattractive. I hadn't a clue as to how prostitutes behaved with their clients and for want of something better to say I put on my best seductive voice and asked,

"Would Sir like to unwrap his very expensive present or have it unwrapped for him?"

"First of all, Sir would like you to call him Simon," he took a quick glance at my name tag, "and, Helen, I love opening surprises myself."

He patted the bed, and I think I maybe overacted the provocative walk across the short distance to the bed.

"Don't act like a pro Helen, just be yourself," he scolded.

I lay down on the bed next to him and my thoughts turned from sex...to being found in bed with a hotel guest and I couldn't relax as tension started to creep through my body.

"What if someone knocks on the door, Sir...Simon?"

He considered my question for a second.

"I shout and tell them to bugger off. On this floor nobody argues with us...shall we say, very important guests!"

I was slightly placated to hear it, but it still didn't feel quite right.

"Let's continue where we left off in the bathroom, shall we?"

He moved in to kiss me and I turned my head away,

"No, don't do that, please. We are not lovers, Simon and it doesn't feel right."

He shrugged and looked down at my body. The bathroom scene unfolded once again as he drew up my skirt and pushed my tights and panties down. Although the scenario was totally alien to me, I was excited in a way I had never been excited, yet tense at the same time. The tension was a mixture of wanting...and fear. I hadn't had sex in weeks and could hardly wait for his fingers to once again edge their way teasingly into my warmth and wetness. The underlying fear was intensifying the pleasure. I was feeling rather bad...and shameless. I placed my hands under my bra and fondled my breasts...a new experience. He watched me and I got the impression it was something he'd never seen before, his mouth gaped in excitement. I jumped, but pleasurably so, when he unexpectedly twiddled with my clit for a short time before moving his attention to my pussy. His right hand was awkwardly groping about with the top half of my clothes so I helped him.

"You are eager, Helen. I see that. I think…that you want fucking as much as I want to fuck you, don't you? You take your clothes off while I attend to this beautiful pussy."

I pulled my blouse off quickly, but I was struggling to hold back, the anticipation edging ahead in the battle. His fingers were inside me again, probing and shoving. Every damn nerve within me was alert, waiting and already tingling, ready to surrender. As he bent his finger towards my G spot I couldn't hold back any longer. My body arched backwards as I moaned out loud and my upper thighs gripped his arm, holding his fingers firmly in place. I could feel my juices flow and I wanted more; truly on fire. I let the first wave of orgasm subside. My bra finally unclasped, I threw it to the floor and my skirt followed in one movement, up and over my head. I panted in pleasure…and I was fascinated. I didn't recognising myself *or* my behaviour.

"Wow. I can feel your juices all over my fingers. I want that juice all over my cock. Let's see if you've got more to give."

"Oh, I've definitely got more to give," my voice was raspy. "I can see the bulge in your undies. I want that bulge inside me, fucking me. First, I'm going to pleasure your cock."

I knelt on the bed and pushed his boxers down his legs. They only reached his ankles at the full stretch of my arm so he kicked them off with one of his feet. I was pleasantly surprised when the bulge sprang out of his tight trunks, its hardness twanged as it slapped back against his stomach, thick and superbly erect. I wanted him inside me there and then, but I couldn't be selfish. My aim was to please the man and earn the cash. Again, I wondered what the hell I was doing as I leaned over and wrapped my fuchsia lips around his cock. I teased around the head and tickled its tiny orifice with my tongue...the orifice which would soon be spewing out his cum when he ejaculated.

He moaned almost silently as I stroked the length of his cock with my tongue. I changed position until I was leaning over the bed, my head between his legs. Taking one of his balls into my mouth, I grasped at his cock with my right hand and rubbed it up and down his length, slowly at first and then steadily increased the speed. He was groaning again as, using my tongue, I flicked his testicle back and forth in my mouth. I eased the first one out of my mouth and taunted the other for a minute before also encasing that one with my lips. My hand moved rapidly up and down him, and he steadied it,

"Slower, ease off. I'm getting too eager to cum."

He lifted his back off the bed, and grabbing under my arms, hauled me up his body. My probing tongue licked his body throughout the move, from his pubic bone past his navel and up to his chest. He pulled me upwards until I was poised at the tip of his cock and eased me back down and onto it in one deft move. We both groaned at the same time. It felt awesome and every nerve throbbed inside me. My need was making me light headed.

"You're so wet. It's exciting me. Your pussy feels tight and hot around my cock. Fuck it now, let those sweet juices flow."

I pushed my pubic bone downwards and the feel of his muscle inside me was amazing...tight, stinging and throbbing. I moved with ease, ever the accomplished rider. Sitting on his stiffness I felt the pleasure of every inch as my vagina rubbed at it abrasively, my clit being massaged against his pubic bone in the process. He bit hard into my neck and my shoulder as I rode him. I gave it everything I had, putting it all into getting my reward and it was there, ready to explode, his bites making me gasp in pleasure and in pain.

I came, more explosively this time, so much wetness. He reached down to where his cock entered me and felt around its hardness with his finger. It was so sensitised down there, just the touch of his finger on the lips of my labia sent me soaring to new heights. I gasped for breath and could feel my body was aglow with the heat.

"Is that good, Helen - me fucking you? You have so much cum in only a short time. When were you last fucked?"

I was totally incapable of answering…breathless and still shaking from my orgasm.

"It doesn't really matter. You're enjoying yourself. I'm coated in cum."

He rolled me over onto my back and as he did so, I lost contact with his throbbing cock. It was his turn to go down on me and he thrust his tongue into my newly acquired wetness and tasted.

"So sweet, baby! So sweet, as I knew you would be. I knew you would taste good and you definitely don't disappoint."

His tongue moved beautifully inside me and I didn't know when my orgasm was going to cease, it was so intense. Then the tongue was gone. He eased himself up my body, and his cock found its target again as he mounted me. The stinging tightness, that feeling of being fucked by something so hard and thick was unbelievable! I gripped my vagina around his muscle and squeezed each time he thrust into me and it felt so good. It was hot and…I almost forgot what it felt like to be fucked and released again how much I love it. He was getting faster, thrusting harder and he bit into my neck again, then my shoulders. The nibbling and the hard thrusting was driving me into a new frenzy, my body tensed; so taut I was being driven crazy. I could feel myself going cross-eyed and didn't know what to do next. My nails dug into his back as I exploded again. He pulled out quickly and pleaded urgently,

"Quick! Onto your knees!"

I squeezed my pussy tight around his muscle as he rammed it in from behind and it finally tipped him over the edge. He threw his head back, gritted his teeth, and shouted out in ultimate pleasure as he released his cum.

It took his breathing ten minutes to calm. When he finally lifted his weight from my body, I felt his semen gush out and spill between my thighs. I was still shaking uncontrollably but jumped off the bed in a hurry when the reality hit me in an instant.

I showered in such a rush, desperate to get back to work should somebody be looking for me. He sat and watched me towel myself dry and put my slightly crumpled uniform back on.

"You could do well for yourself, Helen. You love to be fucked, and you certainly know how to pleasure a man. I know some men, wealthy men who...well, would pay lots of money to fuck you and be fucked back as good as you do. Men who need total discretion. I would pay you again. Don't let this be a one-off. Give me your number. I'll get you some clients. Are you interested in making money, Helen?"

I was staggered by what he suggested...'enjoy being fucked and get paid for it'. At the same time I was also trying to come to terms with what I'd just done; prostituted myself whilst I was at work. I could feel my face flush with guilt.

"I...I'm not sure, Simon. I shouldn't have done that...it was completely out of character...I...there are freaks out there. I don't want to be in any danger. I shouldn't, can't."

"I can almost swear to you that any person I give your number to will not be a freak. They will pay you well, no question of it, and you will not be in any danger. Give me your mobile number, Helen. I'll get you the work and I'll tell them you're called…Kat, Cougar, Puma or something equally ridiculous."

He laughed at his little joke and paused in his laughter a second, waiting for my reaction.

More at ease now that I was dressed and ready for work, I smiled vaguely and jotted down my mobile number as he handed me the cash. I stuffed it safely down the front of my tights and we said our goodbyes.

I don't know how I managed to get through the rest of my duties. Every time I caught sight of myself in a mirror my face looked crimson. I imagined that everybody was staring at me, wondering what crime I just committed. One thing I did realise…if I went ahead with this ridiculous suggestion of Simon's, I would be able to have a sex life when I wanted, earn fantastic money and I wouldn't need to fall in love. But the biggest bonus for me, I wouldn't get my heart broken ever again…no more hurt. It was that handsome bonus that persuaded me it was maybe the right thing to do.

CHAPTER 25

$\mathcal{I}$ still cry every day, but my initial disbelief has progressed towards acceptance and the anti-depressants are at last doing their job. I still haven't been able to face going over to my parents' house to sort anything. I asked Anthony to go over to their house and fetch back some items from a list I compiled, things I wanted...mainly some of their personal effects and the family photograph albums. That was all I wanted. The estate agent I called was super-efficient and had the house on the market within a couple of days. He was confident of a quick sale. Hopefully, I would be able to arrange for the furniture to go to auction before long. Mum's was already sold by a local garage and Dad's car had of course, been a total wreck after the accident.

On the Saturday morning, a few days after Simon brought about my initiation into the world of prostitution, I was having a well- earned lie-in for once. Work, along with *the* big surprise, had been hectic all week and I was shattered. I'd already been downstairs, made a pot of coffee and a slice of toast and was back in bed having a quiet read, amongst plenty of tears for my parents. Also at the forefront of my mind, I had mixed feelings about dipping my toes into the sordid sex trade. While I was partly disgusted with myself at the most recent rampant sex sessions with Alex and Simon, I found both experiences dirty, yet exhilarating. I felt twinges and dampness merely by thinking about them again.

A couple of clicks jolted me from the thoughts as Anthony's bedroom door first opened and then closed. I was surprised to hear him tapping on my bedroom door,

"Helen, are you awake?"

My peace and thoughts disturbed, I sighed.

"Yes, I'm awake."

There were a few moments of hesitation from him, maybe pondering what he was going to say.

"Can you come downstairs soon, please? There's… there's…some things I need to…to…tell you. Things you need to know that can't wait any longer." He sounded on edge, tired.

I started to panic, wondering what the hell was going on now. I sensed from his voice that it would be things I didn't want to hear. I felt a sinking feeling in the pit of my stomach.

Do I really want to know?

"Helen…?"

"Okay. Yes. I'll be down in five minutes."

He was still in his dressing gown and sat in his favourite armchair, a fresh pot of coffee on the table and an empty cup, so I poured one for myself and sat at the edge of the settee, feeling tense.

"Well?"

He took a few sips of his coffee, then gazed down into his cup, avoiding my eye, and mumbled,

"I haven't been sleeping well lately, and last night, not at all."

This news didn't move me in the slightest and feeling rather smart-arsed, I remarked,

"Well, unfortunately I'm not your G.P. but it could be down to the many things on your conscience."

He scowled at me, evidently affronted.

"Don't you *ever* let things drop, Helen?"

I felt like bloody slapping him. He was riling me before I even knew what else was coming in my direction. Did he really expect to be off the hook? He obviously had things he wanted to say. His expression was one of pure frustration, so I decided to keep quiet and let him speak.

"Go ahead then. You want to explain why you're not sleeping I presume?"

His face was red, he put down his coffee cup and proceeded to fiddle with and pick at his finger nails.

"I've wanted to tell you before now, Helen. I didn't think you could cope with it on top of your grief. You've had more than enough to deal with."

I couldn't disagree with that, but he'd been the cause of everything except the death of my parents. He took a minute or two to compose himself and finally looked directly at me.

"The business is finished, Helen. The bank has called the official receiver in."

I stood up, started pacing the room. I felt as if I'd been hit with a sledge-hammer. It must be wrong, my father wouldn't let...

"My dad's business? Finished? You...He..."

I couldn't take it in. Then it hit me even more quickly, like a wrecking ball. I could feel my anger building and I unleashed it at him in an instant.

"My father's business, ruined?"

I couldn't stop myself and the decibels exploded from within me.

"HE'S ONLY BEEN DEAD THREE FUCKING MONTHS AND YOU'VE MANAGED TO FUCK IT ALL

UP IN THAT SHORT SPACE OF TIME? EVERYTHING HE FUCKING WORKED FOR! GET…"

"Helen…NO! It's been…"

But I was relentless in my fury.

"WHAT WOULD MY DAD SAY IF HE KNEW? HE FUCKING TRUSTED YOU! YOU BASTARD!"

I was shaking with rage. Of all the things he'd done, even to me, this was by far the worst…destroying my Dad's business. Something that I hoped would live on forever…something Dad started from scratch and built up over the years, and now that had died with him! Such an overwhelming sadness just crept up on me and rendered me speechless as I let that thought sink in.

Taking advantage of my silence, Anthony, who was still sat down, leaned forward and held his hands up as if he could calm me.

"Helen! Helen! Ken knew about it. It didn't just happen overnight, or without his knowledge. He knew. It's been going on for months now."

I glared at him angrily. Was this something else he thought he could talk his way out of? If he was hoping to pacify me, he'd have to do better than that!

"Helen, sit down! Let me explain! You're an accountant, for fuck's sake! You should know that businesses don't just fail overnight!"

I started pacing again, refusing to do as he told me by sitting down. I felt a surge of hatred and violence towards him. He was my father's finance director, in a position of trust, how could he have let this happen?

"COME ON THEN, ANTHONY, EXPLAIN IT TO ME! HOW THE FUCK DID YOU LET IT HAPPEN?" I bellowed.

I lost control and had to sit down, fearing that if I remained standing I would launch myself at him.

Throughout the next half hour, I heard the whole story after finally calming down enough to hear him out. Ten or eleven months ago, Anthony found out through some business contact, that two smaller advertising companies were about to go into administration. Keen to help build up my father's business even further, Anthony saw the opportunity to gain more clients as one not to be missed. He convinced my father to look into the matter further and they'd attended meetings with the receivers for both businesses. Persuaded by Anthony's cash-flow forecasts for the next five years, Dad agreed to purchase both companies for a pittance, along with their liabilities.

They took a big risk and it failed. The trade creditors unanimously agreed to bear with them, receiving an agreed figure per month, pleased to be getting more than the expected nine pence in the pound the receiver would have paid. However, by the time the PAYE and VAT liabilities were settled for both the failed businesses, which far exceeded Anthony's predictions, the company bank started putting pressure on Dad. The expected new portfolio of clients never materialised. Those clients, obviously suspecting that taking on all the liabilities of two failed companies would cripple Dad's business, took their business elsewhere.

"Ken was desperate to save the business, Helen. We were both worried for months. The day before the accident, he made an appointment for us to see the bank. He was going to ask them to increase the overdraft facility or see if they would accept their house as security for a loan."

My head was going round in circles, trying to fathom who was to blame in all this...Anthony, for telling my father about the two businesses? Or subsequently, his worthless cash-flow forecasts? Maybe Dad and his stupidity, his stupidity for placing his trust in Anthony and his judge-ments? I couldn't think straight in my fury and as if to add insult to injury, he added.

"That's why I've been behaving like an arsehole these last few months, Helen. The worry, I couldn't take it anymore!"

He finally tipped me over the edge with his words. I picked up the nearest thing to me, a heavy glass paperweight, and flung it at him with as much force as I could muster. He ducked and it went smashing through the lounge window into the front garden.

CHAPTER 26

*W*ithin ten minutes of dodging my missile, Anthony was dressed and gone. I didn't trust myself to do or say anything else. I was livid. I shot off upstairs with a bottle of wine before he left, determined to drink myself into oblivion.

I lay on the bed trying to get a grip, but it wasn't easy. I tried to work things out in my mind. I couldn't understand how Dad was so taken in by Anthony so much that he even pushed me towards him, thinking he was perfect husband material. Next, I started blaming myself. If only I told Dad months ago; about the rent boy, the rape, the gang bang and the cocaine. It could have prevented all this...and probably my parents' deaths. All the worry caused Dad's heart attack, I know that. But hadn't Anthony just said it was the worry that made him behave badly? So that must mean the businesses were taken over before Anthony's scandalous behaviour. Why hadn't Dad asked me, a qualified accountant, to produce cash-flow figures for him? Anthony had a degree in design, that's why he started work for my father. He had very little knowledge of accounts other than what he picked up from Dad. What the hell had my father been thinking of, making him Finance Director? I went over everything; every conversation I could recall over the last nine to ten months, sifting through to ask myself if there was anything, any words that I should have picked up on that would have given some indication. I came up with nothing.

I woke up at ten minutes to four, my mobile was ringing. My eyes searched for the bottle of wine first. It was still more than half full. I remembered finishing the first glass and there was still half a glass remaining of the second one I poured. Not quite the oblivion I hoped for. I sighed and answered the call.

"Hello? Helen Pawson."

"Helen? Hello, it's Simon speaking. You remember?"

I sat bolt upright, suddenly alert. How could I forget? I'd never be able to forget.

"Yes, I remember, Simon!"

"Have you thought any more about my suggestion?"

I trembled, knowing where this conversation was heading, but not quite sure yet what my final decision would be.

"Yes, I have thought about it, but I've had quite a few other things to think about as well. What answers do you want from me?"

"As I said, Helen, I can get you some clients, good ones that I can vouch for. I have a gentleman who wants to meet you in the next few days, you can do it at the hotel, nobody will know. Can I give him your number?"

It was going way too fast for my liking. The thought of uncomplicated sex was appealing but there were some little matters that needed to be discussed before I would even consider it.

"Have you considered my safety? These people could be…"

He interrupted sharply,

"He's hardly going to murder you in a hotel room, Helen. Come on!"

He was starting to piss me off, being too presumptuous.

"I work there, Simon. It's not a brothel. I won't be able to meet people there indefinitely."

"Well then, you call me before each and every meeting. Let me know where and when. That should put your mind at rest."

He seemed to have all the answers ready. I wondered why he was so eager for me to do this, but then another thought crossed my mind.

"So what's in it for you then? Have you always cherished some weird ambition to be a pimp?"

He didn't really strike me as the type, but there had to be something, some strange reason he was keen for me to be a hooker. I held my breath as I waited for his reply.

"As if! Helen, I don't want your money, I promise."

Swirling my remaining wine around in its glass, I listened rather dubiously, at his attempts to sound convincing.

"Then why, Simon? You're being too pushy."

He hesitated as if thinking of a valid excuse.

"Well, for one thing, I'd quite like to see some of my clients *and* acquaintances stay out of the divorce courts and keep their names out of the nationals. It will end up that way for some of them if you don't go ahead with this..."

He stopped at that point and had my attention, fully, but something else was coming. He needed a little more prompting though,

"So why, Simon? What *is* in it for you? There has to be something!"

Finally, it dawned on me the split second before his reply.

"I get to have you for free, three or four times a year. Think of it as my commission."

I didn't need to give my answer too much thought. I had

my own needs to think about. My mouth was already watering; I needed it so much,

"Okay, that's…ermmm…pretty fair, I'd say. Yes! Give this…erm…gentleman my number then, please."

Hell, I felt horny all of a sudden, wonderful, dirty sex to look forward to, my heart rate was speeding away. I was about to end the call as he piped up again.

"Just a minute, Helen. One more thing you need to be made aware of! If ever you should decide to talk about what you did with your clients, or mention their names, a word of warning, you're the one that will come out of it all looking bad, not my clients!"

I hung up the call.

Within twenty minutes my first client called me. He was booked to stay at the hotel and would be checking in on the following Wednesday afternoon. He gave me his name, told me what he expected from me, and gave firm instructions as to what I was to wear. I would need to go shopping.

CHAPTER 27

*R*ushing down Piccadilly from Green Park tube station on my way to my 'business meeting', I stopped and carried out another quick rummage in my bag, wanting to be certain that I had everything I needed. It was rather a rush getting away from the house, as our neighbour caught me putting the rubbish out. In my opinion he deliberately came out to ask what all the loud screaming, shouting and swearing was about on Saturday morning. He heard the window glass smashing as I launched the paperweight at my despicable husband. He didn't bother to ask me if I was okay. His attitude showed he didn't give a shit about me or anybody else for that matter. There was a not so subtle undertone when he brought the subject up, that implied, 'I hope this is a one-off because I don't want to hear it again, it's not what we expect in our respectable neighbourhood.' Still, I didn't have time to dwell on thoughts of him and quickly put him out of my mind.

Satisfied that I had all the essentials needed for my evening's work, I stepped up the pace and quickly rounded the corner into the little side street that would take me to the rear entrance of my place of work, one of London's top, five star hotels – *the business*. Rather than arrange the appointment for the Thursday morning and take the big risk of being caught, I thought it best to sneak in at night and take the chance that I wouldn't be noticed prowling around the corridors.

As the service lift began its journey upward, major doubts started to creep in regarding what I was about to do. Not about the sex, it was exactly what I needed after all. It was the sneaking around like a burglar that I wasn't relishing. I was bound to get caught, and it worried me. Emerging from the lift, my eyes scanned the corridors and I was relieved to find there was an absence of staff on the top floor. Once I was stood in front of Tower Suite,' I knocked gently,

"Room service, Sir" I uttered, in what was no more than a whisper, knowing that there was a certain VIP in the suite.

"Yes, come in!"

As I walked into the suite and engaged the chain on the door, I caught a fleeting rear view of him in his dressing gown as he swiftly disappeared into the bedroom. Ten minutes in which to get myself ready, in the bathroom, as per the instructions I'd been given. Hurrying through the bedroom, it didn't escape my notice that he was getting undressed so I averted my eyes. After I locked the bathroom door, I quickly checked my make-up, not that it mattered much for this appointment. I started to remove my clothes and hung them carefully on the hooks behind the door. Routing around in my bag, I removed the special clothes; the ones he asked me to purchase. I squeezed my way into the tight-fitting, full body suit. It was made in a luxurious, velvety-feel, black fabric, two cut out holes to expose my breasts and an open crotch that would expose the area from my pussy to my anus. Two minutes to spare. I fiddled about to get my other accessories in place; the beautiful cat mask complete with whiskers and pointed ears followed by a belt which dropped low onto my hips and letting the pussy-cat tail fall over the crack in my backside. I unlocked the door.

I dropped onto my hands and knees and crawled over to the saucer of milk that was left for me by the shower cubicle door and started to lap at it. It was faultless timing on my part; I heard the bathroom door open and looked down to peer between my front and back legs. The dog (aka my client) was padding slowly towards me across the room. Seconds later, I felt his cold, hard nose and heard him sniff around my anus and pussy. His tongue started to slowly tease and torment around the outside of each orifice, taking care to keep me waiting, to keep himself waiting, prolonging this sex game of his for as long as he determined. He was holding his anticipation and excitement in check, while he patiently awaited his ultimate pleasure. Sensing my eagerness, he rubbed his tongue over my clit. It was heaven and I squirmed in delight, my mind totally focussed on the pleasure. Minutes later I pushed myself backwards towards the tongue and got my reward when he started to thrust gently into my pussy. Oh so slowly...and mind-blowing. Shaking violently all over I experienced my first orgasm. He continued to thrust, stopping every few seconds to take greedy licks at my free flowing release, savouring the taste briefly, before thrusting yet again to induce my second explosion. I came faster this time, but not quite as intense. I shuddered. It was an obscene charade I was acting out with him; but as disgusting as it sounded at the start, it was only an act...a dirty act, but no less exciting. As the shakes subsided, I started to feel the weight of him on my back and I could also feel his rock hard and very *human* cock swaying, desperately seeking the pussy it desired; now deliciously wet and accommodating. He soon located my warmth and thrusted harder and faster, pushing and pushing and its thickness throbbed inside me, painfully tight.

My arms started to tire as he grunted away. I could feel my top end slowly starting to sink and seconds later my upper limbs with no feeling left in them, gave way, and my face ended up in the saucer of milk. To save myself from drowning (I wondered how he would explain that one) I shifted the position of my head so that my ear was in the milk, rather than my nose and whiskers. Intense pain followed as he clumsily grabbed me by the nipples and started gripping them too damned hard, as if to give himself greater purchase for each thrust. Each powerful push had us moving around the bathroom, the saucer beneath me scraping its way across the tiled floor, slopping some of its contents on the tiles in the process. The journey came to an end when the top of my head reached the tiled wall. I could go no further, my skull felt as if it would cave in with the pressure as the increasing crescendo reached its finale and the fucking came to an end with his explosion of semen, both inside me and on the floor. To make the act more credible, again, as per his precise instruction, we tried to separate for ten minutes, me, 'pretend' attempting to pull forwards and away, him still ramming into me, but acting as if to pull away, like the dogs I watched shagging once when I was a kid.

For fuck's sake, get that thing out of me!

When he did finally pull out for real, I felt the wetness trickle down my inner thighs and watched it ooze onto the floor. With that, he was gone, back to his bedroom. I ran some water into the bath, soaked and washed out my nether regions, ridding myself of his deposits and prepared for the next onslaught.

I was amazed that the remainder of the evening was quite straight forward. He discarded his dog costume and wanted me to play with his cock, rubbing and fondling it, until he summoned up sufficient energy to start fucking me again, in an assortment of positions of his choosing. His cock never once lost its stiffness, in fact it was unnaturally stiff. I suspected he'd taken Viagra. He fucked me for over two hours and with the exception of a few short breaks to catch his breath, there were no further orgasms to be had for either of us.

Once dressed, I grabbed the things off the bathroom floor and stuffed them back in my satchel. There just one thing left for me to do. Walking through the suite, I snatched up the envelope that was left on the dining room table for me. He disappeared back into his bedroom. No doubt he would shower, rinse away all traces of me and our sordid business transaction. It was quarter past one in the morning when I left through the back door of the hotel.

Not one word had been exchanged between us throughout the night. Other than use me as his sex toy, what subject could he possibly find to converse with me about? He was a Sir…a member of the House of Lords, and a former cabinet minister…and I was just a hooker!

Now that would be a story and a half if ever I felt like revealing all! The Lord obsessed with dog and cat sex…what a headline!!

CHAPTER 28

Since Anthony's revelations about my father's advertising business a few weeks ago, we barely exchanged more than a few words in passing, other than one night when I had far too much wine. I started screaming and shouting at him, blaming his ineptitude for the failure of the business, which in return caused the death of my parents. I was relentless. It all came pouring out of me...everything. His parents' attitude towards me, his rent boy, rape, the orgy and the cocaine they snorted...nothing escaped my vicious attack, with the exception of the envelope. My knowledge of that was unknown to him and I intended to keep it that way, at least until I gleaned some more information.

Towards the end of my drunken outburst, he turned his back on me and fled the house, probably fearing an action replay with something a bit larger than a paper-weight...and with a better placed shot!

He didn't return that night, leaving me to cry in frustration and sleep off the drink on the settee.

I didn't see him again until I got home from work the next day. He'd thrown his jacket and tie onto the armchair and sprawled on the settee. He already looked bleary eyed and soon there was an empty wine bottle kicked over on the floor. His half empty glass in one hand and a second bottle in the other, he acknowledged my presence by raising the glass as I walked into the lounge. He was struggling to keep the glass upright in his hand but managed to slur a toast to himself,

"To me! Unemployed as from today! The receiver closed the doors on Daddy's business at lunchtime."

I glared at him in disgust and went upstairs to throw a few things into a bag. It was my turn to stay out all night. I was eager to avoid another confrontation.

CHAPTER 29

I received a call from my fourth client, right out of the blue and with no prior warning from Simon, who was, it seemed, confidently giving out my contact details without checking in with me first.

Chatting to the gentleman for five minutes, we broke the ice a little. He told me his name and explained that he was a majority share-holder in one of the UK's better known mobile phone businesses. We exchanged a few pleasantries before he requested that I visit him at one of London's finest hotels, which was fortunately, not my place of employment. The appointment was for eight o'clock. During the call, it slipped my mind to ask if he wanted me to bring anything special along, so I filled my satchel with a small selection of outfits and sex toys. After dressing in one of my classiest outfits, a look very apt for the hotel in question, I made a quick call to Simon, bollocked him for not warning me about the client call and ordered a cab. I selected Yves Saint Laurent sunglasses, gave a quick squirt or two of Chanel No. 5 and went downstairs until the taxi arrived.

As usual, I didn't know what to expect as I knocked on

the door of Room 905. His nice sexy telephone voice had me guessing that he was around fortyish, but I didn't always trust my judgement on the matter. For once my guess was spot on; tall, good looking, dark hair with some hints of grey around the temples and sideburns...nice. After inviting me inside the room, he indicated the sofa. I parked my bottom and dumped my bag on the floor next to me.

"Fresh coffee?" he asked.

I noticed he never awaited my reply. He proceeded to pour coffee for me to accompany the one he just poured for himself.

"Thank you," I indicated for him to stop, so there was room for the milk "that's fine."

He gestured to an envelope that was on the coffee table,

"It's all there. Would you like to count it?"

I laughed and shook my head, surprised at him wanting to get the matter of money out of the way first.

"I can do that later, when...you know."

"Right. Yes." He looked a little embarrassed, but smiled before taking a seat opposite me.

I poured milk in my coffee and added sugar. As I stirred the contents of my cup, I could sense him watching me. Interested in reading his thoughts, I watched his expression carefully. I recognised that same curious look that appeared on the faces of previous clients.

"You are one beautiful girl, looks like yours, your body; you could be anything you wanted to be...model, actress. Why this? What makes you do this? I'm told by Simon that you are intelligent and you come from a decent background, so I reckon you don't need the money."

He looked at me quizzically. Yes, the same old questions. The interrogation which yet again, I didn't feel obliged to answer.

I focused on a picture hanging on the wall behind him, instead of maintaining eye contact.

"It's kind of...a long story. One that I think both you and my other clients would find hard to understand, so I am not even going to try. I'm not even sure *I* fully understand my reasons. If I can't understand it myself, how could I possibly begin to explain it to you?"

He digested this for a few seconds as he continued to look at me but the curious look faded from his face...it seemed he accepted my answer.

We talked, drank our coffee and, feeling much calmer, I watched his body language and his face as we continued to talk. He didn't strike me as nervous in any way so I assumed he'd done this before, though I wasn't interested in knowing and I certainly wasn't going to ask him. Watching his hands I noticed the wedding ring. I hoped he wouldn't talk about his personal life. He was rather attractive and the only thing on my mind was getting laid.

Once he cleared the cups and removed the tray, I showed him the couple of outfits and sex toys and enquired as to whether he had a preference?

"It's your day job, isn't it? Let's have you in the maid's outfit" he enthused, "with the stockings and suspender belt. Wear the thong as well."

Gathering up my belongings I headed to the bathroom to change. I was a little nonplussed already, I hadn't envisaged him wanting me to wear any clothes; I was thinking along the lines of lots of cuddles, sex in the missionary position and perhaps make him feel like somebody cared. Well, it takes all kinds. The next eye-opener followed when I walked out of the bathroom, he was sat on the sofa, still fully clothed, playing with what must have been a few thousand pounds worth of Nikon D4 SLR camera.

"Just go about your business, Helen, I'll be with you shortly."

"That's what I'm here for…business. I can't really do it *alone.*"

"Clean, darling. You're a maid, yes?"

What the fuck? Was he for real? He wanted me to clean his hotel suite for the wad of cash I was to receive? Now I heard it all!

I was more than a tad confused. Another idea occurred to me in a flash,

I wonder if the camera is the type that also takes videos and if he intends to film himself fucking me.

My insides tingled at the thought of starring in a porn movie.

"In case you haven't noticed, I don't carry cleaning items around with me, in *this* line of business." I offered gently.

"Erm…No. I don't suppose you do. Use the face-cloth. Start in the bathroom, pretend a bit. Improvise"

Obeying his orders, I did as I was told and went to the bathroom. Picking up the face-cloth, as instructed, I bent over the bath pretending to clean it. I found the little scenario rather amusing…pretending to be a chambermaid and getting paid the rates of a top-class whore. I wondered what the bullies from school would have said if they could see me now. I smiled to myself at that notion then I heard the bathroom door open.

"Lose the skirt, darling."

It sounded promising. We were getting down to business at last. I unfastened the skirt and allowed it to fall to my ankles, flicked it up with my foot, caught it deftly with my right hand and hung it behind the bathroom door.

"Carry on. Sort of…pretend to clean the bath. Bend over, but stand with your legs apart."

I expected him to come up behind me as I bent over; my anticipation had made me clammy down below. I felt movement between the tops of my thighs, but it wasn't his hands or his cock. I heard him whisper,

"Your other client, that is, my friend, has told me that you have the most beautiful pussy he has ever seen. I'm going to see if that's true very shortly."

It was his camera lens I felt moving between my legs. I heard the whirring, clicking noises as he took multiple shots, the lens almost touching the crotch of my thong.

"Now, just stay where you are, put one leg up on the side of the bath, then pull the thong to one side so we can get a better shot," he ordered.

The camera did its work again. We moved through to the living area and I continued to do all that was asked of me; bent over the sofa, legs apart, then one leg on a dining chair, I bent over the bed for him, got down on my hands and knees on the floor, sometimes with my thong pulled to one side, sometimes not, and patiently waited for the next instructions whilst his camera lens moved ever closer to my pussy.

"Remove the thong now, please. We will start in the bath-room again, all the same poses."

What the hell was all this about? What pleasure was he getting from almost sticking a camera lens up my depth? The suspense was killing me...as was my need. Perhaps he would start feeling horny once he'd taken all the shots he wanted!

Thong off, I posed yet again for the same shots. I got quite turned on by the suggestion of penetration that the camera lens was giving, wondering how long it would be before he wanted to fuck me. How long until I could climax. I needed that. We repeated every last shot and finally he said,

"Go and lie on the bed, Helen. On your back, open your legs, please."

The camera remained in his hands and he still had his clothes on. I would be here overnight at this rate. I was desperate for sex and frustrated that things were moving too slowly.

"Oh wow! That really *is* the prettiest pussy I ever saw. He was right, your client...so right."

Get any closer and that lens is going to be up it. In fact I might grab the lens and shove it up myself if you don't get on with it soon!

"What I want you to do now sweetheart, is really show me how pretty that pussy is. Pull the labia aside, let me see the vagina, and your clit as well, let me photograph their beauty."

I opened up and the camera responded to his push of the button, more shots were taken at every imaginable angle.

"Right, I've got it. Now stick your fingers in there, right up, all the way up." I happily complied.

"Yes! What a shot!" His voice was full of excitement.

More snaps and plenty more followed, but I'd had enough. I felt so undignified; on a bed in a posh hotel suite, my own fingers delving inside me.

Un-fucking-believable!

"Hey! Is there a remote chance that you are going to start fucking me at some point in the near future? I'm getting quite bored now with you poking me with nothing but that bloody camera lens," I urged.

"I'm through, sweetheart. You can get dressed now."

"What is this? No sex? I'm kind of ready to be fucked if you know what I mean. I *need* to be fucked right now."

"Sweetheart, you got me all wrong. I don't fuck with anyone but my wife. I don't need to. See this...?"

He grabbed his genitalia through his trousers to show me...soft in his hands.

"Does this cock look excited to you, honey? I love my wife, and I make love *only* with my wife."

"Then why? What are you paying me for if you don't want

to fuck me?" I could hear the tone of my voice…a little piercing with irritation.

"I collect pictures of beauty! We appreciate beauty. *You* are being paid to provide some of that beauty. I didn't realise that you were in this business for anything other than the money. I never imagined that you would actually *want* to be fucked."

Ten minutes later I was paid, dressed and out of there. In the lift, going down my breathing was fast and ragged. I was flushed with anger. An experience of the proverbial itch that I couldn't scratch. It didn't happen very often, thank goodness. I was never too good at getting off by myself. I could never get it right. It would be a waste of time even to try. The more I tried to concentrate on coming, the further away it always seemed and I usually gave it up as a bad job. When I arrived home that night, I indulged in a long, cold shower before climbing into bed.

CHAPTER 30

J can't understand what Anthony is up to. I've been puzzling for a couple of weeks and my mind is in over-drive. He said he's officially unemployed since the receivers closed the doors on my father's business and yet he still goes out every morning before me. Sometimes he dresses smartly in a suit, at other times he's smart casual... expensive jeans and a sweatshirt.

Each evening, he's arriving home after me just like he always did. Not once did he volunteer any information and I am determined not to ask him. I can't pose the question in case it gives him the impression that I'm interested. The truth is, I don't really care what he is doing. The main thing that concerns me is that it looks like it will be down to me to pay the mortgage and bills until he is earning. I know he will be expecting some statutory redundancy pay but that won't go far.

I expected him to be depressed, but unless he's an extremely good actor, which I sincerely doubt, he doesn't appear to be down in any way. We still don't communicate, unless it's to snap at one another, but he seems cheerful;

whistling and even singing at times. It's crossed my mind that he's spending his days at his parents' house. I can't come up with an answer for the suit and tie though, unless interviews are on his agenda.

I sat at the kitchen counter drinking my coffee, lost in my thoughts about Anthony and his new found unemployed status when something came flooding back into my mind. The envelope in the greenhouse! With everything that happened recently, the funeral, grief, my O.C.D., my job at the hotel, *and* my new side-line, it hadn't occurred to me to keep a check on the greenhouse. I know that he probably only used the greenhouse as a last resort, an emergency hiding place when I arrived home early, but would *he* think it to be less likely that his goods would be discovered in there than in the house? He didn't know that I found them...so maybe.

Excited all of a sudden, I got up and rifled through one of the kitchen drawers where I recall seeing an old notebook. I hurried out, enlivened, to the patio and checked the pots in the greenhouse – nothing! I made a note of the dates the first envelope arrived and disappeared as they were firmly imprinted on my brain. I added today's entry and I would keep on checking *every* day and log my findings. I felt positive that, whatever Anthony's involvement was with the envelope, it wouldn't be a one-off. I even started to wonder if the drugs were his new career move. I hated being suspicious in case I was totally wrong but his behaviour didn't inspire much confidence.

A call from the estate agent affected my mood drastically later in the day. It was pleasing in a way, to hear that my parents' home had attracted a lot of interest, with more than sixty viewings, but an incredible sadness caught me in its grasp the minute I ended the call. The home where I spent my childhood, my parents' dream home, would sometime in the near future be occupied by strangers. They would change things for sure, as anybody would want to. I could understand that, but the thought of it sickened me. I played around with the idea of forcing myself to make one last visit, but I was worried about the effect that it would have on me.

CHAPTER 31

*H*ere I am, sitting in a top notch executive hotel room in Paris with a guy I only just met...my seventh client since I started out. Seventh client! I hoped I would have started to get accustomed to the idea of having sex with total strangers after six clients, but I still couldn't shake off the apprehension. My stomach churned as I walked into the room and I desperately hoped that the beads of perspiration on my forehead had gone unnoticed by him.

Two days previously, when he first called me, he explained that Simon, my first client, handed him my mobile number after a meeting they both attended some weeks ago. After introducing himself as David, he offered to pay for my return air fare from London Heathrow. I accepted the offer and agreed to the flight times he suggested. When I collected my tickets at the airport I was amazed to see the words 'business class' printed on them. He was financially secure, obviously. I prayed the husky warmth of his voice matched the image I conjured up in my mind. When you're being paid for sexual services it certainly helps the mood to find the client...at least a little attractive, particularly as my business arrangements were also a means of trying to fulfil my own sexual needs. Having been badly hurt twice in my past, I intended that my new career would totally eliminate the need to have boyfriends and emotional involvements in the future. I didn't want or need the hurt that always seemed to go hand in hand with love.

When he met me in the hotel lobby I wasn't disappointed. He wore an expensive suit with an equally expensive white shirt, his tie loose at the open collar. His eyes captivated me. They were a striking, brilliant green, with a glint of mischief to them. There was a few tinges of grey in his otherwise dark hair. I could sense it was going to be both easier and harder this time. Easier because he was so sexually attractive, but harder for that same reason. During my previous sexual encounters with clients I was able to close my eyes to their imperfections or vague attractiveness and just fantasise. I remained emotionally detached and managed to thoroughly enjoy the physical waves of orgasm in the places where my wildest fantasies took me. I would have no need to fantasise with this guy, but how would I ever be able to close my eyes? How could I possibly avoid looking at him?

I felt quite heady, too hot...my instant infatuation with this guy the prime cause. Trying not to be too blatant, I struggled to keep my eyes from drinking in his physique and his designer stubble. He was a little too attractive for my liking. I needed to keep emotional distance from my clients and *too* attractive would mean too much temptation; temptation to look too deep into those eyes and search his soul. I wondered if David could sense my eyes burning into him. He finished pouring the wine, turned around quickly and stared back at me, his eyes shining with desire and pleasure as they roved over every inch of my body. I was thrilled in one sense to be found so desirable by this perfect specimen of masculinity, but the excitement that I could barely contain, I perceived as an unwanted threat to my resolve. He came over and handed me a large glass of white and said,

"You're shaking and tense. Relax. I don't want anything perverted or anything that you're not willing to do. I want your warmth, your company, and your body, but later... much later. We'll spend a couple of hours getting to know each other a little better. Is that okay with you?"

Was that okay with me? Phew! It certainly was...or was it? There was an element of doubt creeping in. I didn't really want to be in this situation. I didn't want or need to know anything about this man and yet I couldn't resist playing along with it all. Perhaps the alcohol was to blame for giving me that sense of bravado. I'd rather it was that, than any genuine eagerness on my part.

I heaved a huge sigh of relief but instantly hoped he didn't read too much into it and maybe think I was reluctant in any way. I was anything but reluctant, but not quite ready just yet. I wanted to wallow in the anticipation for a short while...undress him in my mind...and get my head around what I wanted and needed. I needed to enjoy his body and show him the good time he was paying me for. My intent was to fuck him senseless and at the same time achieve my own selfish pleasures. The thing I really didn't want to do was to let this guy into my head, to mess with me!

"I suppose that would make sense." I uttered, barely audible.

"When did you last eat?" he asked, passing me the menu, "I'll order up some room service, just have a look and choose whatever you like."

I felt a slightly sickly feeling descend in my tummy. I didn't think I would be able to eat and I told him so. Yet whilst I struggled to understand what was wrong with me, I was vaguely aware that I allowed him to coax me into ordering something light. He opted for something similar, placed the order over the phone and turned to me again,

"Right! Music or a film? I'll leave it up to you."

I could feel my eyes well up, touched by his kindness and consideration. I smiled up at him, thinking I'd struck gold, but not in the financial sense. He paid for my airfare, was wining and dining me and now was allowing me to choose our evening's entertainment. I imagined that he would afford me that same consideration in the bedroom. In the short time I had been in his company, I was confident that selfishness would not be in his nature. Although I usually managed to achieve orgasms during my assignations with some previous clients, that was at times due to my own exuberance rather than any attempt by *them* to pleasure me.

Given my short experience in the profession, this to me, was rather unfamiliar; a new approach from a client. I liked it. It was lovely to be treated in this way, as a person with real feelings, rather than as an object of which every orifice was to be used and abused. I had to keep reminding myself it was a business arrangement, he was paying for my time. Also at the back of my mind was the fact that he would be fucking me at some point, as had already been agreed, and I devoured that thought with relish, another novel feeling to me. I felt a sensuous warmth and tingling course through my body, the wine glass trembled in my hand. It wasn't just the sex...I was beginning to really like this guy. The trouble was...I didn't want to like him. I wanted to feel indifferent towards him and his personality. I don't want emotional involvement with any man, I'm too insecure; the insecurity caused by two men, my two longest relationships. The unfaithfulness, the hurt... and how I feared ever having to deal with those emotions again. I don't think I could ever trust another man with my heart.

"Have you decided then...what is it to be?" He asked softly, jolting me out of my brooding.

"I f-feel like a t-teenager on her first d-date...being g-given a choice." I stammered and giggled nervously.

He laughed, and it was natural; unforced. I don't know why I felt so uneasy, or perhaps it was because I could sense that I was being sucked in, against my will.

"Come on, Helen. Help me out here. You're my guest." He smirked as he threw out his arms in a gesture of mock helplessness.

My heart fluttered on hearing him speak my name for the first time, and slightly bemused by his insistence and amateur dramatics, I considered the options...a film or some music? Was I actually interested in talking to the guy and getting to know him better? No, I certainly wasn't. It was a business transaction. I amazed myself when the words came out.

"If we are meant to be getting to know each other, then a film maybe isn't such a great idea, is it?"

"Good point. I'll find some music first, then I'll pour us another glass of wine."

He held out his hand for my glass, so I quickly sipped the small amount of wine that remained and handed it over. I almost recoiled when our fingers touched briefly, not wanting to feel that connection, that chemistry.

"We'll unwind and chat, yes?"

Taking the lead in our chat, I purposely kept the conversation general, skirting around any subject that may lead to questions about me and my life. He gazed intently at me and I could sense he was watching every move I made. I could have sworn that in his mind he was already having sex with me and wasn't really listening, though he smiled often and asked or answered questions in the appropriate places. The conversation between us jumped from one subject to another and I marvelled at how amusing he was, how intelligent and how…charming and sexy. There was a sudden lull in our tête à tête as he stood up and went to fill our glasses again.

Even though the time was flying past since we ate, the wine was taking effect and my nerves settled down considerably when unexpectedly, he slowly turned towards me, head tilted to one side and asked,

"Why are you doing this, Helen? Why are you here in this hotel room with me when you evidently have so much? Tell me, why the sudden career change?"

His face showed such a puzzled look…a look of bewilderment, that I could barely contain my sudden urge to satisfy his curiosity. It was another first, a client who was interested in me enough to ask why. It filled me with warmth, although it also rendered me speechless because I knew that if I was to answer one or two of his questions, he would bombard me with even more.

Maintain your silence, Helen!

"You don't want to answer me."

There was a genuine tinge of disappointment in his eyes as he spoke and he let his shoulders sag in an over exaggerated manner, but only momentarily. I was relieved to see his face break into a smile once more and I smiled back, amused by his attempt at acting.

"Can I tell you what it is I can see about you? Would you mind? Or is that being too impertinent?"

I gave my approval with a slight nod, and lowered my eyes as I did so, not wanting to make eye contact as he delivered his observations. I wasn't even sure I *wanted* to hear his about his thoughts and what he could read about me.

"You have class. Your intelligence is impressive. I'm guessing you attended private school?"

I glanced up at him for a moment, gave a half smile and a

nod before I looked down at my hands again. I didn't want to hear compliments from him. I was trying to keep an emotional distance, for fuck's sake!

"You are well-spoken, beautiful, and new to this way of life, right?"

I looked up again, straight into those wonderful eyes; eyes that continued to read me. I was overwhelmed by the compliments. My heart was racing, but this was in total conflict with what my head was saying. My thoughts told me to get out of that room and away from him and what I was feeling! I tried to steal my eyes away, knowing that he was reading me too well.

I decided to play it down so, desperate to put emotional distance between us, I gave a pleasant sigh, curled my legs up beneath me on the sofa to give him the impression I was relaxing in his company.

"We've only just met, David. I know nothing about you...I don't want to...and you don't need to know about me. I take it you're not sorry I'm here?"

"Certainly not!"

He laughed, his puzzled expression expired. If he felt any disappointment at my reluctance to open up, it wasn't evident. He joined me on the settee, leaning back with his hands behind his head and his legs stretched out in front of him, eyes fixed firmly on mine.

Hoping to put the ball back in his court and get the conversation onto a somewhat safer topic, I asked,

"So what are you thinking now?"

"My thoughts?"

Once more in amateur dramatics mode, he placed the heel of his hand to his forehead and raised his eyes to the ceiling as if in deep thought. His mouth turned down then in mock disappointment.

"Well, as I'm not going to discover anything about you

and your life...one...I can't wait to make love to you. Two... I'm going to have a bath and I would like to join me. Three... I want more wine."

Make love? What the hell?

A warning bell rang in my head. Only two men in my life ever made love to me and they were not clients. He was paying me for sex, so why did he use *that* terminology? It suddenly dawned on me and I relaxed again. He was just a gentle natured guy and far too polite to say that he wanted to fuck me. He just opted for a much nicer way to express it. I was pacified.

"Make love to me, David?" I chuckled, shaking my head at him in disbelief. "Clients want to fuck me, do perverted things...not make love to me!"

He grinned at me saucily and chuckled.

"Do they indeed?"

He moved closer and put his arm around my shoulder. Leaning in even further he kissed me on the cheek and asked in a more serious tone,

"Does all that meet with your approval then? Do you want to be made love to or do you want to be fucked, Helen? Either will work for me."

Whilst the thought of being made love to excited me, I knew that I couldn't let it happen. I wanted this to be nothing more than a fuck. I leaned towards him playfully and returned the kiss on his cheek, ruffling his hair as I stood up.

"After all the taxis and airports I could certainly use a soak in the bath, if it's big enough for the two of us. As for the sex, as long as it's good we can call it what we want can't we? Let's see what category it falls under once we get started."

I was determined as ever that once we started, it was going to be one mammoth, dirty, fucking session, where the words 'love making' didn't exist. It would be sexual gratification without the heart strings. I already felt the warmth and dampness in my panties that accompanied the tendrils of a wanting ache that was spreading within the deepest parts of me.

I watched, fascinated, as he removed each item of his clothing to reveal a truly beautiful, tanned and toned body. I wanted to reach out and touch him, if only to confirm that I wasn't dreaming. His eyes roved up and down my body and I couldn't help but notice his delectable cock was getting hard as he watched me. While we indulged in plenty of eye contact, the conversation was minimal whilst we bathed. I sat in the soothing hot water imagining what it was going to feel like to be fucked by him and I played those thoughts through my mind with relish. I wondered what David was thinking, but with his demeanour and his eyes taking in every bit of my skin, it already seemed as though his thoughts were not far removed from my own. Without even speaking, we playfully sponged each other down, but there was no awkwardness in our silence. I was comfortable with him, confident that he would treat me right. It was pleasant to relax and take in every detail of his body. Every last inch of him was perfection. I was finding it hard to breathe and my body ached to have him inside me. We fondled tentatively for a short while before getting out of the bath. As he held a bath towel in his hands I noticed that he hadn't started to dry himself, but was transfixed as he watched me gently pat my towel up and down my body.

"Your body is so sensual, Helen. It's beautiful."

It pleased me to see the appreciation in his eyes and I beamed back at him.

"You've got a sexy body yourself. I bet you work out at the gym a lot?" I asked.

"Not quite as much as I would like to. I enjoy a really good workout. It makes me feel good about myself. I think the best workout I'm likely to get this week is the one that I'm planning with you very shortly."

I was getting somewhat hot and bothered by this man, there was something totally scorching hot about him, but I couldn't pinpoint why I should be so bothered. He already told me that he wasn't into perverted sex, so why was I worrying?

I checked my make-up before putting on a very short, lacy robe that I packed. David grabbed one of the bathrobes from the hook behind the bathroom door and I noticed he dabbed a little men's fragrance on himself before leaving and closing the door behind him.

When I went back into the bedroom, he had put on some classical music in my absence and was laid on the bed, propped up on the pillows, hands behind his head. He looked and smelled amazing. I was looking forward to having sex with him, but I allowed one or two reservations to creep into my thoughts. Perhaps he was going to be a let-down in the sex department? You can never really tell. Of the clients I had over the previous few weeks, I did tend to think it was the plainer looking guys that were the best lovers. Somehow I think they always seem to try harder. David wouldn't need to try. I was turned on already just seeing his body reclining on the bed.

"Come here, Helen. Come and lie down next to me. I've poured us another glass of wine."

Not wanting to seem too eager, I casually fiddled with a few of my cosmetics on the dressing table before joining him on to the bed. I noticed that his towelling robe was slightly apart which exposed the tops of his thighs. I was flushed. I could feel the heat on my forehead and an excited tingle in my nether regions...I wanted him so bad. I needed him to fuck me that very minute. It occurred to me that perhaps *I* should be paying *him*. I made myself comfortable next to him and leaning across towards me he didn't fully open up my robe, but pulled the sides apart slightly to reveal some cleavage.

"You really are beautiful, do you know that? You are also a truly lovely person. I was told that by the friend, well...acquaintance really, the one who gave me your number. If he hadn't told me, I could see it for myself...in your eyes, the moment I met you tonight."

His eyes locked on mine, and he whispered his next words.

"It can't be easy, doing what you do."

I didn't look away from his gaze. I couldn't, although I tried hard enough.

"It certainly makes my job easier, having a client like you. You are very hot and extremely good-looking, what more could a girl want?"

"Money, apparently."

His comment stung a little and he must have noticed it in my eyes.

"Touché!"

"I am sorry, Helen. I didn't mean it to come out sounding as rude as it did. I never meant to imply anything."

He looked mortified at the thought he offended me so I giggled,

"I've had much worse things than that said to me over the years, even before I was...before I made a career out of *this*."

He leaned further towards me as if to kiss me, and I kissed the side of his cheek and down towards his neck, though I so badly wanted his lips on mine. He caught on quickly.

"Ah. I see, that's fine."

I felt as if I had been scorched when his lips first touched my cheek in return and then copying my first move, he kissed my neck ever so gently. I winced and he asked,

"Are you OK?"

Rather than answer him, I openly displayed my pleasure by gently nibbling his neck and moaning. He was setting me on fire so quickly I could feel the burning and wanton desire in the pit of my stomach and I tensed even further as he fully opened my robe and his lips traced a path down to my breasts, slowly outlining a circle around each of my nipples in turn, tormenting, and whilst his tongue barely made contact, my nipples stood proud and erect. He was breathing heavily and his hands were gently massaging my belly, first around my navel and then edging each careful finger width towards my pubic area. Suddenly, I needed more. My need was urgent. I was experiencing an awakening...something that had lain dormant for months. It was re-emerging; an uninhibited desire to fuck and be fucked was taking over me. I was not going to wait. I was going to take the lead in this, such was my craving for him. I pushed him onto his back again and planted my lips firmly around his wonderful manhood.

He groaned out loud,

"Wow! What a tigress! Taking the lead, huh? Are you turned on already? Do you want it bad tonight? Do you want me to make you cum?" I muttered a reply as well as I could manage, my lips caressing every inch of his cock all the while. "You...are...turning...me on. I'm not...wanting *it*...bad, I want *you*...real bad. I want you...to fuck me...want to make...this...the best...fuck...you've ever...had in your life."

"I'm sure you will, but...hey, go steady there...don't make me cum too soon. I'm finding this..."

He broke off his words at that point and stroked my breasts again, tweaking and pulling at my nipples. I was feeling ready to explode and he wasn't even inside me yet.

"I'm going to fuck you now...wherever you'd like me to

189

fuck you, let's do it...I want to shove my cock hard into you...feel you cum all over me."

I reluctantly moved my mouth away from his cock and took his hand. I led him over to the dressing table and pushed aside all the bottles. I sat myself at the very edge. He bit into my neck again at the same time his hands eased his throbbing piece of muscle inside me. I gasped in ecstasy on penetration. As his movements inside me got under way, he grabbed hold of my breasts and I wrapped my legs tightly around his bottom. I held him firm as he thrust into me and he reached all my nerves with one hard thrust...my g-spot, my clit and I gripped onto him tighter still. Every inch of him was inside of me. It felt beautiful...like Heaven. I tensed my inner muscles around him and felt the nerves of his cock throbbing inside. The power of his thrusting was driving my desire to new heights but I wasn't ready to cum yet. I didn't want either of us to cum. I needed to stay locked like this, feeling the growing intensity of my emotions...the exquisite anticipation. I don't know how I managed to hold it back for the new few minutes but somehow I did. His movements back and forth were not full on, his cock was moving in and out maybe just an inch or two, but the euphoria was beyond my expectation. His pubic bone stimulated my clit, perfectly.

"I...can't hold...much longer...can you...cum quick, babe?" he gasped.

"Go for it, David....just fuck me...but fuck me hard. When you cum I'll explode too. I know I will...just let me have it, let me have your cum now."

His pace quickened, his thrusts became harder, much deeper, almost pulling out completely before thrusting in again, hard and deep, hard and deep, and it was breath-taking. My every nerve was at its pinnacle and the instant I knew he was coming, I finally let go. Oh my God, I was drenched in the flood of our warm fluids and struggled to catch my breath. My whole body shook from the orgasm that was deliciously slow to die.

"That was…so good…beautiful!"

He struggled, too breathless to get the words out as he rested his chin on my shoulder.

"And I don't need to ask if it was good for you. I can see that you enjoyed that, babe."

We stayed in our position at the dressing table for a short while and it felt so good to have his arms around me. I wanted to lay on the bed with him, be cuddled by him for the rest of the night. It was so good…too good. He cuddled up to me and we talked for a short while before both drifting off to sleep. I could feel him kiss the back of my head just before I finally dozed.

When I woke up a few hours later he was stirring. Catching a glimpse of the clock I saw that it was six forty five. I jumped out of bed and went straight over to switch the kettle on. Using the complimentary coffee and sugar sachets I prepared two cups for us. With the noisy kettle coming to the boil a couple of minutes later, he was soon fully awake. Heading to the bathroom, I went to freshen myself up and brush my teeth. He followed me in there to take a pee.

"Kettle's on. Coffee? Or would you prefer tea?" I asked.

"Whatever you're having will be fine by me, babe."

"Coffee it is then. Get back into bed, and I'll bring it over."

He kissed me on the cheek when I got back into bed, and asked if I slept well. I assured him that I had.

After I finished my coffee I went into the bathroom and got under the shower. I closed my eyes as I washed my hair, lost in my thoughts about him. A shudder of excitement about him fucking me the previous night…not wanting to be overjoyed about it…worrying…about what? Frightening thoughts…So lost, deep in thought…until I felt his hands around my waist. I opened my eyes, blinking the lather of the shampoo from my eyelashes. He raised me up quickly and as I wrapped my legs around him he shoved his cock hard into me and my back slammed against the tiles. I was in heaven, his hard slamming sending me into a new dimension. His cock felt like a rod of iron. I rubbed one lathered hand all over his back as the other held tight around his neck trying to stop myself from sliding down his body. I didn't want to slide away from him. His throbbing was intense, it felt beautiful. My insides were on fire. After two or three minutes his knees couldn't take any more and they started to buckle...his cock slipped out of me and we moaned together, in urgent frustration,

"Helen...get...on the...floor...quick!"

I half slipped on the tiles in my rush to the floor, onto my knees... eager to be fucked, for him to cum inside me. I barely made contact with the floor when he rammed into my warmth again, so hard...so deep, and in an instant I was there, climaxing...screaming out in pain and intense pleasure. As I yelled out for the second time, I felt his cock spurting, and with each pump of cum, I came again...and again. David groaned out loudly and bit into my neck. Throwing my head back and closing my eyes, I could hardly cope with the intensity of my orgasm as I felt the last squirt of his cum shoot up high inside me.

As my flight took off from Paris CDG five hours later I heaved a sigh of relief. I was finally away from him. Not being in his company strengthened my resolve. Much as I enjoyed David's company *and* being fucked by him, it was a one off. I hoped he wouldn't be in touch with me again, yet I couldn't explain why the thought also traumatised me.

CHAPTER 32

*M*y mobile phone rang at six o'clock on Sunday evening. Anthony was at home, getting pissed, as was his new found habit, and nodding off to sleep every few minutes during a Top Gear Special. He was getting on my nerves, as always. I walked out into the garden to take the call as the screen showed an unknown number. It was a new client, my ninth. I'd been expecting his call around eleven that morning. Simon called me the previous day to ask my permission this time. The guy was a television presenter. I saw him fairly regularly on a particular programme and never much cared for him but…business is business. Simon called him 'a good man,' so…

After answering the call, he greeted me politely and introduced himself, but in a manner that seemed a little offhand, or perhaps I was being judgmental because of my limited knowledge of him. I noted he was well-spoken, but I already discovered in my short time as a call girl, that that didn't mean a thing.

"I'm booked into the Kensington Suite at your place of

employment and would like to use your...um...services tomorrow morning if at all possible?"

I was livid about having to do another session during my working hours at the hotel, but he insisted that he already had a busy schedule for his time in London. I explained that I couldn't guarantee a time as we have certain routines at the hotel that must be adhered to. Our appointment would depend on how much work was involved in the first three suites and Kensington would be the last. He sounded disgruntled.

"I will wait until two o'clock and no later. I have some-where to be by four."

It sounded as if he thought *he* was doing *me* a favour, not the other way around. Irritated, I managed to keep my voice steady and polite before asking,

"Would you like me to bring anything special along, Sir?"

There was silence at the end of the phone...maybe he was considering his answer. I cast an anxious glance towards the house and noticed Anthony watching me from the kitchen window. I hoped he would stay where he was while I finished up my call.

At the end of the phone the client finally barked his answer at me,

"Like what for instance? Just your presence will do!"

Still polite, but getting increasingly rattled by Anthony's presence at the kitchen window, I asked,

"Do you have details of my price for the transaction, and you know that the payment should be in cash?"

"I have everything that you require, young lady, just be sure that what I need is there no later than two, please."

His manner completely riled me and I was beginning to wish I said I couldn't do it. I assumed he wanted sex, so what would he do for his fuck if I failed to turn up before two o'clock? Go to the street corner where he may end up with more than just getting his leg over? Go back home to his frigid or frumpy wife to try to get what she doesn't normally give him? That's exactly why these guys want a hooker, isn't it? Because their wives don't want sex, or perverted sex at least! Sixty percent of the time the sex wasn't the least bit perverted, some guys just needed the company, or so I've been led to believe. These thoughts rumbled around in my mind and I felt half inclined to ring him back and cancel.

I was more than a little nervous as I made my way into work. I decided when I woke up that I would go ahead, but I'm always wary with new clients, you just never know what ideas they've come up with - what they could inflict on their whore. Another reason for the apprehension was the dangerous game I was playing, again...being a whore to some of the hotel's very important clientele *and* during my working hours. However, it was the mere presence of this type of prominent client that made staff very reluctant to cause more intrusion than was absolutely necessary. It was unlikely that even my superiors would come to check up on me.

My first two suites turned out to be easy. In 'Garden' there was nothing to do. The bed hadn't even been slept in. Clothes had been deposited in the wardrobe by its occupant, female, who loved her designer clothes. I took a peak into the bedside cabinet drawer and half concealed under 'The Holy Bible' was a gigantic, nine inch, black cock vibrator with quite a sizeable girth. Hell! My eyes started watering and all I was doing was *looking* at the bloody thing. There was quite a little stash of other interesting sex toys too, some of a type that previous clients used on me a couple of times. Carefully shutting the drawer lest I disturb anything, I started tiptoeing towards the bathroom.

I'm tiptoeing? Why, for fuck's sake? Guilty as charged, Helen!

I just invaded the privacy of this faceless person,

someone who likes big cocks. Feeling a brief rush of shame, I sniggered to myself and went about my business as usual, minus the tiptoeing. The bathroom clearly hadn't been used either; clean towels still neatly folded on the rack provided. Perhaps this female got lucky the previous night. I felt quite horny. I'd stared at the black cock and other paraphernalia for a few seconds too long. It had been a long fortnight.

I caught the very distinguished looking gentleman in 'Thames' just as he was about to place the 'do not disturb' on his door knob. He was wearing an expensive silk dressing gown. He beamed at me, a twinkle in his eye. Extra-marital sex? I doubted it somehow, he didn't look the type to have a mistress. He pressed £20 into my hand and winked,

"We don't need cleaning today, pet. I'm sure you have other things to do."

I smiled at him, touched by the gesture.

"Sir, I don't want your £20. Enjoy your...morning. I still have plenty to keep me occupied," I said, pushing the £20 note back into his hand.

He gave me a final wink, closed the door and I assume disappeared back to his wife.

I filled the rest of my time easily. I cleaned and re-cleaned 'Garden' twice over, which helped feed my O.C.D. needs for the day.

My client in 'Kensington' was already naked and waiting for me. He stepped aside as he opened the door, out of view of the main corridor. I wheeled the trolley in ahead of me and his hand came around the door to pass me the 'Do not disturb' sign to hang on the door knob. Surely, he couldn't fail to have seen my eyes bulge when I noticed the size of his cock! For a good minute or so, I didn't notice anything else about him. The black dick vibrator I spotted earlier must have been an omen. This guy's cock almost matched it, both in length and girth. I could hear my own gulp and a sudden constriction in my throat.

I was visited by an overwhelming desire to run; utter panic that this cock would never get inside me. Not a black cock this time, but a purple veined variety. It was already at full stretch, the credits still rolling on a 'pay per view' movie. Obviously he'd been preparing for me. I hardly got chance to close the door when he leapt on me and planted his lips firmly over mine. I jerked my head to the side in horror, already on edge,

"Don't kiss me!" I snarled my warning.

With a nonchalant shrug of his shoulders, he bit hard into my neck instead. His right hand shot up my skirt and straight down my panties. Three fingers delved inside me. I felt tension building in my neck and shoulders. He was hurting me and I winced in pain. After a few minutes of his finger nails scraping the walls of my vagina, he tried to shove his cock in the side of my panties. I was still right up against the door. Being much taller than him there was no way that was going to work. Grunting to himself he stuck his fingers back in my pussy even more roughly than before, and with his other hand, he tried to tug my panties down at one side.

In his desperation to get at me, he didn't seem to comprehend that it was his poking hand that was preventing the undies coming off. I pulled his hand away from my crotch and rolled the panties down for him.

"Shouldn't I get undressed before you go any further?" I suggested.

He shrugged impatiently.

"Just the knickers and skirt, leave the rest."

"No bra? Don't you want to see my breasts?" I offered.

"I want to fuck this" he said, grabbing at my pussy again, "not look at two useless pieces of muscle, tits don't do anything for me."

I felt a sense of impending doom, a panic attack in the making. Beads of moisture formed on my forehead, I needed to fight this thing. He carried on regardless, oblivious to my inner struggles. Once all my lower clothing was removed, he grabbed my arm and lowered me to the floor. I was still no further than the two metres into the room. Just as I feared, he struggled to get his cock inside me.

Stay focussed, girl! Stay focussed!

The pain was excruciating, even with his lubrication the whole act was abrasive but …on a new level. His pre cum slime coated my inner thighs before he tried to ram his cock in; seminal fluid dribbling away steadily. Minute by minute he seemed to make more progress, inching his way further in until that was it, it wasn't going to get in any further. I was sore already, stinging. My normal, natural lubrication non-existent.

Once it dawned on him that he couldn't get any more in, he started to make violent thrusting moves at me, but it wouldn't go in at all. Despite the force he put into his thrust all he succeeded in doing was to move me further along the carpet. The burn on my back added to my other sores; yet another thing to strengthen the regret I already felt.

After ten long minutes of me feeling nothing but pain, I placed my arms around his shoulders and rolled him onto his back, determined to get something from this other than pain and money. I lowered my body on top of his and rode him, stimulating my clit expectantly, the first bit of pleasure I felt since stepping through the door. Almost instantly I produced some lubrication, his cock was moving freely inside me and…I was tingling and ready to cum. A sharp stinging slap to my left cheek left me reeling.

"Stop trying to finish me off, you bitch. I'll cum when I'm fucking ready to cum!" he growled.

I was furious, my eyes filled with tears, I lashed back at him with my tongue,

"Who's trying to make *you* cum? I'm trying to make myself cum, which you seem incapable of doing!"

The second blow came, the other cheek this time, but I turned my head slightly before contact was made, the stinging not quite so severe.

"I'm not paying you colossal amounts of fucking money so *you* can cum. I get to fuck, you get the fucking money, got it?"

With that he rolled me onto my back once more and resumed to fuck me around the room. I lost track of time, but after what seemed like forever he pulled out and rolled me face down. His finger edged into my anus and I screamed at him.

"DON'T EVEN FUCKING CONSIDER DOING THAT!"

He must have thought better of it. After he pushed his dribbling cock back inside, he reached both arms around my hips and rubbed at my clitoris with his fingertips and rammed into me like a man possessed. I came just in time before his cock twitched. He grunted like a pig as his seed exploded into me.

Fury, hurt, irritation, disgust, I felt them all…but the transaction took a turn, a surprise! I was astounded. He walked into the bathroom with a cup of coffee and some of the complimentary chocolates. As I soaked my body in the bath, he held ice to my cheeks and apologised for his behaviour. He sat on the edge of the bath and watched as I tried to cover the red marks on my face with a concealer. Handing me an envelope containing the cash he muttered,

"Could I…call you again please, Helen? I'll be in London again in a couple of months."

I couldn't resist a dig and the words came readily.

"Wife neglecting you these days?"

He rammed his hands into his pockets and shot me an icy look, so I quickly added,

"Sorry. That was out of order. Yes, by all means ring me, but I can't use the hotel again. You will have to meet me elsewhere."

One last look in the mirror confirmed I made a decent job with the make-up. Checking my full appearance carefully, I left the suite and headed to 'clock off' my shift.

I couldn't resist calling Simon later that day and telling him what I thought about his idea of 'a good man'!

CHAPTER 33

A Saturday evening in late June came out of nowhere and we were experiencing an extreme heatwave in the U.K. I pulled out of the drive and as I headed down the street, I breathed in the familiar smell of barbecues. Earlier that day, the supermarket was crammed with shoppers; the shorts and T-shirts out in force, the women filled their trolleys with sausages, chicken drumsticks, burgers, bread buns and a variety of salad items. As for the husbands…they were the usual fright; beer-bellied, T-shirts riding up, proudly carrying 2 or 3 multi-packs of 'on offer' beer or lager (instead of putting them in the trolley). It seemed to me as if they were trying to make a statement. What the image portrayed was…'look at me, I've got my beer, I'm tough, no-one messes with me'. It was a sight I detested – no class. It's rare for my snobby persona to make an appearance but…

…if only they would put their packs of beer in the trolley…

I headed for the countryside and away from the suburban areas, in the hope that it would be quiet. The young and the not so young singles would be heading out to the pubs and clubs. Families would be heading home from the beach or having friendly gatherings to serve up their charcoal-tinged offerings, cheap vodka and beer, and with bouncy castles and paddling pools for the kids.

I arrived at Hollow Hill Wood at six thirty, pulled off the main road onto a narrow dirt track and drove slowly for five or ten minutes until I came across a small clearing where my car would not be seen from the main road. To the best of my knowledge, it should be safe for a couple of hours while I walked.

After locking up the car, I ventured further into the wood. I took deep breaths to the back of my lungs, enjoying the cooler, fresher air. The lower temperature under the dark cover of the trees was more pleasant; much less humid than it was in the scorching sun. I was glad that I grabbed my light weight cardigan to bring along. There was a stillness and beauty about the woods that I loved and had done since my childhood. My parents regularly took me on Sunday outings to local beauty spots; woods, waterfalls and parklands and I was thankful I grew up with their appreciation for nature. The woodland flowers enhanced my surroundings and various leaves and needles crunched under foot as I saun-tered along. Birds chattered to each other and I enjoyed the solitude of my rambling, gazing at all of nature's delights as each came into view. I picked my way carefully through the trees for the next ten minutes or so, trying to keep to tracks others used before me and taking care not to wander too deep into the darker depths. I looked behind me on two or three occasions, having the notion I heard the crackling of undergrowth snapping…noises that hadn't been caused by *my* footsteps. There was nothing, nobody to be seen. Perhaps the noise was made by a wild animal; a rabbit hopping along or a young deer trying to remain elusive. I stopped and listened again when I heard yet another noise. I turned my head to look over my shoulder and in that split second, somebody launched himself at me from my left. I screamed. A hand planted itself firmly over my mouth and nose. I started to panic, my clean breathing disabled. A voice whispered into my ear,

"Quit the fucking screaming or you'll get hurt, understand?"

I nodded at him, my eyes wide with fear as his other hand struggled with the button on my denims, and then the zip.

"Push your shorts down your legs."

The pressure over my mouth eased and I instinctively tried to bite on his fingers, determined not to give in to his intentions without a fight. I wasn't going to push my own shorts down for him. His intent was obvious. I knew he was going to rape me…but I certainly wouldn't make it easy for him.

"Stop the fucking biting, you bitch," he snarled, as he forced my body down onto the undergrowth.

Once I was on the ground, he threw his body over mine to prevent my escape, one hand remained over my mouth and the other fought to push the shorts down my legs. I pushed at him and kicked out with my legs, but struggled to make contact as he dodged the kicks. One of my arms had become firmly trapped between my body and him, but with my free arm I made a wild blow to his head. I tried to scream again…the sound that escaped between his fingers sounded like a strangled yawn. Frustrated, I bit into his hand. He flinched and slid it down to grip my throat tightly. I felt his cock slap on to the top of my thigh. Struggle though it was for him with one hand, I felt my shorts being manoeuvred down to my knees. The reality dawned on me, there was no escaping him. The outcome was inevitable.

I was about to be taken against my will. Painful memories of being raped by Anthony came flooding back to me and I was now being forced to relive them. The tears started to flow. Unable to push my shorts further down my legs and without releasing his firm grasp of my throat, he used his foot. The rubber sole of his shoe painfully abraded the side of my shin as he kicked down at the shorts until they were free. His bodyweight shifted. After a battle with his own attire for a few moments, the penetration happened. His cock stabbed into me with tremendous force and more pain racked throughout my body. He fucked me, violently and I sobbed throughout, partly due to the pain down below, but most of it I could attribute to what was happening in my head… reliving that horrible night nearly one year ago.

The pressure on my throat was to hurt even more so, as with each powerful thrust his grip became tighter and more restricting. I kicked out again with my feet and I tried to dig my nails into any of his bare flesh I could see or feel. Yet with his free hand he fought to, and succeeded in getting both my wrists together and pushed them way back over my head. I sobbed quietly as his brutal and frenzied shagging went on. After what seemed like an age he pulled out, forced my arms down by my sides, and positioned his knees so they were holding my arms firmly in place. He was sat on my chest. He lifted my head off the ground and forced his length into my mouth. Placing his hands either side of my head he pulled and pushed it back and forth so that his cock was going in and out. I gagged and tried to turn my head away from him.

"Close your mouth! Make it tight around my cock or you'll gag all the more!" he ordered.

I tried hard to be optimistic; if I obeyed, maybe there was a chance we could get it over with quicker and I could go home. I prayed he didn't have plans to kill me. I hadn't seen a knife or a gun but he was very muscular and would soon overpower me; I wouldn't stand a chance but I wouldn't stop fighting. He plunged into my mouth for what seemed an eternity and my throat hurt with gagging. I was ready to vomit. My attempt to shut off my mind to think happy thoughts or sing songs in my head were futile. I did whatever I could, knowing it was the panic that was making me choke. I recognised the signs; he was on the verge of spurting cum into my mouth. As his cock entered for another thrust I closed my mouth tighter, grazing his length.

"You bitch, you've nicked my cock on your teeth!"

He slapped the side of my head and pulled out of my mouth. I opened my eyes and noticed that his erection had softened during the last minute; no cum, no erection...result!

One deft move and he was off me, rolling me so I was face down and he was on top again. I feared what I knew was coming. He tried to ram his softened dick into my anus. I laughed inwardly feeling confident that it couldn't happen... his cock was almost flaccid. He wasn't to be deterred though. He delved in with a finger alongside his cock and I felt him getting hard again.

Once his excitement was aroused to new heights by the buggery about to take place and his cock made initial contact with my arse, its length and stiffness were soon regained. My attempts to fight were feeble and all I was physically able to do was kick at his backside with my feet. My fingers were nipping or gripping any area I could reach, fingernails digging in, but the bruising that I was inflicting on him would be nothing; nothing compared to the broken nose, the head injuries or the blows rained down on him in the boxing ring.

He fucked my arse for... not long but the pain was infinite. He was going to damage me internally and I couldn't wait for it all to end...for his final explosion into me. The moment arrived at last and as he climaxed, he bit into the back of my neck. His strength sapped with the last bit of exertion and he flopped, my body taking his full weight while his breathing returned to normal.

I was free at last as he stood up; free of the weight that held me down for so long. I stayed put, rolled my head on one side and watched as he zipped himself up and looked down at me with a smirk on his face.

He nodded and was gone. Two minutes later I was dressed but bedraggled, re-tracing my steps back through the woodland and back to my car. Through the trees, I could see the brake lights of his Porsche 911 some distance away as he negotiated the twisting dirt track. An envelope was tucked under one of my car's wiper blades.

The envelope contained my payment for services rendered; I was paid to act like a rape victim! Although no rape actually took place this time, I knew it was in bad taste. The guy hinted during our first phone conversation that if he was happy he would likely contact me again, probably in a few months. The client liked the 'turn-on' of the fight, the screaming, kicking and nipping, the knowledge that his victim didn't want him and the power of being able to force himself on a woman; take what wasn't his to take. While acting out this grossly indecent charade, I took some consolation from the knowledge that I probably saved an innocent woman from being violated. I saved some female from having to re-live that nightmare every day of their life, and probably being unable, *ever*, to have a normal sexual relationship. No female should ever have to endure what Anthony put me through. He was the one to blame for the lack of regard I had for my own body.

CHAPTER 34

eeling more than a little shaken I stared into space; rooted to the spot in the greenhouse. My mind raced ahead and I wondered where things are headed for Anthony. I checked the greenhouse each day for the last ten days and had found nothing. Today is different, it's Friday and there's another envelope containing the same squishy powdery product. It has been hidden there by Anthony at some point while I've been at work. I lifted the top plant pots off again, as if my eyes had deceived me the first time…but it's still there. I haven't been hallucinating.

He was wearing a suit when he left home before me this morning. Amused at myself for digging deep into my mind to recall what he'd been wearing, I felt like a private investigator. My main issue is that I'm not usually around between Monday and Friday. I wanted to see if somebody would call to collect the envelope or whether Anthony himself would retrieve it and deliver it to…God knows where. It's bugging me, but I don't think there's anything I can do about it. I doubt he will make any arrangements to move the stuff on a weekend when I'm around home most of the time.

I headed inside next to make myself something to eat, but all the while I couldn't get the envelope or its contents off my mind. Having no desire to be in the lounge once Anthony comes home, I poured a glass of wine to take upstairs with me. I jumped, suddenly startled as he walked in the back door. Lost in my thoughts, I hadn't heard his car pull in the drive.

"Would you mind pouring one for me?" he asked before he even closed the door, "I've had a hell of a day!"

Cheeky bugger!

"Yeah, sure!"

I smirked to myself, thinking he couldn't have given me a better opportunity if he tried. I was immediately excited with the thought that maybe I could use this chance to find out anything else that might help.

I grabbed another glass, and casually commented,

"I thought you were unemployed. How come you've had a hell of a day?"

I don't want to ask any direct questions if I can avoid it; living in hope that he'll unintentionally volunteer what I want to know.

"I'm not unemployed. I got a job almost straight away. In advertising, of course!"

He knelt down on the pretext of re-fastening his shoe-lace. Shoes he would be taking off when he went into the lounge? I knew it was done deliberately to avoid eye contact with me.

"That's good then. At least I'm not left paying the mortgage and the bills," and as a little afterthought, I added,

"I thought the suits were maybe for interviews."

He grunted something I couldn't quite make out. He didn't bother to answer my question about his day, so I asked again,

"So…your day? Hell, you said!"

I turned my attention to clearing my plate away, eagerly awaiting his reply.

"Oh, that! I've been in Brighton all day. New client... maybe. The meeting didn't go so well."

A little later, as I lay in the bath sipping at my wine and thinking he lied to me about Brighton, a point I hadn't considered before suddenly came in to the equation. Anthony wasn't necessarily the person who put the envelope in the greenhouse. Anybody could have walked up our drive and round to the back of the house...somebody who had been told exactly where to leave it.

CHAPTER 35

 uring the week, I received a call from another new client; another of Simon's acquaintances, who introduced himself as Thomas. All he told me was that he's involved in football in a big way, although he was not and never had been, a footballer. I guessed he was maybe a club chairman or perhaps something to do with the F.A., but it wasn't important to me, whatever he did. He asked me to spend the whole of Friday night with him, so at least I was forewarned.

At seven o'clock prompt, I knocked on the door of his suite in a superb Knightsbridge hotel (thankfully, not where I work). As is usual with a first-timer, I didn't know what to expect, but when he opened the door to me and I saw his welcoming smile, straightaway I liked him. He was shorter than me, with grey hair that showed hints of his natural red. Wearing a smart pair of trousers and an expensive jumper over his shirt, he was minus a tie. I recalled memories of my lovely maths teacher at school and this guy could almost be his double. He had the kindest eyes and such a lovely manner. I held out my hand and he took it between his hands and kissed it.

"Come in, my dear. What a pleasure to meet you."

He nodded his approval and smiled at me, his eyes lighting up.

"Thank you, Sir. It's lovely to meet you too. How are you?"

He didn't answer my question, but politely gestured towards the couch.

"Please, won't you sit down? And it's Thomas to you. Can I get you a glass of wine?"

He didn't wait for me to answer. Perhaps his nervousness prompted him to keep talking.

"Which do you prefer, a red? Or maybe a dry white? If I don't have a bottle that you like I can order from room service."

At last he paused for breath and looked at me expectantly.

"Actually, I would prefer gin and tonic if you have gin?"

"Oh excellent, I do have gin, I'm rather partial to a few G & T's myself."

I watched his hand tremble as he poured two large gins. Amazingly, his nervousness had a calming effect on me. I felt relaxed and confident.

"Are you nervous? I don't bite, Thomas. Most of my clients survive our dates." I laughed to put him at ease, and he managed a chuckle along with me.

"Well, this is the first time, the first time I have, you know, had a...a date with a...ever."

"You can say the word; Thomas...hooker. I know what I am, it doesn't offend me."

"No. Not that word...I was going to say, lady friend. You are my first ever lady friend, besides my wife. I have never...I haven't asked you here for sex, my dear. I just want to talk with you, that is all."

His big revelation didn't surprise me in the least. The guy was certainly not the type to visit hookers and most likely never cheated on his wife or even looked at another woman. I admired his loyalty and regretted the fact that the men I had in my life were not like Thomas.

"Thomas, you have my full attention for (I looked at my watch,) let's say, hmm, I will leave at 8am, it's 7.15pm now, that's twelve and three quarter hours, so talk to me. I am almost as good at listening as I am at…providing sexual services."

I took the G & T he handed to me at last and settled down to listen, hoping that my relaxed demeanour would have a calming effect on him too.

He was slow to get started and I don't think he really knew where to start, but after a little coaxing from me, his words were soon in full flow.

He told me about his privileged childhood, very similar to my own; the private education, private music lessons, horse-riding lessons… money was literally thrown at him. There is however, one major difference between Thomas's childhood and mine. I am fortunate enough to have had loving parents, parents who loved each other almost as much as they loved me. I was saddened to hear that his parents' marriage was one of deceit, selfishness, lies, adultery and more selfishness. The only people to show Thomas any love and affection were his full-time nanny and the hired help at his family home.

There was the gardener who played his beloved football with him on their beautiful lawns while his parents were away on their many business trips, besides a handyman who built him a tree house in the orchard and a cook who made him gingerbread men and let him lick out the bowls. His 'Nanny Jane' nursed him through the various childhood illnesses; the falls and scrapes, the neglect and upset that went hand in hand with parents who didn't kiss, cuddle or tell their only son that they loved him.

Throughout Thomas's revelations of his childhood, my maternal instincts surfaced from within. I was visited by a sudden urge to hug him; I really did feel for him. I tried to imagine how my childhood would have been without the love of my parents. That thought this soon into my personal grieving process was enough to traumatise me, so I quickly cast it aside.

His love of football came from watching the game on television with the gardener.

"Football was not played at my school, it was always rugby. I was always the one who came off the field with ripped ears, missing or broken teeth and a broken nose. I hated it. Mr Tyerman, our gardener, would always let me sit in his shed and watch football matches on his portable television. Once I was past eleven years old, and Nanny Jane's supervision wasn't quite as strict, I stayed awake late on Saturday nights just so that I could watch 'Match of the Day.' I knew that I would never be good enough to play football, but I was determined to go against everything my parents wanted for me and seek a career in anything to do with football."

I watched his eyes as he spoke and I could see and feel his passion. Football is, and probably always will be, his greatest love.

I listened intently as he talked me through his qualifications, his university days and career to date and furthermore, the disapproval he met from his parents at his choice of studies and career moves. They never communicated with Thomas from the day he left university, although he remained in touch with Nanny Jane and Mr Tyerman.

We were rapidly getting down the bottle of gin, and while waiting for room service, Thomas encouraged me to talk,

"Your turn now, my dear."

My worst fear rose to the surface and my stomach lurched. I made it a rule never to reveal my private life to my clients. I stalled for a minute or two.

"Oh dear, do I have to? You don't want to hear about my life, Thomas. I think you would find it pretty mundane, after everything you have revealed about yourself." I groaned inwardly and quickly considered what would be safe for me to discuss.

Keeping it brief, I told him about being bullied at school and then I very sneakily flipped over the subject matter by talking about my favourite films, books, art and music, and started to draw him into a conversation of my choosing. He raised his eyes to the ceiling and then stared back at me.

"You are being very evasive I think...so intelligent...but so transparent. What are you trying to hide? Is your past painful to talk about?" he asked.

I laughed at that.

"No, it's not that at all. I'm asked so often that I get sick of telling the same old stories to my clients. You do understand that, don't you?"

He nodded unconvincingly which left me to wonder if I was completely off the hook. I jumped in quick and threw another question in his direction to discourage further questions.

"Thomas, tell me about your marriage, please?"

I was curious. It had been at the back of my mind all evening as to why he was paying me.

"Which one?"

I raised my eyebrows in surprise.

"Sorry, I didn't realise."

"You couldn't possibly have known, dear, don't apologise."

It took him half an hour to tell me about how he met his first wife. Once married, they wanted to start a family together but it never happened and after seven years of happiness (well, he said they were happy), she left him for one of England's soccer legends. From the tension in his shoulders, I could see some of the old hurt had surfaced and he barely whispered,

"She was pregnant by him within the year, I thought perhaps if it had happened for us…"

His time to leave that subject behind, he swiftly moved onto his current marriage.

"Jenna. My beautiful, Jenna! She married me for my money. I'm no fool…I realised that fourteen years ago. We haven't had sex for…it must be five years now. Since a year or two after we married, we only ever had sex when she was drunk, or when she wanted a few thousand pounds to go shopping."

He sighed before continuing.

"We have a son. I think he's mine. His birth certificate says he's mine. Twelve years ago he came into the world. After the lack of love through my childhood, I never realised the power of the emotion or ever felt such love. He mostly reminds me of me. I send him to a private school, one where they play football as well as rugby. Jenna is indifferent. Oh, she's not horrible to him or anything like that, but I think it's an inconvenience to her to have him around. She doesn't show a great deal of interest in his education, but if he makes something of himself, if he becomes famous or rich, she will then be 'so proud' of him and perhaps manage to find a love for him from somewhere. She is a cold-hearted woman, her selfishness knows no bounds. She doesn't know how to love… she doesn't love me."

Tears formed in my eyes at his last statement and anger rose inside me; an anger at the heartless woman he married.

Due to her snobbishness, dinner parties were frequent at home, and she would spend the evening trying to belittle

Thomas in front of their guests. I found myself disliking her intensely after what he revealed to me and I didn't even know her. He deserved so much better, this true gentleman with his impeccable manners, I found him an absolute delight, but I was puzzled.

"Thomas, why don't you leave her? Divorce her. You need happiness in your life."

"I'm afraid I can't do that. Jenna is a prize bitch, she has affairs, she treats me badly, she's not a suitable mother, but as long as she returns to our home, I have hope. I love her, I will always love her."

We went to bed around midnight. I kissed him goodnight, pecking him lightly on the cheek. I wondered if my naked-ness might arouse what was lying dormant and had been for five years. He faced me for a while as we talked some more. His eyes glanced fleetingly at my breasts at times and once at my full body. I could sense a discomfort in him. He wanted me yet he didn't want me. He turned his back to me and muttered goodnight again.

"Thomas, I don't want you to feel uncomfortable at all, but I am going to put my arms around you, cuddle you and hold you. No agenda, no ulterior motive on my part. I want you to feel loved and that someone cares for you, because no-one has held you for so long. You want to be true to Jenna, I understand that. Just enjoy the feeling of being loved and held, pretend its Jenna. Go to sleep happy for once, with arms holding you tight."

Initially, I felt his body stiffen at the side of me before all tension eventually drained from him and I heard his rhythmic breathing as sleep took him from my hold.

I left the hotel during the night while he was sound asleep. I have no need of his money. *Nobody* should have to pay just to have someone listen to them; someone who showed love and compassion. We were similar in many ways.

I lived a lonely and sad existence like him but our night together made me realise that I had so much more than him. I struggled to fight back my tears as I made my way along the road, tears for Thomas, for his childhood in particular. At least I have memories of loving parents and for that I will always be grateful. My client actually helped *me*. I failed to tell Thomas that I was grieving the loss of my parents, but having heard about the cold, cold people who happened to be his parents, I felt was a turning point for me. I would harbour no more selfish thoughts about how I couldn't cope without my parents.

I wasn't the least bit surprised when Thomas called me on the Saturday afternoon, asking why I left the hotel without allowing him to pay me. When I explained to him about my grief and why I left in the early hours of the morning, I added the fact that he helped me come to terms with my grief. He expressed his deepest sympathy and concern for me and wished I told him of my loss face to face. We chatted on the phone for half an hour and before we ended the call he insisted that I keep in touch…which I promised to do. I had a new friend.

CHAPTER 36

"

Allo, Mees. Fo...give me, my...'ow you say...friend (I gasped in shock when I heard the friend's name, one of Simon's clients) say to give you...a reeng! 'E.. say 'ow you may...'elp...wiz...ze...my...porbelm, oui?"

"Prob-lem, you mean? I offered,

"Oui...erm...yes...prob...lem!" I smiled as I listened to his broken English, totally bemused.

"Is this...a problem of a sexual nature?"

"Erm...yes...je...I 'ave a certain...'ow you say...needs...'eez zis...er ...cor rect?"

"Yes, that is correct, Monsieur. You want to organise a date?"

"Oui, Mademoiselle! Je compren...non...I...er...understan...wot cost 'eez in 'uros (he pronounced it ooros), yes?"

I took advantage while we were discussing money, to tell him how much it would cost him in pounds sterling.

"Certainement. 'Eez zis...er ...prob lem...for you... my.'otel...ze 'Ilton at ze 'Eathrow Aeroport?"

Eventually, we managed to agree a time...seven o'clock. It

wasn't an easy conversation despite my amusement at his pronunciations. This promised to be a fun assignation. He didn't bother telling me his room number, he said it was hard to find and it would just be easier to meet me in the foyer. He would wear a purple shirt and be using his mobile phone, somewhere near the reception desk. He told me not to approach him or talk to him...but to follow him at a discreet distance. I told him what I would be wearing and also that I would use a purple clip in my hair. What could go wrong?

I caught a train to Heathrow and opted for a short cab ride instead of taking the fifteen to twenty minute walk to the hotel. Being a little too early to arrive, I approached the bar, ordered a G & T and sat down on a big squishy sofa. I positioned myself so that I was able to see most of the reception desk and beyond, took a book out of my satchel and made a show of being engrossed in my reading. For the next twenty minutes, my eyes felt like they were doing a dance, glancing first at the book, up towards reception, then to my wristwatch. I was always in the habit of checking my watch every thirty seconds or so when I'm nervous and waiting to meet someone for the first time. Each time I check I hope that the pointers will miraculously jump forward in time, eager to get the initial awkwardness over and done with.

I checked my mobile next, for no other reason than having something different to do; feigning writing and sending text messages. Indulging again, my eyes darted back to the watch, five past seven. I started to wonder if the call was a hoax, one of Simon's crazy friends who he'd passed my number to! On the verge of wanting a second G & T, I stood up to go to the bar but held back as my client appeared near reception. Purple shirt and...taking his mobile phone out of his shirt pocket. It was him.

He stood with his back to me and watched the main entrance door. What the hell would I do if he didn't change position and continued to monitor the revolving door? *He* was late after all, so surely he would expect me to be here on time and waiting somewhere nearby. As I left the carpeted lounge area, the noise of my heels on the tiled reception floor caused him to turn. He noticed me. I looked down on the pretext of searching my satchel for something, ignoring him as instructed.

He walked away around the corner, and away from the reception desk. I sauntered some ten or fifteen metres behind him, still pretending to show more interest in my handbag than in my surroundings. I looked up as he arrived at the lift and when he beckoned me towards him, assumed that no-one was behind me to witness the handsome, dark-haired, French international footballer and a mystery brunette entering a hotel lift together.

We exchanged greetings as the lift began its ascent, his steely grey eyes checked my body up and down. He smiled and nodded slowly several times, hopefully in approval. I did a quick appraisal of him. I heard his name many times, but never having shown an interest in football I never saw the guy before, even though his picture would no doubt have appeared regularly in the sports pages of the national dailies. He was not my idea of handsome, acceptable, maybe! He had a slight bump on the bridge of his nose and a kind of effemi-nate look about him. I didn't feel any immediate attraction and was curious as to how this was going to pan out.

When the doors opened at the ninth floor, he stepped into the corridor, checked the coast was clear and indicated to me to leave the lift. All was quiet and as he used his key card to unlock the door. I stepped up my pace and made a beeline for the room. The door snapped shut behind me and he swiftly put the security chain in place.

He didn't waste a second. I barely had a moment to catch my breath and he stepped forward and started to remove my clothes. He gestured, realising that would be the easiest way; that I was to do the same to him. I unfastened his shirt, leaving it open and moved on to his denims. Once I unbuttoned his flies, my intention was to pull his denims and boxers down in the same move. As I lowered myself with the movement, his swollen cock sprang out of the boxers in front of my mouth. Nice. I reached out for it but he took hold of it himself with both hands and placed it on my lips.

"Sucer…s'il vous plait…pleez…suck."

I was happy to oblige, suddenly realising that my first feelings towards him had been totally wrong.

"It will…make things…easier…if we don't… talk…no worries…about…translation."

I managed to utter between my licks at his cock…an extremely *handsome* cock, and its size…ideal! I carried on sucking, admiring, and he watched my every move, clearly enjoying the feel of my lips as I moved them over his length. Having a break from that action, I trailed my tongue lazily over his scrotum and let my fingers tweak his pubic hair, teasing him. Listening to his moans and feeling his hands stroke and run through my hair as he towered above me, I felt shivers of excitement ripple through my body and couldn't control the urge to taunt him some more. Putting the urge into action, I changed course with my fingers and aimed them towards that sensitive area between scrotum and anus. The move startled him and he wavered, taking a step back. His eyes were wide, I saw the fire in them and felt that fire myself. He panted with delight and pushed the hair out of his eyes, the better to keep a close watch on me as I continued to suck on him. Closing them, he tilted his head up and his groans got louder.

"Oui…oh…oui!"

The tone of his voice made me think he was about to cum, but it was his eagerness showing. He started to thrust way to the back of my mouth and, no longer in control of his cock, I started to gag. He quickly got the message and dragged me across to the bed. Somehow he managed to indicate that I should lie on my back. Once I was in position, he first knelt between my legs and played one finger over my clit, through my Brazilian strip and plunged it into my pussy. Burning up with desire, I wanted more of him and didn't have to wait long.

He repeated the process in no time but using two fingers. His eyes locked with mine, watching me, his fascination evident. The attraction of thrusting his fingers inside me waned and still kneeling, he raised my legs up over his shoulders. With his hand guiding his beautiful cock, he wiggled it through my pubic hair and rubbed the end of it over my clit. It was almost climactic, igniting my inner nerves and I had to try hard to empty my mind. I didn't want to cum just yet. I gazed at the ceiling but it was impossible to close my mind as I eagerly anticipated what would come next; the fire as I waited for his cock to fuck me. I wanted to feast my eyes over it again but it was out of my sight. All I could see was his head while he fucked me with his tongue. I raised my upper body and leaned forwards to pull his head further in. Trying to take control back (I think), he removed his tongue and proceeded to lick all around my vulva, his fingers yet again toying with my clit. My heart felt as if it stopped. I took a deep intake of breath and started to cough and splutter for a few seconds. Recovering quickly, I was aware I could no longer feel his fingers; where were they? Didn't he realise what I wanted him to do with his fingers? I was on the verge of coming, but I wanted more, and he wasn't getting the message, so I showed him...I shoved my own fingers inside and gave a loud groan of pleasure. He caught on immediately.

"Ah...je...I...do...zat,"

He said, and moved my fingers out of the way. He did it more leisurely than I'd done and with it, induced my first release of cum. I quivered in delight. It was a beautiful slow release. The intensity was….intense. It lasted a while, not a multiple orgasm, but long, and slow, and *beautiful.*

"You…er…amour…love…fucking…yes?"

Oh, he'd guessed!

I was hot, sweaty, sticky, wet, and craved so much more.

"Yes, I love it! Keep fucking me, please! With your cock now!"

He didn't keep me waiting; he fucked me as asked, the missionary position, grunting hard with each thrust, and I moaned in ecstasy. Distracted for a second, I became aware of giggling outside in the corridor as footsteps passing the room slowed in their progress. People…listening to the loud and vocal fucking that was taking place, increasing in volume as he neared his climax. Then with a few violent thrusts, he shouted out, before biting hard on my breast, with his final squirt of cum.

I stayed in that position, waiting for him to finish, but I didn't expect the next instruction.

"Leeft…your…'ow you say…bot...tom, pleez." I did so.

"Now…you…pees…dans..er…in…my…mous, pleez."

I froze, not believing I heard correctly.

"Wh…what…the…the fuck?" I stammered, "I don't think I…let me get this right! You want me to piss in your mouth?"

"Oui…er yes."

The humour of the words was not entirely lost, but I was too incensed to be amused.

"Listen. You pay to fuck me. I do dirty, yes! But I do dirty in a sexual manner. I do *not* do dirty as in…of a toilet nature. You will have to pay someone else to do that. Sorry!"

This was something new to me. I thought over recent

months I was well past the stage of feeling such shock, but I found the suggestion more than repulsive.

"I pay for, I get!" he snapped, indignant.

I climbed off him, my earlier enjoyment forgotten. He watched until I was almost dressed, before he came out with the next corker,

"I get disc...er ..discount? Yes? For...er...non...pisser. You...er ...get...five hun red...less."

I wondered if it was a thing with the French. Who actually did things like what he demanded? The sex had been fantastic until that point, but I was totally turned off.

"Fine! I want to get out of here right now. Maybe some street girl will be happy for you to pay her five hundred pounds to piss in your mouth. He shrugged his shoulders dismissively as if it was nothing.

"We...er...fuck...again...one day...oui?"

Amazingly, I got the impression he wasn't too offended by my refusal.

"I don't know! Perhaps, but no...er...non pisser. Not ever! Okay?"

"O kay."

My anger gone, I giggled myself to sleep that night, two words running around my head, oui and piss! I figured I was over the worst of the shock if I could actually laugh about the incident, but I learned about an act that I didn't really want to know about. Before I drifted off to sleep I made a mental note to mention the matter to Simon the next time he called me.

CHAPTER 37

*D*eliriously happy, I sang out loud as I searched my wardrobe for something to wear. Janet, my friend from the Hopkins Partnership, just called and asked me to join her on a night out with all the girls. I can't remember the last time I'd been out, other than my...little business trips! I had plenty of time left to get ready for the evening, but I need to find the right clothes early enough. I don't want to be searching wildly at the last minute, then changing my mind every few seconds.

The taxi is coming to pick me up at seven thirty and the timing could not be better. Anthony left, leaving yet another envelope hidden in the greenhouse, on a business trip the day before, or so he said. At least I don't have to worry about coming home drunk and him...I mustn't dwell on *that* matter too long. I don't want anything to spoil the rest of the day. Janet has kept everything from me; where we are going, what the plans are for the night. I'm just thrilled to have been asked and I knew that whatever we end up doing, I will at least be in the company of my wonderful friends.

I felt really emotional as the cab pulled up. I couldn't

believe it as they all climbed out to greet me with big hugs as I headed down the drive towards them.

"Helen! You're looking great!"

"We've missed you so much at the office!"

"How are you feeling?"

"How are you keeping yourself busy all day, Helen?"

The look on the face of the cab driver was priceless, a typical male reaction to women being overly giddy and demonstrative; raised eyebrows and a shrug of the shoulders. Not to mention the impatient glances at his watch. They all shouted and chattered over the top of each other and I cried, touched by their concern and evident excitement to have me back in their midst for a few hours. I realised just how much I have missed them all. I couldn't wait to ask,

"So, tell me where you're taking me. I'm dying to know!"

They looked at each other sheepishly, and Gillian finally asked the others,

"Should we or not, girls?"

"Please tell me, please!"

I begged like an excited teenager and they all laughed. Despite the giddiness, they were still not inclined to let me in on the secret.

All eyes turned towards me as we approached the last two or three hundred yards of the journey, eagerly awaiting my reaction. The instant I recognized the road and our intended destination, I could feel my face start to drop. I stared open-mouthed out of the cab window as we approached Jigz Club. My stomach felt queasy and I couldn't imagine why this was their choice for our get-together.

"Helen? Helen, what's matter?"

I tried to snap out of it. The girls were doing their best to give me a good night out and I must have looked so ungrateful. I smiled, trying to look happier and said,

"Oh, nothing! I just got..."

"Helen, if this is to do with that guy from your school, Alec Barker-what's-his-face…?" Leanne piped up.

I'm pleased she interrupted me because I hadn't a clue what words would have come out next, had she let me carry on speaking.

"No! It's not that…I'm fine! Really!" And before the subject of Alex cropped up again, I asked, "Are we eating first then?"

I felt such a relief! Everyone's attention was now on food as we settled up with the cab driver and made our way to the restaurant. All through our meal, I listened carefully as the girls chatted about work, their work. While they tried hard to include me in the conversation, telling me any staff news or the client news for that matter, I didn't really feel a part of it anymore. They may as well be talking about aliens. About to change the subject to more common ground, I remembered and was suddenly curious about Leanne and her earlier comment about 'that guy from your school.'

"Leanne, what was it that you were saying earlier about Alex Baker-Thompson? That's his real name by the way, you know, 'if it's about that guy from your school'…?"

"Oh, that! Well…what I was going to say was, if it was about him…why you weren't keen on coming here, well, I don't think you have any cause for concern!"

I couldn't understand what she was getting at. I hadn't told them what really happened that night, but I couldn't wait to hear what she had to say.

"No, it wasn't to do with him. What made you think that?"

I pushed my food around the plate wondering what she would come out with, and didn't understand why I felt so nervous. I even noticed goose bumps form on my arms.

"You said that he tried it on with you. I thought maybe

that was the reason, because if it was, you have no need to worry."

I chuckled at what she just said and tried to make light of the conversation.

"So why have I got no reason to worry? I wasn't worried about him anyway."

"We've…um…been back here three times since…since… you know, your parents' accident. He was here the first time we came, with his friends again. He stared all night, looking over at us all the time, probably wondering where you were."

The other girls nodded at this, confirming that what Leanne said was true.

"Well he hasn't been back since, not when we've been here, at least!"

Gillian added, "He must have really liked you, Helen…to come back looking for you!"

I looked at each of them in turn and they all looked guilty, as if they'd done something wrong. Leanne was tearing her napkin into shreds, Gemma was busy wiping lipstick off her glass.

"Girls, look! I realise that Ted must have told you all that my marriage is over, but you didn't bring me here in the hopes that Alex was here did you? Please tell me you didn't!"

I looked at their faces, trying to read their thoughts, to understand what their true intention had been. Suddenly, feeling tired of the whole conversation, I stood up,

"Enough! Come on, we came here to enjoy ourselves, let's do that!"

We headed to the night club, to the loud music and dancing. The noise was a blessing to me. Conversation was impossible and I was grateful for that. During our meal I began to realise that I was alone…no longer a part of their world. Conversations about accounts, boyfriends, husbands and holidays are just a part of my past. I don't fit in, and if the girls, my friends, ever found out about the new me, they would disown me. It was depressing thought.

When the cab dropped me at home around half past one, the girls hugged and kissed me again. They were delighted that I joined them for the night and told me they were longing for my return to work at some stage. I didn't have the heart to tell them that I won't be returning, ever. I can't.

I poured myself a large glass of wine and sat in the armchair through the early hours, mulling things over. I learned a lot from my night out with the girls. They led normal lives, with loving husbands or boyfriends, nights out together, nine to five jobs. Then there's me; no loving relationship, a menial job that satisfied my mental health problems and a secret life as a call girl. Sordid visits to hotel rooms, taking money for sex, sometimes perverted sex, being paid in addition to achieving my own sexual gratification. I didn't know myself anymore; I used to be a different person, leading a very different life.

Sometime just before daylight and before I succumbed to sleep, I recognised a few similarities between myself and Anthony.

CHAPTER 38

$\mathcal{I}$ stared in disbelief at the name on the caller display of my mobile phone as it bleeped in my hand. The call that I hoped wouldn't happen. I looked around the room then back at the display, half hoping that I was hallucinating, but his name continued to flash up at me in time with the bleeping. Unable to do anything but stare, the bleeping finally ceased, his name was gone. I exhaled at last, unaware that I held my breath for goodness knows how long. My heart raced and as I stared at the phone in my trembling hand, I instantly regretted that I hadn't pressed 'answer'. Annoyed at him for ringing me, and then with myself for not answering the call, I flung the phone onto the settee in disgust as I yelled out loud at him, absent though he was. "What the hell have you done this for? You're getting to me. Go the fuck away and leave me alone, can't you? I don't need this!"

Banging and clattering around the kitchen as I tidied up, my anger was all with myself this time, for being ridiculous. I'd had no wish to see David ever again, so why was I so upset that I hadn't responded to his call? I could have answered and told him...what? That I was too busy? Some excuse like, I was perhaps no longer a call girl? Or be truthful by telling him, 'I can't see you again David. It would be too risky for me to do so?' I put coffee ready in the cup and switched the kettle on but when it eventually came to the boil I ignored it. Instead, I grabbed a bottle of Zinfandel from the fridge and poured myself a very generous measure. Anthony was due in from work within the next half hour and I seriously needed to get my emotions in check before then.

I was about to sit down in the lounge, glass of wine still in my hand, and I noticed the phone light up again. I snatched it up expecting it to start bleeping again. I was stunned to see that it showed two further missed calls from David. Too busy in the kitchen, I hadn't even heard it and I cursed at myself again.

I gulped greedily at the wine, barely pausing for breath. I fought the temptation to call him back, a raging war going on inside my head. As I poured myself a second glass, I was thinking how I had better make a decision and be quick about it. I wouldn't dare take David's call if he happened to ring me once Anthony arrived home. Having taken too long thinking about what to do, and coping with my inner confusion, I looked at the clock and realised I had about five minutes left before he would be here. Ring him...or switch off my mobile? It had to be a split second decision and I decided to switch it off. It wouldn't do for Anthony to walk in while I was in the middle of explaining to David that I wouldn't be available for a business transaction, *or* telling him that for me to see him again would be foolhardy to say the least.

I picked up the phone ready to press the 'off' button and it rang in my hand this time. I almost dropped it in surprise. It was him again. I inhaled deeply two or three times, heart racing and pressed 'answer'. I couldn't get any words out. I listened in silence and shivered. It wasn't a good sign, I knew that. I felt exactly like I had done when I had a crush on one of the teachers in school. There had been no girls to giggle with then, just as there was no friend to giggle with now.

"Hello? Is that you, Helen?"

His voice was just as I remembered. How could I ever forget? I felt sure my heart skipped a beat and I could feel the heat rising up my face. I turned to look in the mirror. I was beetroot-coloured. 'You know you want to speak to him' I silently told my mirror image, 'just do it.' I still couldn't answer.

"Hello? Hello? Helen?" I knew I couldn't wait any longer, I didn't have long.

"Hello." It came out only slightly louder than a whisper.

"Helen, thank goodness. It's David. David Barnard."

My stomach was doing back-flips. My emotions and body language would not be acting the way they were if it *wasn't* him. I took the plunge and I didn't know where the current would be taking me as I finally dived in.

"Hi, David. It's nice to hear from you again. What can I do for you?"

I ranted at myself 'what on earth made you ask that,' 'just tell him no to whatever it is he wants.'

"I was wondering if you were free tomorrow night, for the whole night, if that's possible? I'm in London, so it's easier for you. I assume it will be the same...?" I didn't hear the rest of his words after that last bit, mortified as I watched Anthony's car pull into the drive. Shit! I knew I needed to hurry so I focused my attention back to the call.

"Okay, David. Where in London and what time? I have to hurry now. A friend's car has just pulled up."

I dashed over to the landline phone, where we always keep a notepad and pen. I listened carefully and wrote down the address in St John's Wood. He quickly reeled off the directions from the tube station and I jotted the appropriate L's and R's on the pad. I was to arrive for seven o'clock the next night and he would prepare dinner for us both. As he ended the call, I ripped the piece of paper off the block and stuffed it down my bra just as the back door opened. I headed straight up the stairs to splash cold water on my face, but I flushed the toilet as well so that Anthony would think what I wanted him to think.

I couldn't believe David asked me to stay overnight with him at one of his homes and when I said yes, I hadn't given it much thought. I forgot that I was meant to be working a shift at the hotel the following morning. I would now be waking up next to David. I phoned Mrs Flintoff the next morning, feigned starting with the flu and asked her if there was anyone who I could swap a couple of shifts with. She phoned me back almost immediately and said it was fine, she'd managed to get my shift covered already.

Six weeks had passed by since our first date, assignation, rendezvous, I didn't know the correct terminology for a hooker's appointment with a client. I don't understand what happened to my decision not to see him. I think it was that voice of his, hot, friendly and caring. I closed my eyes on hearing it; imagined hearing him speak in the same room as me, close to me. My mind pulled his image from the depths of my memories. I knew I shouldn't have gone ahead with the transaction, but I was powerless to stop myself.

I left a note for Anthony saying that I was out all night with the girls from work. He still thought I worked at the Hopkins Partnership and as he hadn't ever bothered to get to know any of my friends and colleagues it was highly likely that he would never find out.

Rather than struggle to park my car anywhere near the address, I decided the tube was my best option. It was ten minutes to seven when I knocked on the door of one of the most beautiful mews cottages I ever saw. I could feel the nerves kick in as I stood waiting. I didn't know if I was going to be able to eat; my insides were taking tumbles and making rumbles. It felt like my heart was galloping and for a few seconds I considered *doing* just that. I froze as I heard a key turn in the lock and the door opened. There he was, smiling and gesturing for me to enter with a sweep of his arm and lowering his head. I felt like I was floating on a cloud, lost in limbo between Heaven and Earth. Then quickly coming back down to reality, this guy posed a danger to me and my sanity and I couldn't explain why. I didn't *want* or need to be feeling the very emotion that I was trying to escape from. I should run.

No suit and tie this time, he was casually dressed in Armani denims and T-shirt, an entirely different look to the one I was expecting to greet me. He looked sensational and his eyes positively sparkled. He took my hand in his and as he leaned in to kiss me on the cheek, uttered in the most charming manner, "Helen. How lovely to see you again. You look even more stunning than I remember."

Those compliments again. Why did this *one* man actually make me believe him when he said such nice things? I flushed, more in pleasure than embarrassment and tried to put the thought out of my head and make a response.

"It's lovely to see you again too."

I replied vaguely as I was taking in the beauty of my surroundings for the first time; cream plush carpets and two leather sofas, one coffee table, no armchairs, very minimalist. I always loved my home, but this was something else. The décor was tastefully done and the furnishings and carpets, clearly no expense had been spared. I quickly added,

"Wow! What a gorgeous cottage, David. Are you renting it for the week?"

My eyes scanned every inch of the room in amazement.

"I'm fairly pleased with it myself. I bought it two years ago. I needed a base in London. My two daughters helped me with the design and furniture."

Had I heard him correctly? He just said the word 'daughters.' I slowly turned to face him. I just discovered something about him I hadn't wished to know, and weird...I now wanted to know the rest of it too. He would probably volunteer the information if I didn't ask, but I raised my eyebrows anyway.

"Daughters? So where are they, David? With your wife?"

I blanched at my words. Hopefully, he hadn't detected too much sarcasm in them.

"Yes, daughters. And I expect they will be with their mother, Heidi. She's not my wife, Helen. She hasn't been my wife for over eight years."

That put me firmly in my place and I wondered if I could manage to come up with something to say but he followed on with,

"I've been married again since then. She's called Joanna. We also divorced, four years ago."

It was indeed a revelation. I was finding out things I didn't want to know. I intended that this business transaction should be just that. Knowing personal things about my clients' lives just made it seem like...as if I was involved somehow. I'm telling myself all these things, trying to come to terms with the fact that I have this knowledge and my mouth acted of its own accord as I blurted out,

"So what went wrong then? An affair? Did you have affairs and they...?"

He stopped me with a chuckle and I was instantly sorry for my outburst, after all it was none of my business. I'm his whore. I have no right to be giving him the third degree.

"It's my work. I travel around the world on business three

parts of the year. It was a lonely life for them both, we grew apart. No affairs though, Helen...sorry to disappoint you."

Crap!

I hoped to hell I hadn't offended him and wished I could eat the bloody words that spewed out of my mouth before I had the chance to control it. It was making me a little uncomfortable. I'd hoped for a better start to the evening.

"And no, you haven't offended me in the slightest, Helen, so don't worry. Now, are you ever going to sit down, make yourself at home and let me finish up in the kitchen or should I take you upstairs right now and tie you to the bed? Maybe that way, I'll get to finish the cooking" He grinned.

I picked up on it immediately. How the hell did he guess that I was worried? I hadn't realised I was being so transparent. Or were we just in tune to each other? Yet again, those thoughts increased my unease. I was not supposed to be thinking any of this. I felt a great urge to tell him that he should take me upstairs to bed but he was going to finish preparing a meal for us; a meal I convinced myself would remain on my plate, untouched.

He took my hand and led me to the settee. He waited and watched, smiling at me all the while, while I parked my bottom. He grabbed a couple of magazines from the coffee table, placed them in my lap and departed for the kitchen without another word. I was supposed to be here on business, carrying out a duty that I was going to be paid for, and just like the first time we met, he was wining and dining me. Most of my clients want to leap on my bones the minute I walk through their door, fuck me in any manner they see fit, thrust the payment into my hands and get me back out of the door. I couldn't understand David at all. He was far too warm and caring to be a client, and why the hell would he even need a tart with his good looks and bank balance?

I lost myself in those thoughts for a while. There was an

argument going on between the two halves of my brain. Summing up, one half was saying 'Run like hell, fast as you can,' the other half responding with 'Enjoy. You like him, don't you?' Forgetting where I was for a minute such was my dilemma, I was jolted from my ponderings by David shouting at me from the kitchen.

"Take a seat at the dining table, your ladyship. First course will be served in two minutes."

His cooking was excellent and I was impressed. He served up avocado with raspberries as a starter. The main course was beef wellington, new potatoes and vegetables, which were cooked to perfection. For dessert he'd made dark chocolate soufflés and once they were on our plates he quickly made a hole in the top of each and poured in some white chocolate sauce. It tasted like heaven. Each course was accompanied by a fresh glass of wine, and all the while we prattled on about our favourite foods and restaurant experiences.

After he cleared away the last course he joined me at the dining table again. The reservations I had earlier about whether I would be able to eat had been unfounded. I was comfortable, relaxed and feeling prematurely inebriated.

Elbows on the table, chin resting on his fists, he smiled across the table at me, and I could feel every beat of my heart as his eyes never left mine. I felt tipsy, nervous and excited all at once, a bad mix. Could I trust myself to even speak? I doubted it.

"So, Helen? You know a little bit more about me. My turn to learn now. Start talking. I'm listening."

I smiled back at him following his lead, placed my elbows on the table and returned his gaze, playing a flirting game with him. I tried hard to assume an air of mystery but amused myself with a silly thought that 'pissed' was more appropriate than 'air of mystery'. I giggled, still deciding on what personal details I should reveal to him.

He laughed, "You're relaxed, the wine has seen to that. Time to reveal all. I'll get you started. Do you have a husband, or a boyfriend...maybe?"

Why did he have to ask that of all questions?

It was a topic I hadn't wanted to discuss, but due to my earlier outburst it was inevitable that he would want to know.

"He's an ex, but we still live under the same roof."

He looked concerned, the smile disappeared and a question formed on his lips,

"He's not a pimp, David. He doesn't even know what I do for a living these days. He's not a nice person."

"Then why...?

I already said far more than I wanted but I didn't need him worrying about me or asking any more awkward questions.

"Why am I still living with him? Is that what you meant? He was abusive to me some time ago and...it's a long story." His body tensed and he got up from his chair and walked around the table towards me, "Helen? You prob..."

"Don't worry. He's not abusive any more. The reason I'm still there is...is to see his downfall, and it will be coming soon. I know it will. Can we drop the subject please, David? It's depressing me."

He pulled out the dining chair that was nearest to me and sat down again.

"Of course we can. So what are your reasons for doing this...as a job, I mean?"

He stared into my eyes again, and I wished he wouldn't do it. That all too familiar feeling of unease returned quickly, scaring me even more so I answered him.

"Sex! I can enjoy sex without any need to fall in love again. If I don't fall in love, I can't get hurt."

Even as the words came out I wondered how many of those statements would prove to be true. Needing to break the intense eye contact between us, I leaned over the dining table for the empty wine bottle and waved it in front of his nose.

"Do you have any more wine in the fridge, David?"

He seemed a little distant as he replied, "What? Oh yes… plenty, take your pick."

As I walked through to the kitchen, his eyes hadn't followed my moves as usual. He was staring at the wall straight ahead of him, deep in thought.

On my return with our third bottle of wine, he snapped out of his reverie. As I was about to sit down at the dining table he got up, hooked up both our empty glasses in his hand by their stems and led me over to one of the big leather sofas. I handed the bottle of wine for him to pour whilst I removed my shoes. I wanted to recline with my feet up without causing any damage with the heels. He waited until I was propped up on one elbow at the far end of a sofa before handing me my wine. He then made himself comfortable in a similar position at the opposite end, before picking up his own glass of wine off the floor.

We reclined in silence for a while, downing our wine at a steady pace. I was relaxed in his company. It was nice to just gaze at him and take time to appreciate his sexy good looks, and enjoy those moments without conversation interrupting my thoughts. I smiled at him and he bowled me over when he reciprocated, and moved his legs to intertwine with mine.

It dawned on me what was happening between us, the sexual tension was building. To be so still, our legs touching with no more than a hint of movement from either of us, was the very foundation from which our sexual chemistry would emerge.

I pulled myself upright and leaned over him, reaching down for the bottle of wine which he left on the floor at his side of the sofa. As I reached over, my breast brushed against his hand. He never made any deliberate movement to touch or fondle, it was just a chance contact that sent shock waves throughout my body. That closeness without any sexual action was electric! While still in that position, I poured his wine, topped up my glass and reclined once more. He gazed across at me and I saw it in his eyes too...the longing, sparked by that hint of contact. He opened his mouth as if ready to speak and I placed a finger to my lips, silencing him. I wanted to enjoy the tension, the anticipation and feel every formula, every element of the chemistry and wait for the conclusion of the experiments that were playing out in my thoughts.

I wanted the occasion to pass slowly so I could savour every moment. I could feel the wine starting to take effect, rapidly. My thoughts started drifting away from David fucking me to...waiting, we must wait, waiting would make it better, no rushing, the sooner it started the sooner it would be over and I didn't want it to be over. It was making me giddy. Such illogical thoughts, drink induced. I giggled. David reached out to touch both my hands, he held them, and giggled with me.

"Helen?"

It was his voice. I opened my eyes and his face was almost touching mine. It felt as if I had been asleep for a long time, but I glanced towards the wall clock and the pointers indicated I only closed my eyes momentarily. As I brought my eyes back to meet his, his lips touched mine and he kissed me, tentatively. I was so shocked I couldn't respond immediately, but his warmth and tenderness seemed to meld with my lips. I felt the passion and intensity radiate throughout my entire body and fill me with need. Before I realised it was happening, I was kissing him back, softly at first, and then, as his tongue parted my lips, I knew I wanted him. My self-imposed rules about kissing were broken. The wine; my downfall. Self-control had deserted me.

Kissing each other with a sudden urgency, we rolled off the sofa huddled together and onto the carpet. David was fighting with the buttons of my shirt as I pulled his T-shirt over his head. I had to pull away from the kiss to feast my eyes on his chest and biceps. I ran my fingertips through his chest hair caressing his skin, stroked his biceps then, holding his cheeks in my hands I found it hard not to stare at him in amazement. He was perfect. He finally managed to undo all my buttons and I pulled my arms free of the white cotton sleeves.

We rolled together until he was on his back and I started to remove his denims and boxers. I only managed to get them to below his hips and became too distracted by his cock; it was rigid and the temptation too great.

He moaned out loud as I took him into my mouth for an instant. I loved it and I shuddered with delight to know that I was pleasuring him. Hearing him groan and shout out in pure bliss, I deliberately tormented him, wanted to send him over the edge. I licked slowly around the head of his cock, my thoughts drifting and my own excitement bringing me wave after wave of longing.

"Oooh, yes! Helen…you're…" he stammered.

"Shush, David. Enjoy!" I whispered.

I let my tongue wander lazily up and down every inch of him, but was forced to stop. I needed to remove his denims there and then, freeing his lower body to allow me better access. Once I pulled the lower clothing from his feet, I took off my skirt, panties and bra and lay down between his legs, focusing my attention on his inner thighs, his cock and his scrotum. I felt sticky, hot dampness between my thighs. Tantalising his sac with my tongue, I slowly averted my gaze up towards his face, my eyes not missing one inch of him, his cock, his stomach, chest…so masculine, his neck, so kissable and biteable, his face…so handsome. My heart was like a beating drum; loud within me, pounding, beating out a sound of passion and need. My stomach had an empty feel to it. I craved him; needed so much more from him.

"Swing your body round babe, bring your legs up…over my head. I want to kiss your pussy…massage your clit. I want you to cum for me. I want to taste your cum."

The temptation to 'just let go' on hearing his words was phenomenal. His voice sent an electric current through my body. A sixty-nine, my favourite…and with *him*. Perspiration formed on my forehead, the fire raged inside me. His voice, his words and the promise of what was to come made me shudder in delight. I needed to climax and soon, yet I also wanted it to last, for both of us. I couldn't wait though; I had passed the point, there would be no return once I let go. Much as it was hard to do so, I let his cock slip out of my mouth. I swivelled my body round until I was kneeling, my backside over his face. He immediately thrust his tongue inside me and played his fingers over my clit. He goaded me, so I taunted him in return. Tracing my tongue lightly over his scrotum and thighs, I barely made contact, it worked. I could feel the tension course through his body and he groaned his frustration. I found it hard to focus as his fingers stopped tweaking my clit and entered me, tasting and exploring as far as they could possibly reach. Using his other hand he started to caress my clit again. It was pure heaven. With hardly any warning, I felt a fire inside of me, exciting flames, threatening to engulf me and I shuddered in ecstasy. I cried out in delight through every second of my orgasm. It felt amazing. Before my breathing steadied, I once again gave my full attention to his cock. I wanted him to feel that same beautiful intensity. My hand moved up and down his cock faster and faster as I sucked on him. He groaned louder with each passing second. He was still exploring my depths with his fingers and working on my clit again. I never wanted it to end.

"Helen…don't…suck…so…hard! Don't! I don't…want…to cum…in…your mouth!"

I raised my eyebrows at him. I thought that was every man's dream. I was prepared to let him squirt into my mouth, taste his juices. I never willingly did it before, but I was prepared to do it for David.

"Why…not? I'm…I…want…to do…that…for you."

He pulled out of my mouth and shuffled away from underneath me.

"On your side, Helen. Quick! I feel it, I'm coming!"

I couldn't answer, I just did it. I wanted his cum. I got into position. He cuddled up behind me like spoons and rammed into me from behind. He gripped around me, holding my hips tight in place as he gave three or four quick thrusts and I could feel his spurts of cum as they were released. His cock throbbed beautifully inside me. His fingers rubbed hard against my swollen clit, and my juices seeped into his as I climaxed again. I was soaring through the universe with my eyes closed. I was aware of nothing except for the two of us, the passion and excitement of what we just did. Nobody else existed. As his breathing gradually slowed, he kissed my neck and continued to hold his perfect body tight to mine. After ten minutes he pulled me around to face him and kissed me passionately on the lips. I responded. During that kiss I suddenly remembered our lips meeting earlier, how much I enjoyed it. It had been full of fire…and not something I'd intended to do. But I had no regrets. The wine had weakened my resolve!

His lips gently broke contact with mine and I felt them touch my ear as he whispered,

"Oh shit! Helen, I've got something to tell you!"

I was suddenly tense, not knowing what to expect. What now? Was it something I wanted to hear or didn't want to hear. I wasn't even clear in my head what words I would like to hear. I wondered if it was at all possible to...No! I told myself I couldn't think like that, not if I was to get through life without complications. I was feeling slightly nauseous throughout my thoughts, dreading what he might say next.

"Yes? Go on then...tell!"

I closed my eyes, realising after a few seconds that I was holding my breath.

"We have been down here, naked, and fucking!"

I let a big sigh escape me.

"Yes? Your point being, David?"

"Look at the window, Helen."

I lifted my head off the floor. It took all of ten seconds for me to realise what David brought to my attention. It was dark outside. The wall-lights were on in his lounge and the blinds were not closed. We had been indulging in gloriously naughty sex in full view of anybody walking past who chose to look through his window.

We looked at each other in horror, and started to laugh uncontrollably. We went to bed half an hour later.

I was aware of David's hard-on tapping on my back. Looking at the alarm clock I noted that it was approaching six thirty in the morning. Within five minutes we were at it, shagging like a couple of dogs. When each of us were fully satiated some thirty minutes later, he turned on his side and tried to kiss me, but as I tilted my head, his kisses fell on my cheek instead. I couldn't forget that we kissed the previous night, and it had somewhat troubled me before I drifted off to sleep. I didn't want to be involved with him on that level. I had to make a valiant effort not to fall into that again. I put it down to too much wine and a lack of control on my part, due to intoxication. I knew I had to be in control in future.

Not too much to drink when with clients, Helen!

David needed to be at a business meeting in the city for eleven. After he served breakfast, I showered and dressed and was in the lounge preparing to leave. He sat at the dining table sorting through his briefcase while I fastened my sandals. I wasn't looking forward to going home. I already had a kind of empty feeling in the pit of my stomach. David would be flying out to Geneva later in the evening. He already told me that he wouldn't be back in the country for two or three months, and the thought left me feeling lonely. I couldn't understand why. He was not my partner or husband. I wasn't used to being with him all the time, and yet the thought of not seeing him for so long filled me with dread.

I would miss the mind-blowing sex. That was it!

He came to the door with me as I was leaving and moved towards me once more in an attempt to kiss me. I longed to be able to kiss him back, lovingly and then urgently, but I knew I mustn't do that. He held me by my shoulders and as I moved my lips away, he asked,

"What are you scared of, Helen?"

I wanted to tell him. I really wanted to tell him that it was him I was scared of. Scared of what he was doing to me. I was frightened to kiss him, frightened of what I might feel. I looked him straight in the eye.

"What do you mean, David? Scared?"

"You know exactly what I mean. You won't let me kiss you."

I had to get away from him. I couldn't get in too deep with this conversation. I couldn't let him know any more.

"But you're my client, David! I must go now. Take care and have a safe trip."

I leaned forward and gave him a quick peck on the lips, not giving him enough time to respond. I turned and walked down the street, not daring to look back at him. I could feel his eyes watching me all the way, until I turned the corner into the next street.

CHAPTER 39

en minutes before I was due to finish work for the day, my mobile phone rang.

"Hi, Helen! It's me. Sorry about the disruption to plans. Our flight from New York was delayed nearly twenty four hours because of the weather in the States. I cancelled last night's hotel booking when I realised."

I hadn't been happy that previous night, sneaking about in the service lift and hotel corridors to find that his usual suite was unoccupied. I'm taking a big enough risk as it is, conducting my illicit business in the place where I'm employed. He went on to ask if I was free in the evening. Being as I had nothing else planned I told him it wouldn't be a problem. After he explained when and where; a lodge, part of an estate, and a fellow actor's residence, I hung up. I sent a quick email to Simon once I was ready and set off walking up our street. After I turned the corner and out of sight of Anthony, I hailed a black cab.

Twenty five minutes later I arrived at the destination and knocked on the door. The guy who answered the door took my coat and showed me into a tastefully decorated sitting room where a beautiful log fire was burning and where my client waited. He jumped up and smiled as I walked across the room towards him. I couldn't help but notice the blonde highlights in his sandy coloured hair. He looked much hotter than I remember, but not quite as hot as the sex that I was looking forward to. I could feel my tingling starting down below, memories of our last steamy session re-surfacing quickly.

"How are you, Helen?" he asked as he kissed my cheek "How long is it since…?"

"Two mon…" but before I could finish he cut in rather rudely,

"Helen, there's somebody I would like you to meet tonight."

And as if that had been her cue, she walked in from what I imagined to be the kitchen; about five foot six, with a body so painfully thin. Her hair was blonde and cut in a shaggy style. She was very pretty with cheekbones many girls would die for. It dawned on me that I'd seen her before. She had a small roll in a film in which my client was the leading male, but her total exposure throughout the whole film had been five minutes, tops. I didn't need any warning bells here, it smacked me in the face instantly…he wanted a threesome.

"Phebes, this is, Helen. Helen, this is…"

Still feeling irritated by his interruption seconds before and the fact that I was not particularly happy about this little twist, I couldn't resist snapping back,

"Phebes? Yes, you just said!"

She never approached me to shake hands and although it occurred to *me* to do so, I was too bloody annoyed. This had just been sprung on me at the last minute and my head was in complete turmoil. I had never been touched by a woman sexually, neither had I ever been involved in a threesome. I felt repulsed. My stomach lurched in disgust and I felt half inclined to leave.

Remembering that I was getting paid to give what the client asked of me, I nodded when he inquired as to whether I wanted white wine. I didn't trust myself to speak. I was so shaken, but I knew the wine would relax me, it usually did the trick so I said yes. Phebes poured herself a whisky and sat down next to me. I felt only slightly more at ease after I downed a couple of glasses. We indulged in some idle gossip and although I still had nagging doubts I did my best to contribute to the conversation. Over and over in my mind I was telling myself,

You're still here, you could have gone home thirty minutes ago!

Phebes eventually moved onto a rug in front of the fire and immediately started to remove her clothing. I felt nervous but found it hard to look away. My skin was hot and clammy, but it also felt as if a giant icicle resided within me. I wondered if it would thaw. Glancing over at my client for some indication of what I was expected to do, I shrugged my shoulders at him. Sensing my apprehension and naivety, he tried to put me at ease. Leaning towards me, he almost whispered in my ear,

"Why don't you go and sit with Phebes on the rug, get to know her better?"

My insides were cringing, but after taking a little longer than normal to finish off the dregs in my glass, I did as he suggested. I stiffly plonked myself down about two feet away from her and followed her lead and started unbuttoning my top. Shuffling closer towards me she put her hand on mine and held it still. I winced at her touch and she looked directly into my eyes.

"Don't, Helen. *I* will do that. It will be *my* pleasure," she said eagerly.

She moved in to kiss me, but realising from my grimace

that kissing was not on offer, she kissed around my throat and neck instead. A little unsure how I felt about having a woman's lips kiss me, I was tense...but...it wasn't entirely unpleasant. Her hands continued the unbuttoning I started and she followed by unfastening the clasp on my bra. Looking into my eyes for a reaction all the while, she slid my denims down my legs and flung them into a chair. The effects of the wine gone, my body tensed and I tried to resist but she moved her hands teasingly up my thighs and let her fingers edge their way inside my thong. My head was telling me that it didn't feel right but my body surprisingly experienced the early ripples of an excitement I can't begin to explain.

I looked across at my client, expecting him to join us. He nodded back at me...a nod that told me 'just get on with it'. He started to unzip his trousers though. I gave a sigh of relief. *This* was not my normal sort of business. Phebes had no inhibitions whatsoever though. She behaved as if this was something she was more than familiar with. She ran her fingers through my pussy hair while with her other hand she fondled my breasts, biting occasionally on my nipples. I squealed in pain as she sank her teeth in. Suddenly, she yanked on my thong and it snapped. I glared at her!

She grabbed my hand and thrust my fingers towards her own pubes and alarmed by the move, I sat bolt upright. I had no desire to touch her.

"Don't think for one minute, that *I* am going to fuck *you*, Phebes!" I snapped, "I don't *do* the fucking. I *get* fucked!"

"And I am *happy* to fuck you, honey. I just wanted you to feel me before we get down to it. Relax, you don't have to touch me if you don't want to."

I looked over at him again, wondering why he wasn't joining us. I needed some normality to ease my panic. I tried to put thoughts of Phebes to the back of my mind by concentrating on another client, a special someone, special sex. I laid down again, slightly more relaxed but...not quite resigned to this.

"Lay on your stomach, Helen."

As I rolled over I caught sight of him again; completely naked on the settee, his hand slowly massaging his piece of muscle. Phebes leaned over me and passed me three cushions off the settee.

"Put these under your tummy. Raise your bottom into the air," she ordered, rather bossily.

I was hardly in position before I could feel her tongue licking all around my buttocks, her hands around the front of my thighs, yet again stroking my pubes. She teased, tormented, brushing her fingers gently, but swiftly, over my clit and away again. Her tongue barely touched my anus, and was moved quickly away. I closed my eyes. I didn't have to, but I couldn't see her anyway, so I imagined the tongue and fingers to be those of a man, a special man. I was always good at pretending when I had to, and it was essential for me in this new situation. It was feeling good, I was enjoying every second of the anticipation...the waiting...waiting for the tongue to lick my pussy, waiting for the fingers to slide into it, then for the tongue to lick my clit.

This had to be a man pleasuring me, preparing me to be well and truly fucked. I didn't have to wait too long. His tongue, (I almost believed it *was* him), started gently stabbing into my anus, gentle thrusts that made me shudder with delight. His finger, a lovely male finger, replaced the tongue which moved to my sensitive area between anus and pussy. He was rubbing it, moving more rapidly. He slid his tongue quickly in my pussy and out again. Such torment as next, his fingers were hard in me, in and out, in and out. They entered my warmth again and again as his tongue worked over my clit with deliberation. I moaned in delight, savouring every second as I felt my juice flow, coming and coming again, and I wanted the feeling to go on forever. I placed my hands on the floor and raised my upper body, throwing my head back in intense pleasure, before lowering myself down a few seconds later.

I lay there still shaking from the multiple orgasm that rocked my body and aware that the contact between us had broken. There was a movement, I'm not sure what, but somebody passed something over me, it happened in a flash. At last he was inside me properly, not his tongue or his fingers but his cock, fucking me like crazy. His cock felt strange; different, knobbly even. But I loved it. The knobbles were massaging every glorious nerve ending contained within my vagina. I held on as long as I could, which wasn't long. I had no choice but to let go as one *giant* orgasm sent me soaring into the universe and back. It was delicious and I cried out with the over sensitivity as his cock continued to fuck me hard and fast, thrusting furiously.

"Stop...please!"

I was spent. I let my body flop onto the cushions. He stopped and rolled me on to my back to face him and I realised with horror that it was *her* that was looking down on me. *She* made me cum. *She* fucked me with *her* cock; a nobbled, strap-on cock. As I lay there, reeling in shock, she got onto her hands and knees, bent over me and kissed my throat and with one hand she guided her cock back in and started to fuck me some more. My client, fully hard at last, came and bent over her. He shagged her rather roughly, up the backside, holding on to her tight as he thrust inside her thrusting into me. His powerful thrusts into her gave more momentum to her thrusting into me.

I was on fire. The dirty fucking was taking me places I hadn't been before. I was almost euphoric. I orgasmed again producing fresh spurts of wetness, caused as much by the *thought* of crudity as the physical feelings inside of me. I lost all sense of control in that moment. I raised my head and sucked hard on her breasts. Reaching down with my hand, I stroked her clit before sliding my fingers inside her. It didn't take her long. She climaxed quickly and moved out of the way still moaning. After removing the strap-on cock she sat on the edge of the settee, shoved it up and proceeded to pleasure herself with it. As I was already on my back, he didn't waste his time moving me. He quickly forced my legs in the air over his shoulders and rammed his cock hard inside me, thrusting as if his life depended on it. His balls smacked hard against my backside and it was me who got his cum ten minutes later as he climaxed, yelling out loud.

She invited herself into my bath afterwards. I suspected that she was maybe seeking something extra, but I was totally wrong. She was in fact trying to act like she was my new best friend, though I never had a friend who wanted to share a bath with me. I played along in an amiable manner, discussing fashion, our favourite designer labels and our favourite stores to shop in London.

After drying myself off, I dressed and went back into the lounge to collect my payment. He offered me a glass of wine or something a little stronger. I quickly checked my watch… fifteen minutes until my cab was due to return for me…so I accepted. He handed me the wine and my payment and we indulged in small talk until Phebes joined us in a beautifully made, silk kimono. Feeling unusually out-spoken, I asked about the relationship between them. His reply was to say that they didn't regard what they did together to be an affair. They considered it a business arrangement that takes place once or twice a year. It sounded as if she would also be getting paid for her services and would be spending the whole night with him. I wondered how much that extra service was costing him.

Hearing a car approach the lodge, which would more than likely be my cab, I picked up my satchel and said goodbye to them. Sitting in the back of the cab, I gazed out of the window throughout my journey home, lost in my thoughts...shocked at what I'd just done, but not denying how much I enjoyed the experience. I climbed into bed forty five minutes later, fit to drop.

CHAPTER 40

*A*s I expected, the last envelope that I found in the greenhouse stayed there all weekend. I made the effort to get up early on both the Saturday and the Sunday mornings. Whether it was because I was either working or reading in the kitchen, I don't know, but Anthony went out both days without retrieving the envelope. I checked the greenhouse again just on the off chance that he stayed awake during the night to get the envelope whilst I was sleeping.

It was sometime during Tuesday, and when I was at work, that the envelope disappeared. Another date to enter in my secret log.

CHAPTER 41

As I walked down the street from the tube station, I made a brief stop to check in my mirror. I want to see if my make-up looks perfect before I announce my imminent arrival to David with a text message.

There was no need for me to knock on the door. He was there waiting already with it wide open. As I stepped over the threshold he gave me a hug and a kiss on each cheek. He looked amazing as ever and was wearing some gorgeous, seductive fragrance. His tanned face and arms, acquired during his recent business trip to Indonesia gave him a healthy glow.

"You look breathtakingly hot, darling," he greeted me.

I quivered with excitement at his compliment. He was like a drug to me - his every word a turn-on.

"Compliment back at you, David. I love the tan."

His eyes sparkled as he held me by the shoulders. He was taking in every inch of me. My mind raced ahead. I couldn't wait to take every inch of him into me. I know I shouldn't feel things for him, but I'm struggling to control it. I'd been battling with the feelings for some months and I feared how things would end. He was a client, after all.

"I've got champagne chilling. Sit down, Helen!"

I made myself at home, sandals off, legs curled up and comfy. I heard a bottle chink against glasses in the kitchen as he poured our first glass of the evening. a Bollinger Rosé.

"Bollinger Rosé." He announced, handing me a glass. "How are things? Are you still putting up with that abusive boyfriend of yours?"

I cringed, I had forgotten that David assumed that Anthony was only a partner and I never corrected him at the time. I flushed a little, I don't like being deceitful, particularly with David.

"David, don't worry about me, I can handle myself. He will get what's coming to him, sometime over the next few months I think, maybe sooner! He's going to wonder what's hit him, by the time I've finished." I assured him.

"I don't know what you're planning, but I'm sure he deserves it. Just stay safe, Helen. From what you've told me he can be dangerous and I worry for you."

He looked genuinely concerned. My heart melted at his warmth, I felt a rush of affection and I wanted to hug him and never let go.

"True – he can be nasty, but he can also be very naïve. He is totally in the dark, trust me. Shall I put some music on?"

He seemed to be deep in thought but managed to nod his assent.

"Bizet do?"

"What? Oh...yes, Bizet."

I inserted the CD and pressed play, wondering what he was thinking, wondered if he could read my mind. We lazed around listening to beautiful music for the rest of the evening and flirted silently with each other. It was all part of the game we played during our sessions, the anticipation being almost as enjoyable as the sex. We finished the bottle of Bollinger and started a second one.

It was late when we went up to bed. For some reason, David asked me to get ready for bed in the only other bedroom in the cottage to have an én suite. I wondered what on earth he was up to. Whatever the surprise he'd planned, I was more excited about the sex that would follow. Feeling the pleasant naughty tingling start within me, I dressed in my new underwear; a pair of white, high leg, lacy panties and white hold-up stockings. I picked up the matching bra and decided not to bother. David loved my pert little breasts so they would grab his attention immediately. I carried out a quick check of my make-up once again, before I crossed the landing to the master bedroom, excitement rippling through my body.

He was ready for me, totally naked, bottom on a towel and some equipment laid by his side; scissors, shaving foam and a battery razor. My face must have been a picture, eyes wide and mouth gaping in shock. He laid there smirking at me. I laughed out loud, totally bemused,

"David? What…the…hell…are…you…doing?" I could hardly get the words out for my laughter, "Is this…your new…perverted…idea of foreplay?"

He snorted with laughter.

"I want to make it more pleasant for you tonight. I recall you almost choked last time on one of my…you called it a… wait a minute….yes….you called it an…an obscenely coarse pube!" he carried on snorting, "Get rid of them for me. I can't have you choking on me, Helen. How would that look in an autopsy?"

I waited until our laughter calmed down before I dared to start work on his wonderful nether regions. Both my hands and his body were shaking with raucous laughter. I started with the scissors, carefully trimming back his wiry pubic hairs around the base of his cock and his nether regions. Putting his complete trust in me he relaxed, enjoying my touch; his stomach muscles tightened as I worked my way down. I couldn't keep my eyes of his cock as it expanded, but I didn't want to think about my temptation to climb on top of him and ride him. I kept on trimming until all his pubic hair was short enough. After squirting the shaving foam into my hand, I gently lathered the whole area and started with the razor until it was all clean shaven. I was amazed with the result His cock appeared longer. It looked fantastic, rock hard and hot as ever. David and I both enjoy oral but had to exercise some restraint for a little while longer as there were a few stray hairs to deal with.

I filled the bath for the pair of us to share, to wash away all traces of pubes and shaving foam. I found tea-lights and candles in the bathroom cupboard, lit them and placed them all around the edge of the bath. We took a glass of champagne each and sat in the bath indulging in some dirty and wildly erotic foreplay. Twenty minutes or so of wonderful fun passed and we both shivered, the water had lost its warmth. We headed for the bedroom, far too excited to bother about drying thoroughly. The anticipation had been wonderful but I felt taunted and tantalised enough. I wanted it for real.

Once he was lying down on the bed, I immediately sat astride his face, leant over him and took his cock into my mouth, my favourite sixty-nine. I let my tongue slide up and down every inch of his length and he moaned longingly for more. I fondled his scrotum at the same time, not for one second giving thought to anything other than pleasuring his cock in any way that I could. All the while his tongue tantalised inside me, twisting in all directions, his nose rubbing my clit as he strived to push his tongue further in. It was pure ecstacy. My mind was on him only. I was his toy for the night and I wanted to give him all my attention, sexual and otherwise. I felt hot, I wanted more and didn't want it to end. He pulled his tongue out every minute or so and poked me with his fingers while he captured some air before diving in again and each time he thrust his tongue in, it was more pleasurable than the last. I wasn't ready for it to finish too soon, so when I felt in danger of climaxing I changed position, moving my body down the bed with my pussy well away from his face. When I bent over the bottom of the bed I licked each of his testicles and he whimpered in delight. Wanting him to groan some more, I diverted my attention to his backside. I quickly flicked my tongue over it time and again and he moaned even louder. Sensing his impatience for things to move on, I sucked his cock again giving sharp little flicks with my tongue around its head.

"Come back up here, baby – I want to tongue fuck you," he whispered.

I was ready for it. I shuffled my backside around the side of the bed with my mouth not once losing contact with his cock. He raised my leg up in the air and over him, lifting his head eagerly to get his tongue in my pussy as I lowered myself onto his face. It felt so superb. I shuddered in delight, my enthusiasm for sucking his cock matched that of his explorations with his tongue. If his nose wasn't rubbing my clit, his hand was, it was all so intense! I could feel the onset of a climax. I wanted his cock inside me and needed it badly. I was damp with perspiration and shivering with excitement.

It seemed to me as if he was determined to make me wait for his cock. He stuck three fingers inside my warmth and his tongue flicked around my labia and clit. His bottom started thrusting upwards and forced his cock to the back of my throat. I sucked harder until I could feel his muscles twitch. His salty cum spurted into my mouth, salty and warm. I climaxed at the same time. It felt as if I would shudder forever as he continued to lick my vagina. A little of his semen dribbled down my chin and onto his stomach as we moved apart after five minutes or so, both satiated for the time being.

We snuggled up like two spoons and I enjoyed being able to lie next to a man and feel his arms around me. It was a terrifying thought to me, something I never intended to do again. But just once in a while it was nice to feel somebody's body warmth up close to me. Before I fell away into the grasp of sleep, I wondered if David was in a relationship with anybody. He never volunteered the information and I never dared to ask. I was scared of what his answer might be. The thought made me feel insanely jealous, and the memories of our oral sex and my orgasms faded away as sleep claimed me.

I woke up not knowing what time it was, but guessed I'd been asleep maybe a couple of hours. Glancing at the digital clock, I noticed it was around three o'clock. David's hand squeezed my left boob and I felt his stiffness between my thighs. I was instantly aroused. He pulled me over onto my back, kissed and licked my breasts for five minutes and then he was inside me, his cock needing no guidance, thrusting away hard and fast. He lifted my legs over his shoulders, thrusting even harder and his cock felt beautiful; fucking me hard and reaching my G-spot. His pubic bone ground into my clit and I came, again and again. When he shot his load this time, he stopped thrusting, his cock as far up my warmth as it could go and the feeling inside me when I felt each squirt with the pounding of every muscle in his cock blew me away.

I lay there and smiled to myself, (long after David started snoring) trying to recall every session we had and how he always made me feel. I loved being fucked by him and in so many different ways, and had done from our first encounter. He made me feel…and I couldn't explain where the thought suddenly popped up from, he made me feel like I should run. I didn't want my head and my heart to feel like this – like they were constantly at war.

Just before seven o'clock we were awake again, enjoying coffee and cuddles in bed. I was first to the bathroom for a shower and to brush my teeth. After I emerged from the bathroom, David went in, slapping my bottom playfully as we passed each other. Oral session number two commenced after that. An action replay of the previous evening's antics was well under way, our tongues and fingers, poking and probing each and every orifice. This time as I felt my shudders and tingling begin, I begged him,

"Cum inside me please, David. Cum inside, *please.*"

"Yes, baby. Quick then, hands and knees, its coming."

A quick scramble about by both of us and we were just in time, he ejaculated as his cock entered me, spurting his semen, which met my own juices. We cried out loud at the same time. For fifteen minutes we stayed in the same position, our heartbeats taking time to slow down, panting, sweating, and for five crazy minutes, I started to think that I never wanted to leave that room; I wanted to stay, locked in there, with David forever. I tried to convince myself that I'm not in love with him, not really, and that it was only because the sex gets better and better, the orgasms, *more* beautiful, and even more…*violent.* I truly love being fucked by this man. It was the fucking, not him that I was in love with, it had to be!

After we finished in the bathroom, I got dressed and was almost ready to leave. David was lounging around downstairs in his bathrobe as I was upstairs putting the finishing touches to my make-up.

"Come down here, babe, I have something for you."

Before I was even half way down the stairs he held a little gift bag up in the air to show me. I was astounded! I never once received a gift from a client. I never expected to, they paid me, in cash!

"What's that? What are you buying me a gift for? You don't need to do that, David," I scolded.

"I know I don't, but you are one very special lady and I couldn't resist. Now open it!"

My hands trembled as I removed a gift-wrapped box from the bag, wondering what the hell he was up to. He didn't need to be giving me a gift of any kind. Removing the paper and the ribbon from what was obviously an item of jewellery, a thought crept into my mind,

Perhaps I should pay David for the pleasure he gave to me, instead of the other way around.

Opening the box, I was almost blinded by the dazzle a rather large, diamond pendant sat on the black velvet lining. It was exquisite. My mouth gaped, not knowing what to say next.

"Do you like it, babes? What's the matter? You're not saying anything!"

I didn't know what to say; I was unable to voice my thoughts. Thoughts I didn't want or need. Suddenly, the words spewed out. I couldn't stop myself.

"David, can I ask you something, please? No…that's stupid…I'm being…a bit presumptuous…you're not…you're not in love with me by any chance, are you? No! Of course you're not…how silly of me…to suggest such a thing. Please, tell me you're not!"

He chuckled, but I recognised the gulp of a nervous swallowing on his part.

"Sweetheart, I couldn't possibly let myself fall for you. I couldn't. I know what you do…go with…other men. It's just a gift…for a beautiful lady, and you are very special to me, special moments. I care for you, Helen…but I'm not in love with you."

I felt an icy hand of disappointment snatch at my heart, but I let it pass. It was on the tip of my tongue to say that if I did love him and if he loved me, I would give it all up for him. But I didn't! I don't really love him. We just had, like he said, special moments together.

Don't go confusing this with love, you idiot!

His denial sounded convincing enough. He handed me the envelope with my payment but I waved it away,

"I can't do it, David. I can't take money off you. You've bought me a beautiful gift and I've had excellent fun. Let's leave it at that. I can't take money off you again."

"Accept the gift for what it is, babe…a treat for a special lady. I haven't got anyone else to spend my money on, apart from my two girls. I can afford it. Take the money as well, it was a business transaction, after all. You deserve it all. Now go! It's not up for discussion. I will be back again in a couple of months. I'll ring you and I'll look forward to it."

I gathered up my belongings, we had a hug, pecked each other on the cheek and I was out of there. Missing him already!

CHAPTER 42

S imon called me on Wednesday night. He passed my name and number to another client of his. The man was in one of the F1 Constructors teams, involved in the design of the cars. When he called me, he asked first if I would be willing to collect him and take him to my house for our business transaction. With having the rather large problem of Anthony living under the same roof and not knowing where *he* was planning to be, I told the client that my house was out of the question. The next option he offered was for me to travel to his house. He rented a country cottage near Silverstone. It would be a fair drive for me, but as it was well out of reach to anyone who knows me, I thought it shouldn't pose too much of a problem. Simon, as usual, had vouched for him.

"He's a great guy. You'll like him, Helen."

I had my reservations but as always, I would make my own judgement after our first meeting.

I arrived at 11am the following Saturday morning as instructed. Even though I planned to arrive ten minutes earlier, my sat-nav had its limitations and I ended up first of all at a farm that was one mile beyond the programmed destination. I quickly turned around in the farmyard and drove away, before someone came out to enquire if I was lost.

My new client wasn't exactly what you would call rude but he was not particularly friendly or welcoming either. He pointed to where I could go to get ready and suggested we get started as soon as possible. Apparently, he had somewhere else he needed to be by 4pm and a car was coming to collect him at 3pm. During our call I asked him if there was anything specific he wanted me to bring and he told me that he was into 'uniforms of some description,' but wasn't too bothered what I chose. Other than kinky underwear, school uniform, a maid's outfit (from work) and a nurse's attire, I didn't own much else. I decided to visit a fancy dress shop the previous day and purchased, especially for this date, a policewoman's uniform.

In the tiny little bedroom he took me to, I stripped off and dressed in a black suspender belt, black seamed stockings and black bra. I purposely took my panties off. The uniform once on, completed the 'role play'. I dashed into the bathroom to check my make-up and went in search of the guy, not knowing where he wanted me, but thinking it would be the master bedroom or the lounge. I found him in the kitchen. He was stood near the sink swallowing some tablets. He spun around when I entered the room and for some reason, I thought I saw a look of anger flash across his face...which disappeared just as quick.

He moved one of the chairs away from the kitchen table and pushed me backwards until I was sort of sitting on the edge of it. He tugged the front of my white shirt, ripping the buttonholes and a couple of buttons scattered across the floor. With the front now gaping open, he yanked my bra upwards and exposed my breasts. Not wasting any time, his teeth bit into my left nipple, his hands dragged the skirt up my thighs, feeling first for the suspender belt, stocking tops and yanked hard at my pubic hair. My heart raced and I could feel an overwhelming sense of dread. Using his body, he pinned me in position at the table, his hand left my pussy and I heard the tell-tale sound of the unzipping of denims. My head started to play games. Terrified, but at the same time I felt hot and yearned some vulgar sex. It had been over a week and I wanted to be fucked; bad, dirty fucking, fucking that would satisfy me…and hurt. He poked the tip of his cock between the suspender elastic and my thighs, rubbed it through my pubic hair and roughly shoved it inside me.

"Fuck it! Come on! Let me see if you can fuck me good. I need it."

My wanton desires got the better of me and I put my terror to the back of my mind. It turned me on, talking to him like that…telling him to fuck me good. I held my breath in anticipation.

"Suspenders and stockings, nice choice, Helen! They make me feel like indulging in pure filth," he snarled in my ear,

"And I *am* going to indulge in filth. I'm going to fuck you. And I'm going to hurt you as much as you've hurt me."

I enjoyed the first orgasm as he rubbed his cock over my clit; I shuddered in pleasure, as much from his dirty talk as well as the friction he applied to my clit.

My mind drifted from my vulgar thoughts for a few seconds to wonder who hurt him…who he wanted to punish…after all, it wasn't me who hurt him. I was jolted back to reality again as he pushed me back over onto the table. He fucked me rough and hard, grinding his pubic area hard into mine, the edge of the table cutting into my buttocks. I released more cum, the excitement and fear combined bringing it about. I lost track of time. Mixed up emotions swirled through me. I found myself hating this guy, yet I wanted more. His fingernails dug hard into my thighs and then my breasts, especially the nipples. He thrust his cock hard into me as far as he could go (it felt like he was trying to get his testicles in as well). My stomach began to hurt, in fact, I hurt all over. I cried out in pain and he punched me in the eye. His hands went to my throat and squeezed in a threatening manner as he growled,

"Is it hurting to be fucked like this? I hope so, because I want to hear you cry out. I *want* to hurt you, you're filth. I want to hurt your fucking pussy, and I'm going to hurt more than your pussy, you're going to experience what pain is all about."

He was relentless. He carried on squeezing my throat with one hand whilst with his free hand he slapped me across the face half a dozen times. Fear took over again. I didn't want to cum anymore. The sexual excitement had passed and all I wanted to do was go home. He bit hard into my bottom lip and the fleshy part of my boobs. I prayed that this was going to be the extent of the pain. This guy could fuck, yet he was better at hurting. After what seemed an age, he was nowhere near to coming and I was sore, my wounds on fire. I was finding his behaviour increasingly intimidating.

Without any warning, he pulled out of me and rolled me over so that I was bent over the table face down. He pushed my head down towards the table, his cock found its way into my back passage, and just as he promised he would, he hurt me like hell. I screamed out in my desperation, several times…which made him thrust still harder. He yanked at my hair at the same time, pulling it hard and hurting my scalp. After what seemed like forever, he pulled his throbbing cock from my anus, and flung me onto the tiled floor,

"Hands and knees, filth!"

Hurrying to the floor I obeyed, lest I should get a fist in my other eye. I expected him to stuff his cock up my arse again, but surprisingly, he started to fuck my pussy once more, and already sore from his previous battering of it, I felt like it was on fire as he fucked harder, and harder still. I finally felt that dead give-away, the throbbing of a cock about to explode and I heaved a sigh of relief. He pulled out of me, Hauled me over onto my back and cock in hand, ejaculated all over me; my hair, my face, my breasts, stomach, and pubic region. It was over. I held my breath in disbelief, but still scared that he had more to inflict on me.

"You asked for that, so don't start fucking complaining," he said as he watched me stand at the kitchen sink, dabbing at my face and eye, with cold water, "...and you're getting well paid for it."

I was mortified. I couldn't understand what it was he implied.

"I don't recall asking for anything that you've put me through. How did I ask for it?" I challenged him, acting far more confrontational than I felt. "You are the one who asked me to come here!"

"You're the one who chose to dress as a fucking police-woman! I never told you to do that!"

I was bewildered, near to tears and hurting everywhere. Somehow I messed up, but I carried on fighting my corner and started to be alarmed at my own cockiness, but I couldn't stop myself. I was seething at the way the meeting turned out.

"You said any uniform, you weren't too bothered! I wasn't to know ...what that would make you do to me!"

I indicated my face and the eye that I patted gently with the towel.

"Well, the bitch caught me drink driving. She lost me my fucking licence for two years! I need my licence for work.

She made it difficult for me! The shower is through there…" he dismissed me, pointing to the bathroom door, "…and your money's there." He indicated a white envelope on the kitchen worktop, "Next time, don't come as a cop, and you won't get hurt."

"THERE WON'T FUCKING BE ANY NEXT TIME, YOU ARSEHOLE!!"

I hurled at him before slamming the back door with a tremendous bang.

I couldn't go in to work the next week. The skin around my eye was black, the white of my eye was bloodshot, cheeks, breasts and thighs were badly bruised. I was also bleeding down below and my back was hurting from being thrown onto the hard tiled floor. I'd taken a beating or two prior to this one, but this guy won hands down, the prize for causing me the most pain. I called Simon and told him exactly what the guy had put me through and that I didn't want to meet with him again.

"You'll love him, Helen!" With my best whining tone, I mimicked his voice. "FUCKING TWAT!"

"Yes! I agree, Helen."

"BOTH OF YOU, I MEAN!!" I bellowed at him.

He promised me faithfully that he would deal with it. On Wednesday, I received a call from Frigid Flo at the hotel, telling me to be back at work the following Monday, or I would be receiving a P45.

CHAPTER 43

*M*y Monday shift ended, I was still in the changing room removing my uniform when my mobile started to ring. I recognised the phone number immediately; the estate agents. I was half expecting it. They spoke to me two days previously, the Friday, to tell me that they received an offer on my parents' house at last. The offer was quite a few thousand below the asking price but they advised me to wait a little longer. Apparently, there was another couple very interested who needed to speak with their mortgage advisor before making their first offer.

I felt cold. Since the call of two days ago, my O.C.D. had been bad. On Saturday I emptied the kitchen cupboards, cleaned them all out and put everything back. Two hours later, I repeated the whole process. Anthony never went out that day, nor had he spoken to me, but every time he came into the kitchen, I could feel his eyes burn into my back and almost visualise the expression he would have on his face. He thought I was losing it.

Telling him that I was going out with the girls from the

Hopkins Partnership, I left the house at six thirty and returned around midnight. In truth, I visited a client in his Belgravia apartment. It hadn't been a particularly pleasant experience, and it niggled me even more when I arrived home to find that Anthony was not only *still* at home, but he hadn't gone to bed. I couldn't help being nasty to him, telling him it wouldn't be long before I would be gone from the house for good. I didn't hang around downstairs too long. I thought it would be more sensible to go to bed instead of causing yet another fracas.

The estate agent's words kept coming back to me before I finally dozed off and I was saddened at the thought of my parents' house being occupied by strangers. A crazy idea suddenly occurred to me; I would go and live in my parents' house. It was mine now anyway. Anthony could keep our house. This way, I would sign our house over to him. I would also make sure he had no claim on what had been, and still is my *real* home.

When I woke up on Sunday morning, I realised that my plan would be impossible. I know I couldn't return to my Mum and Dad's house. I had learned to better cope with my grief since getting to know Thomas. To return to what had once been my home, would have a detrimental effect on me and my ever present, O.C.D.

I finally answered the ringing to be told that the first people had upped their offer to the asking price. A cash buyer and they wanted the sale to go through as quickly as possible. I told the agent to accept the offer and instruct my solicitor.

I kept it from Anthony. I didn't see the need to tell him. He didn't know about the villa in Marbella or the Paris apartment that Dad purchased in my name while I was in my teens. It was only after my father's death that their solicitor informed me that I am already owner of the title deeds for both the villa and apartment. I'd been puzzled at the time as to why Anthony, long trusted by my father, was never made privy to that little snippet of information.

CHAPTER 44

*T*he phone call from David came as a big surprise. It was only three weeks since our last date, so I certainly wasn't expecting to hear from him for at least another five weeks. He wasn't in a rush to get off the phone, so we chatted for twenty minutes or so. It was lovely to hear his voice. I tried to picture him as we spoke, but in my mind he wasn't in his car, or at his desk, he was reclining on his bed in his mews cottage in St John's Wood. I enjoyed that thought and let my heart race. If only.

He was overjoyed. His daughter, Catherine, had been accepted at the University she wanted. She excelled with her 'A' Levels and achieved much better grades than was been required. She hoped to become a Forensic scientist and I could hear the pride in his voice as he spoke of her. The pride quickly changed to concern though. His ex-wife recently caught their other daughter, fifteen year old Ruby in bed with a young man, also fifteen and in the same school year. She was, apparently, going through a very rebellious stage and it sounded as if Heidi was finding her quite a handful. He was upset and concerned about the risks she was taking; S.T.D.s, unwanted pregnancy and his biggest concern, drugs. I did my best to bolster his mood for the remainder of our call but I couldn't help but think that despite managing to elicit a few laughs from him, he sounded so down.

Maybe after his jetlag wore off and he'd been to visit his girls he would be feeling much better about things before our next date at the weekend. Even though I listened carefully, hanging onto his every word, I managed to control my excitement.

Before we started chatting about our news he had asked me for my company again. It was a real bonus this time. We were actually going to spend almost the whole weekend together...'a special weekend' he'd added. From Saturday morning at ten o'clock until late Sunday night at his cottage. It would feel like two full days. I'd never felt the rush of excitement that coursed through my body. The thought was...positively orgasmic!

A mini spending spree was called for. I wanted to look stunning for my favourite client. I needed something sophisticated so I could dress for dinner, which was going to be delivered by caterers. I wanted new undies, shoes, a silk robe...and I needed to find a gift for him. I considered getting a new perfume too, but I remembered how he always loved still smelling my perfume on his clothes for a few days after our dates, so I decided to stick with what David liked.

I took three days holiday from the hotel and went shopping in Knightsbridge. I made the search for a gift for him my number one priority, after all I had plenty of clothes to choose from at home if I couldn't find exactly what I had in mind. From my little knowledge of him, he seemed to have everything he wanted. I didn't have a clue what I could buy for him. At least, I hadn't...until I stopped to look at men's watches in a jeweller's shop window. My eyes were drawn to a watch with a beautiful face, and for some reason, I found I couldn't take my eyes off that watch face. I was seeing David's face, and his beauty. After staring for some time I snapped out of my reverie, entered the shop, and asked if the watch could be engraved with a few words on the back. I was assured it wouldn't be a problem and I would be able to collect it the next day, Friday, so I paid and went off to get the rest of my things. I was thrilled about the watch and I hoped that David would be as delighted to receive it as I was to give it. I expected, of course, to be severely reprimanded.

The clothes somehow didn't seem important anymore after I'd bought the watch. I had lots of gorgeous clothes anyway and many that David hadn't seen before. I did buy some gorgeous new undies though and a sexy but classy, silk robe, as opposed to sexy and tarty. I booked an appointment for a manicure and French polish, and at the same salon I decided on a facial. When I arrived home, there was lots to do, and my first task was to select my clothes carefully. I wanted smart clothes to arrive in and clothes to leave in. Bloody Hell, I hadn't even got there yet and already I was choosing an outfit for when I would be leaving! I was getting myself organised, but I had to put the thought about leaving him out of my mind...I didn't want to dwell on it!

Armani blue jeans, a pair of diamante mules on a wedge I found in Harrods and an expensive, plain white cotton shirt, worn open over an equally expensive vest top. I tried on my choices and reasonably happy, decided that this was the arrival outfit; simple, stunning and classy. The little black dress collection was next and I um-ed and ah-ed for ten minutes, before opting for a little jade number, not too low-cut or too short; on the knee and with a pair of jade sandals. I already decided that I would wear David's diamond pendant as my jewellery; my 'special lady' gift. Three or four different searches that night and my wardrobes did not have anything to offer, in the way of a leaving outfit. I always considered myself very fortunate to have such a selection of beautiful clothes, so why then, could I not see anything appropriate? The answer came to me in an instant. I couldn't face choosing a leaving outfit simply because I didn't want to think about the leaving part.

The ringing of my mobile woke me at seven o'clock on the Friday morning. It was a regular client of mine, calling to see if I was available that same night. It was totally out of the question. I didn't want to have sex with anyone the evening before my weekend with David. I told him that I was spending the whole weekend with another client. I got the impression that he was not too happy about it. He was due to fly out to Frankfurt again first thing Monday morning so there would be no further opportunities for sex with me on this visit.

"If you can call me two days in advance next time you are in the country," I told him "I will make sure your needs are my priority." It seemed as if I managed to pacify him, although I imagined he would seek alternative female company during his travels rather than wait until a next appointment with me.

"Okay. You can't offer fairer than that, thanks." Before he ended the call, he gave a much friendlier, "Goodbye, my dear."

David's watch was ready on time as promised by the jeweller. The engraving of my little message was exceptional and I was confident that he would be touched by my gesture. Cross with me, yes, but secretly very pleased. I had one more appointment before returning home; a quick visit to my dentist for a scale and polish, two months ahead of time. Everything had to be perfect. I soaked for over an hour in the bath, painted my toe nails, and then I carefully moisturised every square inch of my body with a product that contained a very light tanning agent. Since my morning coffee, I detoxed the rest of the day; I wanted to feel good as much as I wanted to look good. The last part of the day's feel good treatments was to apply my night creams, one for the eyes, and one for the rest of my face. An early night after that. I needed my beauty sleep.

By nine o'clock next morning I was ready. I quickly laid my hands on a leaving outfit that would fit the bill, but I was still unwilling to entertain that part. I applied my make-up with the utmost attention to detail; the natural look, no eye shadow, just the right amount of mascara, a hint of foundation in a moisturiser and subtle lipstick and blusher. I was happy with the result; natural looking, instead of being too painted. I called for a cab as I didn't want to risk travelling the underground system with the contents of my handbag and travel case being valuable. My bedroom door was locked so that Anthony wouldn't be able to go nosing about. He was at home when the cab arrived for me but I didn't feel the need to offer any information.

CHAPTER 45

*W*hat a welcome I received when he opened the door. He looked me up and down, stunned into silence for a few seconds. He took me in his arms for the biggest of hugs and we kissed the air beside each other's cheeks. Pushing my hair behind my right ear he whispered,

"I need you, Helen. Now!"

I was relieved to hear this as I wanted him badly. I'd been thinking about sex with him from the minute I opened my eyes, yet I was a little surprised it would be happening this soon.

"What? No champagne chilling, David? You're sacked. I need my champers to put me in the mood."

"You're a liar, Helen! When have you ever needed champers?" I couldn't help but giggle.

He grabbed my hand and led me upstairs to the bedroom before stating once more,

"You need to stop with the fibbing, Helen. It's not quite chilled enough anyway and I didn't plan on wanting you this soon. You just look so…ravishing. We don't need the champers anyway."

Once in the bedroom, he sat me on the edge of the bed and, not letting go of my hand, he sat down with me, looking into my eyes as he did so. Returning his gaze, I wondered why he looked so serious. I also noticed how tired he looked around his eyes.

"You look *exhausted*, David. Are you sleeping properly?"

He was fast to fob me off.

"A bit of jetlag, babe, too much flying in too few days. I'll be okay."

We sat there for ages. For somebody who said he wanted me badly he was wasting valuable time. He rubbed my hand between both of his and continued to look into my eyes, maybe trying to read me. The air was full of tension. I could see a question coming but he was being pretty hesitant about it. I leaned my head on his shoulder in the hope it would give him the prompt…and it worked.

"Babe, I want to ask if you will do something different for me this weekend. I pray it won't be a problem for you. It's something I really want."

I was shocked. He never seemed like a client with perverted needs. I was suddenly wary, not wanting to commit myself before hearing what it was he wanted. Maybe *that's* why he gave me the diamond necklace first, payment up front for something a bit different?

"Tell." I ordered.

"Babe, what I want you to do is…please will you let me kiss you? I understand if you…"

I cut him off mid-sentence and planted my lips firmly on his, kissing him tenderly. His eyes opened wide, his turn to be shocked for a few seconds, then he kissed me back. Our bodies were shaking, a little nervous with each other, finding ourselves outside the confines of what was our normal comfort zone.

We took it slowly and gently, enjoying a new and beautiful experience, (stone cold sober this time), teasing each other every now and again, our tongues doing nothing more than tasting each other's lips. Eventually, we leaned back onto the bed and I felt his hand unfasten my denims. He moved on by undoing the buttons of my shirt and slipping it off my shoulders. Following his lead I unfastened his denims and placed my hands up his tee-shirt and stroked his chest. We carried on undressing each other slowly, our mouths seldom losing contact. I stroked his hair, his cheeks, I nibbled his ear lobes and it was beautiful to be touching him and him touching me in return. We explored each other at our leisure, every square inch and I hardly dared to breathe in case I woke up to find it was a dream. Making new discoveries about each other was exhilarating; our ticklish parts, our sensitive parts, and for the first time the sensitive parts were *not* our sexual organs; not my breasts or vagina, not his penis, not bottoms! The sensitive parts were behind the knees, the backs of arms, our feet and our necks. This was sensual, loving foreplay, not sexual, animal needs.

As was inevitable, our explorations became urgent. Our hands started to wander to the tops of thighs, edging closer each minute towards ultimate excitement. Our mouths parted, tongues probed as our desire increased. Each move still gentle yet we could sense each other's wanting…wanting more, wanting that fusion of when two become one, when we couldn't possibly get any closer than we already were.

The moment arrived at last and as he entered me, we both moaned in ecstasy. He kissed me, gazed into my eyes and for the first time I saw love in his eyes. I wished and hoped that he could read me; see through my eyes into my mind and instantly know that I loved him too. His thrusting was gentle and I pushed myself upwards to meet the moves, to show him my eagerness, my willingness to take part, to get ever closer to him. I cried with emotion, taken aback at the direction our relationship was taking, and suddenly that fear was back. I felt as if it was all a dream and was frightened to believe in him. We continued our movements, my hands on his buttocks, stroking and then pulling his bottom towards me. I helped each gentle thrust until it became faster and deeper.

"Are you ready for me, babe?"

I knew in that instant that I would always be ready for him, my heart ached for him.

"Always!"

We climaxed together a few minutes later and we both cried out in ecstasy at the intensity. An intensity that was not born of sexual gratification, it was a deep emotional intensity from a coupling that for the first time, was about passion… and making love. I was unwilling to move afterwards, to break the connection. I lay there in his arms and let the tears fall. My head was on his chest, and he stroked my hair, his breathing finally started to slow down.

"Babe, why is my chest wet?"

"I…um…that was…emotional!" was all I could manage to say.

He laughed and tilted my chin so as to look directly into my eyes and I was surprised to see his cheeks were also wet with tears. Before long the bed almost seemed to vibrate as we laughed. For me it was a reaction of happiness, a relief; that we both felt our relationship changed… into something more deep and meaningful. Yet words of love had not been uttered from either of us.

It was two in the afternoon when we finally made our move from the bedroom. We showered together in the wet room, embraced and kissed as we sponged each other's bodies. No ulterior motive, no sexual innuendo; just a mutual desire to do things together and enjoy each other's company. We dried each other with the fluffy towels, then after donning our bathrobes we made sandwiches and coffee together in the kitchen. Once we'd taken our snack through to the coffee table in the lounge, we sat and indulged in some surprisingly normal conversation at last; maybe an unconscious effort to try to bring things back down to earth and to skirt around the subject of what had taken place earlier.

"Tell me what you've been up to since I saw you last." I wanted to know. "Where have you been on business? How are things with your daughters?"

He pulled a face, shrugging off my questions.

"No. I don't want to talk about me and my life. It's been business as usual. What have you been up to?"

I also screwed up my face. I didn't want to talk about my husband, or my cleaning work, or…anything.

"I have been busy preparing myself for you, David. Beauty treatments, shopping for the right clothes for this weekend, I hope you like them, by the way. And…I've been shopping. I bought a present for you. But I will give it to you tomorrow… before I go home."

"You didn't…you shouldn't have…I…"

"Neither should you." I cut in, "My present is for a very special man. You! Tit for tat, getting even, doing something similar in return, you do it, I do it…."

"Okay, okay, I get the message. Shut up. Now!" and to make sure I did, he kissed me hard on the lips for a minute, "But you didn't need to, babe."

"You shut up." and I kissed him back, to shut *him* up.

We started laughing again, raucous snorting laughter, picked up cushions and started a very juvenile cushion fight, jumping over the back of the settees and chairs, chasing each other around the room, laughing uncontrollably. It was a long time ago that I'd had this much fun and I loved every minute of it. I could tell that David was enjoying himself as well. We ended up flopping down on the settee together, out of breath, our laughter dying down but for the odd giggle here and there.

"I'll put the T.V. on and find us a film to watch. *If* I can find one at this time on a Saturday afternoon, that is."

"Sure, sounds great to me."

He flicked back and forth through the channels and settled on one film, an old war movie, for a few minutes. Without me saying one word he realised he should look for something that was more light-hearted so he flicked through again until he found an old *rom-com*. I grabbed the bottle of champagne that David put to chill much earlier poured us each a glass. We snuggled up and watched the film. Every now and again he would turn towards me and plant a kiss on my cheek or forehead, or my lips and it struck me that things seemed normal, couple thing, and normal felt good to me.

Towards the last half hour of the film I heard David's breathing get much deeper and a little nasal, familiar sounds of someone who just started to doze off. I didn't bother to disturb him. I could see that his jet-lag had kicked in and he looked peaceful so I watched the remainder of the film by myself. I hadn't watched a film in ages and thoroughly enjoyed it. For once I felt happy...everything was looking positive.

When the film finished I carefully tried to extract myself from his arms without waking him. He stirred for a minute or so, shifted position slightly and within minutes was snoring softly again. I busied myself in his kitchen for a while, washing the few plates and knives from our sandwich making. When I went back to the lounge I poured myself another glass of champagne and sat down in one of the armchairs to gaze in wonder at my lovely man as he slept.

I pulled back to reality and reminded myself… I didn't know if he actually *was* my man.

I watched him sleep until after six o'clock, when it suddenly occurred to me that dinner was being delivered at some point, courtesy of a local firm of caterers but I couldn't recall whether David mentioned a time. I knelt down on the floor next to the sofa and pressed gently on his arm,

"David?"

Oh hell. He was so sound asleep, I hated having to do it but was reluctant to let a meal go to waste. However, we both needed to eat, so I shook his arm this time,

"David? Wake up, sweetheart." I whispered.

His eyes opened and he was a little disorientated and surprised to see me there. I stroked his arm gently and kissed the top of his nose.

"Oh. What…?" He was evidently confused.

"What time is the meal being delivered, David?"

"What? Meal? Oh...seven thirty…I think."

"Okay. I'm going to go and get ready then. I'm dressing for dinner; formal. Take your time."

I made a pot of coffee and left it on the coffee table for him as he struggled to get his eyes fully open. I went to the bathroom for a freshen-up. Fifteen minutes later I'd nearly finished applying my make-up when I heard him come up the stairs. I shouted to ask if he would mind getting ready in one of the other bedrooms.

"Yes, no problem, babe," he answered, sounding more alert. "I take it you want to surprise me then? Good! I love surprises."

"Go downstairs when you are ready and I will make my grand entrance, I hope you like it." I shouted back.

"One hundred percent guaranteed."

I felt like a teenager, going out on my first ever date and could hardly contain my excitement. I smiled to myself.

Looking in the mirror, I was thrilled with my reflection as it smiled back at me. The dress looked stunning, the diamond pendant sparkled and there was a glow to my face that was nothing at all to do with the blusher. I heard David go downstairs just a few minutes before I finished. Time to go. I started feeling rather nervous again as I made my way down the stairs where he waited at the bottom, his back to me and his hands held over his eyes.

"Can I look yet?"

When I reached the bottom step I paused, took a deep breath and said he could look. He turned around, took my hand, and in that superb old-fashioned manner of yesteryear, kissed the back of it.

"Your ladyship, forgive me, but you are looking extremely stunning this evening. The dress brings out the colour in your eyes and the overall result is breathtakingly beautiful."

My heart raced at his compliments and I flushed in delight. It felt like no-one else existed in the world but the two of us.

"Thank you for the compliment, kind Sir." I acknowledged "And if I may return the compliment, Sir is looking handsome and... fit as fuck!" We giggled as he led me through to the lounge.

"Would your Ladyship care to partake of a small libation, perhaps a nice glass of jolly old Bollinger?" he carried on in his mock, poshest voice.

"Yes, she bloody would." I laughed.

He sat down opposite me.

"Because I want to sit and stare at you." he explained.

I was more than delighted to sit and stare at him too, he looked... total perfection. He was wearing one of his business suits, charcoal grey and well-tailored along with an expensive looking shirt. He even wore a black evening tie. I hadn't seen him dressed in this way before. He was usually attired in smart casual, a bathrobe or completely naked when we had our dates.

The caterers were prompt, knocking on the door at precisely 7.30pm. I was impressed with the service, they laid the table, served up the starters and went on to serve each course in turn. Everything was cleared away and the dishwasher loaded ready for when we finished dining. They discreetly stayed out of the way in the kitchen whilst we ate each exquisite course.

Before we tucked into our starter, he surprised me by asking,

"Babe, will you stay with me until Monday morning?"

He explained that his flight would be leaving Heathrow at five past three in the afternoon and that an appointment originally in his diary for nine o'clock had been cancelled, leaving him free for the morning.

"Of course, I would love to. There's my shift at the hotel, but I'll call in sick. I've never done it before but it won't matter, it's not as if I have a bad attendance record."

The presentation of all three courses was faultless. For a small local catering company, the chef was excellent and the food was better than some meals I have been served up in a few top class restaurants over the years. I didn't know what each dish was called, but there was very little left on my plate. David's appetite was not as good as mine but again, I think it was all down to his body clock being out of sync. After the caterers left we still sat at the dining table, working our way down the second bottle of wine.

"Can I still give you your present tomorrow, David, or does that have to wait until Monday now?"

"No, babe. It has to be Monday. I have another present for you as well…but don't start protesting, please." he added, just as I opened my mouth to do so.

We sat in silence for a few moments longer before he

took my hand, led me from the dining table, switched off the dining room light and headed up the stairs.

We made love for the second time since my arrival. I noticed the difference with our oral sex too this time. It was all part of our love-making session, carried out with passion, tenderness, exploration, and pure joy. There was no urgency to climax, at least not at the start, though our actions left us breathless. When I sensed that he was ready to enter me, I urged him to sit on the floor, with his back resting against the bed. I sat astride him and he was inside me, already moaning with need. He was tired so I told him to him to leave it to me. I rode him, my inner muscles gripped around his cock, gently at first, then more tightly. I was ready to take his cum and feel my release explode from me too. It was our shortest session yet.

I slept well, other than waking briefly in the early hours and glancing across towards David who was laid on his back. I just managed to make out by his silhouette that his eyes were open and looking up towards the ceiling. I hoped he would soon get back into his normal sleep pattern as I didn't like seeing him look so exhausted. I asked him to turn over so I could cuddle up close to him until he was fast asleep.

He made us breakfast on the Sunday morning and brought it upstairs to bed. He'd been busy and even popped out to buy Sunday newspapers. It was a novelty for me. I'm not really a breakfast person but to have it brought up to bed, along with the papers, yes I could cope with that, with David by my side at least. He removed his clothing before getting back into bed with me. Thankfully, it was a light breakfast; fruit juice, some cereal, croissants, some toast with a variety of conserves and freshly ground coffee. We ate and drank our coffee in silence as we scanned the main news articles in the papers after which we shifted those off the bed and cuddled up together,

"What would you like to do today, sweetie?" I asked him.

"I'll leave it up to you, Helen. I'm not too bothered. I want to enjoy every precious second with you."

I couldn't believe I was hearing those words from David, a client. Words I loved hearing, though they filled me with fear. Again, I started to think about Monday morning, about saying our goodbyes. I turned my face away from him as my eyes glazed over with tears and I felt overwhelmed with sadness. We never left the house for most of Sunday, making love once in the morning and again in the afternoon. We listened to music much of the time, played two games of chess... and talked.

David decided on a drive into the country that evening to find a quiet pub where nobody would be likely to recognise us. We were hungry, not having eaten since our breakfast in bed. Fortunately, there were only one or two locals in the pub we found. We ordered two chicken salads and within an hour and a half and hunger satisfied, we heading back. I didn't feel like talking on the journey back and he kept asking if I was okay. I wanted to open up and tell him I didn't want to leave him the next day, but he didn't seem to have a lot to say either so I thought it best not to mention it. He still looked very tired. I hoped he would get a good night's sleep before his week's agenda.

"Early night for us, sweetie. Let's make love first and then you must get plenty of sleep." I told him.

"That suits me."

Not bothering with the usual wine or champers we headed straight upstairs to bed. We lay there doing nothing except kiss for half an hour until we both started to explore with our hands. I couldn't wait to make love one more time but for some reason, no matter how much I fondled, and tried to coax his penis along, it did not want to play. He said he wanted me badly but after ten minutes or so it was clear to us both that a hard-on was not going to happen any time soon. He started to get angry with himself and his cock,

"Babe, I want you so much and this fucking thing is not bloody having it. I'm sorry."

Disappointed, but more concerned about his fatigue, I tried to pacify him.

"It's not a problem, David. You're too tired. We can leave it until morning."

Neither of us slept well. I was busy fretting about parting the next morning, not knowing when I would see him again. I lay there staring into space and faced the window all night. David was restless and tossed and turned constantly. I think I finally gave in to sleep around four o'clock and when I woke again it was ten past six. David was asleep, but as I didn't know how long it was since he dropped off, I carefully climbed out of bed so as not to wake him.

I got things ready for breakfast, putting David's present next to his plate. I was looking forward to seeing his face when he saw the watch and when he heard what I wanted to say to him. Sitting in the lounge in silence, going over time and again what I already rehearsed in my head, I heard footsteps padding across the bedroom floor and then on the stairs.

"Helen. Where did you go? What are you doing down here? I missed you."

"Come and sit down. Let's go in the dining room, breakfast can be ready in five minutes. I want to give you your present."

I was excited. David however, looked a little preoccupied.

"I need to talk to you, Helen."

"I need to talk to you, too."

I grabbed his hand and dragged him through the dining room, plonked him on the chair in front of the present and urged him,

"Go on, open it."

"Babe…"

"Just open it, David."

I watched on as with shaking hands, he started to peel off the wrapping paper.

"I…oh, hell, babe. You…shouldn't..."

His eyes registered the shock as he stared at the watch. He handled it tentatively and looked at it in disbelief.

"Turn it over. See the engraving on the back."

"Oh, my god! It's truly…beautiful. Thank you, Helen."

Tears began to form in his eyes as he read the tiny words.
♥♥ Came together! All my love, Helen xx

"Two hearts…came together. I like the sexual innuendo that you cleverly worked in." he chuckled "It's beautiful, Helen. I won't ask how much..."

I was puzzled, he'd chuckled, smiled and been emotional when he had seen the engraving, but now he looked serious. I felt an uneasiness in my stomach that I couldn't explain and alarm bells started to ring in my head.

"No. Don't."

"I will go and get my present to you. Then we must talk." he made his way to the sideboard in the lounge.

He came back with an identical gift bag to the one he handed me those few weeks back. I opened it slowly, savouring each second of excitement. He watched me with eyes that were glazed over, doing his best to hold back tears. I began to realize that amongst everything else that it was, he was also not afraid to show his emotions. This time his gift was a diamond bracelet that matched the pendant I already had - eight diamonds, smaller than that of the pendant, but no less beautiful. I was stunned.

"Here, let me."

His hands fiddled shakily with the clasp for a moment or

two until my right wrist displayed the new bracelet. Without a word of warning he dropped his bombshell.

"Babe…Helen…this is the last time we can see each other. I can't…"

The very words I dreaded. My gut feeling was right. I felt physically sick…devastated as my world started to crumble.

"What? But I thought…?"

"That…I loved you? Yes. I do. Believe me, I do."

"Then why? I love you. I…is this because of what I do?"

"Yes. No, I mean…"

I butted in, alarm bells ringing in my head, dreading what he was going to say if I didn't cut him off.

"Because I would give it all up for you, my clients, the lot!"

I felt such desperation. I needed to plead with him, beg him not to do this, I had to try.

"Helen, I know you would give it all up. I hope you will one day. I'm doing this to protect you…because I love you."

"Protect me from what exactly? You don't have to protect me from anything if we're together, David. I just want…"

"…to be with me? I know. But you can't be, Helen. It's my job, we wouldn't get the time together. You'd end up being hurt by me, like my two ex-wives…and my daughters. The distance…and the time apart, it has *killed* my relationships in the past, not just wives, there have been girlfriends too that have fallen by the wayside. I can't be in a relationship, Helen. People get hurt. That's what I'm trying to protect you from, the hurt. The loneliness…it's not what I want for you."

"But I'm used to the loneliness. I am actually *married*, you assumed he's my boyfriend. I have been *very* alone every day during that marriage. I could cope. I could even come with you, everywhere."

"It's not a holiday, babe. It would mean you being alone all the time in a hotel room while I'm in business meetings and some go on until late at night. Or you would be wandering around a city alone. It's not the same. It's not the life I want for you."

"Please, David...?"

"No, Helen. This is my final word. It is hurting me like hell to do this to you...to hurt you, but I have to for both our sakes. Please try to understand."

He let his tears start to flow and in understanding that he meant it, that he was not to be talked out of it; this was his final word...I cried too. He came and held me and we stood for an age, holding each other, weeping with mutual sadness until I broke away and demanded,

"Make love to me, David...one last time...please. Because you love me...?"

"I can't, Helen. That's why I couldn't do it last night... because I knew I had to do this today. I can't do it again. It would hurt me all the more...and it would hurt you even more afterwards, I know it would."

He was right. I was hurt already. I felt as if the bottom had fallen out of my world. I wanted to crawl into a corner and never emerge. I couldn't even bear to look at him.

"I've got to get out of here, now. The longer I stay, the worse it will be. I won't be able to leave you."

I showered as fast as I could but skipped putting on any make-up for once. There didn't seem to be any point. As I threw my belongings in my overnighter he sat on the bed and watched me. His tears almost stopped, but he was powerless; unable to comfort me, trying hard as he was to deal with his own hurt. As I zipped up my bag I cast him a quick glance and made for the bedroom door and down-stairs. I just wanted to be gone, away from him.

He ran down the stairs after me and clutching at straws, I turned around hoping he had a last minute change of heart.

"Here's your money, babe." he said, holding out an envelope.

"I'm not taking it from you. I don't want it." I snapped "What are you paying me for, David? For…for…loving you?"

This was the first time I ever snapped at him and he reeled with shock, almost staggering backwards. The hurt in his eyes was genuine and I softened towards him.

"I'm so sorry, David. I shouldn't have said it in that manner. I *do* love you."

"I'm sorry too. Please, don't let's part on bad terms, Helen. Come here."

We shared a final embrace and a final passionate kiss and I let go of him. I didn't dare look back as I walked away down the street.

I put a call in to work when I got home. I said I was really ill and would be visiting my G.P. later that day. My doctor signed me off for an interim period of two weeks. I used my O.C.D. as an excuse and the time alone to try to get over him. I convinced myself that I hadn't really been in love with him. He was the first person to show me affection and warmth since my parents died and I think I somehow latched onto that and believed I was in love with him.

I didn't receive any client calls while I was off work and was relieved about that. Two weeks later I returned to the hotel feeling not a great deal better. I started taking client calls again that same week.

CHAPTER 46

I'd been chained to his bed for four hours seventeen minutes (and counting) and since the first hour I was feeling extremely pissed off. He always paid me extra for the hours involved, but I question at times whether it's worth it. I detest the whole bondage thing. It's undeniably restricting and I hate lying on my back unless I'm being fucked. Without freedom of movement I never seem able to achieve a decent orgasm. Plus there's the boredom of all this client's messing about to contend with. The sexual action during the past few hours since he chained me up was roughly ten minutes every half hour. That was barely much more than seventy or eighty minutes in the time I'd been there. Not once during the course of events did he unchain or even loosen the shackles while he returned to his office on the ground floor to do some work. He would claim to be working but I had my suspicions. I imagine he was searching the house for anything he could find to shove inside me; phallic symbols.

During the last four hours he used a candle, a banana, a

295

vibrator, and the last idea he'd just put to use with its rough knob on the end…one of his microphones.

"I'll still be able to smell your pussy on it when I'm singing at my next gig."

He proudly announced as he removed it and proceeded to sniff every inch in delight, purely for effect. I couldn't help but wonder about his upbringing. I glowered at him but I knew there was more to come. I closed my eyes and let my mind drift for a short time…to pleasant memories of my other encounters – with David.

This guy also has an obsession. Except for my panties, which he'd ripped off me and thrown across the room, I was still fully clothed. Grey socks that came over my knees, grey school skirt and cardigan, white blouse and school tie. I was attired like a certain young pop star in one of her finest videos and that famous track had been playing on repeat in the background since I arrived.

I could hear his footsteps on the stairs again. I wondered what the hell he was going to poke me with this time. Surprisingly enough, as he walked through the door I could see that he didn't have any objects in his hands. He was minus his T-shirt now and his flies were undone. Despite my opinions of him, he did look quite attractive; his jet black hair with plum coloured highlights slightly mussed.

"Okay, I'm going to undo your ties so you'd better be good. I want you to oil my body first, all over, every last inch of it, and I want you to do it sensually, not like the masseuse at the parlour I was at yesterday, rough as fuck she was."

Irritated by his challenging remark, I was quick to defend myself.

"You know I do a great job. That's why you've called me a second time."

He shrugged his shoulders and pulled a face,

"Well, you'll have to show me again, won't you? I've forgotten. You'll have to be good. I don't like naughty girls."

I felt a sense of relief at last. Some action sounded imminent, he was making positive moves. I'd been in one position too long and my body was numb.

Once he unfastened all my bindings, he thrust the bottle of baby oil in my hand, turned his back on me and peeled off his denims. From sitting at the edge of the bed, he quickly flipped into a face down position without me catching even a glimpse of his cock. I chuckled to myself and wondered if he turned shy all of a sudden.

I started on his shoulders and gently massaged the oil in, careful not to use too much. As I concentrated on smoothing out a few small knots of muscle, he moaned out loud,

"That feels good. Keep at it."

Rubbing every inch of his back, slowly and in a sensual manner, I worked my way down towards his firm and nicely rounded buttocks. With a sudden urge to torment him, I rubbed one finger down his crack and his body tensed as I taunted him with my finger dancing so near to his anus.

"Tease it, baby, tease it!" he urged.

My client was bad, yet my whole body was aching to be touched by him. I started shaking with my need and my head was telling me to be brave, speed things up.

"Would you like me to remove my clothes or should I remain the naughty schoolgirl?" I asked, in my throatiest of voices.

I was feeling hot, wanting him that very moment but I still had work to do. I wondered what his fans would give to be in the room with him right this moment.

"Okay, as a treat. Just leave the socks on, I fucking love the socks."

Moving down his thighs, I continued my torment of his body with one hand as I struggled to remove the rest of my clothes. As the last item, my bra, landed on the floor, I quickly got both hands to work again, still intent on mocking his thighs and edging my fingers in between them towards his scrotum. When I reached the backs of his knees I was amazed at how he squirmed beneath me. It was evidently a very sensitive area for him and I caressed each, though only briefly. I was getting impatient, I hadn't had sex for a week and I was ready for it, hungry for it. My every nerve tingled as I oiled his bulging calves, his ankles…and then I grabbed his waist and rolled him onto his back…

My eyes were drawn straight to his cock and what surrounded it. I felt my eyes bulge out in surprise. I found out why he kept his back to me when he got on the bed. The backdrop behind his amazing shaft was fire, a very recent and painful looking tattoo of fire…cavorting flames of fire, not a pubic hair in sight. Hell fire!

"You silly little girl, I wasn't ready to show you just yet!" he yelled, and sat bolt upright, "Now bend over…no, over my thighs, you deserve a good slap for seeing your present before I was ready to show it!"

I moved into position, obeying his order and he spanked my backside…softly to start with. Every twenty or so slaps he stopped and poked his fingers in and out of my pussy for a few seconds. I didn't want him to stop probing, it was nice and my first hint of better things to come. I wanted him to keep shoving them in. I was on fire like his wild crazy flames, I wanted to be shagged. I wanted to orgasm without waiting much longer.

The slaps on my arse kept coming and every short session of slapping got harder and stung more, the fingers delved further inside me each time, rougher than before, his nails seeking and finding my G spot. It was hurting, I was on fire, and…I was salivating. As fast as the slapping started, it ceased without warning when he rolled me off him and laid on his back again, his solid rock of muscle almost tapping on my lips. I nibbled gently around the head of his cock and tantalised his foreskin with my tongue, careful to avoid catching his ring piercing with my teeth. He whimpered as I fondled his scrotum at the same time.

Reaching out with both hands he stretched towards me to cup my breasts and nip hard on each of my buds. I squealed out in pain …and delight. I took the whole length of his cock in my mouth and sucked, tracing my tongue around every inch, slowly working my hand up and down that beautiful muscle, the rod of steel that nearly reached his navel. Faster and faster with my hands and I could feel his throbbing through my gums, my tongue and my teeth. I could taste his release of pre-cum, hear the guttural noises trying to escape his lips, and he reluctantly lifted my head away from his manhood.

"Quick, sit on top of him. You want his full length, don't you?"

I could hardly answer, my breathing heavy and every inch of me wanted him to fuck me. I moved to straddle him and before I was in position I could feel the gold ring rub against my labia and I lowered myself heavily and felt his hardness push its way into my depths, thick, throbbing and probing. Clenching my inner muscles around it I held it tight and the tighter I clenched, the more I felt it throb. My excitement was ready to peak.

I gripped tightly and for a few seconds it almost felt as if he was going to cum, but I knew him better than that…this guy possessed excellent self-control. I waited and the impending release subsided. I started to ride him, pushing my clit down onto his pubic bone and rubbing it against his new and raw artwork. He squeezed a hand between our lower bellies and fingered my clit, flicking, nipping until I could feel the onset of my own climax. With his free arm around my waist he pulled me along, joining in with my rhythm.

"It's time, baby, let it go, cum onto my flames now. Rub your clit baby, feel it, fuck my cock and cum for me."

I tightened my muscles around him once more and gripped tight whilst I rode on, imagining my pussy to be milking his juices from him, and that thought brought about my explosion. I shuddered as my wetness seeped around his cock. Exhausted, I collapsed onto his chest and he eased me over onto my back and parted my legs. I expected him to start fucking me, but he lowered himself down the bed and put a pillow under my bottom. His put his tongue to work this time, my clit still hard, the spasms of my orgasm not yet silenced. He worked quickly, thrusting his tongue into me greedily, his hand firmly pressing circles over my clit, one finger occasionally poking into me, vying with his tongue.

"Your pussy juice tastes delicious...so sweet...so sweet, baby."

He put his hands under my cheeks and raised my bottom in the air and I felt his tongue around my anus, licking, teasing...I arched my back in anticipation. He carefully lowered my bottom onto his little finger and rammed two fingers of his other hand into my vagina and sucked at my clitoris. Determined, I pushed down onto all his fingers and my body was racked with the throes of a second orgasm. Damp with perspiration, sore, and shaking, I felt drunk with ecstasy.

"I'm going to fuck you from behind now. I'm going to hurt you. You like being hurt, don't you? You deserve to be hurt, don't you? Too many treats for one day, don't you think?"

I was breathless.

"Answer me!"

"Yes. Too many treats...I deserve to be hurt." I whispered,

as I turned over and he stuffed the pillow beneath me to raise my bottom into the air again.

Not prepared for the force with which he entered me, I screamed out as the top of my head was shoved up hard against the headboard. His cock felt like it was trying to break through my cervix. Each time he shoved harder than before and my stomach was wracked with pain at each ramming, his gold ring scratching its way to the top of my burning depths. He pounded and pounded, his balls slapping against me and after ten minutes, the tell-tale twitching of orgasm. He gripped me tight, stopped pounding, pushed his cock harder inside me, and ceased all movement. I felt the intensity of every last spurt of his cum pumping as he climaxed with loud groans of satisfaction.

Ninety minutes later I was back at home. Anthony eyed me suspiciously as I walked through the lounge and straight upstairs to bed but I wasn't in the mood to converse with him. I needed to climb into my bed and sleep...after I relived the latter part of today's business meeting in my mind.

CHAPTER 47

*H*alf past eleven, Saturday morning. It was late for me to get up at this time, yet I'd been awake since eight thirty, been downstairs early and taken a coffee back up to bed with me. On the Friday night I'd had a late night meeting with Simon at the home of one of his friends who was out of the country on business. It was a freebie, my payment to him for the number of clients he sent my way over the last few months. He was a gentleman and someone I trusted. His sexual needs were often vulgar but he never failed to excite me... or, fuck me senseless. He loved that I did exactly the same to him. He liked me to tell him 'fuck me rough, Simon'; or 'put your cock up my pussy' and 'let me feel you cum'. He was always nice to me, so I indulged him. It was his big turn on to hear the crude expletives from me; a well-educated, well-spoken, fairly posh and attractive...whore.

I intentionally stayed upstairs out of the way until after I heard Anthony leave the house. He'd been slamming doors and drawers searching for things he needed to pack for his business trip to Brussels. He hadn't actually told me about it. I saw the tickets for the flights on the coffee table along with his passport. Checking the dates on the tickets, I realised he would be away for a full week. I was ecstatic. (I already considered telling one of my clients that he could have his session at my house for a change, but as he was another prominent figure in politics, the idea might not be so attractive to him). As soon as I heard Anthony's car race off to the end of the street, running late as always, I showered and went down to the kitchen for my second caffeine fix of the day. Feeling more relaxed than I had in a long time and in the knowledge that he was out of my way for a week, I nibbled on a croissant while the coffee was filtering. Once it was ready I carried a cup through to the lounge, where I could sit in total peace for once. I couldn't help but grin...some 'me' time. I gazed around the room in wonder...all my space...a whole week! Feasting my eyes around the room once more...I spotted it...sat on the coffee table. A newspaper...with a quarter of the front page taken up by his picture...my grin faded fast as I snatched it into my hands.

BRITISH MULTI-MILLIONAIRE BUSINESSMAN, DAVID BARNARD 43, DIES AT HIS SWISS HOME

"David Barnard aged 43, died on Thursday morning, a Company Spokesman announced last night. Mr Barnard was diagnosed with terminal pancreatic cancer, some thirteen weeks ago. His daughters, Catherine, aged 18, and Ruby, aged 15, were at his bedside when he died, being comforted by the presence of their mother, Heidi, 42, first wife to Mr Barnard. It is understood that Mr Barnard had remained single, since being divorced from his second wife, Joanna, 38, four years ago. His daughters flew out to Switzerland with their mother ten days ago, when they were informed by their father that he was in the final stages of the disease. Mr Barnard, born in 1965, graduated from Kings College,

Cambridge with an Honours degree in Civil Engineering......"

The report droned on, giving details of his academic achievements, his upbringing, and of course, his successful businessman story, but I couldn't bring myself to read any further. I read those first few lines over and over again until the reality of it started to hit home.

I looked at the date of the newspaper…Friday's, no doubt left on the coffee table by Anthony yesterday and I hadn't even noticed it. The story would also have made the National News, but I rarely watch T.V. Suddenly, it was extremely important to me to remember what I was doing on Thursday, *and* since David's body had been laid in a Chapel of Rest somewhere, spent and cold. I was working at the hotel on Thursday…and yesterday. With a jolt I remembered Friday nights' antics; me, being shagged by the barrister who put David in touch with me in the first place. I was mortified. I was doing *that* whilst David was gone from this world and me…forever. My body was racked by violent shaking, as my sobs of guilt, grief, and sadness all came pouring out. I howled the place down. I felt broken, like somebody just wrenched out my heart. I loved David so much and until reading that newspaper report, I had been totally convinced it wasn't the end for us. I genuinely thought that I would definitely see him again in the not too distant future. Now, it had all just been snatched away from me; that hope. Hope that was now laid to rest…along with the man I loved.

When I woke up in bed in total darkness, I glanced at my alarm clock to see that it was quarter past nine. I couldn't even remember climbing the stairs. At some point during my outpouring of grief, I'd obviously gone upstairs, where I continued my crying and, exhaustion taking over, had cried myself to sleep. I hadn't touched any alcohol but my head felt painful and my eyes were stinging. I got up to go and wash my face, and switching on my bedside lamp, I noticed the newspaper on the floor at the side of my bed. A distressing thought suddenly occurred to me; I didn't possess one solitary snapshot of him. All I had to look at to remind me of him was the bloody picture on the front page of a newspaper that announced his death. Still, it was better than nothing. I lovingly picked up the newspaper, as if by doing so, I was being gentle with him. Not wanting him to suffer any more pain or hurt. I carried the paper back downstairs.

I sat all night in the lounge in total silence, my mind running through our few special memories, time and again. I thought back to every conversation we ever had. I tried to recall every delicious moment of passion and excitement; of when we indulged in sex, and more recently, our love-making, and I relived those times in my mind. The laughter we shared, our meals together; every tiny detail. I was digging deep for every precious moment. I tried to console myself with those memories as they were all I had left, but at least they would always be with me. My mind and body were exhausted and I couldn't muster enough energy. I gave in when my eyes started to close. I woke on the settee sometime around daylight. I recall hearing the morning chorus and thinking how sad it made me feel that morning. That awakening of life at a time when my sadness for the end of David's life was all consuming, caused my sadness to sink to new levels and it hurt so much.

I made coffee and sat around, not knowing what to do. What could I possibly do? I felt so helpless. Other emotions started to surface. I felt a terrific thirst to glean more information about David, anything about him that I didn't already know. I scoured the newspaper report again and again, greedily clinging to every new little snippet it revealed about him, no matter how trivial. I felt anger towards him for cutting me out of his life when he needed me the most. I was livid with the mother of his daughters for being at his bedside when he died, when it should have been me. I was seething at the fucking cancer that took him from me. Most of all I felt furious at the fact that I was probably the last to hear about his illness and death. The thing that was the most devastating though, was that he had *known!* That last weekend we spent together, he *knew* he had cancer and didn't tell me. I got to hear about the cancer and his death, from a fucking newspaper. There would be his funeral to come, 'a private family gathering', the newspaper said, and *I* just couldn't turn up unannounced as a chief mourner, taking my rightful place as the woman who loved him. That wouldn't be the 'done' thing. His daughters wouldn't even know that I exist. How could I do that to them at the height of their own personal grief? I couldn't pay my respects.

Throughout the morning my emotions swiftly changed with every passing minute and I eventually snapped out of the anger. An idea came to mind and I shot into action. I *could* pay my respects to David. I would do it in private. Focussing on nothing else but David, I ran upstairs, had a shower, then I searched my wardrobe for a favourite black dress of his. It was a dress I wore during one of our private dinner parties when we decided to dress formally. I applied a little make-up without any mascara, picked up David's gifts of jewellery and lovingly caressed each piece before putting them on. Before I dressed, I searched the house for four beautiful candles. I don't know why, but I just knew in my mind that it had to be four. I placed them on top of the fireplace, two on each side of David's newspaper photo which I carefully removed from the rest of the newspaper. Choosing some Beethoven music he loved, I grabbed the CD and placed it in the player in readiness. Once dressed, I lit the candles and pressed the play button on the CD player. His music played softly in the background, the candles burned, and I sat gazing at his picture, relived my memories and cried silently.

Mid-afternoon, my mobile phone rang…a client trying to contact me. I ignored his call and turned off the phone.

On Monday, the doubts started to kick in. Questions I had no answers to, but I asked them of myself time and again.

Had he really loved me? He said he did. But if he did, surely he would have wanted to spend his last few weeks with me? Why did he buy me the jewellery? I can't have been as special to him as he made out. He was very rich and money no object, so did he just buy the jewellery because he had nobody closer to him than I was at the time? Had he perhaps bought the jewellery for a previous lover, and the relationship had broken up before he had chance to give the gifts, so he gave them to me? Had he perhaps just thought that he loved me and confused our sexual compatibility and our rapport for love? Had he really liked my present to him? Or was he just being polite as he knew it was our last weekend together? Why had he lied to me about why our relationship couldn't continue? Did he really end it because of his cancer? How was that going to protect me from the hurt, when he knew I would be hurt to hear about his death in the way that I just had been? Was it really because he couldn't have a permanent relationship with me; because of the way I earned money? Had he thought that I was a gold-digger? That wasn't true. His money was not important to me. I would give all his money back, all my clients' money back, give all my parents' money to charity if it would only bring David back to me. Why had he asked me to stay that extra night? Was he just lonely and needed my company after he was diagnosed?

These questions and doubts, contradictions, and let's not forget, *the hurt*, just kept coming at me, relentlessly trying to knock me down.

CHAPTER 48

On Thursday, that same week; the week I mourned David, the week Anthony was away on business, I was in the kitchen when I heard the postman dropping letters through the box. I wasn't in any rush to go and pick them up, assuming it would be more bills for Anthony; garage bills, (there was always one of his three cars getting some expensive part or other), subscription reminders, credit card statements, or even a package in plain brown jiffy-bags (usually his dodgy porn DVD's). There was very rarely any personal mail for me.

I carried on with what I was doing and forgot about the mail until later. I was on my way through the hall to go upstairs to the bathroom. There was about eight envelopes in all and I gave them a quick shuffle, one for me and the remainder just as I expected, were all for Anthony. I left his mail on the bureau that stood in the hallway. Climbing the stairs, I didn't give much thought to the white A5 envelope as I peeled it open. I sat on the edge of the bed and pulled out the contents…a solicitor's letter and another standard size envelope which was addressed to me and marked 'Private and Confidential'…in David's handwriting! My heart skipped a beat, my hands trembled and my head refused to take in what I was seeing. I turned the envelope over in my hands a few times barely able to take my eyes off his writing, as if by doing so the contents would be magically revealed. I hesitated, not sure whether I wanted to open it, certain that I didn't want to read the contents. I picked up the accompanying letter and started to read,

[xxxxxxxxxxxxxx]
xxxxxxxxxxxxxxx
LONDON
14th November 2008
Client Ref: BA546/D131108

Mrs H Pawson
xxxxxxxxxxx
xxxxxxxxxxx
Dear Mrs Pawson
<u>*RE: MR DAVID BARNARD DECEASED – CLIENT REF*</u>
<u>*BA546/D131108*</u>

It is with deep regret that I write to inform you of the death of our client, Mr David Barnard on Thursday 13th November 2008. Due to the inevitable media coverage of Mr Barnard's death, I feel sure that you may already be aware of this sad news.

During the last meeting with my client, some two weeks prior to his death, I received various instructions, mainly with regard to his estate, but one further instruction I received was that after his death, I was to forward to you the enclosed letter which he had already penned, the night before our meeting. I understand that you had a very close relationship with my client and I sincerely hope that the contents of his letter to you can offer some comfort and peace of mind at this very sad time.

If I can be of any further assistance to you, please do not hesi-

tate to contact me on the above number, quoting the client reference.

Please accept my condolences for your very sad loss.

Yours sincerely

William J Douglas LLB

The waterworks were in full flow by the time I was halfway through the letter, leaving one or two tell-tale splashes on the page. I needed to quickly compose myself so I grabbed a handful of tissues off the bedside cabinet. I needed clear vision to read David's one and only letter to me but I also needed a stiff drink to give me the courage to open the second envelope. I wasn't sure if I was ready to read it. I was fearful of what it might contain, things I perhaps didn't wish to read. Somehow, I found the courage.

My darling Helen,

Where to start? We were both hurting so much when we said our goodbyes all those weeks ago. By the time you read this letter my suffering will be over Babe, but the hurt for you, will continue for some time to come.

I am so deeply sorry for all the hurt I caused you by ending our relationship, and for the excuses that I used to do so. You now know just what I was protecting you from and I will always be happy that I made the right decision. I did it for you and you alone.

I never told you this but I watched my father die from cancer eight years ago and I was with him when he passed away. Helen, I was never able to rid myself of that vision of him in his final hours, his body wasted away, his loss of dignity, his pain and discomfort and his fear. These last eight years I have tried hard to focus, picture him when he was happy and healthy, and I do, but for seconds only, then it all just melts away into that horrible vision. It haunts me constantly.

What I am going to tell you next will cause more hurt for you I know, but I hope that, in a strange way, it will also make you happy. Can you remember the weekend when I gave you the pendant, Babe? You asked me if I was in love with you and I said that I couldn't let myself fall for you because of what you do, and that I bought you the gift 'for a very special lady'. I lied to you again, Helen. I have known for some time now that I love you, special lady. When you left me after that weekend I was determined that on our next date (do you recall that I said it would be a couple of months?) I would tell you how much I love you, and if you loved me also I would ask you if we could try to make some sort of life together. It was devastating for me when I was given the diagnosis, but the most devastating thought was not that I have terminal cancer, but that I have been cheated; cheated for not being able to spend my life with you, Helen. I knew that I had to see you again very soon, (hence the wait of only three weeks) and that I had to take some more special memories from our last weekend together. Those special memories are with me now, my darling, and they will be with me until I take my last breath and beyond.

It seems my letter is a fully signed confession. I have already confessed to lying to you and there is more to come. I knew that I would need to know your address so that this letter would find you, along with the accompanying letter from my solicitor. I stayed awake all night waiting for you to go to sleep so that I could go through your handbag to hopefully find something which would provide me with your details. Your credit card only confirmed your name but I found your driving licence and took the address from that. So once again my darling, I apologise for sneaking about and nosing through your handbag. I know I have invaded your privacy by doing so.

I enjoyed every precious moment we spent together since our very first date. You are intelligent, funny, caring, and very beautiful, and you have put a sparkle back into my life, a sparkle that any diamond would be jealous of. Please remember these words and try to smile about them each time you wear my diamonds, special lady.

I have organised my own funeral and I will tell you this,

Helen...my treasured watch will be coming with me, reminding me that, 'two hearts came together.'

Over these last few days I have told Catherine and Ruby about you! Not everything. I have told them about your career...in accountancy! They know that you are very special to me and they know how much I love you. They always wanted me to find happiness and someone to love since the day their mother found happiness. It is my dearest wish that they get to know you and that you get to know them, so that they can see what it is about you that I love. I think they will be in touch with you when all the fuss has died down. Please do this small thing for me, Helen. I want them to know you, it means a lot.

You told me that you would give up your work for me. I know you don't have a life with me to look forward to anymore but would you please consider giving up your work now? I worry for you, Helen. I want you to be safe and happy. Make this decision only when you are ready though.

It hurts me a lot that I can't see you for one last time, but it would hurt me much more to see you. The knowledge that I can't make love to you again, hold you in my arms and tell you how much I love you is just an added burden for me to bear.

I know how much you love me, my darling, and I also know how much you will be hurting when you finish reading this letter. I sincerely hope the day will come soon, when you can cry no more tears and that you can be happy...happy that we found love with each other and that we shared very special moments together, and happy now that you have the knowledge. The knowledge that I love you so much and that I really wanted to share my life with you had things been so different. You have no reason to doubt anymore, Helen.

Stay safe, darling. I hope one day we will be together again, in a better, kinder world, and where love is infinite. In the meantime, I truly hope with all my heart, that you do find happiness in this life

with someone else who cares for you the way I do, nobody deserves
that more than you!
    All my love, special lady
    From YOUR David
    Xxx

I can't begin to describe every emotion that I felt as I read David's dying words to me. I have a letter that will be treasured. I know in my heart that I will read and re-read it, many times over. It is so irrational, but suddenly I can't help being terrified by the thought that my tears might somehow obliterate his words to me.

The following few weeks were surreal. Once Anthony returned from his business trip, I tried to be out of the house as much as I could. I wandered around the parks, and shops, not shopping, just walking. I went everywhere but not seeing anything. I only returned home at times when I knew Anthony would be out. I don't need any confrontation. I don't need any distractions from my thoughts and memories of David…I needed to grieve. And I did grieve.

CHAPTER 49

*A*fter the first couple of weeks of grieving for David, it crossed my mind late one night that I hadn't checked on the greenhouse situation during that time. It was a welcome distraction from my tears and hours spent gazing longingly at his picture. It would give me something else to focus on the next day. It was the first thing I planned to do the following morning, once Anthony went out.

My hands trembled as I lifted the top section of plant pots, wondering if there would be an envelope there or not. I didn't really know how to feel when I found yet another envelope hidden there. I told myself that feeling pleased wasn't appropriate. How could it be appropriate to be pleased about the fact that Anthony was drug dealing? Yet, I couldn't help smiling. The reason I felt like smiling was because I fully intended that Anthony was finally going to get his come-uppance, and soon.

When I returned to the kitchen, I made a fresh pot of coffee and sat at the kitchen table. I needed to get myself fully awake and do some serious thinking. Just a few weeks back, it occurred to me that if Anthony was actually going to work then somebody must have either come to the greenhouse to deliver and/or collect the envelopes. Over the last few months my car had mostly been left in the drive as I had been taking the tube to work. Maybe Anthony told whoever it had been who called that I go out to work on the tube so they needn't worry about the Mazda in the drive. Also, over the last few weeks, even though I hadn't been at work, I was going out most days, indulging in my walks of grief around the city and its numerous parks.

I couldn't take my eyes off the record I kept of the envelope deliveries and collections. I almost willed it to speak to me and point out to me exactly what I was missing. I twiddled a pen around between my fingers and doodled a border around the edges of the paper. Transfixed though I was, nothing jumped out at me. I asked myself what I gleaned already...nothing! Other than the fact that the envelopes came and the envelopes went...zilch! That was all...only those two facts! Somebody had to be coming sometime soon for the envelope that was sat in the greenhouse. Oh, crap!

I shot up from the kitchen table. After quickly checking the back door was locked I tore through the lounge and up the stairs like a lunatic.

I suddenly realised just how vulnerable I was sitting at the kitchen table, and without net curtains or blinds to hide my presence from any visitor to our greenhouse. With the conifer hedges between our house and our neighbours' houses we'd never thought it necessary. Still shaking, I sat on the bed for a while wondering what I could do. While I showered and dressed the only answer that I came up with was that it was down to me. I must stay holed up in my bedroom, a very slight gap in the vertical blinds and wait for whomever...for however long it takes. The thought filled me with dread.

CHAPTER 50

*A*round six to seven weeks after reading of David's death followed by the letter he had written just days before he died, I picked up my mail to find another envelope. I recognised it instantly to be from his solicitor's office. I tore into the letter hoping to find yet another letter from David…something else he'd perhaps written in his final days. But I was disappointed to find there was no letter marked 'Private and Confidential' within the envelope this time.

No more words of love penned by my man…there was nothing inside that I could add to my treasures. I gave a loud sigh of disappointment and started reading the correspondence from Bill Douglas asking me to make an appointment to see him as I was to be one of David's beneficiaries. He apparently left me something in his will.

I started to wonder about his daughters. I felt sure they would have inherited everything as I imagined that David, having been a shrewd businessman but also a sensible father, would have been certain to make sure they never wanted for anything. Even in the short time we spent together I could almost guarantee that there would be trust funds. They wouldn't have access to vast amounts of money until they reached thirty years old. I know he wanted them both to have a career; to understand what it meant to work for a living. He didn't want them to be two rich bitches doing nothing but shop, take expensive holidays, attend wild parties and take drugs. Nor did he want them to become alcoholics, who perhaps once a year, would join many celebs who needed to check in to The Priory for a drying out session. I felt cold. I grabbed my dressing gown and put it around my shoulders, though the house was warm. The time that David and I spent together could be measured in hours, I provided a service to begin with and we fell in love. It felt to me as if, whatever I inherited would be an increase in my hourly rate. I felt cheap. I didn't want David's money, I wanted David.

Although I felt very strongly about not wanting David's money, I badly wanted to meet Bill Douglas. I was curious to know exactly what David shared with him. I called his office and made an appointment before going along to meet Bill. He turned out to be a lovely and charming gentleman who, at almost seventy, still worked full-time in the practice. He shook my hand and held it gently between both of his while expressing his sadness at David's death. He subsequently enquired as to how I was coping. I found it difficult to find the words to answer him and although I hadn't cried over the last three weeks, the tears threatened to make a re-appearance.

Once our pleasantries were out of the way, the subject turned to David's will. Bill informed me that there would be a pro rata distribution from the current funds available. David left me a substantial amount and I was to receive an interim payment of £500,000 for the time being, which Bill handed to me as we spoke. I struggled for words and my hand quivered as I stared at the cheque.

"I..."

Bill looked at me kindly and interrupted,

"David was clearly, very much in love with you, Helen. We had many conversations in his final weeks and he expressed to me his own personal grief for having to make the decision to break off your relationship. I can see that you are still hurting, it shows in your eyes, as it did with David. I do understand though, his reasons for ending it. He told me how he wanted to spend his life with you, and you with him. His cancer would have made those final weeks even more hell had you been together, for both of you."

I realised I'd started to cry again only because Bill thrust a box of tissues at me that had been sat on his desk. I felt that I was so used to crying that I wasn't always aware of my tears, until I found it difficult to see with the blurred vision.

"David's girls..." I started, but he cut me off again,

"...are extremely well provided for. This is David's wish, Helen, that you have this money now. The balance will be paid out at some future date, which cannot be determined at this moment in time. There are assets to be sold, mainly properties and shares. The shares of course, will be sold when the bank's financial expert deems the FTSE prices more favourable."

I didn't wish to hear about the money I didn't want. My selfish grief demanded to know more about David.

"Did you read his, er...David's letter to me, Mr...Bill?" I asked.

"I did, Helen. David always valued my opinion on... certain matters. He asked me to read the letter, from the point of view of you...erm, the recipient, and he wanted me to ascertain if his correspondence would leave you in no doubt as to his true feelings for you. I assured him that the message was conveyed loud and clear."

So David spoke openly to his solicitor about our relationship. I felt at peace about his love for me at last, and I had to make Bill aware of my feelings.

"Then please understand this, Bill. I am in no doubt whatsoever of David's feelings for me. How could I possibly be in doubt, after his letter? I loved David with all my heart. Therefore, I cannot accept this cheque. Give it to charity or something. What good is this money to me, without him?"

"He knew you well, Helen. David predicted that you would be, in his words, troublesome, about accepting the bequest. That is the reason behind my request for an appointment with you. His instructions were clear, 'do not let her out of your office without the cheque, Bill. Do not let me down.' I cannot let you leave the office unless you agree to take the cheque, Helen, or I shall have failed to carry out my client's last instruction. Please take it."

I looked at him and wondered how often he had to plead for someone to accept a cheque. I knew David always held him in very high regard, and deservedly so. Also, I couldn't fail to notice Bill's continued loyalty to his deceased client and his genuine desire to fulfil, down to the last minute detail, everything that had been asked of him. I folded up the cheque and placed it in my handbag.

"Thank you for your loyalty to David and your kindness, Bill. You've given me the cheque. You've carried out David's instructions to the letter, so I will also thank you for that on behalf of him. He regarded you as a personal friend."

I was very close to crying again. I'd only met Bill for the first time today. A guy much admired and respected by David, and this had been the first time I discussed our relationship with anyone. It had felt right to do so.

"There's just one more thing to mention, Helen. Catherine, David's eldest daughter has told me that she would like to get in touch with you, and hopefully meet you at some point in the future when she feels more able to talk about things. She asked if it would be acceptable to write to you, if you don't mind me giving her your address, that is."

My first thought was, what if Anthony found her letter? I mumbled some excuse that I would possibly be moving house.

"Can I give you my mobile number to give her please, Bill? If she is a little apprehensive about calling me herself, you could always call and we can make arrangements through you. David wanted me to get to know his daughters and I will. I am sure of it."

Before I left his office Bill shook my hand once more and said he would look forward to meeting me again in the near future. I smirked as I stepped out of the main entrance door and into the street. I had a cheque in my handbag; but no intention of ever paying it into my bank.

CHAPTER 51

*T*he envelope was picked up only three days after I discovered it, but I'd been wrong in thinking Anthony would be delivering it somewhere.

An Audi A5 convertible pulled into the drive behind my car. I heard the car door open, but because the car pulled up too close to the house it was a bad angle for me to get a decent look at the guy who climbed out of it. While he went around to the back garden, I opened the blinds a little and took a picture of the car with my mobile phone. This was the only use my phone had in weeks. It was turned off most of the time, which allowed me to avoid the never ending calls from my past clients…and Simon.

It was impossible to capture the registration number since the car had been parked in the drive, but I took another shot once it reversed out of the drive; the driver facing forwards ready to cruise up the road. I felt a chill down my spine, but also buoyed by the feeling that I was doing something positive.

I uploaded the image from my mobile phone to my laptop, printed the picture of the car and locked it in my briefcase. I kept checking the greenhouse each day and carried on with my log of the envelope activity. It reached the stage where it was becoming a very regular occurrence, with up to two envelopes appearing and disappearing within the same week. I was growing increasingly worried though. Something wasn't stacking up. I photographed each car as it drove away, then ten minutes later, I ventured down to the greenhouse to find each envelope gone. No longer did I find any envelopes *appearing* after the presence of the strangers' cars in our drive. The thought made me extremely uneasy but it had to be true... somebody was depositing the envelopes during the night while we were asleep. But then where was Anthony's involvement in it all? Finally, it hit me and I cried out in jubilation. I had my answer...*he* was putting the envelopes in the greenhouse while I was sleeping. It had to be him!

I tried to stay awake at night but the medication I was taking persisted in making me far too drowsy to listen out for Anthony's nocturnal activities.

A week passed by with no greenhouse activity whatso-ever, so I stopped hiding away in the bedroom, although I still preferred to stay away from the kitchen during daylight hours. In the middle of watching a chick flick one Thursday morning, I was jolted back to reality as a car door slammed in our drive. The vertical blinds were closed so, not having a good vantage point, I stayed away from the window. I already made sure the door was shut between the kitchen and the lounge. I felt fairly safe in the knowledge that nobody could see me. I turned the volume of the TV to mute...and heard a noise I hadn't been expecting...our garage door opening...and it closed two minutes later. As I heard the vehicle reverse out of the drive, I chanced a look out of the blinds, the Audi convertible again.

I felt as if I was a complete wreck, I dashed through to the kitchen and poured myself a large gin, with only the tiniest drop of tonic. I paced around the kitchen, puzzling over the use of the garage. Yet again, I had another question to ask myself…when did any money change hands? It was at least thirty minutes before I decided to take a look in the garage. I'd rarely set foot in the place since Anthony and I bought the house but I scoured every inch of the place for the next twenty minutes.

It was the last place I looked, one of those large, rigid, folding tool-boxes. I felt like vomiting as I opened it. I should have realised much sooner and wondered why it was even there. Why would Anthony own a large tool-box? He wouldn't have known what to do with any tools! In a plain brown box under the bottom section there must have been about twenty or thirty of the envelopes containing the soft squishy powdery substances. I had him!

CHAPTER 52

The weeks had passed me by in a total fog. I opened my purse each morning before work and looked at the cheque that Bill Douglas handed to me. Five seconds was all it took each time. I returned it to the secret zip compartment after its brief airing. I couldn't bring myself to do anything with the damn cheque, yet it made me incredibly sad to look at it every day. I couldn't get out of the habit. It became yet another of my obsessive routines. I didn't want to bank it, yet I didn't want to tear it up and put it in the garbage.

I recently started a new cleaning job at a different hotel, having been fired for the considerable length of time I took off after David's death. From a financial point of view I didn't need to work. My job was merely a way of escaping from the house, and I needed to clean somewhere, anywhere. My obsessions were at an all-time high. Anthony hadn't failed to notice how many times I cleaned throughout the house in the previous weeks, and I felt sickened by his vicious remarks,

"You seriously need help, Helen. You're mentally unstable." And then,

"Get a life. Get a job."

"I had a life, and a job, until you fucked it all up for me, Anthony!" I bit back.

I still felt unable to return to my career in accountancy. My ability to concentrate on business, figures, or simple matters like reading a novel or watching a movie had taken a slump, in fact it was non-existent. I knew it was only a matter of time before I'd need professional help again for my mental problems. I could not carry on like this indefinitely. I didn't need to be told why it was happening to me again. I knew the cause, but was unable to control the obsessions.

I told Anthony I had a new job. He assumed it's an accountancy position. I didn't lie to him, just failed to correct his assumption.

My mobile rang at ten o'clock one morning, and looking at the screen I saw it was Bill Douglas calling me.

"Good morning, Bill, what a pleasant surprise. How are you?"

"Hello, Helen. I am very well, thank you, my dear. And yourself? I hope I haven't caught you at an inconvenient time?" Considerate as ever. I laughed.

"It's always convenient to speak to you, Bill. I'm keeping busy, it's the best way to deal with things. I'm just about learning to cope. What can I do for you?"

"The reason for my call, Helen, is that Catherine…um… David's daughter has been in touch. She would like to meet up with you, fairly soon if you can manage it. She… um…mentioned tomorrow, if that is not too short notice for you? She understands if it won't be possible."

My hand was shaking, nerves kicking in as I took in what he was saying. I wasn't really ready for meeting David's girls, but I would skip work. I was past caring.

"That is fine, Bill, I can meet them at any time she wants and Catherine can choose where she would like us to meet up. Would you mind asking her and getting back to me with the details please?" then as an afterthought,

"Bill…would you mind telling…asking Catherine…that I don't have a nice picture of David, if she could oblige please…all I have is the picture from the newspaper."

"Certainly, Helen. I will call you back as soon as I have made contact with Catherine again."

He ended the call with that.

Thirty minutes later he called me back to tell me to meet Catherine and Ruby at St James' Park, near 'Inn the Park' at eleven. I had no idea as to how I might recognise them, so asked if he would call Catherine again, to say that I would wear denims, a black jacket and I would carry a black Radley shoulder bag.

My nerves really kicked in the next morning and I could barely think clearly. My thoughts were backward and forwards like a ping pong; wondering what his girls would think about me, or even whether they would like me. I also wondered how much of David I would be able to see in *them.* Would it be David's eyes I saw, when we finally came face to face?

I intended to be early for our meeting and planned to stand somewhere out of sight so that I could catch a glimpse of the girls if I could recognise them, before they saw me. I didn't know if it was a good idea or not. I thought I might be tempted to run, should I see any hint of hostility in their faces, although they had no reason to be hostile towards me I couldn't help feeling a bit like 'the other woman'. Also running through my head were feelings of guilt that David left me money that rightfully belonged to *their* inheritance. It somehow didn't feel right having this meeting at all, but I was doing it for David…he wanted it.

It was ten minutes to eleven when I arrived at St. James Park. I kept a little distance from 'Inn the Park' for a few minutes, but eagerly looked in that direction to see if I could manage to pick out the girls before I made my approach. But for the fact that I was looking out for *two* young ladies, I might have spotted Catherine sooner than I did. She was obviously looking around for somebody she agreed to meet, so I took this as my cue to start walking towards her. I could see that she was tall, about 5ft 10" and dark haired and, when I was just ten yards away from her, I knew I was looking at Catherine, David's eldest daughter. Her eyes were those of her father, in fact all her facial features were unmistakably his. She saw me walking towards her and gave a quick glance at my attire. Finally, she looked up and made eye contact with me. She walked tentatively towards me and offered her hand, which I took in both of mine,

"You are Catherine, am I right?"

"Yes. Catherine. And you are, Helen?" She enquired.

We gave each other a nervous hug and I could feel the tension in her shoulders, a tension that matched my own.

"Sh…shall we walk for a little while? Or would you rather go inside and have coffee, or tea?" I asked.

"Yes, to the walk. I'm sorry my sister can't be here. She is being rather troublesome at this moment in time. I thought it best to come alone. I hope you don't mind, Helen? She can come along next time, if she's in the right frame of mind."

So there was going to be a next time. She didn't even know me yet. I was touched by her confidence.

"That's not a problem, Catherine. If she wants to, I will look forward to meeting her next time in that case."

We walked along the path for a few seconds, and her next words stunned me,

"You loved my father?"

"Very much! He was special, we would have been together now, if it wasn't for..."

I couldn't bring myself to say the word and she looked at me sympathetically and immediately understood,

"I know. I hate the word too."

She turned to face me as we continued to stroll.

"Dad told us about you, Helen, and how much he loved you. You were very special to him too. You must be hurting? That he ended it with you...to protect you? *And* that you found out about his death through the media? If only we thought to look for his mobile phone. We found it three weeks later. Your number is on there...I could have called you. I'm so sorry. It must have been awful for you."

Her eyes glazed over, but her grief was plain to see.

"No more so, than the way it must have been for you and Ruby. I want you to know that David was everything to me. I never understood why he ended our relationship. He told me that it was his work, the amount of time he spent travelling. He said it caused the break-up between him and your Mum, that was the reason he gave me. He said he was ending it to protect me from all that. Somehow I didn't really believe it to be true. I know now though, don't I? I've forgiven him for keeping the truth from me...even though it still hurts."

"How did you meet?" she asked me after a brief silence.

My insides did a flip and I panicked for a few seconds. How was I to answer that one? I didn't want to lie, but she didn't need to know the truth.

"Ermm...I met David through business. A...a mutual acquaintance introduced us. It...it snowballed from there really."

There! I spilled the words out and I hadn't lied.

We walked on for a while in silence. She linked her arm into mine and I was touched by the show of warmth from someone who had been a stranger to me just half an hour before. I liked this girl, she came across as genuine; she wanted the cold, hard facts about my relationship with her father, but she showed compassion for my loss whilst still dealing with her own.

"Would you like to go for a coffee, or perhaps something to eat, Helen? Or are you in a rush to return to work? I have no wish to hold you up, if so."

"I've booked a days' leave. We can do whatever *you* would like. I'm quite hungry too. First eating place we come to okay with you, or did you have somewhere in mind?"

"I like Pizza Express, there's one in Victoria Street."

"Pizza Express it is then."

We ordered food and found a quiet corner where we could sit and talk without the distraction of the comings and goings of other customers and staff. She talked about David and I loved hearing all about him; what type of father he was, the practical jokes he played on them all throughout his marriage to Heidi, his hobbies, anything at all...and she obliged. We went on to talk about University and her dream to become a forensic scientist. Another topic, which I saw caused her plenty of distress, was Ruby and the havoc she caused before David's death and continued to do.

Our food arrived so there was a lull in the conversation for a few minutes as we ate. We ordered a second bottle of wine between us. I was certainly not expecting the next question she threw at me and my stomach sank.

"Why haven't you paid in the cheque that Bill gave you? You've had it for months now."

She looked straight into my eyes, waiting for the answer that I struggled to find,

"I...I...never wanted David's money. It was David that I wanted, still *do* want. I can't take it. I don't need it, Catherine. I have more than enough to keep me comfortable. It belongs to you and Ruby. It doesn't belong to me."

"It is not *our* money, Helen. Our father wanted you to have it, *and* the balance when the estate is finally sorted. Ruby and I are already wealthy enough. We have far more than we will ever get through. This is rightfully yours. Dad wanted you to have it, so do it for him, for *your* David. Pay it into your bank…tomorrow."

My emotions got the better of me, I couldn't look into her eyes at that point, I didn't want her to see the tears that rolled down my cheeks; but she knew. She quickly moved around to join me on my side of the table, put her arm around me and laid her head on my shoulder. I turned towards her and enfolded her in my arms. We sobbed silently on each other's shoulder for a few minutes, then giggled together like schoolgirls when we realised that we had a small audience. She moved back to her side of the table. I told her again,

"I loved him so much, Catherine, he was everything to me."

"I know that, I can tell how much you loved him. I would not be sat here with you otherwise."

After I settled the bill, and with much protest from Catherine, we left the restaurant and wandered aimlessly around London for most of the afternoon. Sometimes Catherine's arm was linked in mine and when it wasn't, my arm was linked in hers. We called into a bar or two, a gin and tonic for me, a pint of Fosters for Catherine, (it was good to tell she was at Uni), the odd shop here and there…if and when something in the windows caught our attention. I was not looking forward to saying goodbye. I needed to be near her. David felt closer than ever when I was in her company and I liked to think that he was looking down, giving an approving nod at our new found friendship.

The moment of parting came around all too soon and at seven o'clock we exchanged mobile numbers and promised to stay in touch. Catherine said she would try her best to get

Ruby to come along to meet me next time. After we embraced for the final time that day, her hand rummaged in her handbag and she passed me a white envelope,

"A couple of photos of Dad. I remembered. The one of him by himself was taken just a few weeks before he was diagnosed."

"Thank you, Catherine. I won't look just yet. I'll save them for when I'm alone as I know I'll get upset. I've enjoyed today very much, thank you." and quickly added, "I will pay the cheque into the bank if that is what you want me to do."

"It is. Bye, Helen," She started to walk away and added, "We'll speak soon, yes?"

"Count on it."

I watched as she walked away from me. I felt such a rush of affection for her. She was certainly a credit to David...and Heidi; so mature...and so like David. It crossed my mind that maybe that was the reason behind my feelings towards her.

CHAPTER 53

*A*fter my pleasant afternoon with Catherine, I went straight home. Fortunately, Anthony was out. I poured myself a large glass of wine and went upstairs to the privacy of my bedroom. Once I took a few sips I gingerly opened the envelope that Catherine gave me. Both pictures were mounted and had been facing each other in the envelope as I removed them. The first one I turned over was a picture of David with the girls. It was dated May 2007 and had been taken in Sicily on the top of Mount Etna. I remember David telling me about that particular holiday during our pillow talk all those months ago. The skies were incredibly blue yet there was plenty of snow on the ground. All three of them were huddled together shivering with their fleeces on. I recognized Catherine easily now, but have to say that Ruby's looks were neither like David nor Catherine. I assumed she would perhaps take after her mother. She was certainly an attractive young lady. David told me how hot it been on the beach in Taormina and yet, just an hour's drive away, at a height of 3350 metres above sea level, the temperatures had been -12C with the wind cutting through them like knives.

The second photograph was of David...my David. He smiled up at me as I gazed lovingly at him and stroked his cheek. He was almost as handsome on paper as he was in life. I smiled back at him, watery-eyed, and asked him in a whisper,

"Why did you have to go and leave me, David? I miss you so much and it hurts."

I allowed my sadness to engulf me for a while and I sought an answer in those beautiful eyes but they couldn't give any response. His lips, whilst smiling, could not produce any words to console me. I propped the photograph up against my bedside lamp, sipped at my wine and my eyes scanned every corner of the room, hoping for, and trying to catch a glimpse of his hazy image watching over me. I took some comfort from that possibility.

On Monday when I finished work at the hotel, and after a full weekend of giving the matter some careful considera-tion, I went to my bank and paid in the cheque. Had it not been for Catherine questioning me as to why I hadn't done so, I think I might have just added it to my collection of keepsakes. Once the cheque cleared, I would transfer the money to my offshore bank account. It was time to bail out of the marital home, and furthermore, time that Anthony got the life that he deserved.

CHAPTER 54

I needed to make a few phone calls so I finally turned my mobile phone on, for the purpose of making and receiving calls, rather than taking pictures of drug dealers' cars. My phone beeped constantly for five minutes notifying me of almost fifty missed calls and even more incoming text messages from the past weeks.

Simon's voice sounded more than a little cross to hear my voice.

"Helen, where the FUCK have you been? I've been ringing you, again and again. I've had your clients pestering me, wondering where the HELL you've been. What's going on?"

It was nice to hear a friendly voice again, angry though he was. I felt a bit wary. He wouldn't like what I would tell him over the next few minutes, but I had to do it, it was only fair.

"I've had a bereavement and it's taken a long time. It's been very difficult for me, Simon!"

He sighed down the phone and I raised my eyes to the ceiling, I knew what was coming next.

"Well, yes, I'm sorry! But you already told me about your

parents, Helen. You started having clients *after* that. It never stopped you before."

I took a deep breath,

"Simon, it…wasn't my parents this time. It was the man I loved. You knew him. David. David Barnard."

There was a long silence before he finally asked, incredulous,

"David Barnard? Helen…you fucking fell in love with a client?"

It was out at last, and it took all of five seconds to tell him,

"Clients? I won't be having any more clients, Simon!" and I ended the call.

Over the course of the next two days I packed some suitcases with the clothes and personal items I would need and loaded them into my car. I also helped myself to one of the incriminating envelopes from the toolbox in the garage. I needed it to put the next part of my plan into action. After I left Anthony a letter on the kitchen worktop, telling him that I would no longer be living in the house, or cramping his style, I checked into the 'Kensington' suite at the hotel. The classy hotel where I'd first been employed as a chambermaid, and the very suite where Simon had fucked me, and a little later, talked me into becoming a hooker.

Using my laptop I started composing a letter; a letter that would be sent without my signature or name at the bottom. Once it was complete, I placed it into a large 'jiffy' bag together with the envelope I stole from Anthony's toolbox along with the images of all the vehicles I managed to capture on my mobile phone.

My second letter was for Leanne, the young trainee at the Hopkins Partnership. I drove out to where she lived with her parents and, after parking my car in their drive, posted the envelope containing my car keys and registration document through the letterbox. She always loved my Mazda. I took the tube back into the city centre and returned to the hotel. Using the telephone in my suite, I hired a car for what would be my last twenty four hours in London.

CHAPTER 55

*M*y late night timing was perfect. I dropped the envelope into the doorway of the Thames Valley Police station in Windsor and made a follow up call from a public payphone shortly afterwards to make sure they received it. I already knew they found it though. I watched a young constable pick it up as he entered the station at ten o'clock, either just starting or finishing his shift I expect. From there I drove towards Anthony's house in my rental car and parked a discreet distance away, under the shade of some trees. I waited for what felt like hours; eighty four minutes to be exact, until three or four police vehicles turned into the road and parked at the front of the house, blue lights flashing continually. Fascinated and feeling triumphant, I watched as he opened the front door to them. Ten minutes later the police entered the garage. After one hour and fifty three minutes Anthony was led out of the house and bundled into the back of one of the police cars.

My luggage already in the back of the car, I drove straight to London Heathrow where, as was arranged, I deposited the rental car. As I made my way to the check-in desk, all I felt was an incredible sadness, accompanied by overwhelming relief. I had done the right thing…not as soon as I should have done had I not had my grief to contend with, but I finally set the wheels in motion!

I took my window seat and, bemused as always, indulged in a little 'people watching.' Folks who pulled their tiny cabin cases on wheels, too busy looking up at the seat numbers and totally unaware that they were dragging their luggage over other passengers' toes or grazing a few ankles in the process. People who messed about stowing their carry-on's in the overhead storage compartments and blocking the aisle, two hundred or so passengers at a total standstill; those who sat down in an aisle seat and immediately fastened their safety belts and then gave a vicious scowl because they had to unbuckle again when the window seat passenger finally turned up. It was a constant source of amusement.

As the wheels left the tarmac and the pilot subsequently started to bank the plane, I looked down on the city lights and wondered what else life had in store for me. I felt elated to be leaving it all behind, but nervous at the same time. I had no clue what I was going to do and wasn't sure whether to get a job in Paris or not. It crossed my mind as to whether I should seek some serious help for my O.C.D. and would it would work if I did?

I didn't know anybody who lived in the apartment block or anyone in Paris for that matter. The only people I expected to see in the next few months were Catherine and Ruby, David's daughters. I've yet to meet Ruby but I promised Catherine they could come to stay with me for a week.

I seriously hoped that living in Paris would be the start of a new life for me and a chance to recover mentally, from all that had been wrong with my life. I was still dealing with the tragic death of both my parents when I heard the devastating news about David. I still felt bitter that the three people I loved more than life itself were taken away from me; the most caring, loving people I ever knew. I don't think I did anything wrong but there were times I wondered if I was being punished for sins committed by me in a former life. Before David came into my life, I first loved Gavin, and he and my one and only best friend broke my heart. My disastrous marriage to Anthony followed along with the numerous stunts he pulled that broke my heart for the second time. No more falling in love for me.

On the approach to Paris CDG, I looked out at the terminal buildings as they quickly grew larger. My thoughts drifted again. I've done it. I've left London and my problems well behind me. I'm no longer a chambermaid or a call girl. I have no friends in Paris who I could have a social life with, plus…there would be no more boyfriends or husbands.

As the wheels hit the runway with a loud thud, a sudden thought passed through my mind…

What would I do for sex?

COMING SOON!

THE HEALING

(A Trilogy – Book 2)

ABOUT THE AUTHOR

Eva Bielby was born and raised in North Yorkshire in the North East of England. From the age of seven, she became a member of her local library, and was backwards and forwards perusing the children's section at least twice a week. Eva still lives in her birth town with her son and daughter, and their respective families being in close proximity.

Having worked in accounts offices since leaving school, Eva passed her accountancy qualifications when her children were very young. She has spent over thirty years of her working life as a company accountant.

Eva has always been interested in writing and has written many poems over the years. She started writing seriously in 2014 when she completed the first part of the erotic Goings On series. Book 2 followed in 2015. These two books have now been revamped and given new titles, 'The Hurt' and 'The Healing'. Book 3 is completed and will soon be released as 'The Scars'. Being a reader of many genres of novels, Eva would also love to write a suspense thriller in the future, and possibly a comedy, which she would carry out under an alternative pseudonym,

Eva has many hobbies, which include playing badminton and going on long country walks. She has a keen interest in spiritualism/mediumship, and has attended several workshops to develop her skills further.

Eva loves nothing better than to have fun with her

grandchildren. During quieter moments, she enjoys a cryptic crossword, sudoku and gardening.

Milton Keynes UK
Ingram Content Group UK Ltd.
UKHW020618120923
428513UK00014B/428